Darling, can we start over?

A NOVEL

MONIKA MEENA

Editor: Komal Meena
Cover Design: Monika Meena
Visit my Website at www.monikameena.com

For those who believe in **Second Chances**

Prologue

What's the worst thing that could happen at your wedding?

Being an over-thinker, I had imagined every possible scenario that could go wrong today. From tripping in front of everyone while walking down the aisle to uttering the wrong name by mistake, I had prepared myself for everything. Nothing could go wrong today. I was going to have my dream wedding without any hiccup.

I just wish I could breathe properly in my wedding gown.

Glancing back at the reflection in the mirror, a smile fondled my flushed lips. I couldn't believe the stunning girl in the wedding dress staring back in the mirror was really me.

This was it!

My day had finally come.

To begin with, my teenage life was a major blunder. Plus, adulthood was not any breakthrough. All-in-all, life has never been much generous on me. But somehow I had landed a decent job. All I was proud of in my twenty-six years of existence was that I'd stolen a spot as a Resident Doctor at one of the reputed hospitals in Florence, Alabama and owned a small apartment there.

But this was something else. Something far enduring, but in a terrifying way. This was serious. Because I was freaking getting married today!

My hands stroked the marvelous texture of the dress. As a vintage-lover, I always adored laces. And the wedding gown felt like my second skin. Exquisitely wrapped around my curves, with the long lacy sleeves beautifying the appeal of the gown.

However, I was having a hard time holding back the cold tingling that surged in my chest. I couldn't help but nibble on my lower lip. Battling to conceal the edginess from flickering on my face. Yet, it was the kind of worry that mingled easily with the great excitement ripening inside my heart. Rendering the emotions flow throughout my body like a thousand fireworks bursting at the same time.

My thoughts soon drifted to the present when Ashley, my best friend and maid of honor, tapped on my shoulder. I released a sharp breath turning towards her. I smiled while bending a little as she fitted the veil on my head. These heels made me quite taller than my actual five-four stature.

"I never thought I would ever say it, but I wish I was wearing that gown. This dress is a real killer, girl." A chuckle left my mouth when she let out a teasing whistle, making my mother clear her throat. Ash was the one person who had stood by me through all the ups and downs of my life, and I was blessed to have her beside me on this big day.

"Okay, ladies, it's showtime. Everyone! Take your position at the altar." All heads swiveled towards the door when my lovely wedding planner, Marcus, entered the room. And I witnessed Ashley letting out a deep sigh. "What position is he talking about?" I almost rolled my eyes at her dirty mind and nudged her shoulder to pop the daydreaming bubble that had started budding inside her head.

"Okay, are you ready, Mrs. Future Romano?" Ash chirped with a wide grin.

It felt weird yet so alluring to hear my future name from her mouth. I nodded in bliss and right at the moment she held my hands and we squealed in glee. Everything flew out of my mind but the notion of walking down the aisle and beholding Lucas Romano, my boyfriend of two years. I wondered if he would cry seeing me in this beautiful wedding gown. *He better, or I would walk the hell out of there.*

"Okay, Ashley, you're the maid of honor, so you should be on your heels too." Groaning at Marcus she hugged me for one last time and whispered in my ear, "I know it's random, but don't run away from the altar. That is too cliché!"

"I promise!" I assured, squeezing her hands. Marcus shook his head at us, and then I was left alone.

Once again, I rushed towards the mirror while adjusting my veil and let out a deep breath. "You look stunning, Sarah!" My dad gave a light squeeze to my shoulders to bestow some rest to my jiggles. I nodded at my reflection and turned around with a grin engraving my face.

"Let's get hitched then!"

⚘

With the beguiling melody pervading in the air, I placed my first foot inside the hall. I sought hard to settle down my racing heart and appreciated some people standing up from their seats. As for now, I had captured all the attention in that enormous hall.

It was the moment I had been envisaging for a while now. And now that I was living it, I could tell it was nothing like I had imagined.

The aisle fright was real.

The walk, down the aisle was much longer than I had foreseen.

My heels were not comfortable like that sales lady had made me believe. And the room was not swelling with silence, waiting for me to say 'I do'.

Squeals of children, who were still running around and screaming at the top of their lungs, filled my ears. I feared one would bump into me and make me fall face-flat in front of the whole crowd.

All my senses were in overdrive, and my heart was struggling hard to jump out of my chest.

Beads of sweat built over my forehead when I felt my father's hands lightly squeezing mine. I looked back at him from the corner of my eyes and met with his subtle, reassuring smile. His mere gesture helped me to breathe a little and being less bothered about the fact that there was a good chance of this fairy-tale going straight down the hill. Or maybe I was just apprehending too much.

Walking further down that artistic petal engraved aisle, my fingers grazed around the bouquet of red roses. The plastic wrap was making my hands sweaty, and I tightened my grasp around them.

My head lifted towards the altar, appreciating my man eagerly waiting for me. My lips curled up into a smile. Just a few more steps and I would be holding his hands. But right there something happened. Something bad that I had already envisioned in my nightmares.

A little girl bumped into me, making me flounder a bit. My hands held out to my father for some life-saving support. Muffled gasps filled the room as I steadied myself back on my feet. My bewildered eyes lowered onto her when she just giggled at me innocently.

Okay, you are cute, but don't ruin my special day, angel.

I smiled at her with tight lips and then she ran away, leaving me swelled up with the fear of embarrassing myself in front of all these people. But I focused on the brighter side of the moment. I was still very much standing on my feet. No major mishap had occurred. Yet!

The music was still flowing, and my man was still waiting. I had to be strong and prove to be decisive about the situation. Thus, I kept on walking. Not allowing the worries to settle down in my heart and consequently ruin my special day. I sauntered with the same grace that I had practiced and we eventually arrived at the end of the aisle.

I turned towards my dad and smiled as he gave my hand in Lucas's. "I'm so proud of you, Ray. Always keep shining as you do." I nodded warmly, barely holding myself back. He planted a kiss on my forehead and stepped back.

"You look incredible, dear!" I bit my lower lip as he stole the perfect moment to lean closer and whisper the compliment in my ear while helping me step on the altar. The moment was so precious that I wished I could hold on to it forever.

My eyes beamed with warmth, savoring the moment. Though my veil was an heirloom and had been passed down to every bride in my mother's family tree, I was having a hard time looking through it. It was too opaque for my comfort.

As if reading my mind Lucas lifted the veil and I caught a glimpse of Lucas's captivating smile. It did a perfect job of putting my troubled heart at ease. He was everything a girl could ever wish to find in her partner.

The priest continued his sermon of addressing the guests. Narrating the wellness of our love. While all I could think of was how entrancing Lucas's eyes were. He had enthralled all my thoughts. For the onlookers, we were merely smiling at each other. Holding each other's hands. But on the inside, our anxious hearts were racing against the turbulence in our minds.

The officiant stepped back a little, as it was now the time for our vows. And every single voice hushed down in the deepest corner of the room. Lucas let out a deep breath and squeezed my hands before jumping into his script.

"Sarah Rose Walter." My heartbeat commenced to rise to the unbearable threshold as he continued. "You're the girl of my dreams who has brought..." He was curtailed short when a dreary commotion rose from the end of the hall. The pin-drop silence of the guests was interrupted by the clanking sound of now shattered glasses. The clatter echoed back through every corner of the room. It happened so quickly that before I could understand what was happening, my jaw hung open, witnessing the dancing curves of the flames swallowing the curtains. One after another.

Almost instantaneously, the comforting glorious moment of the wedding whirled into a ground of utter chaos. Mayhem painted the area as everyone broke into a struggle to flee the place in great haste. The room stretched with screams and shouts, striking my heart with fear.

Within a flash of seconds, everything around my eyes was burning down to ashes. A tear escaped my eye witnessing so many lives falling into danger when I heard my mother's scream at my back.

My head jerked towards the source of the voice, and a dreadful terror rose into my chest. Sickness crammed into my stomach, noticing her having difficulty in breathing. She was progressing too close to asphyxiation. My legs were weak, yet I fought to hurry towards her, only to be pulled back by my gown getting stuck into something. I had no time or patience to look for the cause. I plucked the garment as violently as I could, letting the fabric tear into chunks. But regardless of that, the hem of the dress remained tangled somewhere.

I was imprisoned around the flares. The scorching heat of the flames was flushing my skin. My head swirled in every direction, witnessing the fire starting to devour the altar. The entire section was ablaze. With hot black smoke encircling my essence, making me choke on my breath.

"Sarah!" My head jerked towards the call, but it was hard to tell from where it came across in between all that pandemonium. I covered my face with the back of my hand when I felt something wrapped around my body and in the next moment, Lucas was by my side.

"I got you, baby!" My terrified face shook at him in acknowledgment when I felt a weird sensation at the back of my mind. The feeling was so potent, yet so terrifying, that it made a chill run down my spine. I wanted to turn around and encounter the eeriness prevailing in the air. But Lucas held me unduly close to his torso, restricting any movements.

We started to head towards the back door, yet I could sense my suspicion getting fierce. As if someone's gaze was digging its claws into my back. It hurt in an unusual way, like a long-lost agony, and the wound was getting deeper with every step.

I was withering away under that sensation. Settling my mind on the upheaval, my hands pressed on Lucas's forearm when finally, I dared to jerk a little out of his grip and turn around. Only to welcome the worst, as my eyes met with the ghost of my past, 'Ethan Stanton'.

And that's when I lost consciousness.

One

Ethan

The gates slid open, revealing the colossal house as my car entered the driveway. Arriving at the porch, the wheels came to a smooth halt, and I let out a sharp breath. The day had finally come to an end.

A shaft of cold air greeted me upon exiting the vehicle, suggesting the entry of mild winter in San Francisco. After yet another hectic but successful week of traveling all over the country, nothing felt more relaxing. Home is after all, home.

At the mere age of twenty-seven, I had made a place for myself in the vast hotel industry as the heir of 'Stanton International', a fast-emerging hospitality giant. I had expanded the business well beyond my father's imagination. We had opened numerous hotels and resorts all over the world at almost all major holiday destinations. At first, my father was apprehensive of my big plans, but now he had realized I was really a man of my words.

No doubt, I was entirely exhausted, burning the candle at both ends. But it was worth it. These past few hectic days did buy vast emoluments for the company. Another exquisite beauty of Stanton skyscraper would soon be decorating San Francisco's skyline. I was satisfied with the labor I'd put into it. These sleepless nights were definitely paying off as the company shares were skyrocketing.

Entering the living room, my eyes fell upon my sweetheart asleep on the couch. I knew she would be waiting for me even at this late hour. Despite countless messages conveyed to her to not wait for me as I was running late. She was not like the rest of the people in this house who would sleep peacefully in my absence. She was a beauty inside out. Every time I looked at her, I tried to remember what I did right in my life to deserve a soul like her.

I couldn't hold myself back from admiring her. Pulling out a chair, I settled down beside her. Resting my chin on my palm, my eyes settled on her, noticing her striking face resting against the cushion and my mouth curved into a smile. She looked so calm and serene that I didn't want to wake her up. Her wrinkled face told so many stories of her worries for me that I felt terrible for keeping her awake during these busy nights. Thus, planting a small kiss on her forehead, I slowly stood up. Carefully, not daring to make any noise, I turned around to exit the living area.

To my dismay, my elbow brushed against a vase. I nearly jumped out of my skin when a loud clunking sound of the vase breaking into pieces echoed in the room. My head yanked towards her, noticing her abruptly sitting straight. I couldn't hold back the chuckle that left my mouth when I noticed her looking all over the place. As if she was evaluating what century she had arrived in. She rested a hand over her heavily beating heart, panic overtaking her features. But the smile on my face fell flat when I realized she had caught me.

"You! Stop right there!" Shit! You're in big trouble, Ethan Stanton. I winced when my eyes squeezed shut. Assessing the Medusa that had woken up to turn me in stone. I cursed under my breath, measuring the intensity of wrath I was about to face at that moment.

"It's just a dream, sweetheart. Go back to your wonderland. A land full of fairies, pumpkins, and handsome princes." I attempted to sound as magical as possible while I tried to glide away.

"How old do you think I am, five?" I slowly turned towards her, smiling sheepishly. My breath caught in my throat when she pressed her hands flat on the table, holding my eyes with a death glare. And before I could have saved myself, she launched daggers of oranges in my direction. "Ethan Robert Stanton! You can't run away from me. Where were you? Have you seen the clock?" I tried to duck as many bullets as possible. I was handling an open fire, and all I could do to save my six feet tall body was to hide behind a stupid, tiny briefcase.

The oranges were big enough to break my nose, and I had absolutely no chance in front of her. Good Lord, tonight this lady is in her real form. The ultimate incredible hulk.

"You're like a ray of sunshine..." I ducked another bullet. "... on a dark, drizzling day. Come on, Nanna. Why are you acting like a mad girlfriend?" And I welcomed another blow at me.

"Because you've made me freaking nuts! Where have you been these past six days? Do you have any idea what time it is? Did you even have dinner? I swear, child, if you continue to starve yourself, I'll be forced to push a pipe down your throat!"

"And now you are smiling at me. Do I look funny to you?" She kept throwing fruits till she ran out of them. My amused face was making her mad enough to earn that little pout on her lips that melted me right away. I was enjoying her tantrums. The adorable fight, her delightful voice, just as she kept on yelling at me. I threw my head back, cracking even harder when she stomped her foot on the floor.

"Well, if that is what you want, then don't blame me when I'll be at your office to kick your butt." Her threat set my mouth in a hard line, my body now paralyzed.

"The crazy, scary, clingy lady, says what?" I gave her a look that screamed she had one last chance to correct herself. But she just stood there, tall and presumptuous. With crossing her arms over her chest, the corner of her mouth lifted in a devious smug.

That's it! I have a reputation. If she is not going to back the hell up, then I'm going to make her.

I took a good hold of her cheeks and pinched them. Till they turned crimson. A loud screech left her mouth, and I realized I had signed my own death warrant right there.

"I love you, Nanna. But don't ever think about coming to my office." And I bolted. Ran in the opposite direction to save my life.

"Get back here, you little monster." She yelled in pain, rubbing her face all along.

"Get some beauty sleep, gorgeous. You are getting old!" The corner of my lips lifted when I heard her whining about my behavior and then I climbed upstairs, fading away from her sight.

My smile faded when I knew she no longer could see me. I felt bad for carrying it along with me all the time, but it was my best defense against the darkness of my soul.

People like me walk around this earth with fake smiles and hollowness in our sad eyes, making others believe that we are happy with our lives. But that is all just bullshit. Why can't we just accept our circumstances and stop pretending that we are alright? It's okay to not be okay. I guess maybe we are too scared to reveal our true identity. Too scared to get hurt again.

After taking off my jacket, I entered the password on the safe to keep the documents in safety of my room when a red file captured my attention.

'You are a disgrace to this family!' My breath quickened when a painful memory flashed in front of my eyes. The air in the room thickened and I couldn't hold myself back from retaining it against my pale, cold hands.

The sheer touch of the fabric of that old tattered file ran a shiver down my spine. The papers inside the folder had aged to the extent they had turned pale. But their imprint on my heart was still fresh, like a recent wound. It was no longer bleeding, but the pain and suffering were still there.

My hands started to tremble when I turned over the cover of the folder. My mind already knew, but my eyes still begged to see what was behind that closed record. Fingers pleading to feel the touch of that beautifully carved handwriting, the photographs. But I was a coward, who had no strength to face it. My heart couldn't take it and instantly, I put the file back into the case and shut the door, as if my sanity depended on it.

And then, memories of the day that had been plaguing me from the past nine years came back to haunt me again…

Shaking my head on the beat of the music, my forehead furrowed, hearing some commotion in the background. The voices were just mumbles. And my brows snapped together when the intensity increased with every passing second.

"For God's sake, please tell me what happened, Jonathan?" My Mother's voice echoed in the house.

Plucking down my headphones, my eyes narrowed at my closed door, and right then, I heard a loud hammering on my door. My body jerked up in alarm from the bed. The color drained out of my face as my bemused eyes stared at the door.

"Maria, don't you dare come between us this time!" My breath quickened. A shiver ran down my spine at hearing my dad's hysterical, sharp voice from downstairs. My hands squeezed into fists, not daring to twirl the dial of the door. I felt safe in my room. I believed if I stepped out, I might face some trouble.

I was stoned out of my mind and had no idea if it was happening for real or if it was all just another wild, vivid dream I was experiencing. My legs were shaking, and all I wanted to do was to hide under my bed and never to be found by anybody.

"Ethan! Ethan Robert Stanton!" I jumped out of my skin. His voice rooted me on the spot. I was breathing hard, struggling to inhale some air in my lungs. My hands started to shake, just as loud empty gasps expunged from my trembling lips. Terror overtook my mind, and I continued to blink at the closed door.

"Get your ass down here!" And in no time, I was sprinting downstairs, with my mother at my heels. My heart was pounding like anything. What has gotten into him? The intensity of his voice was enough for me to calculate the rage searing through him. I was so terrified that even the thought of being present in the same room with my father raised a panic in my heart. I wanted to run far away from him and hide in a safe haven.

Just when I descended the last step, I dared to look up and gasped, witnessing my dad simmering with anger. I never for once dared to meet his eyes. I didn't realize when my Mom passed me and was now standing beside my angry father, trying to calm him down while his eyes were desperately searching for me. And at last, he turned around, resting his intense gaze on me. I hastily bowed my head, struggling to keep my senses on track. I couldn't move, nor could breathe. Beads of sweat built against my forehead, and I winced when his voice assailed my ears.

"There you are!" My eyes were cemented to the floor. While my mind was struggling to find the reason behind his wrath.

"Do you know this girl, son?" I flinched at his menacing tone. But then my brows snapped together. What girl? I perceived there was someone else present in that big space except the three of us.

Slowly and steadily, I lifted my head, flickering my eyes in between. I noted he was pointing his finger towards something or someone. At first, my eyes rested on my mother's face. Her eyes reflected the truth of how scared she was. Her beautiful features conveyed concern for her son, but she couldn't express it with words. She was struggling to hold herself back, and I begged her with my eyes to save me.

My arms remained at the sides, fists clenched tight till the knuckles turned pale. The strange thing was that I was still contemplating the purpose behind all this. My school was over and I had completed it with flying colors. Moreover, I already got accepted into the top-class college of the country that my dad himself had picked. So, maybe it was something not related to my studies. And then my eyes fell over her.

Clouds of uncertainty cleared up when I saw Ashley bundled up in the corner. Staring right into my soul with so much hatred and disgust that I knew she was going to change my life that night.

"I asked you a question, son. Do you know her?"

"I...I. I don't… N… no. No, sir!" My trembling mouth was barely able to put my thoughts into words. The answer left my mouth, and I quickly dropped my gaze to the floor. My body was shaking in horror. I couldn't dare to look at him while struggling to utter the lie. I felt like withering away under his gaze.

"Liar! You bastard, grow some balls and admit what you've done!" I twitched under her shriek, gritting my teeth in angst.

"You coward!" She took some steps in the direction of my weak body, and I winced, squeezing my eyes shut. Fear settled up inside me, like someone's cold hands wrapping around my neck. I was choking, no words dared to come out.

"Language, young lady!" The mere firmness of my mother's words was enough to make Ashley halt her steps. She struggled against her anger.

"Are you sure about this? She claims you two attended the same school!" My father's threatening voice was testing me. I could feel his suspicious eyes all over me, and I shook my head once again in denial.

His stare was burning a hole in my soul and I could feel pain rising in my chest. The unbearable twinge heightened with every passing second. A sense of startling anxiety engulfed my body. And perhaps that's why I never for once put up the nerves to meet his eyes. Because I knew if I did, I could've lost all my senses to even stand in front of him under the same roof.

"You son of a bitch! How could you? After all…" she shouted again.

"I'm sorry, but I would like you to stop right there, whatever your name is. We don't use such language in our house." My mother spoke in utter distaste as she backed me. She stood beside me and then exchanged a look of empathy, giving me an assuring smile. I forced a smile, but I knew no one could save me tonight. My insides were dying slowly with fear.

"Do you have anything else to say?" All eyes were glued to my father when he asked her a straight question.

I noted his features were gravely plain. His jaw clenched against the expressions that were stiffened. He waited for Ashley to say something in her defense. I watched when her eyes swam with tears. She exchanged a look from my father to me and I felt bad seeing her on the verge of breaking.

"What did you think? You would come here and build a tragic story trying to convince us that our son is a monster. How dare you try to tarnish our family name! If you were not this young, I would definitely have called the police." My mother was utterly disgusted by her sheer presence.

"Jonathan, why are you still listening to her rubbish talks? We know our son is innocent. You should be ashamed of yourself, young lady!"

"Maria! Enough!" I shuddered at his high call. He made sure that his voice would be heard. Loud and clear. My mother struggled to hold herself back. She passed a look of displeasure to my dad. An expression of absolute loathing for Ashley was furnishing her face.

"We are sorry for your friend's loss, but my son has denied all the allegations. Therefore, I don't think we have anything further to discuss in this matter. You may take your leave, child." The politeness in his words simply indicated she was testing his patience.

Ashley gathered her bag from the floor and gave me a last disgusting look with tear-filled eyes and left without uttering another word.

My head jerked towards my parents and my lashes fluttered, struggling to distinguish between reality and a nightmare. For a moment, my eyes met my father's, and I gasped, witnessing them flaring in rage. He could read my eyes now. He learned I had dared to lie to him.

And that little lie changed my life completely.

"Mr. Stanton?"

"Sir?"

"Ye… Yes?" I stuttered, just as a faded mutter in the background intruded my thoughts, making me aware of my surroundings. I was sitting in the office conference hall, surrounded by a dozen brooding eyes upon me, all dressed in blue and black suits just like me.

I was pulled back from my little troubling past into that enormous room. My eyes noticed a man across the table, standing near the whiteboard, presenting something that I had missed. I was lost again; I let my thoughts overpower me, taking me far away from reality. It felt like I had left my body, allowing my mind to roam around somewhere in the past. Trying to find some answers from those unsaid words.

"What are your views about this, Mr. Stanton?"

Shaking my head a little, I bowed down at my sunken reflection in the glass of the table. And then cocked my head on one side, letting my mind get comfortable with the present. It was not the baffled stares that made me loosen up my tie a little, but it was the feeling of being trapped. It was making me uncomfortable. The hall was too crowded for my likeness. My core stirred restlessly, and I took in a sharp breath of air to stay calm.

"I'm sorry!" And with that, I excused myself and turned around to step outside the room. Straightening my suit, I swung open the door before they could've judged any emotions from my troubled face. My forehead was covered in sweat, my lungs craving for some fresh air. I was distressed while hiding the broken pieces of my soul inside, and it was getting difficult day after day to survive under those stares.

It was a sensation similar to drowning. I couldn't breathe, I couldn't think. It was all blurry, incomprehensible. My consciousness faltered, like my body was becoming numb and my heart was losing all the warmth. I knew the shortness of breath was the first sign of an oncoming panic attack. I needed to go somewhere less swarming.

Climbing the emergency stairs to the roof, I felt my heart pounding. I was hyperventilating. My headache was getting worse, and I began to sweat badly. It was panic overpowering me. I tried to breathe and calm myself down, but it all went in vain. I felt like all the air was sucked out of my lungs and got replaced with weights.

"Are you okay? What happened there?" Just as I was beginning to relax, a thick voice fell into my ears.

Thomas barged in knowing too well where to find me. Restlessness was written all over his face, and I lowered my head, feeling the sudden surge of vulnerability hitting my soul. I couldn't meet his eyes. How could I, when he could clearly read mine and find out what exactly was wrong with me?

"You know; you can't avoid me forever." Tom started.

"What is exactly going on with you lately? You've never shown such a laid-back attitude before!"

'Because maybe I have had enough!' I yelled inside my head. I wanted to pull my hair in frustration and scream at the top of my lungs. But I couldn't do any of those things. I was chained, trapped in these filthy etiquettes. And I kept my poker face on, burying my inner demons.

"Nothing! It's just a bad headache. I'll be fine. How was the meeting?" I swallowed down my frustration, but I was terrified, terrified of being exposed. I feared he would read my mind merely from my voice. After all, it was Tom, my best mate I was talking about. We have been together since high school and attended the same college. We are pretty much each other's shadow and he knew me from inside-out. He knew what I had suffered. He had seen me in my worst days that almost broke me. We were not related by blood, but by heart, we were brothers.

"Sarah is gone, Ethan, and perhaps, for your own good." He said in a soft voice while placing a gentle hand on my shoulder.

A swirl of emotions welled up in my chest hearing her name. I had no control over it. I shrugged his hand and moved away. Taking deep breaths, I tried to calm myself by concentrating my mind on the traffic moving in front of the building.

I knew it was my heart that was going through the emotional pain, but my mind denied accepting it. Maybe hearing her name after so many years had triggered it. But whatever it was, I couldn't breathe.

All these years, I'd strived to forget her, erase her name from my memory, but everything about her was still very much alive in me because she had carved a niche in my heart. Memories flashed before my eyes when I heard her name. Sarah! A delicate and modest name, just like her. The name that had been haunting me for nine years, eating me alive, bit by bit.

"We need to talk, brother!" The resentment grew inside me like a tumor when Tom's voice prodded my ears once again. I kept my back to him, but I could sense the impatience in his tone.

"Buzz off, Tom!"

"Dude, you have to stop this! We did everything possible in our hands to search for her. She just vanished into thin air."

"What the fuck do you want, Tom?" I snapped. My temper had returned.

"What do I want? I want you to get your shit together. I want you to move on from whatever the fuck happened in your past. This is going nowhere, man. You certainly know, we searched every damn place on this earth. Hell, we have been doing this for the past nine years. Trying to find even a single sign of her, but nothing, not a single trace. Either she just disappeared or she definitely doesn't want to be found. I don't know, probably, she wants to live her life without the tint of her past on her present."

"Not today, Tom. I don't want to talk about it! Just leave me alone, for Christ's sake!" I begged.

"I can't, brother. I might be sounding cold-hearted to you now, but you need to take a look in the mirror. You are going mad. Jesus! If I could be brutally honest with you, I would confess, you're losing yourself; you've become obsessed with her. I know we have already talked about it, pretty much fought over it, but I feel you've never stopped searching for her. For God's sake, she was just another girl."

"Don't! Don't talk about her like that." I tried my best to control my rage, but he forced me to the edge and I grabbed his collar into a tight clutch.

"She wasn't just any girl. She was special. A rare soul. She had a fragile core that I broke into pieces. Don't speak of something you can't comprehend, Tom. Don't you dare!" If he wanted to pull the strings till they break, fine, I was ready. I wanted to smash something. But he didn't resist or tried to defend himself. That made me come to my senses, and I took a few steps back.

Lowering my eyes, a wave of regret washed over me. The flash of anger had protected me from the pain that was threatening to leak through my eyes. I put a cigarette to my lips and Tom remained silent while I lit it and took two deep puffs.

"Fine, if this is how it's going to be. But you need to stop obsessing over her. That chapter is closed. The End. And if she really is, what you claim she is, then I guess she would want you to be happy, too. You have to move on, Ethan; at least for her sake."

"But what if one day I find her?" I said, lighting a cigarette.

"Then you better beg her for forgiveness and stop being such a prick." He snatched the cigarette from my mouth and crushed it under his foot before storming away, leaving me puzzled.

He believed she was the one who had been holding me back. Her memories had been keeping me trapped in my past, not letting me move on; but he didn't know what a monster I was. How I broke her beyond repair. I sunk so low that now I couldn't even meet my own eyes in the mirror. I shattered a heart, the heart that once loved me more than anything. Yes, it took me some time, but that night made me realize what it felt like to lose someone closer to your heart.

Love is as precious as those guarded memories we once lived, which give us immense happiness by remembering them throughout our lives.

Tom wanted me to forget about her, to move on, but he wasn't the one to abandon her. I could never end my search, couldn't put a deadlock over my mind to not think about her all the time, to not miss her. The face that held so much pain couldn't be erased from my memories with a snap of the fingers. Standing on the edge of the roof, I looked down at the tiny world and a thought crossed my mind.

What would happen if I jumped right now? Who would miss me when I was gone? And then I stepped back. I was no longer that coward who would run away from his responsibility; giving up wasn't an option.

I know, Sarah, what's done is done. I can't change anything. I can't make amends with my deeds. I know my actions are unpardonable and aren't justifiable. The way I treated you was wrong. But I just want to see you once more. I don't care if it will be the last time, but I need you to understand me.

I know you hate me and perhaps don't want to see me ever again, but I'm really sorry, girl. Maybe, somehow, you have forgotten about me completely; about our past, about those painful memories, but I can't let you go, girl.

Not until I see you again.

Two

Ethan

For once, I was having a peaceful dreamless sleep but had to be jerked out of it in the middle of the night by an emergency call. Just my luck.

"Tell me exactly what happened!" I was shouting at Tom, ready to board a flight at San Francisco International Airport.

"I don't know. I just got a call from John about a major fire breakout at one of our hotels in Houston. I don't have much information, but he said something about five people being injured."

"Oh, Christ!" I raked my fingers through my hair against the turmoil simmering in my nerves.

"How did this even happen?" I exclaimed, against the loud commotion coming from the engine of our private jet. My head spun, still contemplating the news that had woken us from our beds at this darkest hour. And here we were, rushing to reach the site as early as possible.

It was like a pile of troubles had turned over my head. We had endangered innocent lives. People who were my responsibility. And now my father's reputation was in jeopardy. The Stanton name was at stake. And only God knows how many people were going to sue us.

"They are still looking for the cause, but it looks like one of the gas boilers has exploded, sparking the fire." He explained further. *Damn! It wasn't just a minor mishap. An entire floor must have wrecked.* I shook my head in disbelief as we stepped inside the aircraft.

"Good evening, sir." The flight attendant was so calm against my raging nerves, it annoyed me.

"This is serious, Tom. A severe act of negligence." I nodded at the attendant with a short smile, and then stormed off, checking my watch.

At the fastest pace, we would reach there in three hours, which was way too late. But then, I'd no choice. Stumbling down on my designated seat, I had a drink and reclined back in my chair, trying to relax my mind against the unrest shooting in my skull. I closed my eyes, hoping this to be a dream, a nightmare. Praying in my head that something better was waiting for me at the other end.

❦

"This is my personal number. You can call me anytime." My consciousness came back to existence when Tom's voice fell into my ears, waking me from a troubled sleep. My eyes fluttered open at the sight of him flirting with one of the attendants on board. I let out a chuckle, a rather raspy one. The dryness in my throat made my voice hoarse.

My mouth had a strange aftertaste as if someone had spiked my drink. My muscles were sore and my eyelids were heavy, like I had slept too long. When it couldn't be more than three hours, as we hadn't landed yet.

I slid up the window curtains to have a peek outside, shifting against my seat, and glimpsed at the ocean. Beautiful, calm vast ocean with different shades of blue. The beauty of water was calling me for a dive.

Wait a second! An ocean?

My eyes opened wide, my senses coming back online for the assessments. The first thing I perceived was that we were definitely not on the soil of Texas.

"Welcome to Kahului Airport!" A loud greeting struck my ears, making me turn my head towards a grinning face.

"Tom, where the hell are we? What happened to the accident?" His smile got heftier, and a glare contained my features.

"You... little... bastard, you tricked me!" He was bowing down in every direction like he had delivered once in a lifetime performance, and then he turned back at me.

"We are going to stay in Maui for one week! Take it or I'll tell Nanna that you still smoke!" My brows furrowed. "She's already into this? Oh, that evil... evil gorgeous."

Tom wrapped a hand around my shoulder as we stepped down from the plane. "The hell she is, dude! And we are going to get you laid."

As if on cue my phone buzzed with Nanna's text flashing on the screen.

Relax and enjoy Ethan. Everyone deserves a break every now and then. I am sure you will find something magical there. Just listen to Tom.
Love, Nanna

I couldn't hold back a smile that tucked my lips reading her words. I loved that woman more than anything in my life. Hell, she was the only person in my life who was keeping me intact, keeping me sane, keeping me alive. She moved with me to San Francisco when my parents abandoned me. Her warmth served as a patch over the void caused by the absence of my parents from my life. Nanna knew what I had been through and thus it was nice to have someone that had seen you at your worst and still loved you. I knew my mum had sent her to take care of me when she herself couldn't. And I was thankful to her for saving me.

"Man! I already love this Island." I nodded, with a smile engraving my face when I heard Tom checking out yet another beauty passing in front of us.

"He said the same thing five minutes ago!" I affirmed, smiling back at the receptionist, completing all the formalities of check-in. Swirling around, I leaned my back against the reception counter, my eyes drifting to survey my surroundings, and I sighed. My heartbeat was synched to the melody of the peaceful sound coming from the ocean. I had eventually convinced my mind to focus on the present. Enjoy these seven days without worrying about my work. Well, that was impossible; still, I believed in giving it a try.

Plus, it was a good opportunity to check the quality of service our hotel is providing. No one knew my face and so we could easily live here in disguise and observe the surroundings. Just like the stories of Asian kings who used to go out in disguise to get a better understanding of their kingdom.

"Sir, your keys. The bellboy will take you to your rooms. Have a pleasant stay." Before I could've thanked the lady, Tom snatched the keys from her hands and then bowed in gratitude, before turning around to stroll towards the elevator.

I knew Tom's idea of having fun was to drown ourselves in booze for a whole week. But I was surprisingly fascinated by the isle. I never believed it could be this mesmerizing. My attention was pretty much occupied by the beautiful interior of the hotel. The pictures on the walls were depicting the lovely places I needed to visit before reverting back to my monotonous life.

The first and foremost thing I did after arriving in the room was to unfold the large curtains and then unhook the windows. The smell of the ocean had something so sweet that I closed my eyes, taking in a deep breath of air. My body had already begun to relax. The next thing my heart wanted to do was to run out of that room and explore the coastline and I left the room without even changing out of my suit.

The second I stepped outside the hotel, a sense of being 'reborn' swept throughout my body. It didn't take me more than a couple of minutes to reach the shore. The smell of the salty sting of water in the air was so intoxicating that my shoulders loosened. The sunrays warmed up the bleak part in my heart and I calmed down. The happiness of being contented and fresh washed over my body. Blue waves were roaring and hitting the white sand in a rhythm and I was bewitched by its beauty.

The beach wasn't crowded yet. Still, the smiling faces of parents and children stroked me. The small groups of people who were lost in their own little worlds, relishing the morning sun, were enough for me to feel normal again. A realization washed over me and I discovered this was what actually felt like being alive and breathing freely.

Although I was constantly traveling all over the world and had visited many coastal cities, never had I spared a minute to relish the beauty of the ocean; the splendor of nature, love and laughter around me. It was always all business.

I sat down on the white sand and let my skin soak the tenderness beaming from the daylight. Closing my eyes, I could hear the gentle sound of waves crashing on the shore; playful screams and squeals of kids running away from the waves; mothers telling their children not to go any further in the water. I was in absolute bliss. I could spend my whole life here and never wish to go back.

While breathing in the salty waves, I felt a stroke against my right shoulder. I jumped in surprise when next came a girl falling straight onto my lap.

"Oh, I'm so sorry... what a handsome face." Her eyes were a color of deep blue sea, and I felt heat rising into my cheeks when her hand caressed my face. Feeling awkward would be an understatement for the moment, as she still didn't budge from her spot, quite shamelessly enjoying her seat.

"Are you all right, Miss?" Sweet giggles encompassed me, and my head veered around, glancing at a bunch of ladies dressed just like her, rather enjoying the view. The giggles blasted her out of her little daydream, and she scooted up on her heels, offering endless apologies.

I had no idea what to say. Rubbing off the sand from my pants I stood up on my feet. I guess I never felt this shy in my life. So embarrassed and uncomfortable at the moment, I avoided meeting their eyes. They were laughing at my poor condition. And my mouth felt too dry to speak. I nodded like an idiot and then crooked my head.

"You scared the little soul." One of the girls said and then spurred out in laughter. The happiness inside my chest grew with so much beauty prevailing around me. They were looking exceptionally exquisite, wearing identical dresses. They appeared to be someone's bridesmaids.

"Let's invite him to the ceremony," someone whispered loud enough to let me hear it and once again a gentle flush of pink had risen on my cheeks, making me look helpless when they caught me staring at them. They all uniformly bowed at me, and then burst out in countless giggles, compelling me to squint my eyes in embarrassment.

I didn't know what to do at that very moment. So I just grinned at them sheepishly while scratching the back of my head, when one of them handled me over a camera. "If you don't mind." I nodded at her without uttering a word and took some pictures of them.

As I handed back the camera, the girls invited me to the wedding of their friend happening in the nearby resort, but I declined politely and watched them darting towards the main street. The soft fabric of their gowns fluttering in the air looked so angelic and elegant that I couldn't hold back a smile. I turned back towards the waves with a pleasing emotion.

I didn't know what the purpose behind all of it was, but a sudden urge stroked my spirit. Like my inner self scolding me that *'You are on a vacation dude, enjoy yourself'*.

And all of a sudden I decided to follow them before I could've stopped my steps. I caught up to them as they were leaving the beach and introduced myself. It had been a long time since I flirted with someone, but I think the girls liked my company.

The streets were filled with tourists, adorned with the smell of freshly baked bread, and I breathed in the sweet odor. My stomach rumbled at the emptiness. But before I could've walked towards one of the bakeries, my eyes flounced up against the colossal gates of a resort to my right, beautifully embroidered with flowers.

It was an extension of the same hotel Tom and I just checked in, but this part was completely different. This area was specially designed for destination weddings like this one. It had a separate entry and a separate parking space. The resort was constructed as a replica to a palace. It was a true beauty. Glancing up at the lanky palm trees reflecting in the pool at the entrance gave out a heavenly appearance. The artificially engraved rocks framing the water body lend it an impression of a natural water reservoir.

Unfolding my sleeves, I put on my jacket and straightened down the creases on my suit. I had to look less homeless and more a gentleman in that crowd. Raking my fingers in my cluttered hair, I put on my best impressive smile, and ultimately all suited up I was ready to crash the party. My heart was racing up on the fact that I was basically barging in as an uninvited guest, but I couldn't stop now. The girls were practically dragging me in.

As soon as we were inside, they left me alone and ran to take their place at the altar, but not before handing me their phone numbers and taking pecks at my cheeks simultaneously. My face masked with panic, which was soon replaced by a welcoming smile, unearthing myself, I found the place filled with quite a charming crowd. Moving along the long stone walkway, I couldn't help but notice the comfort in the air. It was a compelling, warm day.

The room buzzed with excited chatter and unfamiliar faces scattered throughout the place. I gulped down the huge lump forming in my throat as I stood in the middle of that big hall. I glanced at the guests and let out a deep breath. My brain was telling me to turn back and head out, contrary to my reckless spirit that wanted to experience more.

Making myself comfortable at a corner, I noticed the long aisle leading the way to a center stage and the chairs facing it, cleanly piled up in rows with beautiful blue ribbons draped on them. Being an expert in the hotel business, I could tell the decoration was marking my expectations.

Impressively decorated banquet, with lights, candles, and flowers around the corners, everything in the place called to an understanding that indeed a beautiful wedding was going to be held here. Stealing a glass of champagne from one of the servers, I leaned back at the wall as a loud cheer came fondling across my ears.

My head twirled sideways perceiving a group of men entering the hall. People stood up from their seats and clapped in a gesture of welcoming the groomsmen, best man, and then, at last, the groom.

Strangely, the smile which should have been there on his face was missing. He seemed apprehensive. Nervous, like they didn't have any rehearsal beforehand. However, he strolled confidently towards the altar, smiling on his way to his family.

But then, who was I to judge? I was just enjoying my drink. My glass was already empty, and I grabbed another one from the table. But this time, it was the wine that was doing the judging.

My eyes drifted towards the side of the bridesmaid when everything inside the room fell silent. The light dimmed to obscure everyone else against the spotlight, which was overhauled over the main door. The music pervaded in the air like a gust of fragrance flowing from the bouquets, and I bowed my head in disappointment.

My curiosity had now begun to die down and the alcohol in my blood was having a deleterious effect against my empty stomach. This time, the commotion in front of my eyes had broken the spell. I reckoned it was just a waste of time to come here and enjoy some free liquor.

Shaking my head, I tried to subside down the dizziness overflowing my head. I had too little sleep and too many drinks to be this soaked up in the daylight. I decided to leave when my cell phone started to ring.

"Where the hell are you? Bastard, you already left for San Francisco, haven't you?" A chuckle left my lips when Tom sounded like I had murdered someone.

"You can't guess in a million years where I'm right now." I commenced towards the exit. My eyes briefly roamed back towards the ceremony, perceiving the bride walking towards the altar. Damn! She had one fine-looking ass.

"Funeral. You are definitely at some funeral." I shook my head, enjoying a good laugh.

"Well, no. I'm at a wedding... I was. Sort of." My perviness couldn't help it and I turned my head, checking her out once again. Her lacy gown was gloriously draping around her curves with her beautiful golden locks peeking out from under the veil. And right there I fought a sudden urge to run my fingers through them.

The groom lent out his hand as she joined him at the altar. And I couldn't help but make my eyes roam over that beauty once again. But then I chuckled, slapping the back of my head, comprehending that I should stop checking out someone else's bride.

"Wedding? Whose wedding? Hello?"

Something about the moment made the corner of my eyes catch hold of something. Tom continued to yell at the other side of the call, but I couldn't concentrate on his voice. Every single fraction of my body paused, while my eyes were entrapped by a little nudge at the back of my head.

My head yanked towards the end of the altar, and the truth knocked me out like a gigantic, ferocious wave.

I couldn't move...

I couldn't speak...

I couldn't breathe...

I was struggling to inhale and exhale some air, to do anything that could classify me as being alive.

"Sarah?"

A perishing gasp left my trembling lips. As if asking a question to my own subconscious.

It was her. It was definitely her.

I had finally found her!

My mind wasn't playing any tricks. I squeezed shut my eyes and then unfolded them again. She was still there.

The veil which was once concealing her face was long gone now. Making me admire the face. The face that I'd been scouring like a maniac. The face that had been haunting me all my life. The couple was listening to something the officiant had to say. And my heart sank deeper into my body. She was getting married.

My world came crumbling down in ashes. I couldn't help it. I wasn't ready for something like that. This just couldn't happen. My breath got caught up in my lungs. Nothing but some daunted, convulsing gasps broke out from my mouth. My throat felt arid, like a barren desert.

Everything around me fell quiet. Nothing but an emotion of betrayal scratched my heart. Sarah Walter was in front of me, smiling and sparkling. And she was getting married? Any second now.

But why did I feel cheated? Sarah Walter was starting a new life? She had moved on with her life. She had made up her mind to leave me behind and walk away towards a better future. She had forgotten Ethan Stanton.

I shook my head, half-wildly, struggling to regain consciousness from that damn chilling nightmare. I even slapped myself just to disappear from this nightmare. But she was still there, getting married, listening closely to whatever that guy was saying. Guy? Groom? Vows? You got to be fuckin' kidding me!

She couldn't do this. She had no right to just move on with her life while I was still tied to her. I was the one who had been suffering all these years. Only I knew what I did to find her; I endured the pain every day, withstood every misery just to find her. But, look what she did for me.

Moving on with her life. Getting married to some bastard and dreaming about her happily ever after. But what was left for me? Nothing! Emptiness!

I was the one who was on the losing end, getting cheated. She couldn't do this to me. She had no right to play with my life like that. We needed to sort out so many things. She couldn't just leave me hanging like that. She simply couldn't go and marry any random guy. Jesus Christ! What did she even see in him?

My eyes fell upon her aunt. She was shaking her head at me with a stern look engraving her face. She had noticed me. She had recognized me. And she was alarmed. It was a warning, threatening me not to create any trouble in the marriage. But why? I wasn't here to cause any trouble. But again, why couldn't she notice my situation, the drama in front of her eyes, which was absolute rubbish, totally untrue!

The priest began to speak again and right there, something pressed down on my lungs. Putting tons of weight on my windpipe. My legs started giving out; I sought to take some steps back. I didn't know why, but whatever was happening in front of me didn't feel right. I wanted to flee, yet didn't want to lose her again.

I turned around to leave the place right at that moment, only to get slammed against one of the servers holding a tray full of wine glasses. The collision was so strong that he stumbled back over the chairs behind him. The embellishing pole holding up a portion of tent came down with him, and it was just the beginning of an awaiting calamity.

My eyes bored into the repercussions of his fall. The glasses on his tray went flying in different directions. Beads of liquor sprinkled against the curtains and likewise on the tables beside us. Letting the candles catch the flammable liquid, turning the fiber into the dribbles of wild flames.

The vicious flames engulfed the curtain and right in front of my eyes, the whole wall of curtains went ablaze. The silky material helped them to get charred even faster. The flames spread like a wildfire. Heat scorched my skin, and I had to haul that waiter away from the wall to save him from getting engulfed in blazes.

Screams filled the air, making havoc plunge upon the room. The fire alarm was blazing, and the water started coming down, but it was insufficient. Bit by bit, everything came under the contact of flames, giving rise to an air that was drying and choking.

A small accident had such a huge consequence that in a few minutes, I found almost half of the banquet hall burning down in ashes. The black smoke started filling my lungs, forcing me to cough out against the heaviness on my chest. My hand shot up to my mouth, watching the different colors of flames coiling on the tune of disaster.

I dashed towards the helpless, stranded people, assisting them toward the exit. Wrapping my jacket around a little girl, I hurled her up in my arms and rushed her to safety.

The fire fed on the wood with ease, turning the once pretty wedding hall into a labyrinth of fire. Within the spirals of flames, my eyes drifted towards the altar and I saw her sheathed by the ferocious blaze dancing around her little soul.

"Sarah!" My feet pressed against the floor as I dashed towards her. My hands tossed the chairs out of the way, eyes hooked on her. She was scared, frightened to the bone. A fright crossed my heart, dreadful fear of losing her.

My heart was plunging deeper in the terror. My legs glided against the floor, stopping my body at the very second when I witnessed her fiancé appear around her. He wrapped his coat around her torso, blocking my view. My panicked eyes watched them fleeing from the back door and my body stood paralyzed at that very place.

I recalled wishing every night to get a chance to see her one last time. But was this really the dream come true?

Or a nightmare to cut the ground from under my feet.

Three

Sarah

T he wild gust of feral storm howled, carrying everything with it from dead leaves to the uprooted plants. The fragile shrubs were dancing to its tune, leaving them on the verge of being overthrown. Within the darkness that had overpowered the dusk, leaving the sky gloomy and blind, the storm had started to overwhelm this tiny island with its wildness and I could tell this was going to be a rough night.

The clouds had finished their work of engulfing the sky in shadows. Though it was still twilight, the gloominess had done its best to make everything appear like it was midnight. Another thunder cracked through the bottom of the clouds and I had to shut my eyes to retaliate the fear that had begun to build in my heart. I needed to increase my pace if I didn't want to be soaked to the bone in the rain.

I glanced up and noticed the flickering lamp posts stretched along the pathway. They were making it difficult to see anything on that stormy night. The wind felt thick and frantic, smashing against my face.

"Your mom was right; we should've had tea with her rather than getting our ass-slapped by this insane weather." Ashley was having an equally hard time walking against the harsh wind.

"Come on, hurry up. We don't have time to play who was right," I yelled, and she just nodded at me, hiding her face from that cold harsh waft hitting us.

I failed to notice when the red scarf around my neck loosened its grip and in the next instant; it flew away in the heavy breeze. I twirled around, my hand reaching out to grab it before it could've disappeared in the hollowness. But I was too late. Ash was right if I hadn't been this stubborn we wouldn't be in this situation. I never expected the resort to be this vast. It was like we were walking for ages on this dark, endless trail.

Another thunder cracked against the darkness of the clouds, and all hell broke loose. The clouds could no longer handle their weight and I winced against the downpour piercing through my pale skin. We ran against the slippery path, desperate to reach our destination. My breath heaved as we hurriedly climbed up onto the front porch of our cottage, struggling to catch our breath against the front door. Ash let out a sneeze and impulsively a chuckle escaped my trembling lips. "Bless you."

"I'm going to check on the windows and you go turn the lights on. This place is creeping me out." I confessed, as Ashley dashed towards the rooms.

Rubbing my palms together to provide some warmth to my numbed skin, I ran towards the bathroom. If this dress didn't come off the very next second, I was definitely going to catch a cold.

After taking a soothing warm shower, I changed into my comfortable loose top and shorts and walked out into the living room. My gaze fell upon a pleasing fire burning in the hearth and I strolled towards it. It was the heart of the room and I stumbled down on the chair beside it, letting my body reap some warmth.

"There are no clean towels left in the bathroom. Do you think we should call the room service?" Ash asked, standing at the edge of the table, making some coffee for us.

"We can, but I don't believe it would be useful. Seeing the weather, by the time anyone would reach here the towels would be soaking wet," or maybe everyone was still busy cleaning up the mess of my charred wedding. But, of course, I didn't let that thought escape my lips.

"You are right. Well, I was just hoping we could do something to divert your mind from the fire, but this pig-headed weather clearly has some other plans." She handed me the cup, and I nodded, burying my face in the intoxicating whiff of caffeine.

"So, how are you doing? I know it's a pathetic question to ask, but still... I'm here... you know... If you need to talk or anything." She took three pauses to complete the sentence, and it precisely narrated the thoughts running through her head.

"It's fine. Really, I'm okay. At least, everyone is safe. That's all that matters in the end. Right?" I couldn't meet her eyes. I was positive she knew two things about me at that moment. First, I was lying, me being okay was far from truth and, second, she had realized she couldn't do anything that would make me feel okay.

"Look at the bright side. Even if the wedding would have happened, your reception would have been washed off in this storm." Ash laughed at her own joke.

I gave her an awkward smile when she fake yawned. "Well, anyways, I'm going to knock out in those clean, feathery, luscious, warm sheets. If you need anything, just wake me up." I nodded, and then she disappeared into the darkness.

I turned back towards the hearth. My eyes were gleaming under the spell of the flames dancing on the heap of timber, and I let myself get lost in the vast labyrinth of my unconscious mind.

It was almost dawn while I still lied awake remembering each and every moment of that fire.

After years of rethinking, reviewing every single angle, reconsidering all my life choices again and again, I had finally overcome my second thoughts. Eventually, I had plucked up the courage to start a new life, to give myself a second chance. To marry someone who understood me, and knew me to my deepest buried secrets. But I believe God had other plans.

I realized I was twisting the beautiful gold chain dangling in my neck, absentmindedly. The cold metal brought back the memories of the day when Lucas gave it to me. The day we decided to get married, the wedding date which we finalized. How nervous I was when he proposed to me. However, he was like the way he always is, a lucid water droplet.

I flipped the pendant and my fingers caressed the words engraved on it.

'Forevermore'

I held it close to my heart while squeezing shut my eyes bitterly. *Why do I feel guilty whenever I read these words? As if they never belonged to me. Do I even deserve it?*

My body descended faintly over the soft mattress, and I let out a deep sigh. My mind was still contemplating the fact that I could have died right there. Just in a blink of an eye, everything perished to dirt. Yet, in between the seconds of being shrouded by those screeching flames and getting saved by Lucas, even at that critical moment of life and death, I saw Ethan's face. I knew it was my mind playing tricks on me. He could never be here. But why did I see him? I thought I had overcome my past.

I closed my eyes to give some comfort to my messed-up thoughts. A soft tap stroked my senses, but I didn't bother to open my eyes. The storm was making all sorts of noises. Maybe some tree branch was scraping the window. But the very next second it came again, and this time it was a clear knock at the door.

My body jerked upright, eyes landing on the clock, which was showing quarter past four in the morning. This was an unusual hour to expect someone. Whilst there was still a possibility I was imagining things, but then it came again, louder than before, making me well aware of the certainty, and my forehead furrowed. My head averted towards the window, catching a glimpse of the beautiful drizzle. The storm had finally settled down, but who was the guest it had left behind?

Wrapping a robe around my body, my feet touched the cold floor, and I winced. With my every step towards the door, the vigor of the knock on the old wood heightened. The person on the other side had begun to lose patience, and my paranoia deepened. For a moment, I thought to call the security rather than opening that damn door. But then I thought maybe it was Lucas being sad and depressed over the disaster.

My trembling hands reached for the knob, when I called out, "Who is this?"

It was a futile attempt because my own feeble voice betrayed me. It was barely audible against my trembling lips. I rested my ear against the door, compelled to hear anything that could give me any kind of assurance that I wasn't in danger when I jumped back against the knock. It caught me off guard, and I couldn't stop myself from yanking the door open on reflex.

My whole world came crumbling down in front of my eyes when a bolt of lightning cracked through the air, lending me a moment to appreciate a face.

The face.

Every single thing fell quiet around me, like someone had put my world on mute. My eyes fluttered restlessly, struggling to erase the delusion that they were witnessing. I stood frozen, paralyzed on my spot; nothing could make sense except the dizziness that commenced to creep over me.

It wasn't only my heart leaping against my chest, but my whole body throbbing with angst, battling with the lump flourishing deep inside my throat.

Ethan Stanton!

The boy who betrayed my soul. The boy who broke my heart and shattered it into a thousand pieces. I was staring right at him, numbed to the core, whereas his head was bowed down, perhaps not being aware of my presence. But why? Why the devil was he here?

There were so many unsaid words between us that kept on clenching my heart.

Amazing how some people come into our lives simply to ruin us.

"Hey!"

That voice. That freaking, beguiling voice, which now had a touch of depth, struck me like a lightning bolt.

If you could refer to a situation as your worst nightmare, then this was mine. Standing tall in all his Greek god like glory at my door, soaking wet and shivering in the cold. The chilling wind blew through his sagging wet hair draped over his forehead. The rain and the darkness of night has made his ash brown hair appear almost black.

He was dripping wet from head to toe; the rain had whacked over his body, making the clothes cling to his chiseled abs like a second skin. I could clearly see his muscles throbbing behind his now transparent shirt. There was no inkling of any struggle he had put on to save himself from the storm. And I wondered for how long he had been waiting outside my door.

Our eyes met for the first time in nine years and sparks flew in the air as if we were exchanging electricity through the wooden door we both had been touching. He took a step forward, and I sensed my face heating up.

I was too stunned to react. His hand rested flat on the door and he pushed it open quietly. A combination of fear and desire crossed my features. He held my eyes chained against that subtle gaze, deep and dark, like his own personal dungeon. He was self-mastered in torments and I happened to be his prey today. I could feel electricity flowing up and down my whole length of body.

"You haven't changed a bit!" He spoke again, rather too intimately, looking straight into my eyes. My lips quivered with lashes fluttering incessantly as I fidgeted with my confused mind. I opened my mouth to say something, anything that could make the ground less shaky, but not a single word dared to escape from my arid throat.

"This is so unusual!" His voice had a tint of embarrassment. He leaned on to the door, resting one hand over the door frame while the other swept off the hair from his face. And right there, his enormous shadow engulfed my short frame.

I noticed how extensively he had changed. From the twinkle in his eyes to the gentle smile over his lips, the boy I once knew was all gone now. His features clearly confided how important role time plays in altering someone. Still, his nonchalant gaze at me with those sparkling blue eyes didn't change at all, even after nine years.

My first instinct was to throw myself at him and burry my feeble body in his strong arms. Instead, I strengthen my hold on to the doorknob for my dear life.

I took a step back and dropped my gaze; the doorknob felt icy in my fingers as I shook my head. I was hallucinating. This was a bloody nightmare. This was not happening; it just couldn't be. I attempted to close the door in his face, but he jammed his leg in between, curtailing my actions right there.

First mistake!

"Sarah!" My name fleeing from his trembling lips felt like a long-lost memory I never desired to recall.

My eyes lifted to him, breaking the compulsion that was not permitting me to escape my delusional world. I could no longer run from him. I had to face reality. The truth of him being real.

"Just hear me out first, please!"

"How did you find me?" I muttered under my breath, asking the question to my own fearsome core. I still couldn't comprehend the fact he was here. No logical rationale supported his presence in front of me. It's just plain absurd. He wasn't supposed to be here. He couldn't just find me when it had taken me years to build my own new world far away from his shadow.

And now, the boy who ruined me, hurt me in every possible way, wanted me to hear him out? The boy who broke me beyond the extent of repair, the boy who watched my heart bleed until I withered away, expected me to let him damage me once again?

The creases on my forehead furthered when I heard him mumbling something, as if fighting with himself. His muscles twitched and he fidgeted uncomfortably at his place like struggling to control his body from performing some involuntary action. Then he shook his head dismissively and I noticed him letting out a heavy sigh before he looked up again.

"How are you, Sarah?" His deep, dull voice caused a shiver to run down my spine.

For a moment, anger poured through my veins, and I imagined my body quivering in rage. I reckoned to shout out at him, to insult him, to make him suffer for his misconduct. I wanted to heave out every single retort that he deserved, but I swallowed down everything. He wasn't worthy of my resentment; he wasn't worthy of anything. Not even a tiniest bit of any kind of reaction from me. Because I wasn't the same girl anymore.

"Just peachy since you've asked, Mr. Stanton." I was infuriated. He just couldn't get to appear out of nowhere and ask me how I was doing!

He let out a humorless chuckle. "I see you haven't forgotten my name." His ego poked a void at my tolerance. I wanted to smack that smug off his face. He was dangerously testing my patience.

"And I see you are the same arrogant asshole, just like I remembered." He was getting on my nerves. I couldn't recall a single person who deserved this much bitterness but him. My hands pushed the door once more, but his hand jammed against it, wasting all my efforts.

"I need to apologize, Sarah!" He looked straight at me.

I watched him reduce the distance between us, and my breath got caught up in my throat. My heart began to race up against the thoughts in my mind, all muddled up. I froze, bewildered when he halted just in front of me, securing his place in the room. His big muscular body hovered over my small frame. His hard gaze never abandoned me.

His eyes were dull, so tired. As if it had been ages since he last slept. I couldn't tell if it was just weariness engraved on his face that compelled me to melt underneath him or the heat disposing off his body.

I felt something softening inside me, witnessing the sadness in those astonishingly pale blue eyes that had lost their spark over time. Behind my paralyzed body, there was a windstorm that wanted to elope and touch his face. I wanted to kiss the sadness out of those ocean deep eyes.

Leaning further into me, he deepened his gaze, perhaps to catch a glimpse of my soul. His hand drifted towards my face when his alcoholic breath blew over me, enough to wake me up from the trance.

If I were in a good mood, I would have appreciated his amazing acting skills, but the thing is, I was furious. I was immune to his dirty tricks now. My eyes burned with rage when I noticed him taking another step towards me.

Second mistake!

"Get away from me." I pushed him as hard as I could. Hatred was the only emotion that overwhelmed me now. The sheer audacity he had to come and make me fall into his ploy all over again.

"You're so wrecked; you've no idea where you are right now. Possibly you don't even know me."

"Sarah, I'm not that drunk to not know where I'm. Please, listen to me. I know, my actions have caused you pain, a mistake that I deeply regret and I've come here to correct it. Please understand."

A humorless chuckle left my mouth after hearing the word 'mistake' from his mouth. Had I been a sheer mistake to him? I let out a sharp breath and looked into his eyes.

"It's sad how some people can fall so low to manipulate you for turning into something so disastrous that you lose your own worth... I won't say it again. Just leave. I'm done playing games with you."

His head shook vigorously, with his frantic eyes searching for something on my face. I started to walk towards the door, calmly waiting for him to be gone when I felt a strong grip on my wrist, and without a fair warning, he swirled me into his arms.

My body collided against his unmistakably hard chest, with him claiming both of my hands under his captivity. I struggled in vain. He was so strong that I couldn't even budge from my place. One part, a very strong part, of my brain was begging me to stop struggling and just hold him in an embrace. I hated how my body was reacting to his touch but my mind was still in control.

Third and final mistake!

"Get your fuckin' hands off of me." Anger rose in me like one fierce tide. My smoldering eyes bored holes into his soul, seething with angst. "How dare you touch me?"

"Not before you hear me out. Sarah, I know I've disappointed you. I've played with your emotions. But please trust me, when the reality struck me I didn't waste a second in trying to find you, but I couldn't. It was like you had vanished. As if the earth had engulfed you alive." He freed my hands and took several steps back, holding up his hands in surrender.

"Please try to understand. I'm regretting every single second of my life when I wronged you. Believe me when I say I have suffered enough in these nine years. I've withstood enough remorse to make a man lose his sanity." I felt nothing but utter loathing for him. He sickened me. His sheer presence in front of me made me see those flashbacks I never wanted to remember again.

"You have to understand. I've changed. I'm not the same Ethan I once was. I just want to tell you, if I knew... You know... Reality... I would've done things differently between us." If he wanted to be a stubborn asshole, then let it be.

"I'm calling the security if you don't leave this minute." I dashed towards the phone and hurried to dial the number. I was about to explode in rage. Resentment grew inside me like an untreatable poisoned wound. I have had enough. Holding the receiver in my hand, I glanced back at him.

"Please, I only came here to apologize. I have no intention to hurt you or cause any trouble. You need to know my mistakes are still tormenting me even after all these years, Sarah. They are making me insane, bit-by-bit, demanding answers, pushing me to the height of madness."

"Good, and trust me, you deserve worse. Now move." I gestured towards the door, as I was almost on the verge of screaming by that time.

He reckoned a stupid apology could change everything. He believed I would accept his apology and overlook everything that had occurred in the past. What was he sorry about? Was he regretting ever loving me? Wait, no, he never did that. A cold-blooded man like him could love nobody but himself. Oh my goodness, I never loathed someone that much.

I felt tears threatening to build in my eyes, but I struggled to push them away. It stung to recall the memories that came back with him. The love I gave him, and how he crushed it so brutally that I blamed myself as if it was entirely my fault.

"Sarah, please, for God's sake, just try to understand me. I might have hurt you beyond repair, but I still care for you. I know how you felt. Please don't take me wrong." He was not leaving, and I concluded this was not going to end easily.

"Is this some kind of joke to you? Do you have any idea how much pain I had to go through because of you? How foolishly I blamed myself for everything bad you did to me. Do you have the slightest idea how does it feel like to wake up in a hospital all alone and not knowing what day it was? Mr. Stanton, you're supposed to be there to know how it felt, so don't give me that shit."

"Hello?" There was a sound from the other end of the receiver in my hand that I had almost forgotten I was holding.

"Yeah. I want security in cottage 17, right this minute," I yelled at the person and then hung up.

"Just leave, man." My eyes drifted towards the source of that voice, and I saw Ashley standing at the edge of the living room. I had no idea for how long she had been standing there witnessing all this drama. But I was thankful that she had my back.

"I've called the security. It would be better for you to leave immediately, or possibly your little ego will get hurt."

"Sarah, you are still taking this all wrong. Can't you see how much I've transformed? I'm done playing around; I even joined my dad's company and have been working my ass off. So much that I even own this..."

"Ma'am, we received a call from this cottage? Is there a problem?" All heads turned towards the door, witnessing two men running towards us, carrying steel batons in their hands.

They were lightly soggy and panting, but thank goodness they had arrived on time. They glanced at me first and then towards him and I reckon they perceived easily who was the source of the trouble. I noticed them striding towards him, and I chose to put my back at them. I didn't want to witness any kind of turmoil.

"Get him out of here, and if he appears near this cottage again, I'll make sure to talk to the manager," I spoke firmly.

"Sarah, please, I'm not the man I used to be. I've become better. You changed me; your pure heart altered me. Please believe me, I just came here to say how sorry I'm. I had no intention to offend your feelings or insult you." I shut my senses to his words. They were a pile of lies that meant nothing to me.

"Sir, you have to come with us!" I believed they had by now begun to force him out of this cabin.

"Get your hands off of me! You have no idea who I am." He was struggling for sure, but it was two against one.

"Please, at least look at me. Don't turn your back at me." I sensed his voice started to curtail in the background, like they had commenced to drag him out of here.

"I know this is not you. You are kind enough to forgive me." He yelled again. And the edge of irritation had returned in my head and I turned back to yell at him.

"You are wrong again, Mr. Stanton. Unlike you, some people do change." They were certainly doing a nice job of throwing him out of my sight. I no longer wanted to hear anything from him.

This was no doubt the worst day of my life, first the fire and now this. I wished I would wake up from this nightmare like all of this had never happened.

Ashley came rushing towards me as a commotion broke out at the front door. One of the security men was lying unconscious on the floor while another was struggling for air in Ethan's grasp.

"I warned you not to lay a hand on me, bastard. Do you know who I am? I'm Ethan, Ethan Stanton. This bloody hotel belongs to me, you belong to me, and the fuckin' sign on your uniform belongs to me." Witnessing him barking on the face of the security guard, my jaw slacked in shock. I noticed him clenching his collar like he wanted to rip his head off. He was almost breathless with anger and I took some steps back when he turned towards me after letting go of that man.

His gaze startled me. His eyes were burning with an unmistakable blend of anger and hurt. His ego had been dented. I had damaged his pride. He appeared vengeful with his shirt in a mess and so were his ash brown hair.

And a red scarf was dangling out of his pocket.

Four

Sarah

NINE YEARS AGO

My senior year was almost over and, with it, an awesome experience. I would always treasure these memories.

Usually, I preferred to walk to school, just fifteen minutes away on foot. I liked to walk, alone and serene. It gave me immense pleasure to witness the little things in my neighborhood that we missed often. Just like Elizabeth Bennet. Not a day goes by without a solitary walk.

But Aunt Rose offered to give me a ride today, and I didn't refuse. She was my mother's elder sister. But I could bet they were twins. So synonymous in every way. She was widowed at a young age and never remarried. Though she couldn't bear a child, she had every quality a loving mother could possess. As a child, I loved spending my summer breaks at her house in Fairhope, Alabama.

When I was just starting middle school, Aunt Rose asked my parents and I, if she could take me to stay with her on a long-term basis. My parents resided in Montgomery and were struggling with the newborn Angus at that time. Mind me, he was a crybaby. So, they gladly agreed, and I was thrilled.

Thereafter, whenever the question of my return to my parents was raised, I refused with one or the other excuse. I loved it here and didn't want to lose my friends. I visited my parents almost every holiday and we go on vacations together.

Though I wasn't legally adopted by Aunt Rose, she had practically been my mother ever since. I never felt uncomfortable sharing anything with her. It was like talking to Ashley, but with slightly better words.
I also knew offering a ride was her clever way of monitoring what had been going on in her teenage niece's life.

"So, you are graduating soon!" Her eyes stole a view at me.

"Hmm, hmm!" I replied while texting Ash that I will meet her at school.

"I just want to tell you that I'm so proud of you, dear." I turned towards her when she was sneaking a look at me and then turned her attention back to the road ahead.

"I know it's a little stressful starting everything once again in college as a freshman. But I know how strong you are, Ray. You'll be just fine. Just don't be afraid to accept change!" She passed me her trademark sweet smile.

"I'm a little nervous, Aunt Rose! New city, new friends! I bet I'll barely enjoy their food!" I shrugged when she enjoyed a good laugh, placing a hand over mine.

"You've got this, Ray! Some days are hard, sometimes people are hard to deal with too, but you just need to choose what is right for your mental health." She was looking at a distance with emotions in her eyes, which made me believe she was reliving her own experience.

"Learn to let go of things which you can't control. And accept things that make you happy. Just like how beautiful you are looking today. Oh, I love this white dress. You are looking like an angel." A smile tugged on my lips, running a hand over my dress.

Soon, her legs pressed on the brakes as the Fairhope High School came into view. I quickly climbed off the vehicle, tugging my bag on my shoulder. "I'm going to miss your puddings very much, that's all I know for now. Now I really got to go!" I said, closing the car door, and she nodded at me with another heart-warming smile.

I watched as the vehicle faded away, and I inhaled a fresh breath of air. The day was just pure, bright sunrays warming my skin, with the perfect amount of breeze caressing my hair. I let the positivity from Aunt Rose's words seep into me.

I had been performing like a badass throughout the year. Almost every teacher was proud of me, and above all, I was certain of being accepted in Johns Hopkins School of Medicine to pursue my bachelor's degree. My life was perfectly planned out. Plus, I was in love with the school superstar, Ethan Stanton, who loved me back equally. What more could I wish for?

A short clamor attracted my attention towards the parking lot. A clique of seniors were surrounding the school bus. Tugging my bag on my shoulder, a smile was furnishing on my lips. I strolled ahead and my eyes adjusted on a big banner that was hanging in front of the entrance.

'CONGRATS FAIRHOPE PIRATES'!

"We won! We won!" Suddenly, the entire crowd roared with an ear-splitting cheering and the vibration complimented my pounding heart.

The whole crowd applauded for the cheerleaders joining the area while doing some amazing backflips. My eyes glistened with amazement at two guys following them with their cymbals. And then ultimately, all the cliquey jocks in varsity jackets marched out of the bus, parading their toned muscles, and the school entryway blared with endless cheers. The squad was bouncing in pure joy, communicating with the crowd through whistles and roars as they entered the hallway. A football flew above my head and I had to duck, saving myself. And then my fearful eyes fell over him.

Is it possible to fall in love with somebody so much that you feel incomplete without them? It's a beautiful feeling, yet so dreamy. The person runs through your mind all day and night, overpowering all your rational beliefs.

His handsome face gleamed with the best-crooked smile. Enough to make my day. Now that he and his unruly football team had won this year's championship, it undeniably made him the biggest star of the school, as he was the captain. The whole crowd roared with praise.

"GO PIRATES!"

The leader was followed by his whacky teammates as they leaped on beside a few cheerleaders. The crowd went wild, applauding even louder with hurray and pounding the lockers when he lifted the golden cup in the air. This was the biggest achievement for our school.

My heart was overwhelmed with pleasure of seeing him at that spot. His proud face made me so happy that I forgot where I was. But then I saw one of the cheerleaders flirting with him shamelessly, and my smile faded. Ethan Stanton was not the one to back away. As he always said, 'How can I disrespect a hottie when she is throwing herself at me? That's rude.' So he replied fully, throwing his right hand over her shoulder, bragging about his muscles in front of the mass.

I hanged back in a corner besides the lockers and observed him. I could hear his laugh even from above all the cheering. And then, he turned and flirted with another girl, wearing a deep neckline tank-top. As I said, he put his charm to its best use. Girls could go naked in an instant if he asked them.

Suddenly, my head jolted upright, noticing him leaving his squad and coming towards me. And I straightened up, beaming from head to toe while fidgeting nervously.

"There comes your manwhore." The corner of my eyes creased, and I glanced to my left to see my favorite person. Ashley, my best friend, my other half, had the uttermost disgusted face when she rooted down in front of me, throwing her backpack and books in her locker. I giggled and shook my head at her.

"You are the dumbest girl on this planet! Oops, did I say that out loud?" I just passed her a sweet smile on her sarcastic remark. She just couldn't understand what was in between us. Because it was hard to have an understanding of true love when you had never experienced it yourself. Have you ever fallen in love? So much that it almost blinded you.

I knew it sounded too corny. But what if that mushy love was for real, and what if you had that in your life? The feeling was too good to put in words. Like, it left you smiling all the time, even when you had no reason to smile about.

The songs you listen to become more than just words, sung in perfect tunes. The hot water shower becomes more than just playing under that water. You fall short of dresses to wear, but then you wear a crazy combination thinking about him. When you feel everything is perfect in your life, and you want nothing more.

I was that lucky. I had that kind of love in my life. And he was walking towards me, with the best hotshot smirk on his face, passing flirty looks at the girls ogling at him and exchanging handshakes with guys. Ethan and I were in a relationship since he randomly asked me to be his girlfriend at the night of the homecoming after-party in the beginning of our senior year. And nothing stayed ordinary in my ordinary life since then.

We were considered 'the very-unlike couple.' If I could describe myself in simple words, I belonged to the 'infamous intellectual club' of the class. Only that, I didn't have any glasses or braces on my teeth. But, I was quite nerdy, and the teacher's favorite type, which automatically earned me the odd one out place in Ethan's circle. Ethan, on the other hand, was 'His Majesty' of our high school. He was the most charming guy that even a few teachers passed him clean chits for his pranks in exchange for a few favors. He gladly obliged them, too. Everyone called him the most kick-ass player at the school. He was the captain of the school football team, was blessed with the richest parents in the town and girls swooned over his handsome face.

I couldn't clearly explain when exactly I started liking him. But my mouth did go dry and the butterflies in my stomach took a weird whirl when I first saw him in my freshman year. We shared a class and the day he called my name while passing me the test sheet, my heart skipped a beat. The slightest touch of his fingers on my skin left me lightheaded. Back then, he was just a typical boy, far from the limelight, who enjoyed making people laugh at his silly jokes.

We took a few classes together back then and were not that secluded from each other's friend circle. I used to share my aunt's homemade pies with him, which he used to love. But when puberty hit him, it hit him hard, and he forgot all about me. He joined football and transformed from a cute, funny guy to the school hot-shot. He only hung out with his teammates and was always surrounded by sexy cheerleaders. And so our worlds fell apart until that night of homecoming.

Well, now you could easily assess what happened when he asked me to be his girlfriend. It was not like I was only attracted to his sexy physique, but I had seen the real him. In this relationship, I was the listener, and he was the talker. I treasured the moments where he had opened himself in front of me. It made me stand out from all the girls that flirted with him. We had something that was not built on infatuation. We had a special bond that couldn't be broken so easily. Some even considered us as a fling, and perhaps that was okay; because they didn't know what we really had between us. We didn't want to prove anything to anyone.

Ash had gotten tired of convincing me that he was a bad choice and I deserved someone better. Many a time, I had caught him flirting with girls, but I trusted him because I knew him like others didn't. Despite his friends always mocking him for having a girlfriend like me, he never listened to them. He always said I was his Plan B, of course, to drive them away. Our love didn't have an expiry date, and it made me the happiest girl on this earth.

Suddenly, I felt his strong arms encircling me and the floor underneath my feet floated away, as I found myself swept off of my feet. I let out a shriek and squeezed my eyes shut.

"Put me down. Please... for love of God, put me down!" And in the nick of time, the roller coaster ride came to a halt, and I was settled back on the ground in one piece.

"Hello, darling."

"Ethan, you almost gave me a heart attack. Don't ever do that again!" I let out a breath of relief, still holding my head.

"How can I give you a heart attack when your heart is already with me?" There goes Sarah Walter. His stupid grin made me surrender myself in his arms. I almost felt giddy, deeply inhaling his cologne. We perfectly fit into each other's embrace.

"We won, darling." He whispered in my ear, and I felt butterflies doing somersaults in my stomach. I could feel his heart beating recklessly. Then he slowly separated us out, gazing straight into my green orbs. His eyes were stealing glances between my eyes and lips, and I knew what he was thinking.

My heart skipped a beat, watching him coming closer. My chest rose and fell with rapid breath. Although we had been in relationship for a long time now, still every time he came close to me, and particularly in front of his squad, it made me break out in a cold sweat. I always starved for his touch, yet his presence always made me so nervous. We were seeing each other after an entire week and I couldn't wait any longer. The moment his lips locked with mine, my entire body was set on fire. At first, it felt like a touch of rose, but as things got intense, the rose withered into petals.

The kiss slowly slipped into my body like a dark spell, making me lose control over myself. His mouth was warm and perfectly savoring mine. I let myself drown deeper into him, as his firm hold was securing my face underneath him. My hands rested over his chest, spotting his racing heart.

Feeling the urgency in the kiss, I bit his lower lip, and to my surprise he pulled me closer as if that was even possible. I didn't notice when my hand slipped its way in through the back of his shirt, but it startled me when he shivered. I was shamelessly pleased, taking in the fact that I had this kind of effect on him. Right at that moment, I needed nothing from my life but to stay under his haven.

"Get a room, you two. There are other human beings trying to breath here!" Ash's voice echoed in the background. Ignoring all the clues my body was sending me, I pulled apart, already regretting it. I blushed a deep red, remembering how many people were surrounding us. Burying my face in his chest, I wished we were alone, but it was somewhat difficult between all those whistles and applause in the background.

On the other hand, Ethan was not even trying to make me feel less embarrassed. He was making it worse, with his hands wandering on my back, sending tingles down my spine, fluttering a thousand butterflies in my stomach.

"I missed you, girlfriend." He finally greeted, placing a hand underneath my chin, compelling me to look into his eyes. This was my favorite spot to get lost. Those blue orbs held so much love for me. It was magical.

"Congratulations, boyfriend," I whispered and smiled tensely, staring into his eyes. My heartbeat accelerated when he placed his hands around my waist, pulling me closer. We were just staring into each other's souls when someone's groan interrupted us. I turned my head towards the sound, only to stumble upon Ash's disgusted face. However, Ethan beamed at her, and there I knew this was not going to be a pleasant encounter.

"Were you born this ugly or something happened before you were rescued from the woods?" Ethan teased her. They had a special fondness for each other that I didn't think I would ever understand. I always found them amusing as well as cute. She suddenly turned around and sneered at him with smoldering eyes. They exchanged a hateful look that drove me back to my place. I squeezed his arms, and he winked at me and turned towards her.

"My bad, let's start again. What bad did exactly happen to you?" He gave a lopsided smile, and I covered my face with my hands in disbelief. When on earth these two are going to stop fighting?

"Well, I didn't know Jesus gave you the license to judge people." She spat back as she folded her hands on her chest. Her gritted teeth and piercing gaze challenged him to fight back.

"What? You don't know? Being a ripper, I'm allowed to wash away ugly faces from this earth." He replied, stepping closer to her face. They glared at each other like trying to shoot lasers with their eyes. I could see Ash was ready to scratch his face, and he was unquestionably ready to return the favor. As their expressions hardened, I concluded it was time to end the staring competition before it could take an ugly turn. Placing one hand on Ethan's tensed muscles, I turned to Ash, pleading with my eyes.

"Well, congratulations on ruining my day, but do you know, a scientist named an S.T.D in your honor?" Ash said sarcastically, breaking the eye contact.

"Holy crap, how do you know that? Oh, I see, you are the first patient!" That earned Ash's middle finger toward Ethan as she stormed off, cursing him with some excellent choice of words. She would have murdered him a long time ago if it was not considered a capital offense.

Ethan turned back at me and began to narrate the whole game. The center stage of his narration was his moves that ultimately led them to victory. I kept on admiring his delighted face with a thousand expressions jumping from one to another. I stood there, feeling extremely proud, watching him let go of himself, just like the fourteen-year-old boy I fell in love with.

He cupped my face in his hand, making me look into his eyes. "Jason is having victory bash at his home tomorrow and I want you to come as my girlfriend." Quickly, I released him, gawking at him for any kind of amusement on his face, but it had none. This was my first ever invitation to a high school party and I squealed, jumping in his arms once again.

"Only if you want," he whispered, stroking my now reddened nose, and I chuckled.

"Yes, please!" I was bouncing in contentment. Just the thought of accompanying him at the party gave me chills. I always wanted to experience one of the high school jams and finally, he was making my dream come true.

He was leaning in for probably another hot breathtaking kiss when unfortunately, we got interrupted by a call from his gang. I felt him groaning under his breath.

"Coming!" He leaned in and gave me a quick peck on the cheek. "I'll wait for you," he breathed in my ear, leaving me light-hearted and then he hurried towards his crew.

I was left breathless. My eyes noticed him running towards his team, giving me one last glance. I was glowing from inside, waving my goodbye to him while my eyes followed them until the bell for our first class rang.

Grabbing my bag, I headed towards my class but not before stealing a last glance at him with a smile that he couldn't catch. But I loved him from my heart and soul.

He was my one true love.

Five

Sarah

"And that is my father's second cousin. I didn't even know she existed until the wedding." I whispered back to Ashley leaning towards my right and suddenly we smiled and waved at her, noticing her staring at us.

Saying goodbyes to guests was one hectic job and after the accident, it made my job even harder. Almost everyone had left, except for my immediate family, my best friend and a few cousins, who were here more for the beach and beach boys rather than the wedding.

I was a bit relieved, seeing that all the pity for the almost wedded bride was practically over, and because Ash was with me to share the torment. And also because my most irritating cousin, Sam, was finally leaving with her mother, my not so beloved Aunt Grace.

Aunt Grace hugged my already miserable mother one last time, before wiping off her fake tears. And then it was my turn. I tried my best to not roll my eyes at her. "Oh, my! Why did this terrible thing happen to my little princess? I'm still shaking. You won't believe me, but I couldn't sleep last night, Sarah. I've even lost my appetite, precious. Oh, my baby girl. I'm so sorry." I kept nodding, trying my best to contain my smile.

"But promise me one thing, love. You are not going to get depressed at any cost. And don't ever think about getting on drugs. You are not cursed, precious. It is just your bad fortune." With that, Ashley and my jaws dropped dead to the floor as my aunt finally left.

"My hands hurt. I never waved so many goodbyes in one day in my entire life. I'm going to need a drink after this." Ashley spoke with a hint of discomfort at the edge of her voice. But she never ceased to lend her brightest full-blown smile.

My mother was sitting in a corner clutching my half-burned wedding gown, weeping, as if I was burned alive in that dress, while my almost mother-in-law was comforting her. But it was a futile attempt. My dad came next and attempted to snatch the dress from her hands when it tore into two pieces, welcoming a fresh burst of tears from my mother. I've one crazy family.

My lips parted to provide some comforting words to her, but my eyes caught hold of my luggage being unloaded from the cab boot by a bellman. "Hey, what on earth are you doing?" He suddenly stopped and stared at something behind me. My narrowed eyes followed his gaze, and everything cleared up when they landed on my mother.

"We are staying. I won't leave this place until you are married!" Whoa! Whoa! Whoa! One second she was whimpering like a dying cat and the next second I was witnessing Queen Victoria possessing her body. Dad was right about her. She certainly had some severe mood swings, and they needed to be addressed urgently. I followed her into the main hotel building, whining like a five-year-old.

I didn't want to stay at the same place as Ethan for one extra second. I'd promised myself that day nine years ago that I was never going to talk about him or would do anything which would remind me of him.

I tried to express my concerns to Ash, but she just shrugged her shoulders. "Nah! You are making a mountain out of a molehill, babe. He is gone. That chapter is closed. Don't think about that halfwit anymore. On the other hand, you are not cursed, precious. It is just your bad fortune." She imitated my aunt's words, and that welcomed a scowl from me. Yep, bad fortune. Well, my bad time started the moment I saw his face.

My encounter with Ethan came like a storm and left nothing but havoc at its trail. The confrontation took away my peace. Years of hard work; the wall that I'd built, which was supposed to be protecting me from him, all shattered with one look into his eyes.

I didn't want to see him ever again in my life after what he did to me. I had made sure not to cross paths with him. It would be a lie if I said I had forgotten my past entirely. There were still some loose ends that I wanted to tie, but couldn't. Despite all my attempts at trying to forget him or the memories that were linked to him, somehow my heart always knew it wasn't feasible.

No one can erase one's past. It's an absurd term to believe 'a fresh start'. You simply can't forget your past you just learn to live with it.

But, one thing that he made crystal clear was that he had not changed a bit in all these years. He was the same self-centered man. The same selfish, spoiled brat who could do anything just for his entertainment. What was he trying to prove by appearing at my door in the darkness? All drunk and messed up!

Nice trick, Ethan Stanton. First, go ruin people's lives and then apologize for your own mental stability. But I'm not going to fall for it again.

Shaking my head, in an attempt to fade away that awful night's recollections, we took the last turn and were finally standing in front of our new room. The bellman slipped the card in the socket and we entered a beautiful twin-bedroom suite. As a compensation of almost burning us all alive last night the hotel management was giving us a good upgrade.

"Maybe you are right, Ash. I'm just joining the wrong pieces together."

"See, I told you." She grinned from ear to ear, leaning back on the couch. But then her smile dropped, noticing the bellman, who was still standing at the door.

"And what are you waiting for, dude? I'm broke, and she is doomed, so get lost." I laughed, throwing my head back when I saw him hurrying out of the room, all panicked and pale. *Aww, poor fellow.* The second the door slammed shut, I followed Ash as she entered the twin-bedroom and threw herself flat on one of the beds, letting out a deep sigh. Ashley was very hard to predict. One second she would be all sweet and sugary and the next she could hurt you with her sharp tongue.

"It is actually not a bad idea. I am really liking this suite," I confessed, with a satisfying smile etching my face with appreciation for the room. I made a mental note to ask Luc whether he succeeded in postponing our honeymoon bookings.

"Or perhaps, if we look at this with a whole new perspective, who knows I could find my prince charming at this part of the hotel." *I can't believe this girl.*

"It's been only two weeks, freaking two weeks, since you burned down your last Prince Charming's clothes. And not to forget that deep scratch you positioned on his new girlfriend's face. Had I not stopped you, God knows what you would have done!" This girl is just a limit.

"Don't make me remember all that. That bastard! I should have cut his balls off. How dare he cheat on me? I freaking gave up my favorite ice-cream flavor for that douchebag." She started to pace around the room like a hungry wolf. *Have I ever told you she looks damn scary when she gets angry? Like a real psychopath.* So, I thought not to interrupt her in that unstable state. Let her remember her mistakes. And perhaps my speech would not be needed anymore.

"We dated for freaking three weeks, three weeks! Can you believe it, Sarah? That's the longest I had been with somebody. Still, he cheated on me, just like others. Such a long term I had invested and still got no commitment." I gasped in shock and shook my head while trying my best to conceal my laugh.

"But then, this planet is full of possibilities, and who knows, I might find my man on this island." Once again, she leaned back on the bed, getting absorbed into her fairytale. And I concluded there was no reason to argue with her anymore.

Her love life had little ups and downs. Or maybe she had been searching for love in all the wrong places. Well, what would you expect if you had a friend like me? I shook my head in disbelief, appreciating the lilies in the vase. "Well, as long as you're happy, I'm cool with it." I shrugged, and the next second I witnessed her bouncing on the bed.

There was a knock at the door, and before I could react, it opened. "What do we have here? Long-time no see, cupcake," entered my brother, the devil, Lucifer himself, the soul sucker, the troublemaker. I supposed I could go on and on about his qualities for a whole day. He was going to be a college freshman this year, but he had already achieved his mastery in screwing around. He was the biggest flirt I'd ever seen. And that annoyed the living soul out of me.

Within three seconds, he had already circled his hand around Ash's waist and leaned into her, just as she leaned back in utter disgust. "Did you miss me? I like every bone in your body, especially mine." I cringed at his toilet-licking line. While Ashley appeared like she was going to throw up any second now.

"If you didn't remove your hands right now, there is a very high probability you would lose your precious bone... cupcake!" She snarled.

"Very well, then!" He stepped back at her threat and walked towards my bed. Making himself comfortable, like he owned the place.

He never left a single chance to get on my nerves. No matter what would happen in my life. If I die or get hospitalized, this person was never going to exchange a sensible word with me. Every single person in my family had consoled me upon ruining my big day. But no, my little brother just had to say- "God has given one last chance to Lucas to save his life and run as far away as possible from you." Argh!

"Don't you think she is way too old for you, Angus Fungus?" I folded my hands over my chest and bored my eyes into his.

"It is Angus Walter. And don't you know I have a thing for experienced women?" He wiggled his eyebrows, and Ashley groaned, storming out of the room.

I couldn't tolerate him under one roof, so I followed her in a rush. Climbing down the stairs I noticed a small boy in floral shirt rushing towards me. He placed a small envelope in my hand and ran away just as swiftly. I turned over the envelope, but it had no name on it except the letter 'S' engraved on the handmade paper, and I opened the note.

Good morning, Darling
What a lovely day. Damn that blue dress. Are you trying to kill me already? Just like the sky sparkling with a thousand stars. I wish I were around you.
Have a great day
Yours, Mr. Perfect. XOXO

I stopped dead in my tracks. My heart started to race up in my chest against my baffled eyes, which were scooting over the words. Over and over again. I have a freaking stalker and I'm going to get murdered. OH... MY... GOD!

He knew the color of my dress! Was he watching me from somewhere? I pivoted around and gaped at every single person who was present in my surroundings. But, no one was paying attention to me. Everyone looked busy. Crumbling the paper in my hand, I buried it in the pocket of my dress and hurriedly climbed down the stairs.

Soon I reached the foyer and was ready to exit the hotel when familiar giggles stroked my ears. I tried to find the source with my confused senses, and then found Ash having a rather cheerful chat with a guy. A guy? Bullocks! *Is he the one she was talking about? Her next Prince Charming.* I quite didn't follow his face since his back was facing me. "Hey! Right here!" She waved at me.

"Ryan, this is Sarah, my everything, and babe, this is Ryan." He was indeed tall and handsome with ravishing golden blond hair. Gaze piercing and evaluating.

"Pleased to meet you, Ryan." I tried my best to be polite while he extended his hand for a handshake.

"Oh, the pleasure is all mine, ma'am." He retorted, and my eyes landed on our interlocked hands. Exactly seven seconds had gone by. Still, he didn't let go of my hand. I had to pull it out of his grip.

"I'm sorry, but for now, I've got to steal your brunette. It's an emergency." Giving an excuse, I literally pulled her out of his spell when she blew a kiss back at him. And I rolled my eyes so hard I almost saw my brain.

"What's the matter? You look like you have seen a ghost or something. By the way, I was heading towards your gutted marriage venue." I raised my eyebrows at her.

"Sorry! Your dad has summoned the whole family there." She explained, still stealing glances at her Prince Charming.

Now what? Forgetting about the note, I grasped her hand firmly and marched towards the place.

Arriving at the hall, the intense burned smell pervading in the air attacked my nostrils. The place was torn down into chunks. My mother was standing in the middle surrounded by my almost mother-in-law and they were deep in chat. While a few of my cousins who chose to stay stood at the corner, looking pretty bored. And then there was my brother, already flirting with one of the hotel staff.

A smile crept on my lips, capturing the sight of Lucas. He was wearing loose khaki pants and a blue shirt, looking handsome like he always did. I noticed he and my dad were busy in some discussions with the hotel staff. And then he captured my gaze and walked towards me.

"Good morning, love. I really like your dress." My eyes shot up to him. Was he the one who wrote me that note? But why would he want to be so secretive? Or scare me to death? He had never done anything like that before.

"What's going on here, Luc?" I asked him while looking over at my dad. He was busy chatting with the manager, who was a tall and substantial lady. But at that moment, her face had turned pale like a thin paper with nervousness. A man was standing beside her, but his face was hidden behind my father's. I got tensed for a moment when I felt Lucas's arm around my waist and then we started walking towards them.

"Good morning, Sir, Madam. I wished to bestow our tremendous concern on ruining your wedding. We are acquiescently apologetic for the lives that were put in danger." I nodded to make her feel less awful, and she smiled at me. "But we are more than thankful to your lovely folks for not changing the venue." *What? Who decided that? Dad? Is the wedding still going to happen here?* Before I could've said something, she continued.

"We welcome your decision to postpone the wedding for forty-five days, but there are some things we need to enlighten you about." *What? Forty-five days? That's a pretty long period.* And like Lucas had read the expression on my face, he leaned over my ear and whispered. "Sorry, babe. I have an important case that needs my presence in Court." I nodded at him while internally cursing the decision. Why didn't anybody ask for my opinion?

"Sir, do you recollect the conversation we had... about some changes?" She spoke to my dad, and he nodded with a friendly look.

"I'm afraid, Miss. Walter, but because of the accident, there are some minor changes we had to go through in the arrangements. Which includes some replacement of previous elements, here and there; to make everything perfect as we planned." This time she was addressing me.

I was annoyed and confused at the same time for no one seeking my opinion in making decisions for my wedding when my eyes fell on the man standing next to my father.

"May I present to you your new wedding planner, Mr. Ethan... Stewart!" The manager's voice sounded like it was coming from a distance as I was drowning in ice-cold water now, or a whole iceberg exploded over my head.

Ethan Stewart?

Wedding Planner?

Oh. Come on.

Give

Me

A

Break!

"Isn't he hot?" A familiar voice stroked my ears and when I turned to my right, I almost had to clamp my mouth to cease the shriek that threatened to escape. Because it was my lovely cousin Sam. Why the devil did she come back? Argh, she must have missed her damn flight!

"Please allow me to introduce myself. I'm Ethan Stewart, but you can call me Ethan, or anytime you want." Everybody chuckled at his witty remark and then he winked at my mother, who chirped like a fifteen-year-old teenager.

The room began to load with smoke once again. But only I could feel it. Soon, it started to cramp into my lungs. I could no longer breathe properly. Half of his face was concealed with a black hat. Yet with a swift gaze, he winked at me and my eyes popped out of the socket.

"But what happened to Marcus?" I barely muttered out, but Ethan was already ready with a reply.

"His fish died. I know, such a tragic loss."

Six

Sarah

"Ash, please pinch me. I'm having a dreadful nightmare and I wish to wake up."

"Ouch, not that hard, genius."

I was still letting my mind wrap around the scene that was unfolding in front of my eyes. Ethan Stanton, living and breathing, was having a chat with my father. I might have turned white as snow. Rubbing my arm, I turned around and shared a knowing look with Ashely.

I couldn't believe the fact that I was seeing him. *Is this some kind of dream I'm still living in, or is he standing in front of me for real?*

No, he wouldn't dare to come back into my life after how I treated him last night. Or was it some kind of vicious game of vengeance? He had come to ruin my happy life because he wasn't enjoying his own. And did I hear him right? Introducing himself as a wedding planner? My wedding planner? Had he completely lost his mind?

The whole place was buzzing with chatter and laughter while I was standing rooted at my place, gaping at him distastefully. He was bursting out in chunks of laughter every couple of seconds. As if my dad was cracking the funniest joke of the century. They seemed like long-lost childhood friends. He was so cheerful that I wanted to slap that smile off his annoying face.

"His laugh reminds me of my dad's dead cat. She died choking on the cookies I baked." Ash whispered in my ear without taking her eyes off of him.

"But you can't bake!"

"Exactly!" She paused for a moment, lost in her thoughts. "And just like her, we will have to bury his body in the garden; where nobody would find him." She sounded serious.

Right there my dad burst out into another hysterical laughter on something Ethan had just said, and my eyes narrowed at him. I had to listen to whatever he was feeding my father, so we moved closer.

"Well Mr. Stewart, your introduction has left quite an impression on people here. On the other hand, if my wife has chosen your team for our daughter's big day, then I believe I have nothing more to say about it. Do I?" My dad sounded flattered.

"As long as you have a desire to live, Sir!" Ethan replied and once again, they burst out into a thousand chuckles and I cringed to my bones.

"I don't think you have met the bride personally, Mr. Stewart. Have you?" The manager gestured towards me and my senses heightened. I had a strong gut feeling that this hellcat manager was one of the schemers.

"Mr. Stewart, this is my daughter, Sarah." Ethan turned towards me while my head rose to him and our eyes met. I swear the tension was visible in the air around us or maybe it was just me struggling to breathe here. The very first thing I noticed was the spark in his blue orbs. It was back. He gave me a goofy smile as his one eyebrow soared arrogantly, and all I wanted to do was to punch that stupid grin off his face right there.

"Damn, you are gorgeous!" His words were no more than a whisper. But ample to be audible by me and earn my 'what the fuck' look.

"It's a pleasure to meet you, Miss Walter." He extended his arm and our hands interlocked. Neglecting a sudden sense of fervor, my eyes peeked into his sparkling blue ones. With my jaw clenched, I firmly shook his hand. Making sure to give a sign of 'I'm not backing off, dude'. It was the enemy's pact of hate with our no-blinking competition.

I had to tell my family who he really was. I needed to destroy all his dirty plans or any other agenda he had to manipulate me to earn back my trust, or particularly my apology.

"I wish all brides were quiet and pleasant like you, ma'am. The last one's sharp voice is still ringing in my ears." He let out an awkward snicker, and I forced a smile. *Well, no one plans a murder out loud, Asshat!*

"By the way, Mr. Stant..." I paused for a second to scrutinize his condition of my intentionally made unintentional mistake. He scratched his head, and I couldn't hold back my smugness.

"Sorry, my bad. Mr. Stewart. Right?" He nodded, getting back the colors on his face.

"If you don't mind, may I see your business card? Just to ensure that you are the same person my mother has personally picked for my wedding. You know; I'm very particular about my choices." I folded my arms over my chest, witnessing the beads of sweat forming over his forehead. He quickly wiped off the nervousness while peeping around the people surrounding him, letting out an uncomfortable chuckle.

"What happened, Mr. Stewart?" My eyebrow rose suspiciously, with him turning pale.

"Actually, there is... It's with my assistant. Uhhh... Lucy… she has a little problem..."

"Ladies and gentlemen, I want to apologize for being late. In your service, Mr. Stewart's personal assistant, Lucy." just as on cue, a young man entered.

"You are?" Ethan muttered, just as all heads turned towards a new face popping out of nowhere. Everyone was amused, especially my dad. Because, since when mankind had started naming their sons Lucy?

"You are Lucy?" I rolled my eyes as if this little trick could save him. Lucy shifted in his place as my eyes stabbed into him. He seemed too familiar to my consciousness, and then it struck me. Thomas!

"Yes, Lucy. Short for Lucian! Is there any problem, señora?" *Oh, come on, Thomas. I know you. You know me. So, who are we exactly fooling?* I wanted to yell out the truth, but still withheld myself, trying to find out what the real game was. Thomas kept his poker face on, playing along with his master, and the resentment grew thicker inside me.

I snatched the business card and an obviously fake portfolio from his hands and then my cynical stare skimmed through them thoroughly. It looked damn real. But, how? My eyes drifted towards Ethan, who was by now smirking in return. Of course, he could buy anything with his filthy money.

"I appreciate your concern, Miss. Walter. But the people we hire have to go through a thorough procedure of reviewing and substantiating their quality. You don't have to worry a bit about anything, ma'am." That hellcat spoke again and, God, I wanted to strangle her. Did he buy every single person in this hotel?

"My daughter is a woman of questions Miss. Nobody can outsmart her." Patting my shoulder, dad let out a generous chuckle and strolled towards my mother. *Dad, you don't know how low this prankster could fall to make things twirl on his fingertips.* Fake name. Fake crew. Fake ID. Everything about him was one big fat sham. So, what was next in his plan? Getting me arrested by faking his own death?

"So, did you enjoy the little note I sent you?" Out of the blue, Stanton whispered near my ears. His hot breath against my skin sent shivers down my spine. I could feel my cheeks heating up and something churning at the pit of my stomach.

"What the devil are you doing here?" I muttered with my gritted teeth, stealing a glance at my surroundings. "You will see, Starz," he whispered when we got interrupted by someone.

"I'm really sorry, Sarah. I had to take that call." Luc joined us and settled his hand around my waist. His touch felt unusual, yet so comforting. I smiled, glancing at him as he leaned into me, planting a quick peck over my cheek. I looked at Ethan from the corner of my eyes and he was fuming.

Clearing his throat out loud, Ethan extended his arm for a handshake towards Lucas. "I'm Ethan Stewart, Sir. The new wedding planner. Glad to meet you.", Lucas had to withdraw his hand from my waist to draw it forward.

"Oh, yes, yes, Mr. Stewart, Lucas Romano." They shook hands as Ethan's brows knitted.

"You don't look Italian." Ethan had already started judging my fiancé.

I saw Luc drawing his head back, enjoying a good chuckle. "Shit! I forgot to bring my spaghetti hat to look more Italian!"

"Ha-Ha. My bad!" Ethan held up his hands in embarrassment, but he wasn't finished yet. "So, what do you do for a living, Mr. Romano?" I gaped at him in disbelief. *The hell he is telling you. Who are you? My dad?* And why the hell was he so curious to find out everything about him? It felt like Lucas was being interrogated.

I noticed a change of manner on Luc's face. He looked at him with skepticism now. Narrowing his gaze at him with a delicate smile, against the devil's straight poker face.

"Is he your ex?" Lucas broke a joke and Ethan responded the very next second. "You bet."

"Well, I'm a lawyer and before you shoot me with another question, my mother is American, and I was brought up in Boston. That's why I don't look so Italian." Lucas chuckled and the first time after meeting Luc, the devil smiled. The kind of smile that a serial killer would give you before slitting your throat.

"Excuse me, dear." I took my leave and commenced to turn around.

"Sure!" Lucas and Ethan spoke at the same time and then looked at each other. I tried my best not to groan. I stormed away, clenching my palms into tight fists.

"We can poison him with Cyanide. It's the easiest way to kill someone without being traced." I turned to Ash with bewilderment, starting to guess what types of movies she had been watching lately. She held up her hands with her raised eyebrows, while turning around and sprinting out on her heels.

I didn't know what Ethan was expecting to gain from all this, but he knew I couldn't get rid of him so easily. At least, not without creating a big scene in front of my parents and would-be in-laws, not to mention Lucas. I didn't want to spill all the secrets of my dreadful past in front of everybody.

I had to kick him out before he would even think of hurting my family. I needed to make sure he would be long gone before he even plans to ruin my life.

A knock at my suite door intruded my thoughts, and I turned my head towards the sound, already cursing the person for disturbing my peaceful time.

"My eyes are closed in case you happen to be naked." Ethan's voice yanked me up from the couch. Witnessing him barging into the room with his hand over his eyes.

"What the hell are you doing here?" I straight-up yelled at him. He peeked from behind his fingers and sighed dramatically, looking over at me.

"Here I thought it was my lucky day!" He said, dramatically rolling his eyes. My stunned face couldn't stop him and in seconds, he plopped over the couch bringing me down with him. Reclining comfortably on his back, he placed his hands behind his head and closed his eyes.

"Stanton? You dead, already?" I spoke with gritted teeth. He smiled at me, leaning close to my face. My heartbeat raced up in the acknowledgment of him invading my personal space.

I could smell him; the old Ethan scent I knew so well. A mixture of apple, cedar wood and fresh-cut grass. He was breathing my air, eyes moving to my trembling lips, surveying my face, like jotting down every single detail his eyes were perceiving.

For a fraction of a moment, I thought he was going to kiss me. My heart started beating at rocket speed and muscles in my lower abdomen tightened at mere thought of that hypothetical kiss. I didn't like how his gaze was piercing my soul, and I cleared my throat, pushing him back with both hands on his chest.

"Wh-what are you doing?" My voice betrayed me.

"I just needed to see your beautiful face up close, so right now, I'm ogling at you."

"I mean, why are you here? Crazyhead!" The lines on my forehead grew darker when he again leaned towards me, plucking out a rose from the vase behind me and holding it out for me.

"I want some of your precious time. Alone. Just us!" He said so softly I couldn't believe my ears. I snatched the rose from his hands and tossed it away.

"Did you really think I would agree to something like that? Never happening. Anything else?" I asserted firmly, folding my hands over my chest. I saw his eyes darting down just for the fraction of a second and the movement of his Adam's apple as he swallowed hard finding my eyes again.

"I didn't say it would be easy, but I could foresee that in our near future." He was still smiling in confidence.

"Listen to me, Crazyhead, I want you to be gone by sunset," I said sternly, looking deep into his eyes.

"I'm going nowhere until you forgive me, Sarah. Also, you don't have a say in it, darling. It was your mom who personally chose my crew. You can't oppose her decision." I could hear a challenge in his words.

But I didn't care to answer him and stood up, ready to walk outside.

"Sarah…" He tried to talk, but I raised my hand to cut him.

"I know what you are trying to do. Manipulating people and having your way with them is your favorite pastime. But, unfortunately, my life is not a game, so don't you dare play with it. I'm giving you a good piece of advice here. Just back off." I could feel a nasty headache creeping up on me.

"Sarah, I've not come here to play any games. You are speculating this all wrong. Hell, I didn't even know I would find you here. I'm not asking much. Let's just have a conversation for a few minutes, like two sensible humans." His voice sounded so genuine, but I knew better.

I shook my head, squeezing my eyes shut. This man was not going to back off easily. I let out a humorless laugh, noticing him dwelling in confusion.

"Monsters like you never change. It's all about revenge, isn't it? Just how the hell did this bitch get the nerve to insult me?"

"Don't you dare speak ill of yourself!" He shouted abruptly and stood up straight with a jolt and I sensed a threat in his words and instantly took some steps back.

He saw my action and flinched. Pulling his hair in frustration he took two deep breaths and with clenched jaw he spoke a little gently this time. "You can blame me, scold me or even slap me if you want but please don't say anything bad about yourself." I could hear desperation in his voice.

"Okay, let me make it simple for you, Stanton. I'm not going to forgive you. Not now, not ever. Therefore, you are wasting your precious time here rather than enjoying your glamorous millionaire life. So, go back to where you belong. Trust me on this. It's better for both of us this way."

Before I could storm out of there, my dramatic exit was cut short when the door went ajar and my mother walked in followed by a couple of girls.

"I like that, Starz. Keep that sassiness coming," he muttered, grinning, and then signaled the girls to come forward.

In a couple of seconds, I was surrounded by them as they started to take my measurement, bending my body parts in every possible uncomfortable way. One pulled my right hand up, while another took off to wrap her measuring tape around my neck. Trust me, she didn't know how to take a damn dimension, as she was choking me to death.

"She has put on some weight, Mr. Stewart. Make sure to craft her wedding dress one inch smaller." It was my mom's voice coming from somewhere behind me. With a smooth movement, they let me turn around and then, once again, commenced to grope every part of my body in the name of measurements.

"Mom, you know I'm better with off-the-peg dresses. I don't trust these guys," I pleaded.

"Oh, shut up, young lady. I know your choices. The undemanding and ragged potato sacks. I let Ashely make your first one, but that proved to be unlucky, so now I'm going to decide what you're going to wear!" Did she just tell me to shut up? And that too, in front of Ethan? My image was tarnished. A fresh chuckle stroked my ears, which soon turned into a cough, and I shot my best furious look at that devil.

"But for God's sake, I have forty-five days. Believe me, mom, I'll buy the fluffiest and most expensive gown you have ever seen." I could see she was not at all convinced.

"But Ray, there's nothing wrong with getting it stitched in front of your eyes. And the hotel is sponsoring everything for the wedding in-lieu of almost burning us all down to death. In addition, we are anyhow staying here for another week!"

"What?" I shouted without realizing. One whole freaking week? I yanked myself out of the grip of those stupid girls. "Leave us alone!" I cried out about the unbelievable information my mother just shot at me.

The girls shot a questioning look at Ethan, and when he nodded, they left, closing the door at their back. But Ethan was still there and showed no sign of leaving.

"Excuse me?" I raised an eyebrow at him. He looked at my mother and she held her hand up, permitting him to stay. He was trying hard to suppress his smile. *This is so embarrassing!*

"What are you thinking, Mom? I need to head back to work. And perhaps you too. What on God's earth are you guys going to do here for one more week?" I let out a nervous laugh. Please say yes, just one Y- E -S, but my mom's stare grew into a hard, scary gaze.

"Look, Mr. Stewart, today's generation." Her response confused me. I turned my head towards Stanton and witnessed him shaking his head in disappointment while looking down. *Am I missing something here?*

"Next week is your parents' wedding anniversary, Ray. Have you remembered something or do I have to state the specific date? Mr. Stewart here has convinced us to turn this doomed trip into a happy one. Hence, your dad and I have planned to stay here for one more week and celebrate our anniversary. Isn't it so amazing, Ray?" *Yeah mom, so amazing that I want to choke Ethan to death for planting this idea in your head.*

"But…" I started, but she cut me off.

"And don't make an excuse for work because you already are on leave for your honeymoon," she continued.

"You are so dead, Ethan Stanton," I muttered under my breath, looking over my mother's cheerful face.

"I'm sorry. Are you talking to me, Miss Walter?" He startled me.

"No!" I growled.

"Everything is set, young lady. Nothing is going to change now. And if you have any problem, which I can clearly see you have, you can talk to your father about this," she said in a conclusive tone and turned towards Ethan. "Mr. Stewart!"

"Yes, ma'am." He choked on his laugh.

"I've other important things to do. I'll take my leave now, but make sure the measurements are taken properly. I want that dress to be exquisite." She gave a light pat on my cheek with a soft smile and turned towards the door.

The moment she exited the room I turned towards Ethan with a smile etched over my lips when a flush crept across his face. Flickering my eyelashes, I slowly strolled towards him. He was dazed and alarmed. My heart was pounding, threatening to break free from the rib cage. I reached him, encroaching upon his personal space, breathing his air. And then I smashed my body with his. But instead of my lips, my knee smooched his groin.

He cried out like a five-year-old, plunging straight onto the floor. He clenched his little friend and uttered quite a profanity at the top of his lungs.

"Oh. My. Shit. Balls!" An evil smirk etched my face, noticing him in agony.

"Talk to me one more time with that foul mouth of yours, and I will cut off your balls." Immediately, my eyes drifted towards the girls frozen at the doorframe and found them scared shitless. For a good minute, they kept on gazing at him in disbelief as he was shrieking in pain, rolling on the floor.

I cleared my throat, making them break out of the daze, and they rushed towards him and dragged him outside the room.

"Asshat!" I shut the door and locked it this time. I headed straight for the shower to calm my mind with cold water.

After taking a long cold shower, I came out and sat on my bed tired. Events of the day catching up on me. As I laid my head on the pillow, I felt a paper crumble under my head. I gaped at the same handmade paper from this morning, with a beautifully engraved **'S'** on the top of the envelope. My first instinct was to tear it into pieces, but then curiosity took over me and I opened it.

Good evening, Starz

If you've started missing me already, then remember, I will always be right outside your window, darling.

Have a Lovely Evening

Your Mr. Right. XOXO

Seven

Ethan

DAY ONE

I had Forty-five days.

Until her wedding.

Until she could see me as a changed man.

Until I could win her trust back.

But did I really need forty-five days to earn her heart back? Or perhaps I could do this while we were still here. On this very island! One whole week was pretty much enough for her to forgive me. Perhaps, as much as I knew her, it wouldn't take her more than three days to forgive me and fall for my charm all over again.

Yup, that's what was going to happen, sooner than I had imagined. Or maybe I was being too self-absorbed? But then I had easily convinced her parents to stay one more week on the island, to my advantage.

"Staying in the cottage for almost a week is a terrible idea, dude. I don't know about you, but all my muscles are so sore that I feel like I was working out all night." Tom entered the living space of our cottage, and I looked up from my notebook, witnessing the crankiness etching all over his face.

"Come on, dude, you can do better. It's just a matter of one week." Or maybe less. I didn't know yet. He nodded while stumbling on the couch in front of me and closing his eyes when my mind drove me somewhere far.

Though I was positive about the outcome I'd been working on, the truth was, I had no idea what was going to happen in the upcoming days. I was still struggling with the basics. I didn't know how to earn her trust back, let alone, make her comfortable in my presence. She just didn't want to hear me out. I had made some calculative moves for my chance of success. Still, how was I going to advance when she didn't even want to speak to me?

But the one thing I was sure of was her. She had changed. I didn't know yet if it was for better or worse. Last night I observed that the warmth that used to sparkle in her eyes was gone. It seemed as if her soul was missing.

I wanted to hug her so bad. To keep her safe in my arms. It was physically painful to be so close to her and not able to touch her. My body was acting on its own accord as if it had broken past the control of my brain.

I wanted to drop to my knees and beg for her forgiveness but she wasn't ready to hear a single word coming out of my mouth.

She has grown into a strong woman just as I imagined her to be. But she has also grown cold. Like her heart was frozen behind thick walls with no means to cross over. Maybe in all these years, she had become good at hiding her emotions, but I could sense the little discomfort her voice held. And the fact that she wouldn't smile anymore told so many things about her.

I wasn't talking about the fake smile she had been carrying at that altar. She couldn't fool me. I knew her real smile, the one she used to give me when we were together. I wanted to make her smile for real. The true smile. However, as long as she was planning to strangle me in my sleep, it was kind of hard to accomplish that.

From the fire in her eyes to her lethal blow to my little friend, I could feel this trip had just started to take us to an unusual place, to a different dimension. As expected, she hated me with all her guts. Hell, she couldn't even stand being under the same roof as me. I bet my face annoyed her the most. And what infuriated her further was that she couldn't even do anything about it, unless, you know, she would tell my secret to everyone and voilà!

I was lucky that her Aunt Rose left this morning, otherwise, I would not have dared to show my face in front of her family. Even then, I was scared that her parents would somehow recognize me. But one encounter made it clear that she hadn't shared my photograph with her family members and I was safe until she or that evil devil Ashley would open her mouth.

One word from them and everything would be finished. I chuckled, thinking about the name she had given me. 'Crazyhead,' I liked it. No, I loved it.

"You are getting on her nerves, brother! She is definitely going to call the cops on us." Tom stated matter-of-factly, with an irritating smug on his face.

"Don't worry, dude. I'm not a man to be easily scared." I shook my head, looking away, and the moment Tom left the room, I chuckled once again.

I couldn't deny that I'd been enjoying our little chase. It was quite fun to see Sarah mad. But I wasn't doing all this to torture her. All I wanted was to melt the ice of her frozen heart. I want her to feel human again. To let her emotions flow freely without her concealing them in a glass cage.

I couldn't think of a moment in the past where I had heard her cursing or throwing death threats like she was asking somebody to join her for a cup of tea. I was pretty much relishing the moments, so much, that I loved to get on her nerves. Seemed like it had become my hobby lately. She looked too adorable when I irritated her.

I really needed her to understand that I was doing all this just to make her forget about her past. Forget about all the bad things. I had no intention of ruining anything, nor to take away the happiness she had found in her life. I just wanted her to notice me. Look into my soul and see the difference in me. Recognize that I'd changed, so that she would forgive me and let go of all her bad memories. For that, I was ready to endure anything.

I closed my notebook, settling it down on the table when my smile dropped at an odd suspicion. I felt strange, like I was being watched. A stare burning a hole in the back of my head. I turned around to peek out the window and there was Sarah. Standing at the window of her hotel suite with binoculars in one hand and my note in the other, staring right at me.

I made my way towards the window, keeping an eye on her. She didn't move at all. Though she was too far away for me to make out her expressions, I could sense the malicious smile creeping on her lips, making me almost cringe with fear.

Something mischievous has gotten into her mind. I drew a hand in my hair, trying to fade away the peculiar feeling from my mind when my forehead crinkled. A fear crossed my heart, and I dashed inside the cottage. And as I expected, my notebook was missing.

"Agent Tucker, what's the status update? Over!" I spoke in the walky-talky while balancing myself on a tree and snooping through my binoculars at Romano's room, two rooms down Sarah's. I know, I know, we could have just used our cell phones, but I was on vacation and this was pretty fun!

"No movement on my side, Agent Stanton. Our suspect is clear. Over and out!" Tom replied, and I tucked the walky-talky back in my jeans and further narrowed my eyes on my prey. He was sipping his usual black coffee, sitting in a chair on the balcony while reading the same old book.

He had a delighted smile on his lips that certainly didn't make him look like someone whose wedding just got canceled. I wondered why he seemed so happy. Like he was having the time of his life on this beautiful island. As if he was rejoicing at a vacation. Shouldn't he be sad about his wedding and honeymoon being postponed? Shouldn't he be spending every second of his time with Sarah?

I bet something was cooking in his wicked mind. And I had to find that out before he would hurt her. I had a gut feeling that he was disguising himself from everybody, and in reality, was an evil Italian gang member who was after something precious in Starz's possession. I wondered what she even saw in him. But whatever it was, it was fake. Just then, I decided that my first motive was to expose his real identity.

My brows knitted when Romano's phone buzzed, and he stood up, heading inside. The other side of the conversation made him crack in endless laughter. What's so funny, dude? Maybe it was his girlfriend? Or wife? Or the bounty hunter he had sent to kill me?

I followed his actions from my binoculars, copying his every move. Bending a little to my right, I scanned him closely. He was definitely cheating on her. Or why else would he appear so excited while talking to some random person?

He was getting out of my line of sight, so I tilted further when unexpectedly, I felt like drifting in the air. My body swayed in the air, a bit forth, a bit back. My heart came up in my mouth and I grabbed hold of the nearby branch of the tree for my dear life. Phew! Dude, don't forget that you are crouching on a damn tree ten feet above the ground. Sufficient to break your neck.

Steadying myself, I let out a breath of relief and cleared the sweat that had built on my forehead. And, once again, spoke through my walky-talky. "Target went beyond my vision. Can you spot him, Agent Tucker?"

When Tom didn't respond, I tried again. "Agent Tucker, can you hear me? Over." I was terrified of falling and breaking my ass. The things we do for forgiveness.

Minutes passed, but still no reply. I put on my binoculars again and attempted to discover the target, but he was still past my vision to make out anything. I sighed in defeat and searched for Tom when I caught hold of an image of golden hair and my lips tucked up into an ear-to-ear grin finding Starz.

A weird kind of joy filled my chest just by seeing her. My senses turned pervy as I focused the lens closer on her features. My gaze paused on her rosy, full lips and I felt something stir in my pants. Gosh! They are so kissable. Moving a bit higher, I glanced at her cute nose and the freckles on it, and my finger ached to stroke them.

Climbing further on, I noticed her alluring emerald eyes. They were piercing a hole straight into my soul. Staring straight at me. But why? Holy shit! I shot down my binoculars and saw her glaring at me. And that glare was creepy as hell. I noticed her talking to someone on the phone, while at the same time stealing a view of me.

And then, from the corner of my eyes, I noticed Tom. Sprinting on his heels, shouting and scratching all over his body. He was hysterical. Running wild and trying to take off his clothes at the same time. And the next moment, with a splash, he jumped into the pool, still half-clothed.

"Your agent is compromised!" Sarah's voice came from the walky-talky. "I repeat; your agent is compromised!" Followed by a sinister laugh.

"Dude, what exactly happened back there?" I asked Tom back in our cottage while he was drying his hair with a towel.

"I don't know, man. One moment I was sitting there keeping an eye on that moron and the next moment that devil's angel, Ashley, sprayed something on me from behind and I was itching all over. I couldn't help it and had to jump in the pool to stop myself from scratching the very skin off of my body." He replied in a painful voice. A chuckle left my mouth before I could stop it, and Tom threw his wet towel at my face.

"I'm leaving this island tomorrow morning, asshole. I can't live with this humiliation anymore," Tom blurted out, and I could feel the embarrassment in his voice.

"Man, it was just a dirty prank. Instead of fleeing the battlefield, we should contemplate hitting back. Be a good sport and think of something out of the box." I couldn't let those two birds win so easily.

"They are demons disguised as angels." He muttered.

I had to agree with him.

Eight

Ethan

DAY TWO

The temperature inside my car heightened with every stroke of her lips against mine. It was getting steamier and troublesome with every move, and I could feel myself steaming with the sensations she was provoking in my body.

"Oh, baby! I missed...you so much." She breathed out, her lips hot and luscious. Just as her hips rubbed against my raging friend, I couldn't help but moan against her mouth. She was going to kill me. I should've stopped her, but I didn't want to. My desire heightened with her every move. I pulled her closer. The long trail of her legs feverishly wrapped around my body. I removed her hair out of her beautiful face, kissing her deeply.

"Oh! Starz! I need you." She moaned as I bit her lower lip. My hands were running up and down on her body. Feeling every bit of her gorgeous figure.

Our heartbeat synchronized with each other, pounding like it was going to explode with so much passion infused in the car.

I closed my eyes when her hands began to unhook my belt. The zipper slipped down, and I could feel her hand inside my jeans. My lips parted in an extreme craving, already living the unfailing sensation she was about to give me. Her body shifted upon me and I shivered, realizing her hot vanilla breath nuzzling my ear.

"Are you ready for me, Stanton?" I could barely nod at her as she lowered her head. My breath hitched at the ultimate feeling when someone slammed a hand on the window and my eyes yanked open.

"Stanton! Are you dead inside or what?" A strange sensation jolted in the back of my skull, making me shoot upright on my bed. What is happening? The knock on the door came again, and I clenched my head, doing my best to wipe out the clouds of confusion over my reasoning. The ache in my head gained its edge, and I sprinted towards my bedroom door. I was truly annoyed by the way I was yanked out of that steamy dream with my cottage door being beaten up so early in the morning.

A yawn escaped my mouth as I scratched my head while my eyes adjusted to the sunrays coming from the now opened front door. It took me a while to ascertain that Starz was standing in front of me in real and I was not dreaming anymore. But why the hell did she seem so mad at this early hour?

"Oh, look who came back to life?" Once more, I yawned at her face, rubbing the back of my neck.

"Do you often get this hysterical in the morning, or did I do something special for this pleasure?" My voice dripped with sarcasm. But instead of replying she barged into the cottage, and my squinted eyes followed her till she started scrutinizing the space inside. She was fuming like she wanted to murder someone, most certainly me.

"What is this? Do you really think I adore making love like some poetry? If I may be bold enough to quote in your words. 'Slow and sensual. Like the billows of ripples. Hard and extreme may not be her thing'. What the fuck, Stanton?" My forehead crinkled at her words. I couldn't get a word she was babbling about. Woman, I need a minute to focus on your gibberish. My mind hadn't started working this early in the morning. And then, the lines cleared up when I saw my notebook in her hand.

"I... No... You didn't..." Fuck!

"I'm a sad little damsel in distress? But also in desperate need of getting laid. And for God's sake, who told you my favorite place to get a boner is on top of the kitchen table?" I was beyond mortified at that particular moment. She had read everything I'd gathered, or more precisely, assumed about her. Even the dark sensual details.

"Stanton, I need an answer on your Sarah Walter's Encyclopedia. And how on earth is this related to your little seek to forgiveness?" She shoved the notebook at my chest, and I gritted my teeth. Argh! Somebody shoot me, please. The embarrassment was eating me from inside.

"And why the hell are you wearing soggy pants?" My head lowered towards my boxer and horror etched my face.

"Oh. My. God! What are you, twelve? It is you who need to get laid, Stanton!" By now she had turned around, hiding her flushed face after witnessing the aftermath of my freshly wet dream about her.

"Argh! Do you desire to have that pleasure?" I joked playfully, making my way towards her. But all she did was groan out in annoyance.

"You are so annoying!" She shoved me aside, stamping her leg on the ground, and then stormed off of the cottage.

What the hell just happened to me?

Did you ever feel this weird sensation under your skin when somebody brushed against you accidentally? It came to pass like a blink of an eye, still, leaving you thinking, 'what the hell was that'. I couldn't explain it in proper words, but it was like waves of bolts running through my nerves, putting every part of my body on fire. It was a frightening feeling for a man like me.

It was just a bare shove from her side. But it was a touch that had left me thinking all day. Why did it feel strange, yet comforting? Whoa! I really needed to get laid as she suggested. Anything to get over this stupid touch sensitivity.

The rest of the day was spent between Tom harboring his bruised body and ego and I trying to come up with a brilliant plan to find Sarah in a private moment and make her listen to what I needed to say. To make her understand how I regret the past and strive for her forgiveness. And then I turned up with the worst plan possible in the history of all plans.

Tom didn't want to be part of any more of my stupid plans, but there was no persuading me to abandon it.

"Well then, if you don't want to come, I'm not going to force you. I'm going to deal with my mess alone." And with that, I patted his shoulder and tucked my backpack on. Twisting on my flashlight, I nodded at him and commenced towards my destination. I could feel his stare on my back, but he didn't say a word until...

"You need to promise me one thing for me to come. If worst came to worst and everything went south, would you let me jump out of the window first?" My head yanked back towards him, and I grinned.

"Of course, brother. And I promise I'll follow you after." My word was my bond. And he chuckled softly, already aware of the fact that we were jumping in a hellhole.

"So, what's the plan?" I encircled my arms around his shoulders, easing into it.

"First, you have to loosen up a little for what I'm about to tell you."

After a whole hour of revising the plan with Tom, we waited for nightfall to make our next move. We changed into our all-black attire and reached the first floor of the hotel. Tricking the gateman and manipulating the receptionist was the easy part. And if the manager could have been here, then she would have made our job even easier than this. However, the toughest part of the task was to breathe through our skiing masks.

It was past midnight and, as expected, the whole hotel had sunken in a complete lull. I looked at my back, making sure no one saw us. The corridors were empty and dark except for the dim night lights. I wondered if she was already asleep, or perhaps my thoughts were keeping her awake.

"Hey, lover boy, put a hold on the daydreaming part and keep your steps with me," Tom grumbled and I nodded at him, following towards the long corridor. This is why I didn't want to come alone. Tom was good at sneaking things. Many a time, his particular talent helped us sneak out of our dorms.

While the scenario was yet to unfold, I could feel a strange adrenaline rush in my veins. It was quite exhilarating for me to sneak up in her room like I used to do in high school, reliving the golden past. I could feel explosions in my head. Kind of good ones that carried the possibility of her appreciating my attempts and finally listening to my intentions.

"109. This is it!" And at last, we were finally standing in front of the designated room, exchanging a wicked grin. Previously, in the evening Tom was able to charm his way into the Room Service Supervisor's room and get the master key card.

Within the quietness of the corridor, a thought crossed my mind. We were certainly breaking some laws tonight. But, compared to the fact that I almost put the whole Walter family ablaze on the day of their daughter's wedding only two days ago, it was not that big a deal.

We were now breaking into the bride's room just to have a chat with her. I could have just walked over and knocked like a sensible person, but I knew she would never listen to me and throw me out just like on her almost wedding night. So my only option was to sneak in.

I didn't even want to think about the aftermath of the moment when she would see me in her room at this odd hour. One single scream from her and it would do enough damage to put us behind the bars. So, the genuineness of the situation was-I had to shut her cakehole, foremost.

I asked Tom to stand guard, as I was just turning to open her room. But then my heart came out in my mouth when a door opened to our right. My jaw dropped on the floor while my scream stifled deep down in my throat at seeing Sarah's little brother coming out. That little seventeen years old man-whore was escorting a girl out of his room just two doors down to our right with his boxers barely hanging on his ass.

I shot my head back at Tom, whose eyes were ready to pop out of the sockets any second. We were so screwed. Our straightened backs plastered to the wall, trying to blend in with the wallpaper, as we snuck a look at the little devil panning out from the room.

"Same time tomorrow, sweetheart?" He flirted in a fake, sexy voice. I kept an eye on him, wishing internally he didn't notice us. But, as he turned to leave, our eyes met and my breath caught up in my throat.

I felt Tom getting frozen in his place beside me. His eyes drifted from me to him, and he gulped down the lump in his throat. Fear etched in his eyes and the next thing I saw was his body lying dead on the cold floor, perhaps, to make him invisible. The dead cat act made me roll my eyes and mumble, "Bitch! Are you kidding me?"

But then something unexpected happened. The little devil started humming a tune and my head turned back to him. There was definitely something wrong with this kid. He was all smirking and stretching his arms out like I used to do. He acted like a carbon copy of my own twisted teenage self.

"No one saw no one." He spoke to no one specifically, and I stared at him in disbelief. He casually strolled back inside his room and closed the door without even giving a second glance at us. I noticed Tom peeking through his one open eye, as he carried the same confused look.

Tom stood up, letting out a deep breath of relief, while I was still holding up the perplexed expression. What the hell was that? Why did I feel like we had just been trolled? Or did our attire really camouflage us?

After gaining my wits back, I decided to go ahead with my plan but Tom started to shake his head furiously. Pulling me away from the door, trying hard not to make a noise. But I was not going to back out now. I knew Tom would bolt as soon as I was going to enter the room, so I dragged him inside with me. I hoped I was not going to regret this.

As I opened the door ajar, nothing but complete darkness welcomed us. Tom hid behind me as if we were facing bullets. He hung onto my shirt as a little girl scared to death of rats.

"You know you are not helping! So, suck it up and be helpful." I squealed at him, keeping my voice as low as possible, and he straightened his back, striving to exhibit his fearless facade. But I knew it wasn't going to last long.

With the pace of a snail, we advanced into the suite. The complete room was plunged in darkness. We could barely see anything in our surroundings. I felt like I was walking blindfolded, yet feeling every bit of air coming out of Tom's mouth on my neck. Our footsteps rattled on the wooden floor against the teeth chattering near my ear.

I twirled around and threw a flash of light on Tom's face. "You will lose all your teeth at this rate!" He nodded, shoving his hand over his mouth, and I turned around when the flashlight illuminated a scary painting hung over the wall. A short petrified shriek left our mouth, which we quickly subsided down. I guess even beautiful art could make you shit your pants when you are at the edge.

I'd be lying if I said Tom was the only one who was scared to death in that room. But the thing was, I wasn't that terrified of this room, which almost seemed like a haunted graveyard, nor of the fact that if we got caught, we would definitely go to jail. I was horrified by the person who came between these two. The woman who had a great chance of killing me after this night.

I swallowed down a nervous whimper and continued the exploration. While planning in my head, I was so sure of finding my way in this room, but right now, it looked like a bloody maze. As we passed through the living room, with a sudden skew, Tom's hand brushed against a ceramic lady figurine on the table, and my breath caught up in my lungs. My eyes squeezed shut and my ears waited for the inevitable breaking sound. We were so over! But the sound never arrived as he grabbed the artifice on the time, preventing it from shattering into pieces. My brows scrunched up at him, whilst he gave me an innocent raise of eyebrows.

Despite the pitch-black darkness encircling us, with the help of little glint immersing from our flashlights, we moved forward. The suite turned out bigger than what I had envisaged. We were digging for the particular door that could be our destination. And just when the flash landed over a shiny object, I looked back, exchanging a knowing look with Tom. It was the knob of the door that led to the twin bedroom, to the woman that was the spur of every trouble in my life. I took an eager step towards the door when I felt a grasp on my arm.

"Are you sure about this? I mean, we have already been busted once. What if he is bringing the security right now? Don't you enjoy being alive?" Tom strived his best to persuade me, however, I was in no mood to back down now. Not at this point when we were so close to our target. I swallowed down the lump forming in my throat against my hands, swirling the cold metal of the doorknob. She would certainly bury me alive.

My nose crinkled against the creepy noise coming through the door, which was drawing ajar. The first thing my eyes fell upon was the sleeping beauty on the bed. I chuckled, listening to her boisterous snores. Lovely. I didn't know she snored like a hippopotamus. Her body was entirely concealed within the sheets, which were heaving up and down with her every gasp of air. Only her golden hair was visible, assuring me that she was indeed my Starz and not that she-devil Ashley.

Wait a second! Where is the second wickedly wicked witch, Ashley? I looked around and clouds of perplexity washed over my senses when I realized there was only Starz present in the room, and the other bed was empty.

We moved over the bed and I turned towards Tom while placing a finger over my mouth. He seemed like he was having a nervous breakdown. The moonlight immersing from the slightly open curtains on the window was giving us perfect excess to her.

Shaking my head to cast off all the unnecessary thoughts, I took in a sharp chunk of air and slowly advanced towards her to wake her up from the deep slumber.

"Starz, wake up. Wakey-Wakey, honeybee. Look who has come back!" I wiggled her a bit. However, she didn't move a hairbreadth. Man, she is heavy.

Jabbing the flashlight in between my teeth, I shook her once again. A little too hard this time. I smiled when she finally groaned a little as her body scuffed against the sheet. And drawing on the evaluation that she was planning to go back to her sweet dreams. I yanked off her sheets just as my flashlight slipped from my mouth.

Two bloody things happened at the same time. Tom accidentally turned on the nightstand lamp and a pair of haunting gray eyes glared back at me. Although I had an incredible time living the adventurous adrenaline rush, I wasn't prepared for what happened next.

Boisterous shrieks filled the room. I was screaming because a rage-filled, wrinkled, unfamiliar face was looking back at me. She wasn't Sarah! No freaking way! The only other possibility was that Sarah had been drinking virgin's blood to stay young during daylight and transformed into an old witch at night. Tom was screaming because he was already scared to death. And at last, the woman in front of us might be screaming because she was in her nightie and two masked men had barged into her room, uninvited. And then it hit me. It was one of Sarah's aunts. We were totally screwed.

"Who is it?" She yelled, looking for her eyeglasses lying on the side table. My heart came out from my rib cage and I knocked them off and then looked over at Tom, who was already lying flat on the floor, playing dead. Seriously, dude? Again?

"What are you doing in my room?" The woman shouted, and I fidgeted to my left and then right. I was doomed from every side. There was no escape plan. My whole body was shaking and panicking at the moment. Neither this old woman was included in my plan nor this feeling like I was going to faint.

Everything that happened next spanned out so fast that my head could barely process it.

The woman started screaming at the top of her lungs and gave a hard kick in my nuts and all the lights went out of me. But before she could make her way to Tom, a sheet wrapped around her head. My eyes shot towards Tom, who was standing behind her, pulling the blanket as if his life depended on it. She was struggling with the tight clutch over her head, but his combat form wasn't lending her enough space for the struggle. I feared he was strangling her.

"What are you doing, dude? You will choke her to death." I struggled to talk him out of it, but his adrenaline rush had overpowered him. I knew he was about to let out a bloodcurdling scream.

"Who is she, dude?" His eyes were almost on the verge of bulging out of the sockets. His grip loosened on the sheets as he received an elbow in the guts and fell to the floor with a loud thud.

"Time to flee, brother!" I exclaimed and dashed towards him, dragging him up towards the door, when shortly I stopped dead on my track hearing a knock at the door. Most probably, the hotel staff had come worried if everything was okay inside.

I condemned every living soul on this planet. My mind was all muddled up thinking of a plan, while my body was still suffering from the pain. She began to stride towards us, and I started up to step back. Analyzing our poor condition, Tom stood up while wincing in pain. Our circumstances were so helpless that I felt like we were standing at the edge of a hill and were going to fall anytime now.

"Give me your names, boys, and I'll try not to shoot you." And then I caught a glimpse of the gun in her hand. Come on, lady. Why do you own a gun? She did scare the living daylights out of us.

Fear heightened in my spine when my back hit the glass of the window. Dead end! I turned towards Tom and found him looking at her with the same petrified expression as mine. On the other hand, I didn't quite understand the look on his face. Is he about to puke or going to faint?

"Tom, remember I said I would let you jump first if all goes havoc." His dreadful face veered towards me and I didn't give him a chance to act before I shoved him off the window, his scream echoing in the thin air.

And I followed after him, just as I had promised.

Nine

Ethan

DAY THREE

I cleared my throat, straightening my suit jacket. We came out to get fitted into professional attires suitable to pose as wedding planners and collect some stuff from a real wedding planner we had hired.

"Just to be clear, my doctor has advised me to go easy for the rest of my vacation!" Tom spoke in a complaining tone. He was pretty shaken up from our midnight crisis.

"All right." I asserted while trying to adjust my tie against my reflection in the mirror that the salesperson had been holding all this time at a very wrong angle. I felt the edginess in his tone, but I couldn't help it. For today's business, we were already behind schedule. My fingers tugged back a few strands of hair, which were wet with the shortest shower I had ever taken.

We couldn't afford to waste even a single minute while we were on this island. Only I knew how desperately I needed that pardon for my past sins from Sarah.

I let Tom pay for our little shopping spree in cash, careful not to use our cards. I didn't want the hotel staff to recognize me and raise havoc that the actual owner of their hotel business was staying here. That would destroy all my plans to get into Sarah's parents' good graces. And we headed for the breakfast meeting.

"I'm scared shit. Okay? What if that raunchy-hag rat us out?" Tom continued whining. I turned around and placed my hands over his shoulders, drawing his full attention.

"We were wearing masks, remember? She couldn't possibly know it was us. And, perhaps, she is too senile to retrieve what happened last night?"

"She didn't seem senile to me when she pronounced 'Give me your names, boys, and I'll try not to shoot you.' She had a bloody gun!" I shook my head. My senses crinkled hard while walking through the memory lane for a few seconds as Tom attempted to imitate her not-so-alluring voice.

"Brother! You will have to trust me on this! She can't beat us. We are the survivors of the dark fold!" He nodded, still a little scared. But then, I witnessed him wiggling his body, letting out some seriously amusing sounds.

"Put your shit together. We have to own this day." I said in a stern voice.

He muttered something to himself and then let out a series of 'hell yeah' sharp breaths. An amusing smile etched my face at his determination and I gestured towards the doors that led to the dining space. He nodded once again with his heart in his throat and with an abrupt motion, he turned around in the opposite direction, ready to sprint on the spurs. Hence, I had to drag his ass inside the room, where everyone was having a nice, warm breakfast.

"Buongiorno, le persone!" I announced boisterously and witnessed Starz choking on her tea in shock. I loved to see her change of expressions, full of surprises. I didn't know about her, but it had begun to give me some sort of pleasure.

"Buongiorno, Mr. Stewart! We were just talking about you. It is certainly a pleasurable morning!" I beamed at Mrs. Walter and then towards Mr. Walter.

Straightening my jacket, I strolled towards them. The breakfast table was packed, and I believed it was a perfect time to impress her entire family with my charm. My eyes drifted from Sarah's father to Romano. And my grin dropped, catching a dislikable sight. I found him considerably engaged in a too friendly chat with Starz. Sitting right next to her, his face too close to her for my liking. My smile faded into a frown. My palm clenched into a tight fist, fighting against the growl that was threatening to escape my mouth.

"Please, Mr. Stewart. Join us at the table." Mr. Walter's voice made me avert my eyes. I nodded as Tom and I took our seats. I happened to sit right in front of Starz, who was doing her best to avoid having eye contact with me. *Come on, girl! You can't ignore my charisma.*

I couldn't help but grimace at Romano. It wasn't only that we men disliked people who had their eyes on our girls; it was more like we yearned to scoop out their eyes from the sockets.

Clenching my palms tighter, I gained his attention by extending my arm and seizing the bread he was about to grab. He unexpectedly retreated in surprise and glanced up at me, carrying a fairly annoying expression, which I gladly resisted with a forced smile.

"I hate to bring this on the breakfast table, but here are the layouts you asked for me to bring, ma'am." I passed the file to Mrs. Walter, and her lips curled into a big grin.

"Oh, you know how to impress a woman, Stewart!" Everyone let out a chuckle at Mr. Walter's remark, but Starz didn't even look up at me to even acknowledge my presence.

"These are lovely!" Mrs. Walter's eyes scrutinized the portfolio as she went through the entire file. And I stole a chance to check Starz. She was acting like I wasn't even present in the room. That hurt my pride and my expressions turned grave.

The room was buzzing with light chatter, and my eyes averted from Romano to Ashley. I gave her a death glare for stealing my notebook. I knew her brain was behind every prank thrown over us. Spraying Tom with itch power, telling Starz about my sensual plans and switching rooms with Aunt Grace. Making every day on this island a despicable day of our lives, especially Tom's. She was on the top of my list of vengeance. Grabbing her attention, I passed her a stern smile while she was giving me a toothy grin with her mouth stuffed with all kinds of food present at the table. Never mind!

Beside her was the little devil, and it was still quite a mystery what his influence was in the family. "Oh, I'm so full. See you later, mom and dad." He quickly dashed towards his mother. And after planting a kiss on his mother's cheek, he went straight out the doors. But not before giving me a knowing look. We would do the talking later, fancy pants!

"I'm impressed, Mr. Stewart. With you by our side, I don't think we have to worry about anything this time."

"Huh?" My senses discerned Mrs. Walter's appreciation, and I shifted in my chair. "Oh, it's my pleasure, ma'am." My eyes captured Starz's staring at me this time, and I cleared my throat, struggling under her suspiciously hard gaze. The grave annoyance was written all over her face as she finished the lemonade in one whole gulp. *Easy girl! You're making me breathless.*

I noticed Mrs. Walter showing the layouts to Starz, and she looked anything but interested. Her fake smile and timely nodding at her mother was an indication she wasn't at all excited about the wedding. But why? Didn't she love him? Oh shit! Her parents were forcing her into this pit. Did she need me to save her?

"Oh, Mr. Stewart, you got this sitting arrangement all wrong." I shook my head and found the mother-daughter duo staring at me. I quickly dashed towards them and noted the order of guest chairs. It was indeed wrong. "Bride's family sits on the left side and the groom's on the right." I scratched the back of my neck in embarrassment. But then Romano's phone call captured our attention, and he excused himself. Good for me, as I took his seat.

At the same time, Mrs. Walter strolled towards her husband to show her the plan and I happened to be left alone with my saucy little beloved. "Morning, Starz. I dreamed of you last night," I whispered close to her ear. Putting up an act of showing her some designs for the bridesmaid dresses.

Her fresh morning lavender and cinnamon scent intoxicated me and I had to struggle hard to keep myself from moaning in delight.

My smile broadened, witnessing her shivering underneath my gaze. Strangely, it fed my little ego seeing her vulnerable. I waited for her fierce reply, but not a single word came out from her side. She just smiled and nodded, looking at the edge. And I was a little taken aback. *Wait a second. Are we behaving like civilized beings, darling? Charming! I'm so into this.*

"Was I strangling you with my bare hands or throwing you off the hill?" She replied without a flinch. Well, that dragged me back from my little reverie. "Sorry?"

"The dream, genius!" Oh, right!

"Well, you were throwing yourself in my arms. Our lips were entangled. Your body was melting into mine." Her head yanked up to me, and I grinned. A horrific look colored her face, yet I noticed her cheeks flushing crimson in embarrassment. "Don't ask for details, but it was sizzling, darling!" I continued. Her eyes were back on the papers in her hand as I noticed her taking deep breaths to repress the temper that had risen within her. I never felt so proud of myself for making her blush.

"Mr. Stewart, how many days will it take until I finally get to see my daughter's wedding gown?" *Oh, that thing! Wedding dress? There is no freaking wedding going to happen here, madam. Not before your precious daughter releases me with her resentment.*

"Oh, you don't have to worry a bit, Mrs. Walter. My most loyal dressmakers are executing the best work of delivering some last-minute finishing touches." I tried to diffuse the topic as quickly as possible and signaled Tom to text the outfitter. I had found the best designer for Starz. She had the expertise to handle every type of last-minute call. But her little perfection had occasionally been a little hard to manage. If she wished not to execute this task, Mrs. Walter will surely have my neck for the guillotine.

"So, Mr. Stewart, apart from planning weddings as a profession, have you ever considered planning your own wedding? Or, perhaps, you are still living the player's life? Dark and daring, as they like to call it." That came straight from Sarah's aunt.

When you find yourself trapped in a deep pit, come up with a cheesy, yet impressive, reply.

"I'm a one-woman man, madam. I don't love many, but I love one in many ways." I asserted. Tom choked on his breakfast. And a smile rose on my face, seeing Starz's wild-eyed expression.

"Oh. My. God! I rolled my eyes so hard that I saw my brain. And it's bleeding!" She spoke so quietly only I could hear.

"That means I've been running in your head, darling." I laid my hand over her's under the table, without even glancing at her. She stiffened like a marble statue and my heart was ready to leap out of my chest anytime now. I kept nodding at Mr. Walter's tale about his own wedding nonchalantly, all the while enjoying the sparks flowing from our touch.

"But I have a little request, darling. Just don't imagine me naked." I peeped at her and noticed her failing to keep that happy face. She was staring at me with those big round dolphin eyes as if I had just hopped out of a magic pond. And it took everything I had to not close my lips on per parted mouth.

She suddenly came out of her daze and struggled to remove her hand from my grasp, only to make me grip it even tighter. The touch sent a tingle of anticipation down my spine. I wanted to retreat, seeing the weird sensation go up in flames in my soul. *What's happening?*

In the middle of the swirls of anticipation rising in my head, I felt a shrill pain in my hand. My head yanked down to the spot, witnessing a damn fork piercing my skin. I had to bite my tongue to arrest the scream that almost broke out. I looked up to Starz and noticed a wide smug adorning her face. Damn! It hurts.

"Oh, I almost forgot, Jane. I had a break-in last night." Out of the blue, Starz's aunt declared to Mrs. Walter. Making my breath caught up in my throat while a spoon slipped off of Tom's hand, as he started to cough. Oh. No! No! No! The dreadful silence enclosed us as everyone had stopped doing their work and now gawking at her. I wanted to get engulfed by the bloody floor right there.

"Oh, my! What are you talking about?" Mrs. Walter let out a worried gasp when we heard footsteps in the background.

"Where are you going, Mr. Tucker? And why are you limping?" Every head turned towards the door, discovering Tom sneaking out like a terrified rat. But Mrs. Walter's voice had stopped him dead on the spot. He pivoted around, and it seemed like he was going to burst into tears any second now. All colors had left his face, leaving him paler than he already was. I had a feeling this was not going to end well. The moment his eyes met mine, I shook my head with a look of aghast coloring my face. *Man! You can't leave me like that.*

"Let him go, Mrs. Walter. He's got hemorrhoids. Painful bloody craps, you can't even imagine!" I didn't know from where I mustered up the courage to say anything at all. Everyone suppressed a smile as Tom shot me a glare. I shrugged my shoulders at him. *Desperate times call for desperate measures, brother.*

"Oh, you poor kid. Come with me. I'll give you one fine herbal concoction. Regardless of its taste, it's an excellent remedy." Mrs. Walter walked around the table and started to drag him out of the room as he shot me a look of helplessness.

"Then what happened, Aunt Grace?" Starz's curiosity interrupted the moment. *Oh, we are back to my abomination. No, please, don't utter a single word.* My eyes were fixed on her, mentally planning to tape her mouth shut.

"I'll tell you what exactly happened, girls. I was taking my beauty sleep when I woke up to a strange sound. At first, it seemed like someone was breathing my name. Calling me with compelling passion, but when I sensed someone caressing my soft cheek, I finally rose to my senses and saw two dazzling blue eyes."

"Oh, my goodness. What happened next?" Ashley squealed, and I joined her, offering a fake gasp. *Yeah! This is so intriguing.*

"That piercing gaze was to die for. I never thought a knight in shining armor would come right from my window and wake me like sleeping beauty. And then in a flash of a moment, he was beside me, holding my face in his soft, supple hands and then." *What the fuck? I'm very much certain, lady, this didn't happen.*

"And then?" Mrs. Walter interrupted, appearing even more inquisitive than her daughter. *Wait, when did she come back?*

"He kissed me." *Yeah, right! Just like I blew out my brains now.*

"His lips were so soft. So luscious. I found myself crumbling with every stroke." Everyone eyed me when I gagged at her bloody description. I shook my head, gesturing with my hand for her to carry on and don't mind me.

"But before he could do anything more, his partner entered my bedroom and grabbed me by my waist from behind. His grip was so strong that all I felt was his ripped muscles girdling my tiny waist. His intentions were alarmingly dangerous, girls." I could feel my mouth hanging open. *What does she even mean? It didn't happen the way she is trying to portray it.*

"And then my feathery frame was flung back on the bed like I weighed nothing. I was too astounded to do anything, and then the one with the dazzling blue eyes began to climb over me. I didn't know what he was..."

"Are you sure about that? I mean, it was all so dark in there. You could have judged their intentions wrong!" I never knew I had dazzling blue eyes!

"I'm quite sure about it, boy. Though it's true, it was all dark in my room, but I have eyes on the back of my head. Things could never get away from me. I even assessed their eye colors, age, heights, and even how much they weighed." *Oh, my freaking balls! Is she a cop? That convinces the reason for her holding the gun.*

"One had brown eyes, and the other had blue ones. The blue-eyed one was much taller than the other one. Over six feet tall, 175 pounds. They both seemed young, maybe mid-twenties. But the thing I found odd about them was how familiar they sounded. Almost like..." I swallowed down the lump forming in my throat when her gaze deepened on me. "Your friend, Mr. Stewart." *Shoot me, somebody, please.*

I let out an uncomfortable chuckle. "What a coincidence... huh?"

"But how do you know it was all dark at that moment?" Sherlock Ashley spoke up, directing the question at me, and I searched for the exit if the situation would get even worse. Starz turned in my direction and gave me a puzzled look and I couldn't help but counter her with my best-forced smile.

"Umm, she said night. Night-dark. It is understandable, Einstein!" Sam, the cousin, came to my rescue, and everyone looked convinced except Ash. I was sweating hard, digging my own grave.

"Whatever, where was I? Yeah, climbing! I resisted him with all my strength, but he tried to kiss me again! Can you believe that? He just couldn't resist!" And I wanted to throw up right there. *Listen, old potato sack. I know sometimes I get horny seeing Starz, but kissing a senile hag isn't my style.*

"Then what happened? Are you all right? Did you call the cops? Where was hotel security? I will sue them!" Mr. Walter was getting furious with every passing second.

"Relax, Mark! I said he tried, but did not succeed. When his attention got distracted towards my sexy legs, he loosened the grip, and exactly then I took the right chance to kick him right in his nuts. I can't tell you how much I enjoyed seeing him crying like a baby on the floor."

"Grace, they could've been dangerous. You should have called for help." Mr. Walter spoke with a raised voice.

"But what happened to them?" Starz was interested in me! I knew it.

"He was so wounded to take the next move that grabbing his partner, they jumped out of the window. They were like Batman and Robin. Batman saves Robin. Or the other way around. Anyway, the hotel security came soon and offered to call the cops, but I refused, as no harm was done. I mean, they must have been some local boys bewitched by true American beauty." She completed her story with a blush. *Oh my! She is one delusional woman.*

"And the good news is that the Hotel management offered me a free spa and sauna session along with free stay as compensation, with extra security at my door and that security guard is a real eye candy." She winked at her sister. Starz and Ashley sighed in pleasure as their shoulders slumped. But all eyes got distracted towards the door when we witnessed Tom heaving his guts out.

"I guess the concoction is to blame," I spoke, turning around and finding Starz glaring at me with a cynical look. I was shrinking under her stare.

Man! The shit was about to get real!

Ten

Ethan

DAY FIVE

I bet the dude up there didn't like me. In fact, I bet the dude was a 'she' rather than a 'he'. And she was being personal now. I get that Starz was one of her favorite daughters and since I was bothering her lately, she was making my life a living hell. Right? But how could she forget that I was her cute little son, too? Then why was I being punished here? And I could bet on my life that she was either high on drugs or drunk her ass-off when she made Starz. Because no way in heaven could she achieve such perfection with her.

I was okay with the Karma thing and all the ass-biting moments that had been lately going on with me. I deserved it, one way or another. But now the circumstances were giving rise to a minor dilemma. My life was simple, and so was my goal. But a handful of strange events, or rather I would say emotions, were making it very difficult.

The goddess was very well aware of my fear of surprises and still, she was mailing them one after another like thunderstorms. I was not even talking metaphorically. This was not fair. She should at least give everyone a fair chance to write their own destiny.

Like right now, I was doing nothing but getting bored staring at the rain outside my window. It had been raining continuously since past forty-eight hours. I had a beautiful picnic planned out for yesterday to cheer up Starz's cold persona but it all got washed away in the storm. I couldn't meet Starz yesterday at all and that made me sick to my stomach. I was getting mad sitting here all alone trying to come up with something, anything that could make her see me in a changed light.

I was stuck here, wasting away the precious time I should be spending with Starz. *Just slow down a bit, enough to lend me some minutes to run down to the hotel to see her.* But then the shower turned into heavy pouring, and I sighed. I was not asking for much. *You are nothing but a stubborn woman.*

And another thunderstorm broke out right above my cottage, and I cried out like a dying cat. "Fine! Fine! I take my words back, gracious goddess. Just calm down!"

It was almost noon, but the gloominess in the sky had made it look like late evening already. I had nothing to do but to count the days I'd left on this island. I checked my cell phone once again and groaned in frustration when the internet was also down. I was so done with this island.

Tom, on the other hand, had decided to just sleep all through this remaining vacation. He hasn't left his room since that breakfast incident. Claiming some virus had gotten into him, which was not allowing him to move an inch of his body. It's a relief that this paralysis virus at least lets him move to the restroom.

I reckoned to write something in my notebook, but then I scowled when nothing came to my mind. I knew nothing real about her other than some superficial facts like her favorite color or movie star. I flung back the notebook on the table when someone knocked.

My head spun towards the door and the lines on my forehead grew darker. Now, who could it be? Without giving it a thought, I walked towards the door. And the moment I opened it, my eyes grew big, witnessing the most unexpected person standing at my door.

"What do I owe this pleasure for, Mr. Angus Walter Sir?" My frantic question led him to smile deeper at me. Without even caring to ask first, he barged into the cottage, soaking the carpet into a darker shade of mud. I could clearly evaluate the rain had battered havoc on him.

My expression turned from being annoyed to puzzled; noticing him settling down his wet ass on the chair closer to the fire and rubbing his hands for some warmth. Something told me there was a big deal cooking in his mind, as he had bothered to come here at this hour, jeopardizing his pride.

I crossed my arms over my chest when he didn't utter a single word and continued to look around the room. Analyzing my things. Judging my style.

"I must admit, you are giving up lots of things for my sister, Mr. Stanton." He let out a dry chuckle, putting his muddy boots on my coffee table. Wait, what did he just call me? I froze to my place. But forcing a poker face, I kept fighting up the conflict.

"I'm sorry, but my name is Stewart, Ethan Stewart. I don't know what you are talking about." I pulled a straight face, not giving in a single shade of skepticism. He turned his gaze back towards me from the fire with a rather serpent smile.

"Oh, come on, you don't have to act in front of me, Mr. Ethan Robert Stanton. I've done my homework. Nevertheless, I've come here to discuss some important negotiations with you... Sir!" Shit! Fear finally crossed my heart hearing my real name from him. And maybe he noticed that too when he let out a chuckle. Now he knew my real identity. He could expose me effortlessly. But he hadn't done it yet. Why?

"How?" Now I was curious. He couldn't overstep me. I was thorough in my identity.

"The night I saw you outside my sister's room, you came under my radar. And then some internet clicks and voilà! But you surprised me. I thought you were just some crazy ex, but damn, you're loaded, man. My sister's crazy grumpy behavior made my job easy, surely. It was, in fact, way too smooth to interpret by just seeing the loathing she has for you. I'm surprised how nobody in the family has identified you yet. You are a freaking business tycoon, The Stantons. You even own this resort." Well, hearing a compliment after so long made my chest pump up three-fold in size.

"So, you like her, right?" He asked sincerely, breaking my trance.

"Well, I am still contemplating that, but yeah, I do hate your brother-in-law, if that proves anything." A bitter taste rose in my mouth as I started to think about him. *He is so fuckin' perfect.*

"What can I say! Sometimes I reckon he chose an entirely wrong profession. Rather than being an attorney, he should have been a priest or something." He said so cheerfully as if he has been waiting a while for someone to hate Mr. Perfect as well.

"Yeah, right?" I squealed as we exchanged a high-five, but shortly after, I held myself back. *Behave like a grown-up, dude.*

"Anyway, I have come here to offer you my allegiance. And also enlighten you about the big news, which is, of course, related to my sister." And then he grew silent. I stared at him, waiting for some more words, but the little devil gaped back at me with the same amusing look. Now I get it.

After deducing his motives, an understanding crossed my face as he continued, "Well, it's obvious for succeeding in your endeavors you need an ally inside the family. And the news that I am about to share with you holds substantial value. But it requires some major sacrifices. Also, I believe you wouldn't want your identity to get disclosed and go to jail for every law you have broken, starting with stalking my sister. Am I right, Mr. Stanton?" The devil had started to show his real color. He was smiling at me, pretending to be an innocent kid, asking for a lollipop.

"What do you want, kid?" I hissed angrily.

"There, right at business. I knew I would be dealing with the right guy." He unexpectedly spoke up, appearing cheerful, and I could do nothing but shake my head at the way this conversation was heading.

"I can't believe I am being blackmailed right now," I said in a stern voice, trying to gain some ground here.

"Oh no, no, Sir, how could I dare to blackmail anyone? I am a normal little brother looking after his elder sister. Besides, I want nothing big... Just your car that you purchased... like yesterday? Am I right?" My jaw nearly dropped to the floor. But this time I was the one who let out a chuckle.

"Are you kidding me? That's a 1961 Corvette. Do you know how rare that beauty is? It's not happening. Anything else?" In no way I'm going to hand over my baby to this demon.

"Oh, that's really disappointing. And here I thought you cared about my sister more than anything else in the world. But obviously, I was wrong. A big chunk of metal is more important to you than my precious sister. I get that. It's all right, let Romano take her on a romantic date this evening. At... oh, my bad. My tongue slipped. I almost forgot it is none of your business." His legs hurled back on the floor and then he headed towards the door. I just stared at him silently, unwavering. He was nothing but a total asshole who remind me of my old self in high school. He paused just for a moment and spoke.

"I suppose my sister has some feelings for you, Mr. Stanton. But who cares now that they are going on their first real date on this gorgeous island. And you know what happens when two people in love get drunk. Oops, I've uttered way too much. See you around then." He again pivoted around and started to walk towards the door, and I clenched my palms tighter in resentment. Even if he had his back on me, I could feel the smirk furnishing his arrogant face, because he knew he was soon going to get what he desired. I could buy a new car, but I couldn't afford to lose that date.

"Fine! But until I'm here, if I find even the slightest scratch on her, you will be brutally..."

"No, no, Mr. Stanton. You don't have to worry about her. I'll take care of her like a girlfriend. But the only problem is I don't have one. Seven PM sharp at Midnite Wine Bar. I will be back with more interesting news soon. Good luck, Mr. Stanton." Putting his hood back up, he grabbed the keys from the table, and just like that, he was gone. I suddenly realized that he didn't give me an address. I shouted his name at his back, but he didn't stop for a second.

Aaargh!! God, what level of wrong did I do to deserve the Demon Lucifer on my trial and being accused of attempting assault on an old hag? My life had become one Whacko story.

But then, wasting no time, I darted into Tom's room. The first thing that greeted me were his loud snores. I groaned, seeing him sleeping so peacefully while I was all fucked up.

"This is an emergency, rise and shine, sleeping beauty." I tried to wake him up with my loud affirmation. A smile furnished my lips, thinking about my next move. But it dropped right off thinking about all the preparations to be done and seeing Tom still dozed off.

"Wake up, dude. It's time for our Plan B," I yelled and he stirred a little, but the snoring continued. I had no time to make him understand the situation properly. I couldn't let one more day go to waste.

I walked straight towards him and after finding no signs of him waking up anytime soon I opened the window above his bed so that the natural holy rain would wash down his sins.

"Holy Shit! You son of a bitch! Are you trying to kill me? Fuck you, man!" The expressions on his face were priceless, but I couldn't afford to waste time and got straight to business.

"Calm down. I was just trying to wake you up. Now get your ass up. We have a whole plan to put together. No time to waste. We need a tux and a gift and I don't have a fuckin' car!" I almost shouted in frustration.

"What the hell happened to your car?"

The rain had finally given way to a light drizzle but we were running late. It was already late afternoon and Tom had been on his phone for over an hour, giving me a warning eye every time I tried to talk to him. I started to give up on him, but then suddenly he announced, "All done. Let's go get you that car, Mr. Stanton!"

So, after getting ready, we took a taxi and commenced towards our first destination. I was feeling strange sitting there. It was hard to remember the last time I traveled in a cab. I couldn't help but imagine if someone had made love in the back seat. I was desperately missing my car and simultaneously murmuring curses to that little devil. The taxi driver was too old to be trusted, but Tom just relaxed his back on the dirty seat whilst putting his hands behind his head.

Our first stop was to pick up the delivery of a gorgeous Cadillac CT4 V Convertible that Tom had managed to book at the shortest notice. Man, I wished I knew how he did that. Just name a thing and he would make it available. He was my personal genie.

After completing the first task, we headed straight to get me fitted into a tux. Well, I couldn't go on my first date with Starz in nine years wearing beach shorts now. Could I?

Skillfully putting on my blazer, I closed the buttons and began to adjust my bow. *You have never seen me in a tux, Starz; because if you had, then you would never have agreed to go out with that fake Italian chap. But, I could assure you, babe, you might have the most beautiful green eyes, but my dazzling blue ones are not getting easily dismissed today.*

It was getting dark outside, and I was getting nervous with every passing second. Was I already late for my plan? Had they already reached the venue and were enjoying the sweet wine and slow music? Or had it surpassed to the next level, and they had already commenced to make out in the car? Or maybe the car got jammed up, and she got furious and kicked him in his balls before storming off. My mind couldn't stop imagining things.

"Are you sure you put the right name in the GPS, Tom? I mean, we have been circling this place for the last forty minutes. The island is not that vast to take this much time." Anxiety was clearly dripping out of my words. I was grabbing the steering wheel tight while at the same time my head was hanging outside the window in search of that damn bar which was supposed to be our target, or what that little devil had told me. I hope he didn't trick me because if he did, then I would make sure to remind him who the real boss was in this game. But right now, I was at a vulnerable stage.

"There." Tom pointed to his right, and I read the name *'Il Mio Amante'* and below it, written in the smaller font, was 'The Midnite Wine Bar'. I chirped like a little girl in my seat. I turned to Tom, and he nodded at me. That jerk didn't give me the actual name. I would make him pay, but right now, I had other priorities.

Putting my game face on, I pressed the brakes right in front of the restaurant entrance, making sure every eye in the vicinity was turned at us. I obviously wanted to show off my new car but, unfortunately, Starz was not among the spectators.

Well! Well! Well! Romano chose a place with an Italian name meaning 'My Lover'. When the hell did that workaholic get so romantic? Huh, I shouldn't have taken him so casually.

"It seems like divine cuisine, dude. Romano is not that much a dork as we thought of him, or rather, as you thought of him. Turns out he has good taste!" I groaned at Tom's words and decided to ignore him. Handling the keys to the valet, we surveyed out surrounding.

"I'm going to punch his face so hard that his lips would never curl to say the word 'Love' ever again!" I growled under my breath, but I guess it came out a little louder than I intended because Tom heard it.

He tugged at my arm and said, "But why? Why do you want to kick his ass? He is her fiancé, her future husband. Obviously, he will take her on romantic dates." Okay, that question added fuel to the fire. *Future husband? My ass!* I turned my head back and glared at Tom, who on the other hand gave me an amusing look, raising one eyebrow.

"You want to know why I want to do this to him? She doesn't love him. He is taking advantage of her for being so naïve. I just feel protective of her, well don't you understand, for humanity's sake?" It was as simple as that, and it didn't require any further explanation.

"But why do I smell some tenderness and a lot of jealousy in it? Admit it, bro, it's not just about an apology anymore, you are falling for her again." I huffed out a bored expression and made a 'what the fuck' face.

"Did you just call me a jealous ass?" *Ethan and jealous? No one is born to make me jealous, dude.* Tom had a neat, fascinating smile that he always had while teasing me. But this was the first time I found myself running out of words. I opened my mouth and closed it again, trying to find a good counter back. But failed miserably. *But I don't get jealous! Period.*

"I don't know what you are talking about, man. I just don't like that guy. That's it!" I confessed and again began to scan people who were entering and leaving the restaurant, and then my eyes noticed a familiar car. My sight fixed to the vehicle as it came to a halt just outside the main entrance. Narrowing my eyes, the valet opened the door and there he was, standing beside the most beautiful girl on the island.

Suddenly, Tom pushed me aside, obscuring us from their eyes, behind a tree. A groan escaped my mouth when Romano placed his hand around her waist, and she smiled back at him. She was so faking it! My hands automatically curled into fists to suppress the strange rage that was threatening to come out. My eyes followed them walking inside the diner, holding each other's hands. And uneasiness grew in my posture.

I shook my head in denial because I couldn't comprehend why I was feeling this way. The sheer sight of them made my heart twitch with anger. An odd emotion swirled inside me, and I clenched my teeth tighter. My hands itched to swing out and put a dent in the wall. I wanted to pull Romano's hand out of its socket for touching her. She doesn't belong with him.

My mind was confusing me, as it was jammed with so many unfavorable thoughts that it gave rise to a difficult situation. Finding it hard to ascertain what exactly I was feeling at that split second. Angry? Annoyed? Or, as Tom declared openly, jealous? Furiously, I turned back to Tom, who was staring at me with an annoying smirk.

"I don't know about you, man, but I'm going inside, and this is not at all jealousy." With that, I marched towards them, letting out a deep sigh. The doorman bowed and opened the door for me as I entered the restaurant.

It was warm inside, or maybe my nerves were on fire, impatiently searching the way to their table. I located them and my blood started to boil, seeing him whispering something in her ear. The piano was playing loudly, and he was, in fact, taking advantage of that. *Told you, Tom!*

In between all this, I noticed the receptionist through the corner of my eyes. She was already staring at me like I was her favorite ice cream flavor. I passed her a genuine smile that made her lean further on her desk. *Button up your blouse, madam. Leave something to the imagination.* Clearing my throat, I turned back towards them and noticed Romano placing an order for their best red wine.

Call it resentment that was slowly growing in my veins, swallowing down my rational thinking, but I couldn't watch him looking at her in that way. I noticed the server coming out with their order of wine. This was my chance. I cornered him and slipped a hundred in his hand, whispering directions in his ears. He looked at me with big eyes and for a second I thought he would ask me to buzz off, but then he winked and pocketed the money and moved on.

The waiter did his magic and, with a little slip of hand, spilled some wine on Romano, ruining his suit. He suddenly stood up, saving his remaining suit, and Starz had never looked this fretful before. The waiter started apologizing endlessly and offered him a tissue.

My stabbing gaze noticed Romano apologizing to her and then heading in my direction. My eyes pivoted around and I comprehended he was in fact advancing towards the restrooms. Making a hasty move, I faced the receptionist, and when he was about to pass me; I pretended to be fully engaged in a chat with her. The second I checked him taking access in the restroom from the corner of my eyes, I smirked. Time for some action.

"Do you want more wine, signora?" Starz nodded, still dazzled by the little episode. But in the flash of a moment, she looked confused and quickly shot her head in my direction and my lips crooked into a big smug. She recognized my voice. I automatically smiled from ear to ear. But color left her face, and she sat there with all the astonishment.

"Is this seat taken?" Her beautiful green eyes expanded like she couldn't believe her eyes. Her stair paused on me for a little longer than necessary and I could see that she was checking me out. *Missed me, baby?*

"What are you doing here? No, you can't sit here." She sneered while checking the direction where Romano had just disappeared into. I smiled at her reaction and, ignoring her hatred, I drew the chair back and sat in front of her. The very first thing I noticed was the sparkle in her eyes, they were glittering in the pale light. She wore a plain, long green gown that hugged the sensual curves of her body devotedly. She looked too gorgeous to take my eyes off of her. I was entirely mesmerized.

But then again, she was now giving me that look, like I was the last person she wanted to see tonight. But it all looked forced and fake or maybe it was just my wishful thinking.

"What are you doing here with him?" My voice came out harsher than I intended. I could clearly see my question getting on her nerves.

"Well, first of all, it's none of your business. And second, if you could excuse me, then I would like to enlighten you that the whole world doesn't belong to you, definitely not I." She drew her head closer to mine and spoke again.

"Listen to me very carefully, Stanton, don't even think about spoiling this evening. Or you would soon realize how far I can go for tormenting you." This time her voice got a bit elevated, which attracted the neighboring old couple's attention. She smiled at them warmly and again shot her head back in the restroom's direction.

Her threat welcomed a chuckle out of me. "Meet me at the back in five minutes," I stated and slid off the chair, seeing Romano making his way towards the table.

"Who was that?" I heard him asking.

"No one, just an old friend from a bad old time." She eyed me and I smirked, walking away from them. Resuming my place back by the receptionist, I had a good view at the table with Romano's back towards me. She looked a little helpless now; a little uncomfortable around him. He was saying something to her, but all she could do was survey her surroundings for my essence.

Tonight I became aware of two things. Although it was tough for me to accept them, they were two undeniable truths. One, I was still in love with Sarah and desperately wanted her back in my life.

And second, no matter how much I don't like to discuss it, it was a sheer truth that I never hated this Romano guy just because I thought one day he would break her heart and leave her broken. But I despised him because I did that job myself and he was too perfect in healing her wounds altogether. He was actually good for her and I envied him.

Truth be told, I felt inferior to him. I couldn't even compare myself to him. After all, he was a decent human being with a good heart. God knows how badly I pulled all the strings to find even a single appalling thing about this man. But no, he was one hard-working lad. No dirty past, no criminal background, not even marrying her for money. Hell, he was such a saint that he sought his mother's permission to marry her. *Now, who does that in the twenty-first century?*

More than five minutes had passed, but she was not buzzing from her seat. Maybe the charm of my tux didn't work on her.

Shaking my head to clear all the negative thoughts. I took out my phone and dialed Tom's number for some help. The bell rang, but he didn't pick up the phone. What happened to him now? I dialed again, and it similarly rang for a long duration. And when I was about to hang up, his voice came from the other end and I loosened up a bit.

"Hello! Bro, a little crisis has occurred here!" Now what? "Do you remember your stalker Sam, the cousin, that over-emotional teen? She accidentally bumped into me and now screaming her heart out to meet you. What should I do, man?" *Damn it, man.* I ran my hand through my hair in frustration. Now from where did she fall into the middle of my plan? But then suddenly my mind worked on the right spot and I smirked.

"Tell her to wait for me in her room at midnight. But, before that, ask her to call Sarah and cry on the phone."

"What?" Tom gasped.

"Tell her it's just a little prank. Man, just convince her. She will do anything to get into my pants." And I hung up. This had to work; we had no other option left.

I slowly peaked towards them, and as planned, Starz received a call. Looking distressed, she excused herself from him and began to head towards the restrooms. I grinned, seeing her coming in the right direction, and rushed towards the restrooms and got on with my work. Swiping the signs of 'HER' and 'HIS' on the door, I sheepishly smiled comprehending its after-effects. Nevertheless, this was the only way to get her all alone.

Thus, after my evil work, I ran inside the male restroom that she was about to think was female. My heart began to race up, imaging the things that were about to happen. I knew she was going to get mad at me because of this little trick. Much worse than I'd experienced till now. But I could endure that if it would get me a chance to talk to her in solitary.

Suddenly, I heard the squeaking sound of the door opening, and my mouth felt dry. I took out a deep breath to make myself look less nervous. My palms got all sweaty picturing her so close to me.

"Sam? Why were you crying? Sam?" I heard her worried tone. With every passing second, her voice came closer to me and I made myself ready for the perfect time.

"Where are you? You are freaking me out, girl!" This time the voice came right outside my cubicle and, finding the right opportunity, I pulled her in with a swift motion. I seized her phone and put it in my pocket. A little surprised shriek left her mouth; that I subdued by putting my hand on her mouth. I pushed her back to the wall and made her steady. Damn, I felt like a creepy molester. I studied her face as those beautiful eyes were squeezed shut; her body was shaking in fear. I did feel like a kidnapper.

"Relax, it's just me. Ethan." And damn, those supposedly comforting words worked exactly opposite to my expectation. Her eyes jolted open, and she pushed me away with all her strength. *Wow, what are you eating lately, Starz?*

"You? What the hell do you think you're doing? You scared the living daylight out of me!" She started shouting at me like a hungry lioness while steadying her frantic heartbeats. But I just smiled at her reaction and placed a good distance between us, as much as that confined place allowed. I just wanted to let her feel comfortable under my shelter.

"Did you run away from a madhouse? If not, then you have been acting like you should be in there." She continued, and I again kept on smiling at her.

"Ugh, shoot all this. First of all, tell me why do you smile so much? That too at the very moment when I want to chew you out." Her nostrils were flaring with anger. I chuckled at her question and tilted a little closer, which welcomed her eyes getting rounded up.

"Is it a crime to stay happy all the time, Starz? I smile because I feel pleased whenever I see your face." I uttered every single word with pure honesty, and she became silent for a moment.

We were openly staring at each other now. Words fell silent and our eyes were doing all the talk. I could tell she was trying to find some kind of trick on my face. However I was just dumbfounded by her beauty. My heart thumped frantically against my ribcage. Finding each other in such close proximity had stirred up nine years' worth of pent up sexual tension between us. My fingers twitched to touch her trembling lips. But unfortunately, the moment got intruded when we heard some voices coming from outside our cubicle. If I was right, then Tom had already changed back the signs by now.

"Am I inside the male restroom?" A sacred whisper fell into my ear and I sheepishly ran my right hand over the back of my head. I nodded and her eyes went back from sweet to flaring dragon fire. She opened her mouth to yell at me once again, but the sound of guys outside our cubicle made her shut her sass.

"Do you have any idea if anyone sees me here, with you, what would happen? What will people think about me? How will I explain it to Luc?" Her yelling in mere grumbles sounded too adorable. I just leaned my back on the wall and encircled my hands over my chest, enjoying the moment. I shook my head with amusement ripening in my eyes.

"Oh, you think it's funny! Huh? Wait till I get myself out of this mess. I'm not going to let you go this easily, boy. I am going to report it as sexual harassment!" She threatened me once again and, grinning at her, I began to close the distance between us. Her eyes inspected me as they contemplated every single movement of my body very carefully.

"Don't you dare come near me! I know Kung Fu." She warned me with her pointed index finger and I just raised my eyebrow at her threat.

"Relax, Starz. I'm not going to touch you until you ask me to." I winked at her and she showed her distasteful face at me.

"First of all, let me tell you how annoyed I am with your nickname. It sounds so stupid. Why do you even call me that?"

"Because 'stars' are stunning and unreachable, which is kind of same for you. And the 'Z' thing reminds me of dreams and you are my most beautiful dream, which I desire to turn into a reality." I smiled while looking down when her mouth hung open. Yeah, it surprised me too.

"Oh my God, how touchy! I'm so overwhelmed with all these emotions that I think the wine is coming back in my mouth." She retorted, but her remark came a few seconds late, revealing how my words actually affected her. And then she straightened up. "Look, I've no idea what's running in your empty head or what the heck we are doing in this cubicle. But if you are doing all this just because of our little prank on you and your partner, then I must say this is the dumbest revenge I have seen. You have…"

Closing the distance between us with a sudden forward lurch, I had my hands resting flat on either side of her head in a split second. She took in a sharp breath, eyes expanding to the size of two saucers. Her gaze briefly fell on my lips and she bit her lower lip between her teeth. I could almost hear her pounding heart.

"You were saying something!" I whispered into her ear, letting my lips touch the soft skin. She slowly closed her eyes and then opened them again with a long exhale.

"I ... I ..." Words left her side when her eyes were exchanging glances between my eyes and my lips. I could read in her eyes that the proximity was stirring her buried feelings for me.

"Do you love him, Starz?" I whispered, and her head shot up to me.

"Excuse me?" The irritation was back in her body language. "Who are you? Who gave you the right to ask me that?" Her snigger worked as an intoxication for my blood. I was glad of our closeness that let me study her features clearly. She was still a bad liar.

She scoffed in pity and then pushed me off, turning towards the door. Her hand reached for the knob when further voices pervaded in the bathroom. I could tell she was having an inner battle between fleeing from me and the risk of being exposed for being present in a male restroom with another man. Thus, she remained still, with her senses fixed on the mummers outside the cubicle. But my eyes remained stuck on her. On her every move, ready to run away from me.

"How do you look so beautiful?" I suddenly uttered, almost to myself. But obviously, she heard it. Her back straightened up and the hair on the back of her neck rose. And I could clearly see the blush rising up her cheeks.

"Because I'm a freaking vampire. Anything else? Do you realize what you have done? My engagement could break because of your stupid prank. He is waiting for me out there. If I don't appear soon he will think I ditched him or something. Or I'm not worthy of his love." She was fuming again. But her reply made me frown. She was with me right now, but still thinking about that Romano! I envied him so much. I felt like getting angry for no reason. No, I wasn't jealous! But I had never suffered this way for anyone in my entire life. This feeling was alien to me. First time in my life, I felt the urge to be in the same spot as he was. It was the worst feeling.

"I know you don't love him, Starz. Your eyes have already told me that much. Then why are you marrying him?" I asked straight up, and she scowled at my question. Her face was grimacing in resentment.

"You don't know a thing about me. I-I love him and he loves me back. Period."

"That's a lie, Starz." My words came out soft and slow. I wanted her to hear me clearly. I felt an ache in my chest when she didn't let her eyes meet mine. Slowly I placed my hands on her shoulders and made her face me. Her eyes remained locked on the ground, but I could feel her heart racing up at our proximity.

"Tell me the truth, Starz. Why are you marrying him? Is someone forcing you?" My voice fell out low and flat. I tried to find anything on her bowed face, but she didn't let me study it at all. She looked anywhere but me. The whole restroom went silent. Nothing could be heard except our heavy breaths. Something was buzzing in my pocket, but I ignored it.

"Because I'm done with people like you, Stanton. Full of all the lies and manipulation. Your kind of man makes us believe in things that don't even exist. I am done taking risks. I have no strength to get my heart broken a second time. He is a good man. So good that perhaps, I don't deserve him, but I also didn't deserve a thing you did to me." *People like me? My kind of man? What is she implying to me?*

"So, you are marrying him just because you are scared of getting hurt again?"

"Yes!" She hissed in my face.

I was angry. Furious at her for keeping herself inferior to her dear fear. How could she do that? "Then maybe you are letting your fear triumph over your true beliefs, Starz. Life is all about putting up with risks. I never thought of you to be this frail." My words poked the determination in her face and then I dashed out of there while slamming the door shut at my back.

I was mad beyond my restraining power. I punched a wall on my way out, leaving a stinging pain in my hand. But it was nothing compared to how enraged I was feeling. Anger rose in my veins, and I wanted to beat the shit out of someone at that very moment. Maybe my actions spoke better than words. I clenched my fist, forcing my body to conceal the violent urges it wanted to do. I bit my tongue, literally.

Coming out from the restroom, my eyes fell on Romano. He was checking his watch whilst strolling outside the ladies' restroom and I grinned with evilness. I was back in my vicious phase.

"Mr. Romano, what a pleasant surprise. What are you doing here?" I pretended to act in my best professional look amid measuring the restlessness on his face. And after hesitating for a few seconds, he spoke.

"It's Sarah. I can't find her. I even checked the ladies' room."

"Oh, Miss Walter? I saw her leaving the restaurant a few minutes ago. I know it's none of my business, but is everything all right between you two, Sir? She seemed in a hurry. Almost furious when I last saw her." He looked down and began to shake his head in denunciation.

"It's all my fault. I should never have chosen the venue without asking her first." He mumbled to himself. And when he looked up, he barely met my eyes. After giving me a fake smile, he walked off, patting my shoulder. I rubbed off the spot he had just touched and smirked at his back.

❦

After ruining their whole date, I blew out a heavy, relaxing sigh and made myself comfortable in the passenger seat of my car. This was one hell of a date for them that they would never forget throughout their lifetime.

But why was I even doing that? Why did I even sabotaged her date? It's not like I wanted her to break her engagement and choose me instead. Or is that what I secretly wanted?

I opened my one eye and peeped at Tom, who was staring at me accusingly. But then I closed my eyes back and continued to smile at my work. Well, she had already accused me of being a manic monster, which I had to live up to. Now I would stop at nothing.

Tom was just pulling into the driveway of the hotel when I saw Romano at the door with a puzzled look. Something was odd about him. I jerked up straight, and before the vehicle would have come to a complete halt; I opened the door and jumped out. Panic grew in my nerves as I rushed towards him.

"What happened, Sir? Why are you standing here? Where is Miss Walter?" I tried to make it as casual as possible, but then my heavy breathing and urgency attracted his suspicion. So, I tried to relax and waited for his answer. He looked pissed at something, and I made myself ready to tackle the situation.

"You told me she left the restaurant long before me, but she hasn't reached the hotel yet. Are you sure about her leaving the place?" I nodded, but my heart twisted at his words. A sting of fear crossed my senses. If she was not here, then where was she?

But then our eyes melted over a taxi entering the driveway. I let out a breath of relief when I noticed her coming out of the vehicle and giving the taxi driver her watch. I was confused. Why was she giving him her watch?

The realization hit me like a hurricane. Holy shit! She might have left her belongings on the table while coming into the restroom, and Romano may have taken them with him. I looked down and found him holding her purse. I put a hand in my coat pocket and felt her phone. *I'm so dead.*

She unfastened her high heels and marched towards us, holding them in her hands. She appeared like a walking death for me. Hungry for my flesh. Wrath was evidently dripping off her body. I took some steps back. When Romano turned towards me. And, man, he looked even more terrified than me. We watched her storming towards us, and a shudder ran down my spine. She was definitely going to kill me tonight, and it was going to be a brutal murder. I gulped down a lump in my throat when her dead eyes met mine. If looks could kill, I would've been burned to ashes right then and there, or maybe chopped into a thousand pieces.

I couldn't remember being this scared of anybody in my life. The thumping of my heart could be heard in my ears as she halted in front of us. Trust me, I felt an arrow piercing my heart when she shot a stern look at me. With a quick look at Romano, and yanking her purse from his hands, she headed inside without saying a word. And we let go of a breath.

"I will talk to her in the morning. Good night, Mr. Stewart." Romano quickly spoke up and disappeared in the wind.

What just happened? What should I do? Should I go talk to her now, or wait till the lava cools down? Just like Romano? No. It's my fault. I need to fix it. So I chose to chase my own death.

I hurried in her direction, finding her waiting for the elevator. Seeing me coming towards her, she shook her head and sprinted towards the stairs. She was climbing so fast that it was hard for me to match her pace. Yet as she got aware of the fact I was still chasing her, she stopped dead on the pathway and twirled around. Man, she had one bloodcurdling glare. I put my hands on my heart and tried to calm it down. Reminding it that she was our Starz, the same girl we both liked. But right now she was a little mad to scare us both.

"I'm so sorry. I didn't know you had no money or phone. If ..." I extended her phone towards her.

"Don't you dare bring your sorry ass to me. Do you even have a slightest idea how your silly rage on the cubicle's door got me locked up inside the cabin? God, it was so embarrassing to call for help. Because I was freaking trapped inside a male restroom." Slowly leaning onto me with her hatred, I had to slant back from her furious face.

"Next time, if you try to do anything like this, I am pressing charges on you. No. I'm going to kill you with my bare hands. Do you understand me, Stanton?" She shouted while snatching her phone from my hand, and I could do nothing but nod in that deadly, terrifying glow.

She once again commenced to climb up towards her room, but then she turned around and gave me her best 'what the fuck you still doing here' look.

"I'm really sorry, Sarah. I know it was totally my fault, but it was an accident. I never meant to do something bad to you." I paused and started to think.

She glared at me one more time and knocked at the door. Ashley answered, and she was about to go in when I grabbed her hand.

"Stanton. Leave my..." She was cut short as my grip faltered when the door opposite her room opened and all heads turned towards it. The second I saw who it was, I cursed the day she was born. Sam, the mad cousin, was hardly wearing anything. I felt dizziness start to rise in me. She checked me out from top to bottom and I felt Starz's confused eyes shifting from her to me. "Hey, my Boo Bear!" The moment she spoke, Starz slammed the door in my face.

I was condemned for the day.

Eleven

Ethan

DAY SIX

The bed made a pattering sound as I turned to my right again. I had spent all night tossing and turning, only catching maybe a couple of hours of sleep in between. Dawn was approaching, but it was still dark outside and nothing but the sound of wild waves crashing against the seashore was breaking the silence. As my naked back laid back on the mattress, my mind once again got engulfed with endless thoughts about her. Thoughts that I wasn't allowed to have.

Never once had her face stopped reflecting in front of my eyes since the day I saw her in that wedding dress. Her precious laugh. Her frown. Her emerald green eyes. The way she tucked her hair behind her ear when she was nervous. Her recollections were playing through my head. Again and again, as if my life had halted on those little details. It was all so terrifying. I needed to get away from her, but I couldn't.

I was asking some strange questions to myself. Was this the same turmoil I went through when I saw her sitting on the bleachers reading some book all those years ago? She was oblivious of her surroundings. Minding her own business. Not having the slightest idea that I had been always watching her. I couldn't deny she did disturb my football practice, earning some scolding from the coach. Little did I know I would ask her to be my girlfriend and make some of the best memories of my life.

I never thought a person could play such an important role in my life. It was so appalling that every day I craved to capture a glimpse of her face. Her presence had started to leave a satisfying sensation in my lonely heart.

I just wanted her to look at me. To acknowledge my presence. To notice my sincerity. I never thought I could be so eager for such ordinary things. Like a five-year-old kid teasing the girl he likes because he is dying to talk to her; to hear her voice.

One thing that was hundred percent clear in my mind was that I had lost her once and I am not ready to lose her again.

The realization hit me hard, and I jerked up on my bed, clasping my head in my hands, letting out a frustrated grunt. My heart was beating so fast it felt like it would jump out of my chest and land into my hands anytime. I ran my hands through my hair and pulled them in frustration. I never wanted to feel this weak in my knees for anyone. But then, she was not just anyone. She was special, an exceptionally beautiful soul.

I rolled out of my warm bed and stretched out my sore muscles. The sun had not risen yet, but it didn't hold me back from taking a walk on the beach. Putting on a t-shirt and a light jacket, I yanked my cell phone in my pocket and walked towards the door. Quietly unlocking it, I took my leave with my eyes surveying Tom's sleeping face. The second my body stood outside the door in that open surroundings, I shivered as the cold breeze battered me. It was quite a lovely morning. I pulled my hood up and pushed my hands deeper in my jacket's pocket, and strolled in the direction of the clattering waves.

It was drizzling. Not much to get me wet, but enough to feel the tiny droplets on my face. The wind howled widely, and I cherished it. The sun seemed to be rising from the womb of the deep blue ocean. My skin was cold, but my heart was still beating wildly with warmth.

The wet sand felt like jelly squishing under my feet as I strolled along. But I wasn't alone. My eyes noticed someone standing near the waterline at some distance, and curiosity hit me. I narrowed my eyes to recognize the person, but couldn't because of my nearsightedness. I marched along in the direction of the stranger. After a few steps, I was able to guess that it was a girl. Her back was facing me and her hair fluttered freely in the wind. It was freezing outside, yet she was in a thin shirt, hugging herself.

A dozen more steps and I was hit by her lavender and cinnamon fragrance, which came pounding at me with the cold breeze. It happened just like in my dream, only this time I felt lightheaded, melting in her scent. It was the same fragrance that kept me awake most of last night. Realizing who she was, a smile of gratification colored my face as I walked towards her. God was definitely playing some prank on me.

My steps dropped just beside her, witnessing her striking beauty. She had her eyes closed as the early sunrays were washing over her smooth skin. Her lips were tucked up in a satisfying smile. She sighed, and my heart skipped a beat. It took me off guard when out of nowhere, frosty waves clashed my feet. I squealed like an innocent child in surprise, but she just kept her eyes shut, not surprised at all. "Good morning, Stanton!"

I twirled towards her completely. Standing so close that had I moved forth one more inch, my lips would've caressed her ear. I just stared at her as if my life depended on it.

This angelic face had endured so many terrible things because of me that I felt ashamed of myself. Those eyes bled just because of me. I tore her heart apart, and now I was foolishly living in faith that one day she would accept my apology. *Such a selfish bastard I'm.* I was so drowned in my ego to realize the depth of the agony I gave her. But I never meant to hurt her.

Silence surrounded us like chains of steel, and I found myself trapped with her like the opposite ends of a magnet. She didn't move an inch. Neither did I! The winds came trouncing on our frozen body, but we stood there like a statue. My heart was pounding, and I was afraid she would hear it.

Lifting my right hand, I was about to touch her face when a realization hit me. She was not mine. I had no right to touch her. She frowned a little. Maybe because I was blocking the rays from falling over her face.

"If you could change one action from your past, what would it be?" Her forehead furrowed at my question, and her eyes opened slowly.

"I would call in sick the day I met you." She replied in a calm voice, but her eyes were digging deep into my soul. I chuckled, looking down, ashamed.

Surprisingly, she continued the game by asking another strange question, "If I ever got lost in the crowd, how would you find me?" And I responded with the first thing that came into my head.

"I'll just call you!" I blurted out, lost in her beauty.

"Clever! But you don't have my number. And Nah! Don't even bother asking!" She chuckled, lightening the mood. But I was so lost that I could do nothing but stare at her.

"I am sorry for being such a pain in the ass. But the truth is, I fear the day I will let go of you and your love. I will be lost. And then I'll just be sitting here, unwinding my thoughts on the sand, helping some kid build a sandcastle." I stated, sinking deep in the remorse. I felt ashamed to even meet her eyes. I could tell she was trying to read my face, trying to find the sincerity in my words. I looked everywhere but at her. I didn't have the guts to face her.

Finally, when I found some nerves to look at her, she dropped her eyes and quickly turned around. Not even a single word came out of her mouth, but I heard her taking deep breaths of tenderness. The air felt heavy around us. Geez, I spoiled her happy morning mood. I shouldn't have said that. Damn my stupid, lovesick heart. Dumping the sour mood; I jerked up my head and flashed a broad smile to lighten the atmosphere, though it was a fake one.

"Looks like someone holds a grudge." I tried my funny voice and saw her staring over me with a look clearly asking herself, 'did I fall on my head as a child?'

"Well, you practically locked me in the men's room last night. Remember, Mr. Stanton?" She just shrugged and then started to stroll along the beach, carrying her flip-flops in one hand.

"What else was I supposed to do when you don't even want to talk to me?" I sprinted along as I ran a hand through my hair, willing myself to stop staring at her perfect ass. Focus, dude, focus!

"By the way, I forgive you for ruining my chances with your hot cousin last night." I joked, trying to make her laugh, but she gave me a strange look and moved on, shaking her head.

"But I have a question for you. Why do you always call me Mr. Stanton? I'm just Ethan for you, or 'darling' if you insist." She yanked her eyes at me, but I could tell she was faking the anger. I raised my hands in surrender, but she was still calm. Something was odd with her today.

"Not that I mind, but seriously it sounds like I'm the king of kings, Stanton the fifteenth, Lord of seven kingdoms," I called out and man, it did sound good. After some strides, she stopped and turned back at me with a blank face. However, she had a haughty stare.

"It reminds me of who you really are. And it doesn't let me forget that you are a stranger to me." She replied in such a cold voice that it hit me like a dagger, piercing my heart. Her reply shut my mouth completely.

She commenced to walk away, but I was frozen in my place. I looked down at my feet and then back at her. *Girl, I wish I had the courage to tell you how I feel. I might be a stranger to you, but trust me when I say, sometimes a stranger could bring great meaning to your life, just like you have brought to mine.*

"Sarah Rose Walter!" I shouted, making her turn around almost immediately. She looked straight at me and I stole the chance to capture her beauty on my cell phone. The second she heard the shutter sound, she had her glare back. And man, I was sure my life was in danger. I witnessed her storming towards me, and I knew I was in trouble. Taking several steps back, I turned around, running away for the sake of my life.

"Ethan Stanton, get your ass back here or I swear you will not like my bad side!" She yelled at me, but I didn't stop.

"Is it bad-bad- as in the evil side or bad-bad- as in the naughty side?" I asked, catching a glimpse of her mad expressions. *What if she kills me right here and dumps my body in the never-ending ocean?* I was risking my life here.

I yelped in shock when one of her slippers hit my head. What the hell! As I turned around, the other one also came flying up straight in my direction. I was just able to dodge it at the last moment but then noticed her looking around in the sand for pebbles. Rubbing my head in pain, I ran as fast as I could.

This girl was a freaking ninja. I never thought of her being this ferocious. She had changed so much. Not that I didn't like this side of her, but her feistiness was proving hazardous to me. I turned around to check my progress and witnessed an empty coconut coming right in my direction. Oops!

It hit right across my temple, and everything around me started spinning. I was knocked off in the sand, with birds singing around my head while stars gliding above me. I didn't know what I was saying. I no longer remembered anything. What was my name again?

"So, are you handing me your phone, or do I have to seize it by cutting your hand off?" She hovered over me while putting her hands on her hips.

I was still disoriented. Grabbing my head, I looked up to face her. "Wow, you are scary, babe." She was smirking down at me, so accepting my defeat, I handed her my cell phone. I saw her grinning in victory, and seizing the moment, I tucked my leg behind hers, making her lose her balance.

Her hips landed smoothly over the sand, and I quickly climbed over her, smirking viciously. I was taken aback when she began throwing punches into my stomach. Ouch! Maybe she wasn't bluffing last night and really knew Kung-Fu. I never thought she could ever give me this kind of fight back. She lifted her right hand away from the face, which held my phone, while the second one was giving me a tough tussle.

"Easy, darling." I hastily moved my head to the left to dodge another blow. *Charming! This chick is a freaking cat woman.* But in any case, I was going to take my phone back before she could delete the perfect picture.

I stretched my hand towards her right hand when she started to do something on the phone, and in the flash of the moment, she had her claws on my face. I screamed in pain as her nails dug deep into my face. "Not the face, darling. Not the freaking face!"

She tried her best to dismantle my head, but one tickle on her tummy and her hands freed the phone. With my conquest of the nuclear weapon that she was, I pushed her both hands above her head and fought to steady her body underneath me. I settled my weight lightly on her, and her struggles ceased. No more kicking and thrashing me like a punching bag.

Suddenly, something felt weird. I looked down at her and unintentionally, my lips brushed the corner of her mouth. Her body surrendered underneath me, stopping all movements. We were breathing hard. I could feel her hot, heavy breaths on my face. The sparkles of her wide green orbs were enough to make me go all giddy. She had her eyebrows raised in acknowledgment of our closeness. Still, she remained calm. Her mouth half-opened in a gasp, with sweat furnishing her forehead. I noticed her gulping down the lump forming deep in her throat. While my mouth felt arid. She was my thirst, and I was her fresh air. She was gazing at me like seeing me for the first time. None of us blinked. Afraid the moment would disappear.

I noticed the transitions in her body from our juxtaposition. Her heart started to beat faster. Her chest rose and fell with rapid breaths. Her trembling lips wanted to say something to me, but her voice betrayed her. *Is she really afraid of me? Am I making her uncomfortable under me? Should I stand up?* But I wanted to stay like this forever and to be honest, the sinful Ethan wanted to relive the dream that had left him wanting for more. But did she want the same? No!

I closed my eyes and nodded at her in assurance and placed both hands on either side of her to balance my body. I groaned when I stumbled a little because of that wet sand. And she turned her head away. My face dropped at her revulsion. Maybe she was never going to forgive me. Eventually, with considerable effort, I finally managed to pull my body up, now standing up straight on my feet. Shaking the sand off my hands, I held out my hand for her aid. This time she looked at me and then towards my hand. But then, not finding me worthy enough to be a help, she stood up on her own, leaving me empty-handed. I curled back my hand, a little disappointed this time.

"I'm sorry! I crossed my boundaries." I apologized, looking down while grasping my neck with my rejected hand. But then something unexpected happened. I froze right there when her words reached my ears.

"I forgive you." My head yanked straight to her. She gave me a smile worth dying for. I was too shocked to say anything. I found myself pretty lost for words. I stammered a little, but then ultimately shut my mouth, feeling like an idiot.

"I really mean it, Stanton. I forgive you for the things you did to me. It happened in the past and I'm over it. You should too." She let out a dry chuckle, looking down.

"After all, we can't keep on dwelling on our past. There is no need to beat around the bush. It happens. People make terrible mistakes. They fall apart. Sometimes we do things we regret doing." She continued without faltering. My eyes bored into her, and the realization crossed my mind. She was talking more about herself rather than me.

"So, there is that, and then there is this." She gestured toward the engagement ring on her finger. Maybe she expected me to say something, but my mind was unable to form words.

"Anyway, now that you have heard the most awaited words, you can leave this island and this awful life soon. I mean, I can totally understand how tormented you had been feeling chasing me around." I let my eyes linger on her, and she stared at me with the same intensity. She was waiting for my reply, but I didn't know what to say.

I gazed at her in disbelief. Did I hear her right? *Am I seriously pardoned? Am I really free of the burdens of my sins after all this time?* But then again, the thought of leaving this island, leaving her, wasn't making me feel any contentment inside my heart. I had been searching for her all these years to make her accept my apology. Never was I confused about my goal. Then why was I not bloody happy hearing those words? I shook my head to clear my mind, but the heaviness in my heart didn't curtail.

"Do you trust me, Sarah? Do you see me as a changed man now? The man who can never imagine hurting you ever again, even in his dreams? Have I earned your faith back?" My eyes pierced into her when she let out a dry chuckle.

"Stanton, I'm a good enough person to forgive you, but not stupid enough to trust you again." With that, she left me alone at the beach, more confused than ever.

<hr />

All cards were laid. I was ready to make my next move. Perfect!

The vehicle was ready. The driver was committed, and the plan was on the way. Everything was perfect and eagerly waiting for the Bride to be. *But where the hell is she?*

"Why can't I come?" Mrs. Walter's voice attracted my attention as she came rushing out of the gates, followed by Starz and the she devil Ashley.

"Because it's my wedding and I want to have a dress of my choice, Mom. Just accept the fact that you will never let me choose on my own." Starz replied with a deep sigh.

"Remember, I don't want you dressed like a homeless person or as if you're going to a funeral!" Her mother said, turning towards her.

"Then perhaps you should stop torturing me before I kill someone and we really would need to go to a funeral!" Starz replied with the same grouchiness, and I adjusted my tie. It looked like someone was not in a good mood today. The argument was pretty intense, so I tried to persuade my mind not to jump between them.

But I was who I was, and I intervened, "You don't have to worry about anything, Mrs. Walter. My designer will handle everything. I can promise you that I won't let her buy any potato sacks." I winked at Starz as she descended the stairs, passing me the best grimace that could possibly turn anyone into ashes.

"Maybe you are the one I'm going to murder." She directed that at me in a hushed voice and wrinkled her nose a little, and I smiled in response.

꒰ঌ

"Here we are." Tom declared as my eyes drifted towards our destination. I may not like the idea of Starz marrying someone else but I want her to have the best of everything. And so I tweaked some connections and the best designer from LA, who is also one of my favorite persons, had landed within the hours of my phone call.

A smile etched my face with pride as I witnessed the interior of the boutique. My head spun around at the simplicity yet grandeur of the place. It was simply fabulous. The high-end mahogany furniture, the mannequins embellished with finest gowns, and the Italian floor with LED track lights were making everything gleam. I had some idea that she could do wonders in a matter of just one day, but this was exquisite.

And there she was. The woman standing in the middle of the room with a subsided annoyed look. "Ellen!" I approached to greet her.

"Aha, Ethan. What a pleasant surprise." She was glowing with her perfect, shimmering aura. Her short silver hair perfectly matched her charismatic personality. I scratched the back of my neck in embarrassment when I noticed the piercing look on her face as she walked towards us. She was a little older than my mom, but never too old to give me one hell of a masked glare.

Seeing her calm and composed, I reckoned she wasn't that mad at me. I decided to play it safe and extended my hand to shake as a peace gesture with my sweetest professional smile. But the next moment, she pulled me into a bear hug that knocked the living air out of my lungs. I wasn't able to breathe. She was literally crushing me as if taking out all her anger in that hug.

"I missed my grandson's first birthday party. It better be important or you would be in great trouble, child." She muttered near my ear, and I let out a chuckle, noticing Starz's suspicious eyes on us. *You see, this is the biggest disadvantage of having close friends work for you. You can't get all bossy on them.*

"I found her, Ellen." She suddenly ended her bone-crushing hug and stared at me with her big blue eyes, and I genuinely smiled at her with a small nod. She was my Nanna's best friend and thus she knew my whole story and my endeavor of searching Starz.

She quickly averted her eyes from me and shifted her attention to the girls. Her eyes rambled between Starz and Ashley. "The blonde?" She whispered, leaning sideways at me while her eyes were fixed on them. I blinked at her in approval and there she beamed again. "I'm impressed. She is beautiful." I just scratched my head at her comment.

"Oh my goodness, are you blushing, lover boy?" I was flabbergasted at her question, and hurriedly changed my full semblance.

"Mrs. Pecoraro, this is my client, Miss Walter, and her friend, Miss Ashley. And ladies, this is Ellen Pecoraro. She is the one you need."

Starz smiled at her while extending her hand, but Ellen pulled her in her arms, taking everyone by surprise. I couldn't help but just shrug nervously when Starz stared at me with questioning eyes.

"Oh. My. God. You are 'The Pecoraro'. The one and only Pecoraro." Ashley screamed all of a sudden, making Ellen finally let go of Starz from her bear hug and I let out a breath of relief.

"I am Ashley Ellsworth. Oh, I'm a huge fan of your work, ma'am." Everyone was confused at that moment except Ash. I didn't know she was a fashionista type.

"Oh. No. No. Don't believe everything they say. Paparazzi are guilty of exaggerating my image. I'm a mere amateur designer, who has won only nineteen awards and been listed in the top ten earners of last year. Anyway, I've made the perfect adorning gown for you, dear." She quickly gestured towards her two assistants and they suddenly disappeared deep into the shop.

I saw Ellen getting engaged in conversation with Ashley, as she seemed too interested in her work and I gladly didn't disturb them. On the other hand, I noticed Starz getting lost in the section of party gowns. Her eyes were gleaming like diamonds, and I stole the chance to get sneaky with her. She was so engrossed in beautiful dresses that she didn't even notice me standing just behind her. I buried my face deep in her hair and inhaled the intoxicating whiff of lavender. Once again, I felt like I was in heaven and getting bewitched by one of the angels.

"Just say the word and I will buy the whole store for you." She twirled around, and I smiled when she rolled her eyes at me.

"Oh, no-no. You have done more than I could ever ask, Stanton. I simply can't increase my debts on you." Baby, that sarcastic remark made me go all crazy. *Gosh, this girl is so amazing.*

"But if you give me one more chance, I..."

"Is everything all right in here?" I cursed underneath my breath when the cock-blocker Ashley came, sticking her nose between us. She glared at me like I'd stolen her brain and replaced it with rocks, and then turned towards Starz, smiling brightly at her. God, why me? Didn't we have a deal that you will keep away all the bugs and in return I would not kill Ashley? Just remember, you broke the pact first, madam.

"Never been so perfect." I gave her a forced smile as she took Starz's hand, reckoning to drag her away from my vicinity. But then the dress arrived.

"Oh, my goodness." The girls chirped like a kid seeing an ice cream truck.

My eyebrows heaved up, taking in the extravagance of the dress. I had earlier briefed Ellen about Sarah's measurements, her preferences, her love for vintage and laces and asked her to make the most beautiful dress for the most beautiful girl, expenses no bar. The two girls rolled down the mannequin diligently, and in the end, Ellen and Starz disappeared behind the large white curtain, leaving me with that thief. *Huh, seriously? What a torture.* We rolled our eyes at each other and turned in different directions, ready to ignore each other for the next hour.

I was a little tired from last night's endeavor. Thus, stumbling over the comfortable-looking couch, I rested my head back and closed my eyes to catch some sleep. The couch dipped a little on my right and I sneaked a look and, as expected, found my sworn enemy grinning at me, and my forehead furrowed at her. *Now, what the hell does she want from me?*

"So, how do you know 'The Great Pecoraro'?" Her fingers air quoted her name and I shifted at my place. "I know she works in LA and her rates are sky-high. So how did you manage to drag her down to this island for a small wedding?" Her eyes were burning holes in my skull.

"Just so we are clear, woman. I really am allergic to back-stabbing lying thieves. And if I got infected, no one would be able to tolerate my maniac acts, especially not you." Her eyes lowered for a moment.

"Yeah, about that. Listen! I'm sorry for stealing your notebook, okay? I shouldn't have done that. And also for that itching powder prank. And for everything that made you lose your shit. You know; I was just being protective towards Sarah!" I had no idea whether to feel good about the apology or get mad at her actions.

"But now I want to make everything right. Starting with returning your car!" Did she say my car?

"It was you who sent that goon to me!" That came out to be a shock. I was mad. Pretty flaming mad.

"Obviously, how do you think he got to know about the date in the very first place?" Her aura suddenly changed into a proud narcissist dame and when she palpated my furious face, she was back in her dying cat looks.

"And why are you telling me all this now? Are you going to die soon or something?" I shrugged my shoulders and in the next moment, she plunged to the ground, kneeling in front of me with her hands clasped together, praying up at me.

"Please, do your thing and get me an internship with Mrs. Pecoraro. I know you must have some connections with her to bring her all the way here. I would be eternally indebted to you for this. Please! Please! Pretty Please!" *Oh, now I get it.*

She was about to get a hold of my leg, and I jumped back in shock. "Okay, okay, fine lady, just keep your hands to yourself! But remember, you owe me for this." She quickly stood up and jumped towards me, embracing my scared self in a tight hug. "Whatever you say, man. But I don't do sexual favors. Just to be clear." I grabbed her shoulders and placed one arm's distance between us.

"Thank goodness you cleared that up!"

"You know; this little favor doesn't mean I would let you play with Sarah's feelings again. I know you haven't changed a bit." Okay, that hurt my self-esteem. I knew I had willingly made myself fall to the lowest, but it didn't give an open invitation to random people to insult Ethan Stanton in his face.

"Don't you sound a little rude for someone who was begging on her knees for a favor just a few seconds ago?" I curled my hands on my chest to keep my annoyance in check. I was not the same Ethan Stanton. She shouldn't affect me. Her meaningless words should have no power over me. Yet I was feeling this disgruntled spasm in my chest that I couldn't ease away.

"Ashley?" Our heads turned towards Ellen's voice and saw her confused eyes wandering between us.

"Ahh, okay! Meanwhile, Miss Walter is trying on her dress. Why don't you go upstairs with Miss Lily here? I have a bunch of samples for bridesmaids. And also she will show you our special section of maid of honor. I bet you will like it." Ellen smiled, gesturing towards one of her assistants.

"Great!" She chirped, taking a good hold of my arm, and the next moment she was dragging me upstairs with her.

As we reached, I saw her eyes lit up when she saw endless rows of dresses and as expected she disappeared from my sight, lost somewhere behind all the alluring clothes and I let out a yawn. I needed some sleep, ladies.

"How's this?" My head shot up at her, noticing her holding up a dress, and I smiled wickedly at her. "This is perfect! You should definitely try this one." I pushed her inside the changing room. Bolting the door from outside, I fixed a chair under the doorknob while grinning deviously. Payback bitch.

As I turned around, I saw Miss Lily staring at me with wide eyes and her hands covering her mouth. "Do not worry, ma'am. It's just a little prank on my childhood friend. Now come, let's go and find out how the bride is doing." I took her by the shoulder and dragged her along with me.

"Are you serious? Open this damn door. I will kill you, Stanton!" Ash's threats creased our ears, and I just laughed and kept dragging the scared assistant downstairs. Ash started thrashing at the door, and I helped her by turning off all the lights. "Stanton! I'm telling you last time, open this door right now or I'm going to break it." The clattering sound of the doorknob gave me utter delight.

"Ethan, are you even there?" My smirk only got bigger as she groaned at the top of her lungs and commenced to take out her wrath on the naïve door. No one was going to hear you, girl.

The second I stepped downstairs into the waiting area, my eyes literally turned into two big hearts hanging out of sockets when I saw Sarah's reflection in the mirror. Everything surrounding me numbed. The first thing that crossed my mind was, *who the hell is this girl?* It seemed like I was seeing a completely different person. My Starz, who was famous in high school for her messy bun, baggy clothes, and homeless attire, was nowhere in sight, and in her place, an angel had fallen from heaven in front of me.

I was awestruck by her transformation. All I needed right at the moment was the time to freeze so that I could behold her beauty in my eyes forever. She just seemed unreal. I must have been looking like a terrible lovesick pup, as she simply took my breath away.

Ellen placed her hand below my jaw, which must have been hanging open from captivating her beauty. My eyes wandered on her from top to bottom, and then again from bottom to top. It was a never-ending loop. You could call it gawking, but for me, it was an intense admiration. My mind went blank. It could comprehend Starz and only Starz at that moment.

She was admiring herself in the mirror, and I could see how nervous she was. So unsure of herself. I wish I could make her realize her self-worth. But I found myself lucky enough to witness all this.

God, if it isn't too much to ask, then make her look at me with the same feelings which I had been dealing with lately. At least make her truly forgive me.

I never believed in miracles. But then I met her. Found her once again. And this moment. This very moment with her was no less than some miracle to me.

I walked closer to her, coming into the vicinity of her vision as she stared back at me through the mirror, and I smiled. She gave me an anxious smile and I think I almost died right there. Did she just bless me with a real smile? I was feeling light-headed at that instant. Am I dreaming? Or was it another one of God's dirty jokes?

My breathing went all shallow when she turned around, holding her dress. I was losing myself in her mesmerizing beauty. God, how could someone look so beautiful? It should be illegal.

"Say something, Crazyhead." I shook my head when her words brought me back from the spell. She looked very doubtful about the dress, and I wanted to make her less anxious. But I was back to being dumb. I tried to say something but found myself out of words. I opened my mouth and then closed it again, not finding words to describe how unbelievable she was looking.

"What would you say if I asked you to marry me right now?" The words escaped my mouth before I could've held them back. I cursed myself underneath my breath when her eyes pierced my heart, looking deeper into my soul. She held my eyes for a good ten seconds before she let out a humorless chuckle. The smile had a bitter taste in it.

"Nothing. I can't talk and laugh at the same time!" Ouch!

Twelve

Sarah

NINE YEARS AGO

"**A**re you sure this is the place?" Ash was on the wheel of her dad's antique car as we reached our school jock Jason's house for the victory bash.

Nibbling at my lips in nervousness, I took one more glance at our surroundings, eyes blinking incessantly. Blaring party music and dozens of flashing cars in the driveway; it must be the place. "Yup, this is it."

After driving for around fifty minutes, we had finally reached the venue. It was exhausting to convince Ash. She was skeptical even after three hours of begging. So I had to resort to emotional blackmailing. She finally agreed after I reminded her of 'the oath of friendship' we took in middle school. I was utterly thankful for her company because now I wouldn't be standing in a corner surrounded by unfriendly faces all by myself.

She double-checked the door locks, and I shook my head at her cynical behavior. "What? You know my dad would kill me if anything happens to his car." Her worry made me almost roll my eyes, crossing my hands over my chest.

"Turn around and see the truth for yourself. Do you really think someone is going to steal this scrap over all these beauties?" The look on her face seemed vague for a few seconds. She had a peculiar quirk on her lips when she gave me a lopsided smile. "Old is gold, baby!"

Our heads automatically turned towards the music. And the moment we started ascending the long pathway to the house, I rubbed my sweaty palms against the fabric of my dress. I was dressed in a yellow fit and flare strapless dress that ended around my mid-thigh while Ash had opted for a tomboy look in baggy jeans and a crop top with an open boyfriend shirt draped over her shoulders. The idea of everyone's gaze being fixed upon me started to make my heart beat faster.

I knew I might have gone a little overboard with the dress and heels and makeup, for a fun party like this, but I had missed my senior prom last month because of stomach flu and this might be my only chance to have a proper dance with Ethan before we pass out of high school. To finally fulfill my desire to be his prom date. So, walking tall in my heels we moved forward.

Though the pathway was lightened with fairy lights hanging on the beautifully crafted trees, my skin still tingled in anticipation of what laid beyond. The intensity of music increased as we processed further and just as we reached the last stone, my mind struggled to absorb the wildness of the crowd in front of me.

My unrestrained heartbeat rang in my ears, noticing an enormous pool of people. The ear-piercing music made my heart pound so hard, I could feel it strain against my ribcage. The vibration through the sound pulsated throughout my body, setting my nerves on fire. The sound of water splattering in the swimming pool and people shouting over the music mingled perfectly like a perfect blend of spice and sugar.

Suddenly a shriek echoed around, followed by a guy jumping off from the first floor straight into the pool, making me jump out of my skin. My hand yanked towards my chest, suppressing the little heart attack he just gave me. It was scary, yet made me elated.

"I thought I was going to get bored, but this is insane." Ash's words fell into my ears, but I couldn't respond. I wanted to absorb every glimpse of wildness happening in front of me. I bet my eyes were gleaming in ecstasy, with adrenaline pumping in my veins.

Could it be for real? I didn't know this kind of crazy world existed in real. It was a scene taken out of some YA movie. My mind was not prepared to process all things my eyes were witnessing. I couldn't explain the sensation thriving inside me. The feeling was something to behold, and I felt like I had entered some alternate crazy world.

I didn't think I had ever been

This alive...

This free... And in particular,

This thrilled.

My over-enthusiastic big grin was perfectly narrating the level of adrenaline rushing through my veins.

"Xandra! Xandra! Xandra!

Our heads turned towards the commotion, only to witness a crowd hovering over two not-so-familiar faces. They seemed pretty drunk. The pace at which they were emptying the cups was enough to make anyone pass out, but it was clear their bodies were used to this level of alcohol. From the charged atmosphere it was evident that the 'Xandra' girl was excelling in the game, as the crowd was chanting her name. Just as she emptied the last cup, a loud howl left her lips, making everyone around her cheer in ecstasy.

Somehow, it was a good thing that we hardly knew anyone here. We were easily concealed in the crowd, witnessing everyone going crazy. Some faces were from our school, while others were quite unfamiliar. "He has invited the whole town." Ash's words near my ear made me turn around and my eyes drifted towards the enormous staircase at the end of the hall, twirling like those in a dollhouse. I was mesmerized by its beauty.

Sizzling hot!

They were the only two words that could perfectly describe the things that were happening in front of me. My heart raced up with the deafening sound of metallic music. The hall was filled with faces. Faces I was used to see daily in school corridors and some other faces that seemed much older.

Taking everything in, Ash and I looked at each other and then burst out squealing in excitement like complete lunatics.

"I'll get us something to drink." Ash offered and disappeared into the crowd. I glanced around, my eyes desperately trying to find that one particular face. The face I was dying to catch a glimpse of. I bit my lower lip, with nervousness creeping in me. He must be around here somewhere.

"Drink! Drink! Drink!" My attention got captured by the crowd cheering at the loudest. I found myself getting curious yet again. Maybe they were having yet another stupid drinking game. And before I knew my legs were heading towards it.

Even after standing on my toes, I couldn't see anything. My little self could barely pass through the crowd that was encircling them, and I shook my head. "They are serving something different in the basement; I'm curious what's attracting people down there." Ashely's words made me turn towards her as she handed me a red cup.

"Let's keep ourselves away from that dark part!" We clinked our cups and turned back towards the madness in front of us. My face scrunched up with the bitterness of the liquid in my cup, but I quickly forgot it when Ashely's cell phone rang.

"Shoot!" Her face turned pale when she checked the screen and my forehead creased. Hastily answering the call, she just muttered out some yes and no and then hung up. Shoving her cell phone back in the pocket, she gave me a once over and then hid her face behind her hands, letting out helpless groans underneath it.

"I know it's a crime to ditch your best friend," she grasped my shoulders as I kept on nodding at her as she went on. "But I'm really sorry. My dad… he is once again drunk. Almost naked, and dancing in front of our porch. I really need to get there before our neighbors call the cops." I held her hands to make her stop fidgeting and gathered her attention.

"Just go!" Without uttering anything, she heaved me into a short hug and darted away. My eyes watched her fading away in the crowd, disappearing somewhere. I sighed, gulping down her drink as well. I shook my head, turning away from the door when I noticed a familiar face and my eyes gleamed.

He was one of the close friends of Ethan, and not to forget the only nicer one I knew. Everyone called him Tom rather than his real name Thomas. I watched him standing in a corner, leaning against the wall. Taking a sip from a beer bottle, he shook his head at the cheering crowd with a hint of disapproval. His other hand was wrapped around some girl as he leaned over to whisper something in her ear. I made up my mind to confront him. He might have some idea where I could find Ethan.

Disposing off the now empty cups and straightening my back to look less scruffy, I strolled towards him when my shoulders bumped into someone halfway through. It wasn't hard like a wall, but still firm enough to leave me a little startled. My body turned to the side simultaneously, eyes following the person, only to be stopped dead by the massive shadow looming over me. He was so tall that I was just reaching up to his chest. My anxiety grew stronger, seeing an unknown person smirking in arrogance.

Two of his friends followed shortly, and I felt like a scared little girl surrounded by wolves. I lowered my head, eyes already glued to the floor. I mentally begged Ash to come back and rescue me, but I knew she couldn't. Sweat covered my forehead when my sight of black-and-white tiles started to become wobbly.

"Hey guys, it looks like someone got lost!" The boy in front of me spoke in such a thrilled tone that it scared me. I sensed his hand drifting towards me, and I leaned back. My nose wrinkled just as his metallic breath touched my face. "Why do you look so familiar, sweetheart?" I was stunned when I sensed another hand coming closer to my face. It pressed under my chin, lifting my face to have proper eye contact. A shiver ran down my spine when I stood frozen under his stare.

Just when I met his alarming gaze, something caught my attention at his back. I narrowed my orbs, observing the person closely. The haziness around my thoughts cleared out when I saw Ethan at a distance having fun. Playing some drinking game with a ping-pong ball.

"Knock it off, Bert, you are scaring the blondie." I jumped in fear when a slurry voice fell into my ears. The voice was too close to my back. "Sweet! What do we have here?" I shivered when his breath attacked the nape of my neck. A blend of smoke and alcohol in it, making me cringe.

"I'm Jason. Hey, I know you!" Now he was in front of me. He took a step forward, only for me to step back. "But, from where? From where? From where? Ahh, you're Stanton's chick!" Out of nowhere, he clasped my arm, pulling me onto his chest. My heart almost exploded. Whereas my morale tried its best to mask the fear rising into my chest. Yet my sharp, shallow breaths in panic narrated everything.

"What was your name again?" He asked, jerking me back at an arm's distance. The hungriness in his stare disgusted me. His grip was painful, but I still dared to struggle. I wanted to get free from his sickening touch and run far away from this place.

Ripples of their wicked laughter turned into waves of torrential pain in my head. It was like experiencing a living nightmare, and it frightened me so badly that I felt like I was going to lose my consciousness.

"Sa… Sarah!" I barely let out my name from my trembling lips.

"Wow, you can actually talk. She is not dumb." This time he lowered his head, once again letting his disgusting breath fall over my face. The moment his lips touched the side of my face, I shuddered. He let out a whiff as if a wolf sniffing his prey.

"Do you want to hang out somewhere, private, Sarah?" His low, husky whisper sickened me. I struggled underneath him, letting out some stressed grunts, but it was futile. I was helpless. His grip was so strong that I knew it was going to leave bruises. Right at that moment, nothing crossed my mind but regret. A feeling of disappointment for ever coming here.

"Why are your hands empty?" Suddenly, he shoved a glass in my hand, making the liquid splatter on my dress. "It's my party and everyone here is bound to drink their ass-off." He shouted his last line, making everyone around him laud for him.

I felt nausea hitting deep in my throat. I tried to shove his hand away, which had now settled on my hips, but he didn't even budge. I could feel water welling up at the back of my eyes, from not even being able to defend myself. I wanted to scream, but I knew it would be drowned in that ear-piercing music. The whole room swirled in front of me, making me dizzy, and I just wanted to run far away. I wanted to hide in my closet till this night got over.

Without a warning, I felt a strong grip encircling around my arm, and in the flash of a second, my body was freed from Jason's grip. It happened so quickly that I couldn't comprehend who was behind it until I heard his voice.

"Where were you, bastards? You guys missed my fuckin' victory shot!" Hastily, I lifted my head, only to come face to face with Ethan's smirk. A breath of relief left my trembling lips, feeling him close to me. He made me feel safe. My sense came to ease, feeling protected underneath his warm embrace. His familiar scent calmed my nerves, making me clearly discern that the dreadful moment was over. But then an uncomfortable silence enclosed us.

Suddenly, he sensed something was wrong and grasped my shoulders, making me turn towards him. "What's wrong?" I remained frozen, bowing my head when I could feel his stern gaze on me.

"You know she is mine, still you dared to touch her." My head shot up, witnessing him consumed with anger. The threatening voice had an edge of irritation in it, and it made me swallow down a lump in my throat. I noticed his sharp gaze shooting daggers at Jason, and I wrapped my hands around his arm.

"Chill your ass down, Stanton. We were just checking on her if she needed anything. Weren't we, Sarah?" Checking? If I could be more specific, you guys were harassing me. I glared at him when one of them sheepishly smiled at me to save his ass from Ethan. Jason's mates were having a hard time standing underneath his cold stare. While Jason was, in fact, throwing deadly glares at Ethan, who was gladly returning the favor.

"Don't mess with me, Jason, or next time it won't be a warning!" He circled his hands around my waist protectively. A muscle in his jaw twitched, noticing Jason holding up his hands in surrender. I tightened my grip around his arm, making Ethan believe that we had enough of him.

He loosened up a little, and we turned around, walking towards a quiet place. I smiled when he caressed my face, making me feel better.

"I'm sorry about that, babe. They are just a bunch of jokers. Please forgive me!" I looked into his eyes and found love and care. My face flushed, feeling him so close to my body. I nodded, palpating the delicacy of the moment. Without giving me a fair warning, he shot me his signature heart-warming smile and pulled me into his arms.

"Hey, girlfriend." The second his husky voice stroked my ears, my heart melted away. He intertwined his fingers with mine, giving rise to a spark that flickered through my soul. He noticed the effect he had on me when he drew me closer, his hot breath nuzzling my ear.

"I've never seen something so beautiful." His lips brushed against my ear and I closed my eyes, letting my body be bewitched by him. A sense of tranquility penetrated my body, and I was grateful to the dim lights in the hall for concealing my blush.

My hands pressed against his chest when we stared into each other's souls. I sensed the tilt of his head as he drew in for a kiss. At first, the kiss felt soft and welcoming, but then the urge of possessiveness overpowered it.

His fingers buried in my hair, pulling me closer. His mouth tasted like my favorite candy, with a strong scent of alcohol-infused in it. But there was something peculiar in that kiss, which made my eyes go round at the back of my head. Every part of my body was tingling in pleasure. He nuzzled my lower lips as if telling me how sorry he was for all the things I had to go through and it made a smile creep on my face. I moaned in pleasure as if accepting his unsaid apology.

But then, it only exploded something in him. He inhaled a sharp breath and in the next second kissed me even more deeply. I just wished the time could stand still at that moment. So that I could relive this kiss over and over again. I wanted to be selfish for once in a lifetime.

We had to break the kiss to take a breath and I laid my head on his chest as he wrapped his hands around my waist. At that moment I closed my eyes and let the music soothed my soul. I let myself get lost in that bottomless sweet sensation. His fluttering heart once again made me want nothing but to stay like this forever.

"Ethan?" A silvery voice suddenly intruded on us, making our heads turn towards the source.

"Oh, my goodness. Is that really you?" And before I could complain his warmth was gone. I was once again cold and lonely.

"Natasha? Long-time no see!" Ethan's voice sounded like he was very happy seeing whoever intruded on us. I knew it was bad to feel jealous of someone for no reason, but I didn't like her way of invading our private moment.

My face turned solemn, noticing them exchanging a very friendly hug. Though she was way more gorgeous and maybe older than me, still she had no right to steal him like that. I grimaced when she crossed the line by intertwining her arm around his. She was pretending like I wasn't even present there.

I mentally whined like a little girl who couldn't get the last available toy in the store. Why was it too much to ask for some little time for ourselves? A few alone and somewhat personal moments were all I wanted. I noticed her trying to drag him towards the dance floor, but Ethan turned around and gestured towards me.

"Natasha, she is Sarah!" I held out my hand, trying my best to smile at her.

"And babe, she is Natasha, Jason's elder sister! She is a freshman in college. We used to spend every summer together." Listening to the newfound information, my fake smile slipped off my lips. Evil siblings were ready to make my life hell. I almost gawked when she passed me a quick nod and then turned back towards Ethan. I'd never met such a rude person.

"Those were the days." I gulped down the jealousy when she raked her fingers over his upper arm. "Now, come on. This is our jam!" Ethan tried to pass her overenthusiastic offer, but she was too stubborn to leave his side. My eyes drifted back and forth between them, praying she would give up. But it was not going to happen anytime soon. There was something between them that made me anticipate they had a history.

I almost groaned with jealousy when she ran a hand over his chest. Whispering something in his ear that made Ethan let out a sheepish chuckle. Well, it worked like a charm. Letting his guards down to her repeated whining, they finally ended up on the dance floor. But, the problem was that I was also dragged along, and let me tell you this straight, moving my hips in public was not my cup of tea. I was more of a bathroom dancer.

I didn't want to embarrass myself, as I already knew how bad I was at this. Thus, I kept my feet glued on the floor, watching Ethan and his long-lost friend having the time of their lives. Occasionally, I smiled at him whenever he sneaked a view to check on me between his smooth moves. "Oh, my Gosh!" Out of the blue, a girl stumbled in front of me. My eyes bulged out in alarm, witnessing the glass in her hands tilting over me till I saw the liquid drenching my dress.

"I'm so sorry, sweetheart." A fresh swell of irritation rose in me when I shot her a glare. But she was already pretty drunk to catch anything and simply passed me, once again stumbling on her heels. The fabric of my dress started to soak the liquid quickly, and I worried it was going to leave a permanent stain. My head lifted towards Ethan, who was busy with Natasha, totally clueless about the little accident. And I tapped his shoulders to gather his attention.

"I'm going to use the restroom." Quickly sneaking a look at my dress, he nodded at me. "Do you need me to come with you?" He shouted near my ear, but I just shook my head and turned around, storming off the stupid dance floor. Crossing the hallways, I reached the end of the hall, fighting my way through the crowd, and finally twirled the knob of the washroom. The smell hit me first, while my eyes took a moment to notice a girl puking her guts out, and I quickly closed the door.

"Just breathe!" I tried to wane the fresh waves of nausea that just hit me and went upstairs in a search of another washroom. My hands shook in hesitation to open doors. Though the voices coming from inside were confirming me to not disturb them, I didn't know what should be done with quiet rooms.

My right hand whirled the doorknobs while the other covered my eyes. "Yoho! Is anybody in there?" I finally found an empty room with an attached bathroom. The water soaked the front of my dress as my fingers struggled to rub off the red stain, which was not going anywhere. I gave up dejectedly.

My head turned up to the mirror. A small smile crept up on my face, remembering the moment Ethan actually checked me out and appreciated my efforts of spending hours getting ready for this stupid party. But, I didn't want only a one-time appreciation from him. I expected to spend the entire night with him, talking and listening to the words meant only for me.

Exiting the bathroom, my eyes instinctively drifted towards the ceiling. Glancing at the beautifully crafted roof. It was then that I noticed the glamor of the room. I guessed it was the master bedroom with an aura of allure flowing through it. The gray decadent curtains and white shiny marble floor gave it a perfectly elegant look. But the centerpiece of the room was the mahogany king-size four-poster bed, spread out like it owned the place.

I fought a strong urge to climb under the sheets and just go to sleep. My head was pounding, and my vision was getting blurry. Maybe I was exhausted from all the drama that unfolded downstairs a while ago or there was something in those drinks or both.

My forehead creased when a knock came on the door. My first thought was that it must be just another couple in a quest for an empty room, but then came a call. "Sarah? Are you in there?" The voice pulled me in, so compelling that grabbing my heels in one hand and my purse in another, I ran towards the door like a kid running for an ice-cream truck.

Ethan's apprehensive face confronted my heavy breaths as I pulled the door open. "Sarah, what's wrong with you? I have been searching for you everywhere like a maniac, and you are hiding here. What are you even doing here all alone? Do you have any idea how worried I was?" I chuckled, lowering my head. Maybe it was a tint of alcohol in my blood or just my cheesy thoughts. But his handsome features looked so much more mouth-watering while he was being mad at me.

"I'm sorry. The downstairs bathroom was already packed, and I just found this room empty, so you know I called the shots. It's not like I was..." I was babbling like a moron when, without giving me a clue, he kissed me.

My hands let go of the things they were holding, making them available to clasp the hem of his jacket. The feeling was so strong that I leaned back, almost tumbling, when he wrapped his hands around my waist, pulling me in. He savored my lips like a hungry beast. The short, hungry kisses gave him only enough time to yank off his jacket.

"Is this okay?" His lips barely let out words, lifting me in his arms as I wrapped my legs around his waist.

My head was too fuzzy to concentrate on his words. At that moment, my mind couldn't think of anything other than kissing him back. "Umm... Umm." And, just as he earned his answer in my moans, he let down his guards and melted within me, with my back hitting the wall. How did it suddenly get so hot in here?

I shivered as his lips nuzzled down my lips, fingers stroking the sweat droplets on my neck. He planted a trail of kisses down my neck, and I withered away under his touch. The curtains of my eyes dropped down when he nipped that soft, weak spot on my neck. A light moan left my already parted lips, with the contact of his body heat against mine.

He kissed the curve of my breasts peeking out of my dress, and I shivered as my body begged for more. The sensation was something I had never felt before. The feeling was so explicit that I found myself fading away under his strong aura. I pulled his lips back on mine. This time, he was being sympathetically soft. Warmth spread throughout my body while knocking out almost every ounce of air from my lungs. His skillful hands rested over my breasts, caressing them over the thin fabric of my dress. Pleasure shot up underneath my skin, accompanied by a strange sensation between my legs.

I hardly had a moment to react when his tongue caressed the seam of the neckline of my dress. And when I surrendered, tilting my head backward, he explored my neck, not leaving a single place untested. The kisses remained soft and gentle as our actions harmonized with each other. Heat engulfed our bodies, and my heartbeat doubled with every stroke of his tongue on my skin.

But then, unfortunately, he had to pull apart to take a mouthful of air. We stared deeply into each other's eyes with our shallow breaths. I sensed him kissing my nose, and it made the corner of my mouth curl up in his cuteness. I pressed my forehead on his and closed my eyes, feeling immense tenderness.

"Is this okay?" Ethan's voice came out so raspy that something tightened in my lower abdomen. His warm breath brushed against my wet lips that I felt it climb into my veins and melt my heart.

"Hmmm…" I could not trust my voice so I just nodded slightly.

"Please, open your eyes, Sarah." He whispered, just as his hot breath brushed my lips, sending waves of pleasure flowing down my spine. I shook my head in no. I was not ready to face reality yet. What if this was all a beautiful dream and when I open my eyes everything would disappear? I didn't have the courage to endure that. I was not that strong. I did not care if it was a dream, I just wanted to keep on living in it.

Suddenly, I sensed my body being carried somewhere. I smiled, softly. I was in his protected arms. Thus, there was nothing to worry about. I was content with listening to his heartbeat, which was racing profoundly.

I felt the soft touch of fabric underneath me, and it took me a moment to comprehend I was now lying on the bed. Strange anticipation crossed my heart, urging me to open my eyes. And I witnessed him climbing over me. My heart pounded, catching sight of him cloaking my body with his naked torso, portraying the perfectly sculpted physique. I had no idea when exactly his shirt came off. But the element that struck my heart was in his eyes. A strange 'want' glowed in them.

"Ethan, I'm scared." My eyes fluttered with a strange fear and Ethan froze at his place.

"Do you want me to stop?" He asked breathlessly in a hoarse voice while pulling himself away.

I held him tight and pulled him back upon me while shaking my head and begging with my eyes for him to stay.

"Then, let me protect you!" He obliterated all my second thoughts with a breath-taking kiss in return. I lost all control over my body as I returned the kiss with all I'd got in me. I could no longer think straight. I ran my hand through his hair and felt the softness. He slanted his head further, deepening the kiss. He bit my lower lip, making a forceful way in. I loved his dominance.

He cut the kiss by caressing my neck with his hot lips. His talented fingers slithered down the clasp of my dress. His tongue made soft circles on my breast and then his lips closed on my nipple, earning a moan. My whole body shivered under his touch, waiting for the inevitable.

"I really like you, girl. I need you." His voice was low and husky and I was dumbstruck, staring deeply into those ocean blue eyes. They hold so much warmth for me that I believed they could never lie to me.

He stroked my cheek with the back of his hand, and I knew he was having an inner battle between his need and my consent. He was staring into my eyes as if trying to read my mind through them.

"Tell me you want this too." He finally said with a deep sigh and closed his eyes as if scared of my answer.

I cupped his face in my palms and made him look at me. When he finally opened his eyes I spoke gently, "I want this. I need you too, Ethan!"

Before I knew how it happened, our naked bodies slithered softly together. The touch felt like the finest silk. I realized right then that this storm would be seizing my virginity with it.

Slowly, I felt his hands moving down while our tongues entwined in passionate kisses. My body jerked forward with an impulse when I felt his finger sliding inside me. Instantly, his head shot up, discerning the reason for the tightness. I wasn't able to meet his eyes in embarrassment and buried my head at the nape of his neck in utter shyness.

"Are you trying to kill me, girl?" His love intoxicated me completely as he crawled down, leaving a trail of passionate kisses on my torso. My whole body exploded with pleasure as his mouth closed over me down there. My eyes rolled back in my head and I swear I could see stars dancing above me at that moment.

He came back up, and I tasted myself on his lips. We shared one more soul-melting kiss. "Are you sure about this? Please say something now. Anything if you want me..." My hand pressed over his mouth. I didn't want to hear any of his words.

"Just make love to me already. Will you?" With a playful smile, he slipped inside me. A shooting pain exploded throughout my body. The pain was intolerable and excruciating at first, but slowly the pleasure overtook my body. He sank his hips deeply into me, leaving no space between us. A tear trickled down from the corner of my eye, and he kissed it away.

With every move, my breaths became shallow. I moved with him, and we were in perfect sync. I felt the tension building inside me. I let out a deep moan as he was hitting my sensitive spots perfectly. I felt him reaching closer to the peak. We were so caught up between the intoxication of the climax and losing ourselves in the moment that we didn't realize we had touched the edge at the same time.

We were lying there in a tangled mess, sweating profoundly. Our body temperature was showing how far we'd both come in the last one year. He embraced me within his strong arms, planting clusters of kisses on my forehead. And I smiled, my senses all hazy and inebriated.

Tonight I gave everything to Ethan; my love, my body, and, moreover, my soul. I let down all my guards and fell candidly into his love. I was left with only one thing tonight;

His mark on my heart.

Thirteen
Ethan

DAY SEVEN

Resting my elbows on my weak knees, I held my throbbing head in between my hands. My mind was messed up with so many contradictory thoughts. I never found myself being this puzzled in life as I was right now.

She had finally accepted my apology. But then what on earth was I still doing on this island? She said she would never trust me back, and that was okay, right? But then why did it feel so bad hearing those words from her mouth?

On the other hand, the much-anticipated night of her parent's anniversary celebration was here. I was going to have one last night with her. One last night? *Why does this feel so awful? Just thinking about it raised a sharp sting in my chest. Am I falling sick?*

When I was living my pitiable, monotonous life, time seemed to run very slowly, but now I didn't even realize where this past one week had disappeared. It was like I blinked and the next moment time slipped away like grains of sand from my hand. It was really strange for me to feel something like this. This odd desire to stop the time from passing.

Yesterday, when Starz was busy changing back into her clothes out of that mesmerizing wedding gown, I picked a dress for her. A royal blue floor-length cocktail gown with off shoulder sweetheart neckline and a high-rise cut at the left thigh. I had sent the dress into her room just now with a small note.

Good evening, Starz
If you've really forgiven me, please wear this dress tonight.
-Your Mr. Perfect, XOXO
P.S. If you won't wear it, I would know you haven't accepted my
apology and I will keep haunting you ;)

I was half-convinced she would stomp down my room any second now, throwing the dress at my face. Half of me, on the other hand, was hoping to see her in that dress tonight. It was my last chance to bring a smile to the face which I had filled with tears all those years ago. A few hours from now she would go back to her old life, far away from me. Memories of the past week would vanish from her mind sooner than later.

I would no longer be able to feel her presence in my life, to see her beautiful eyes. But why was I feeling so depressed? I was searching for her all these years just to earn her forgiveness, and now I had it. Then why was I still feeling this weird burden on my heart?

"Dude, I never thought I would say this. But I am going to miss this place." A humorless chuckle escaped my lips at Tom's words.

And in my case, I know one thing: 'I am going to miss her so bad that it's going to hurt.' I confessed to myself.

"They are all going to be there at the same time. You know; I feel a little anxious when it comes to her family. Leave her cousins aside, dude, her best friend alone is enough to take both of us down." Tom was sweating, fidgeting with her necktie.

"Don't worry. I will watch your back this time, especially from that cousin and scary best friend." Adjusting our tuxedo jackets at the same time, we pushed our way through the glass door to enter the banquet hall, and my breath caught up in my throat.

Though I had been to multiple parties, a strange sense of nervousness hit me tonight. A small hint of consciousness crossed my body seeing all of Starz's close relatives in one room. Was I looking good enough for standing a chance in front of that Romano? *Argh! I'm Ethan Stanton. I'm best at everything.*

Although I was the official organizer of the event, in reality, Tom had hired efficient professionals to work in disguise to make the event a success.

The place was jammed with happy people, and I smiled, trying to melt into that crowd. It seemed like Starz's brother and cousins had found dates for the night. The night was growing younger with every passing second. I chucked down a glass of wine and made myself comfortable. It felt strange yet comfortable seeing such a big, happy family having a good time.

The soft music meandering its way from sweet violins had set a dynamic vigor in the environment. Some people were slow dancing, getting lost in the melody, while others were indulged in conversations. There was a strange spark flowing in the room that was filling me with joy and playfulness. While on the other hand, Tom was too restrained. As if ready to run at the slightest slip up.

Various thoughts were running through my mind, but the most important was 'where the hell was Starz?' My curious eyes were dying to get a glimpse of her in the crowd, and the mere thought was making me smile for no reason. I came here just for her, just to get one last chance to talk to her, to hear her cute yelling at me. I frowned when after a whole minute of ducking, bending and even dodging some skeptical stares, I still wasn't able to locate her.

"Look who's here, stalker of the year!" Ashley's voice brought me back from my weird slanting position, peeking at a group of girls, searching for Starz. Straightening my back, I looked at Tom from the corner of my eyes and he was alarmed too, frightened to be precise. Gulping down the lump in my throat, I turned my head nervously, only to find her looking down at me. As if I were some homeless person crashing her wedding reception.

"Well, it is nice to meet you too, thief." I snatched the glass of wine from her hand and quickly gulped down the liquid, placing the now empty glass back in her hands. "Wait for a second. Please, do care to explain why or rather how you are looking... nice?" In horrific shock, I gazed at her dress and then finally halted on her face. My eyes were bulging out. How the hell could makeup convert someone's looks from homeless to royalty?

"Well, I will take that as a compliment. Now tell me you were looking for Sarah, weren't you?" I was about to come up with a sarcastic reply, just when my eyes caught a glimpse of a figure behind her. And I saw a fallen angel making her way inside the banquet. My heart skipped a beat, and my breath got caught in my throat. A strange aura engulfed me in its never-ending essence. My surroundings flipped in silence as she placed her foot inside the room.

"Hello? Are you there? Did he forget to take his medicines today?" Ashley waved her hand in front of my face, but my eyes were busy capturing the exquisite beauty. Placing my hand on Ashley's face, I pushed her out of my sight.

"Damn! You're going to kill me, girl!" I mumbled under my breath.

"Dude, looks like you dropped something." This time I heard Tom's voice, but pushing everything out of my mind, I headed towards her, completely dumbfounded.

"Dude, it's not only my jaw. I believe I just dropped my heart at her feet somewhere," I answered back without looking at him because my eyes were busy admiring her. They were just gleaming with her aura, stuck on the most beautiful person in the entire world.

A cold breeze from somewhere came thrashing on my senses, and I felt lightheaded. I was totally blown away by her magnificence. I never knew someone could look so stunning. It should be illegal to look this hot. How could my heart withstand so much prettiness in one go? She was looking so exquisite that I forgot to breathe.

She had worn the gown I sent to her. Seeing her in that dress was doing strange things to my heart. The trail of her gown fluttered behind her as she walked, giving everyone a fair view of her graceful, long legs. The ladders to heaven. And I was regretting my choice. She shouldn't have been dressed in that, because every single man was ogling at her now. Even the hotel staff paused and started gazing. My body temperature was rising with all that jealousy. I wanted to grab her hand and run away from all those eyeing her. Only I should be allowed to worship this magnificent goddess.

The one thick ribbon on her tiny waist was making my hands ache to tuck around her waist and pull her into my arms. The sexy sparkling heart shape neckline was highlighting her curves so perfectly that I loosened my tie to breathe a little. *God, it's really hot in here.* Maybe the air conditioner was not working or it was all Starz's magical warmth.

My breath got trapped in my throat as she started to walk towards me. She was beaming from head to toe, and I never felt so blessed in my life. She had that heart-stopping smile that was making me go all gushy. She continued walking in my direction, nodding at people in between, and my heart began to thump crazily. She was like sunshine. I didn't think there was a need for lights in the room anymore because her smile was brightening up the whole place, filling up all the emptiness in my heart.

Out of the blue, she waved her hand at me and my heart began to pound harder, if that was even possible. I looked down and witnessed my hands shaking in anticipation. Just a small friendly gesture from her left me all jittery.

I was grinning like a maniac. Her appearance in the room in that dress had made me the happiest man on earth. It only meant one thing. She had really forgiven me. She had understood that I was a changed man now. She had accepted me. I could hear my heart beating loudly in my ears.

"Dude, is she really coming towards me, or am I just fantasizing about her?" My voice came out so huskily that I startled myself.

"Bro, it has never been so real." Tom whispered in my ear, and my mouth hung open in a gasp. I closed it quickly and finally, a satisfied sigh left my mouth. This was not a freaking dream. She was really here. She was coming to me.

But suddenly, out of nowhere, we were shoved aside like ragged dolls. We hardly managed to balance ourselves when I noticed Ashley coming out from behind us. She was dusting off her hands like they became dirty by touching us. She passed me a smirk on the way, and I mentally cursed her. My glaring eyes were piercing holes at her back when she headed to hug Starz. Wait, what? Please don't tell me that Starz was waving at her and not at me. Ugh, I feel like crying.

"Looks like we have some uninvited guests," Ashley said loud enough to make us hear clearly. I let out an 'I'm going to kill you, bitch' chuckle at her. She was the biggest enemy of my life. If we were ever going to meet in hell, I was going to throw her in that boiling lava! After giggling at our poor condition for a few seconds, both the girls strolled off hand in hand, leaving me infuriated.

"I'm going to put some free food in my stomach. You can catch up with those wild cats." And with that, Tom also fled the scene, leaving me alone with my thoughts.

That's it! Tonight I am going to talk to her, straight and forward. She can't avoid me any further. She need to know the truth. She has to see that I am not an egocentric, insensitive person as she perceives me to be. She will have to accept this truth and once that is done, she can go marry whoever she wants. I will not bother her anymore.

The clinking sound of a teaspoon on the Champagne glass interrupted my self-encouragement and when I looked up, I saw Starz in the middle of the crowd, raising the glass to her eye level. Her face reflected a hint of nervousness.

"Ladies and gentlemen, I would like to propose a toast. To express a few words of love and gratitude for my mom and dad." Silence spread throughout the place. I found myself raising my glass while I placed the other hand in my pocket. A few seconds passed as everyone managed to grab a glass, and then she let out a nervous chuckle.

Tilting her head towards her parents, she passed an incredible smile and said, "Hey, Mom and dad, what can I say? Every word is too small in front of the love you've bestowed upon your children." I sneaked a look at her parents beaming proudly at their daughter.

"Well, it's a charming evening, and so are the people who have joined us to celebrate the anniversary of this beautiful day on which two young hearts united to become one. You two are the reason I believe that true love really exists. Your beautiful and admirable bond makes me hope for my happily ever after. I'm more than blessed to have parents like you and wish your love will flourish even more year after year."

She raised her glass, and everyone joined her in the toast. "To happily ever after." My heart was overwhelmed by her soothing voice and spectacular beauty. But my smile dropped when I saw Romano coming over to hold her. Wrapping his hand around her waist, he placed a peck on her head. *How earnestly I wished to be in his place right now.*

Soon enough, her parents and cousins surrounded her. They were all hugging each other and were posing for family pictures. She looked like an innocent charm that was hard to catch. Mr. Walter threw his head back, laughing when she pouted at him at some joke. I felt so lost, yet so content standing there.

Never knew seeing all this would make me miss my own parents. My family. Though they chose to separate themselves from me, cut all ties from me, their blood still flowed through my veins. My heart still ached to hear their voice. Dad's pieces of advice. My Mum's whining about my careless attitude. Never knew this beautiful occasion would bring back so many memories.

I started feeling lonely in the crowd. Just like Ashley had defined us 'the uninvited guests.' There was a loud commotion in my head screaming that 'I didn't belong here.' The cake arrived right then and people cheered for the couple while I took some steps back. Starz pulled her brother close and Romano was on her other side all the time. They were all smiling and clapping as the cake was cut and I took some more steps back. Right at the moment, something stirred in my heart. A realization hit me. I was not part of this family. I'd never been. I never belonged here. I was nothing more than a hired agent for them. Beyond our fake professional relationship, there was nothing between us. I was no one to them.

I smiled, watching them so happy together. Someone has said it right, 'money can't buy everything. Not the ones who love you, who care about you.' A family is everything you live your life for. I blinked several times when a stupid tear threatened to fall out. *I swear to God, one day I'm going to ask my dad why he hates me so much!*

The party progressed when guests forced Mr. And Mrs. Walter to move towards the dance floor. I was at the bar, looking down at my empty glass, feeling a little tipsy. I turned around to find Tom when my eyes fell over a rather chirpy Starz, staring at her parents with contentment. And I thought about talking to her one last time.

"They look so happy. You certainly gave a pretty impressive toast." I leaned towards her and saw her bestowing a heart-melting smile upon me.

"Really? Even you can also see love and happiness amongst them?" Her sarcastic remark made me shake my head and then she continued. "Well, I must thank you. You know; for planting this idea in my mom's head. I don't know how you did this on such short notice, but everything has turned out so good. I really appreciate it." Her sparkling eyes gazed into mine with utter sincerity, stealing my rationality away. I found myself getting lost in them.

Our eyes held onto each other, and I seized the moment by tucking a loose strand of hair behind her ear. We got lost in each other's thoughts. Untouched by our surroundings. Everything around us dissolved into nothingness. Leaving Sarah and me alone in that empty space. I took her hand in mine, tilted my head apologetically, and then mouthed 'I am really sorry, girl.' Her features softened when those hushed but sincere words reached her. But then, to my utter bad luck, we got interrupted. She turned around, her hand slipped away to see Romano standing in front of her with a rose in his hand.

"Would you honor me with a dance?" He extended his hand, smiling comfortably at her. And she gladly took it and I retreated.

Looking down, I scratched the back of my neck and turned around in disappointment. I chuckled at my doomed luck. It looked like nothing was in my favor tonight. I decided to leave and started heading for the door hastily when someone bumped into me. My hands quickly shot up to apologize to whoever was standing in front of me. But it was Mrs. Walter.

"Ahh, Mr. Stewart, I was looking around for you. I just wanted to thank you for organizing such an incredible event. I have no doubt now that my daughter's wedding will be tenfold magnificent." Maybe she noticed the broken phase on my face. "Wait. Were you leaving already? Stay for a while, Mr. Stewart. I insist. Would you like to dance with this old lady?" I smiled at her, fighting back my emotions.

We slowly danced for about a minute, yet she shared the whole story of her wedding. I couldn't help smiling at her. The story was too scandalous. Soon, the song changed to 'one way or another' and she excused herself when Sam, the cousin, replaced her. She grabbed me and yanked herself in my arms. Adrenaline rushed through my veins when an evil plan ripened inside my head. And we started jumping in sync.

She was astounded when I placed my left hand around her waist while my right hand grasped hers as we headed straight towards Starz. Starz and Romano were thrown back in different directions when we jumped in between their glued bodies. They stared at us in disbelief, but we were not paying attention to them. I commenced twirling Sam at full pace. I placed my free hand behind my back while the other swirled her around, making a complete circle. And then, in the end, I pulled her back in my arms and she clenched her head against her body, trying to balance herself.

But then, unexpectedly, she cracked up like she was enjoying her ass off and our crazy dance started to break the floor. Everyone's eyes were on us, but we were not in the mood to care about anything. I took off my jacket and, after swirling it around in the air for a few seconds, I flung it somewhere. My hair was a big mess and my shirt was hanging out. I was out of breath, sweating like a pig, but I was finally feeling alive. Gradually, people joined us and our crazy dance got viral.

A few minutes later I saw Starz had joined the moves too and was jumping up and down, losing herself in the music. I shook my head at her and she copied me. I grasped her hand and twirled her around as she clutched her head, beaming from ear to ear. "You are looking so beautiful you made me forget my pickup line." I shouted near her ear and she threw her head back while hitting my chest playfully and laughing at my honesty.

We were jumping, bumping into each other, and shouting in that loud music. I never felt this alive before. My nerves were on fire, and I was totally turned on. I stopped moving, seeing her laughing, beaming with happiness because of me. A satisfactory sensation crossed my heart; warmth touching my cold soul. Her laugh was making me lose my senses. She was jumping in ecstasy and here my heart was trying to make its way out of my chest. She grasped my arm in between, and a spark flew down my spine.

I was clueless about what took over me when I grasped her arm and yanked her body into my chest. Her smile was quickly replaced by a surprised gasp. I cleared the streak of hair from her beautiful sweaty face as my eyes dropped to her lips. I lost control over my senses when her hot, heavy breaths fell over my face. She kept on blinking at me, bewildered, but my eyes were stuck on those full rosy lips. I was fighting an inner battle and subsequently tightened my grip around her waist. She didn't say anything, just kept staring at me. Maybe she wanted the same. Otherwise, she would have given a sign of resentment or anything, but nothing came out of her and I took it as a yes!

I clubbed her face in my palms and imploded my lips on hers. I didn't know how I had been able to stop myself till now. I realized I wanted to kiss her ever since I saw her walking down that aisle. Pulling her closer, I deepened the kiss, savoring every inch of her mouth. The kiss was so intoxicating that I felt dizzy like I was back on my favorite drug after a long break. It felt like I was kissing her for the first time in my life. Moreover, I had never felt such a strong pull towards anyone before. I was totally under her spell.

But then something strange happened. I was shoved back by a strong force, and her right hand connected with my left cheek, creating a resonating sound. Shortly, the music halted, and ominous silence engulfed the place. My head dropped to one side and my hand automatically covered my cheek, which was burning from that forceful slap. She had that sick expression that made my heart sink.

I was totally taken aback. One second we were dancing and laughing, and the next second I found myself being eyed with pure hate. I took some steps back as her face looked disgusted from being in my proximity.

"Starz... please understand..." I tried to find some words, but before I could complete my sentence, she stormed towards me and slapped me across the face one more time.

"How dare you touch me?" I dropped my head when she looked at me in loath. I couldn't bear that look. I didn't know how to react at that moment. I opened my mouth to offer an apology, but I had no regrets about what I did.

I watched as Romano came to stand beside her. Ugh, how could I forget? He couldn't keep his nose out of our business! I clenched my teeth as he turned towards her to hold her in his arms.

"Please calm down Star... Sarah." Nervously looking at the audience that we both had attracted, I extended my hand towards her.

"Mr. Stewart, I suggest you take a step back from my fiancé." He interrupted, placing one hand on my chest. And man, that triggered something inside me. I glared at him, clenching my palms to settle down my anger. Who was he to interfere between me and Starz? It was our personal matter to sort out.

I felt Tom's hand on my shoulder and I somehow controlled my anger and again stepped towards Sarah. But unfortunately, I observed her glaring at me with nothing but despise. Suddenly something broke inside me when involuntary tears fell from her eyes. I had hurt her again. I misread the signs.

"I'm sorry, Starz. I didn't mean to... I thought you wanted the same. You wore that dress…" I was cut abruptly mid-sentence when a humorless laugh escaped her lips. This made me confused like never before.

"The dress… I wore it so that you would stop bothering me once and for all. You thought I had fallen for your charm again? I'm not the same foolish girl, Mr. Stanton. I'll never want anything from you ever again. Your mere sight disgusts me. You are in a pathetic delusion to even think of something like this could ever happen!" Her words hit me like daggers piercing my soul. I could clearly see the detestation in her eyes. I was about to say something when Romano turned towards Starz again.

"What did you just call him?" His eyes were punching holes in her when she turned towards him.

"I'm sorry I didn't tell you this before." Then she turned towards her family, who by now were surrounding us.

"I've been hiding this from all of you ... God knows why!" And then finally she looked back at me like I was some rotten and rejected piece of apple. My soul stirred at that look.

"This right here, who calls himself Ethan Stewart, is a liar, a cheat! He has been lying to all of you. His real name is Ethan Stanton!"

Panic rose in me hearing my real name. I ran a hand through my hair and pulled them in frustration. When her eyes met mine again, I silently pleaded her to stop whatever she was going to say. But as expected, she ignored me.

"He is no wedding planner... hell, he freaking owns this hotel."

"Please, no!" A whisper left my lips as I squeezed my eyes shut.

"His real face is not what he is trying to show everybody. He is a lying, manipulative, selfish bastard. A vicious man is hiding behind this charming face, who would go to any length to destroy lives with his power and wealth." I kept my eyes glued to the floor and clenched my fist, nails digging into my palms. Everyone was stealing glances at me and soon whispers started going around within her cousins and friends surrounding us. They were looking at me in shock and disgust.

A couple of seconds passed, and she turned towards them, letting out an evil laugh. "Rest assured, he is dumber than he looks. He thought he'd come here, play the 'I am-a-changed-person-now' game with me, impress my family and I'll run into his arms once again!"

I raised my head at that and found her looking straight into my eyes. "You're so pitiful. How low can you stoop than you already are? After everything you did to me, you seek my forgiveness with these cheap acts? You destroyed my life! You took away everything I had! You robbed me off my dreams! My hope! My self-confidence! Hell! You ruined me completely. What more do you want?"

I closed my eyes on her last words. I never felt so ashamed in my life than right there in front of her at that moment. Opening my eyes back, I saw Romano encircling his arms around her in a comforting gesture. But to my surprise, the shock which was furnishing everybody's features was absent from his face. Did he already know about her past? Oh God, why did you make me so bad and him so good? He knew everything and had accepted her in every way. That's why she said she probably didn't deserve him. I was so stupid.

"You made me feel like it was all my fault. I started to hate myself. Heaven knows how much I loved you." She was hyperventilating.

"I curse the day I met you. I'm so ashamed I fell for you, Mr. Stanton." She turned around to hide her face from me when tears started falling freely from her beautiful eyes.

I couldn't bear seeing her breaking down like that. She might hate me. Still, after listening to all this, I couldn't hold myself. Instinctively, I reached towards her to comfort her from sobbing.

"I can never forgive myself for what I did, but please give me another chance. That's all I ask, Sarah. I'll prove my worth to you." I placed a soft hand gently on her shoulder to make her understand. "I'm really a changed person now. I am not faking…" before I could complete my sentence, a punch landed on my jaw, forcing me to stumble back.

I was stunned. I shook my head to clear my head and throw away the pain as I clenched my aching jaw. I had barely recovered from it to see it was Romano who had hit me when another punch came right at me, but gaining my reflexes back, I ducked this time.

"How dare you? How dare you come anywhere near her! How dare you show yourself at her wedding?" He growled at my face, but I remained calm as much as I could. Tom came between us and helped me up on my feet again.

"Look, man, I've nothing against you. I just want to talk to Sarah." I tried to walk past him, ignoring his glare, but he blocked my path.

"Make another move towards her and I won't even flinch in calling the cops and show you your place, bastard." It was a big mistake he made. That threat activated the worst part of my brain.

"Try me." I hissed. Tom tried to push me back by placing a firm hand on my chest, but I pushed him aside.

I heard a growl coming out from his mouth, but before I could grab his collar or ruin his face, to my bad, Mr. Walter stepped in between us.

"Enough!" My head dropped when he started walking towards us. "So it was you! You are the boy who destroyed my little girl's life. You took advantage of her! You are the reason she almost died! She never even told us it was you! You broke her! And you dare come here and play with her again right under my nose!" This time, I had no words or excuses. I looked past him towards Sarah and saw her standing there and looking at me with pain in her eyes. And soon enough, her mother came forward, standing beside her father.

I dropped my head, entirely ashamed to meet their eyes. Her dad grabbed my collar and when my ashamed eyes met his, I saw revulsion in them for me.

"I don't care who you are. I don't care if you own this island! You get out of here right now or so help me God, I'll kill you for hurting my daughter!" I gaped at him, not moving an inch from there. I wanted to say so many things, but words betrayed me. Soon enough, Tom stepped in between us and pulled me back, away from his grip.

I struggled, but he dragged me outside. My tear-filled eyes wanted to catch one last glimpse of Starz. I struggled to see her face, her beautiful eyes. We locked eyes for a split second and right there it came to my senses that she hated me because she had loved me with all her heart.

"I'm really sorry, Sarah! Please, talk to me. Please, believe me."

"Enough, dude! Get a grip on yourself!" Tom shoved me outside the Hotel. Freeing me from his grip, I looked at his furious face. Saying nothing, I saw the first taxi, which was parked outside the gate and I rushed towards it. My head was hurting, and I was hyperventilating. Losing my tie, I threw it somewhere and jumped in the back seat, and rested my head on the headrest. I started to breathe heavily as my heart was thumping loudly in my ear and her hatred-filled voice continued to echo in my head. Her countenance of pure hate and resentment kept flashing in front of my eyes. The cab started moving, and I tried to calm my nerves.

"Stop at the nearest bar," I said, with my eyes still closed. I only realized Tom was sitting in the passenger seat when I jumped out of the car as it came to a halt and he paid the driver for the ride. My legs felt like jelly and my head was throbbing like it was going to explode any second. Squinting at an open bar near the beach, I headed straight towards it.

Soon enough, Tom joined me at the bar. But he didn't stop me from getting drunk. One after another, I let my throat get burned with those blazing shots. But still, after half a dozen shots, I wasn't drunk enough to forget everything. Or maybe my mind was playing tricks on me again.

"I fucked up Tom! I wanted her to see how much I loved her but instead, I made her hate me even more. I am such a mess." I pointed my finger towards Tom, but my elbow slipped from the counter and Tom grabbed my hand to steady me. But I jerked him away.

"You know what Tom; you were fuckin' right. She didn't want to be found. She doesn't want to do anything with me. I searched for her everywhere all these years to apologize to her and she almost forgave me but I ended up screwing everything yet again. Ruined her wedding, her parent's anniversary. I'm such a selfish bastard."

"Calm down, bro. You have had enough." Tom tried to steal the glass from my hand, but I pushed him again and jumped down from the stool on the cold sand. I couldn't actually remember removing my shoes but my feet were bare when I started walking.

I cursed the heavens at the top of my lungs, which might have attracted some glares, but I didn't give a shit about anything. I began to walk away from everyone, holding my drink, but stumbled on a pebble and made it spill in the sand. Tom came to my assistance once again, but I freed myself from his grip and furiously smashed the now empty glass on the stone pathway in outrage.

"She called me a lying, manipulative, selfish bastard." I saw Tom readying his hands to catch me anytime. He was saying something to calm me down, but I was too out of my head to comprehend his words. It was like his words were falling on my ears but not reaching to my brain. I placed both my hands on his shoulders and looked across into his eyes.

"I'm not a bad person, Tom. I'm not such a terrible guy. I loved her nine years ago and I still do. I'm..." I couldn't continue any longer. My voice started breaking. There was such a heaviness in my chest as if being crushed by the weight of a thousand boulders.

Looking down, I said, "I too have feelings, Tom. I'm also a human being. I too get hurt, bro. I'm not as bad as she alleges. I've made mistakes and I regret them, but I'm a changed man now. My heart also breaks and I too feel pain." I guess it started to rain at that moment, or maybe something went wrong with my eyes. I rubbed them as they started flooding. I pulled myself away from Tom and spoke for one last time.

"She is absolutely right to reject me. I don't deserve her. Hell I don't even deserve to breathe the same air as her. I have never loved anyone in my life as much as I love her, Tom. But, I'm never going to tell her that."

"I've lost her all over again tonight."

Fourteen

Sarah

DAY SIXTEEN

The warmth of sunrays felt good on my skin as my body finally slumped after running miles on this beautiful morning. I felt a peculiar, yet familiar, kind of rush flowing through my body. Though my lungs were craving oxygen, it was a feel-good type of breathlessness. With my chest rising and falling against my pounding heart, I opened the water bottle and gulped down a hefty amount of water to ease up my cracked throat.

Although the day had just begun, I could feel it was going to be a promising and pleasant day. As long as I wouldn't get a call from the hospital, everything was planned to go smoothly and stress-free. No worries, whatsoever! It was my first day off since getting back from Hawaii and I was feeling so happy about not having to wake up before the sun. Or not sleeping at all and then tossing my ass in a not-so-hot shower. And mostly, for not worrying about getting late for work. *I love lazy fall mornings.*

To say it was an awkward week at work would be an understatement. First two days everyone in the hospital was congratulating me for my marriage. Painstakingly, I had to explain to each one of them that I was not actually married yet. The whole story about the fire at my almost wedding was a hot topic for the nurses and residents the whole week. Then came "Oh! I am so sorry to hear what happened at your wedding! Such hard luck!"

Even the senior doctors were shocked to see me back from my leaves so soon, for which I had to beg them for ages. Finding out that I had not actually gone on my honeymoon and would be taking another long leave in the near future almost made my senior resident pull his hair out in frustration.

I was about to take another gulp from my bottle when a strange feeling of being watched nagged me. I surveyed my surroundings and then up at the nearby buildings, but everything appeared normal, as on any typical Saturday morning. There was a U-Haul truck parked in the driveway, but no one was visible around it.

My paranoid thoughts got interrupted by Finn's voice and I looked up, already relaxing seeing his face on my balcony. He was loudly calling out to me, and I sent him my best big grin. I waved at him and he happened to get cheered up even more. Waggling his tail so vigorously, I feared he would knock down the flower pots. He was my best buddy. *Who needs a human if you have a wonderful Golden Retriever, right?*

So, wasting no time, I rushed inside while waving greetings at some familiar faces of the building. My legs quickly climbed the steps with leftover energy from the run. My one-bedroom apartment was in a pretty antique building and thus, the elevator part was missing.

Despite the fact that the building was old and worn out, it was close to my heart. Yeah, you guessed it right. I had earned a small home in this brick and stone structure with my hard-earned money. My parents offered to help on many occasions so as to buy a decent house in a good neighborhood but, a mortgage felt much better than owing them a huge favor. Anyway, it was a perfect place for me. Decent locality and close to my workplace.

After finally arriving at my designated third floor, my steps slowed down when my puzzled gaze fell upon someone's belongings scattered in the hallways. I scratched my head in confusion. This was not the kind of view you were usually welcomed at this early in the morning.

There lay a heavily jammed suitcase, some kitchen utensils peeking out of a big box, a loosely tied bundle of books, and a bunch of toilet paper rolls. It seemed like someone was either moving in or has been thrown out in a hurry. That explained the U-Haul truck. But whatever it was, the person's belongings were blocking my way to my door, and I was a little annoyed. I felt trapped. My apartment was at the end of the passage, and it kind of felt weird to climb over someone's possessions.

My eyes wandered over to an ajar door of flat number 22, which was supposed to be vacant. And then at Mrs. Jenkins. The curious-looking, middle-aged woman from the apartment opposite number 22, standing in her doorway, staring at it with the biggest grin plastered on her face. *What is up with this lady today?*

"Good morning, Mrs. Jenkins," I called out with a genuine smile. She looked at me for the briefest moment possible, and soon her eyes drifted past me. As if searching for something behind me.

I looked back, and there was no one to be seen. But she seemed genuinely interested in whoever was about to come. I decided to leave her to herself and carefully made my way forward. Trying hard not to step on anything scattered on the floor, I finally reached my door and kneeled to take out my keys from underneath the doormat. As I opened the door, my phone started to buzz from inside and I wondered who would be calling me at this early hour of the day.

As soon as I entered, Finn came running towards me, barking in excitement while burying his face in my feet. Placing my keys in the trinket bowl gifted by Ash at my housewarming party, I picked up my phone from the entry table. Ash's name was flashing on it with a picture of us hugging at my almost wedding in Maui. I checked the time; it was still quarter to seven in the morning. *Wow, either she has not slept the whole night or maybe she is in another time zone.* Because in no case Ash and morning could go hand in hand.

I took her call feeling so happy hearing her voice after almost one whole week. *Yeah, we are best friends in crazy times.* We were so inseparable that even her mom advised her to move in with me. Good idea, right? But, as we grew older and life got caught up we drifted far apart, but only physically. Our souls are still connected.

"Hey! What's a John Dory?" She started without a greeting. Her cheerful tone spread a wide smile on my face as I kneeled to caress the impatient guy who was aiming to stumble me over the floor and lick my face.

"Are you going to explain, or will I have to generate some superpower to understand random words coming out of your mouth?" I asked her while pouring some dog food into Finn's bowl.

"Okay, okay. Well, you remember Ryan from the island? He turned out to be my Mr. Right. Sarah, I can't tell you how perfect he is. He cares so much about me. And he is too hot. Bonus, right? Oh, and don't forget his panty-dropping British accent. Just so…"

"Hold your horses, girl." She let out a deep breath, trying to calm her nerves. "First, tell me where the hell are you? I haven't heard from you in over a week!"

"Well… I'm on the Sunshine Coast, Australia. It's heaven on earth, Sarah…"

"Put a sock in it. What happened to Pecoraro's internship? Oh my God, you lied to me? You fled directly from the island with him, didn't you?"

"Well, I didn't actually lie. I mean, sweetheart, I said I was going to discover the best version of myself. And this right here is the best anybody could ever get. Private jet. Private beach. Exotic food. What more can you ask for? Trust me, girl, I'm living the time of my life. He makes me so happy. Can you believe soulmates do exist? I found the perfect man, babe."

"Nobody is perfect, Ash!" I exclaimed quickly.

"Okay. Okay, I understand. But he left me with no choice. He had to leave the island. So it was either traveling around the world with the love of my life on his private jet or working my ass off on an internship that couldn't even cover my bills. So, I choose an adventurer's life. And relax, I will get another internship offer. It's no big deal. Or if I'm lucky enough, he will buy me a whole fashion line. Eeep! I made the best decision ever!" I was no doubt happy for her, but everything seemed too good to be true.

"Okay, fine, if you say so. As long as my best friend is safe and happy, it's all good. I'm really happy for you, Ash." Suddenly our conversation was interrupted by the doorbell.

"Hold on, someone's at the door." Heading towards the door, I kept listening to Ash going on about how handsome and perfect her man was.

Looking through the peephole, my forehead creased when I couldn't spot anyone.

"Hey, I got to go. We have a plane to catch. Guess where we are heading tonight? Rome, baby! I'll catch you later. Do text me what John Dory is. Okay? Ciao Bella." I laughed at her killing enthusiasm and turned around to push open the door. My confusion soon cleared up when I saw grocery bags resting adjacent to my front door. Jeez, I almost forgot I had ordered groceries online as I didn't have time to go shopping and my pantry was almost empty.

"Oh. My. God. He is finally back!" While picking up the bags, my eyes wandered over to Mrs. Jenkins chirping like a teenage girl who had just found the perfect dress on sale. *What has gotten into her?* She was standing in the hallway, blocking my view of the person she was referring to.

"Is this an obsession? I don't know, man. But this is definitely something." My heart dropped dead in my stomach when the male voice coming from down the staircase at the end of the hallway sounded too familiar to my liking.

"But I'm going to figure it out, man. And no, I don't need another place. This one is perfectly fine. Plus, there are some nice bars in this neighborhood. I even made a friend last night. His name is Willy, and he works in a strip club." My brain went numb hearing the sound echoing in the flight of stairs getting closer with every word. Mrs. Jenkins started jumping in excitement and I, on the other hand, went all paralyzed with a shiver running down my spine. My eyes must have swelled three-fold with terror etched on my face. Please God, no! Don't let this happen! Oh, for goodness' sake. No!

"No, Tom, I need you to take care of the business. I can't trust anyone else. I can very well take care of myself. Yes! I can survive in a one-room flat. You know, I can clearly see now how God has planned my fate. I feel so positive." The voice echoed in the hallway and my mouth opened in a big O, completely stunned at my damned fate.

"I know, man. I need to dump my arrogant ass to make it work! I also know this is going to be difficult. But I'm doing this, dude. No backing away now. I want her to see me as I truly am. The real, changed, better

Ethan who has fallen…" Suddenly his voice was drowned by the ear-piercing squeals of kids running down the staircase.

"Oh god, these pretty little angels are going to make my ears bleed. By the way, just in case I go missing, I've mailed you my address." His voice surfaced back again and my eyes drifted towards Mrs. Jenkins as she adjusted her already low blouse.

"Wait, what? Of course, I'm not giving up on her. I won't stop until she actually forgives me. I mean it, Tom. Now put the damn phone down. My battery is running low." I could no longer fool my mind now that he sounded too close to my denial.

My breath got caught up in my throat when his face slowly came into view, emerging from the staircase. He was holding a coffee maker in one hand while adjusting his phone and two cups in another. He looked down at his feet and let out a closed-lip smile, like he wanted to punch someone. It was a smile through gritted teeth. The lines on my forehead grew darker when I observed him climbing the stairs in the weirdest way. Like he was suffering from some rash under his pants, making him walk like a penguin. But as soon as his entire body made an appearance, I noticed Mrs. Jenkins's twins hanging from his legs.

Everything stopped existing as soon as our eyes locked. My eyes bulged out of sockets, witnessing him standing there in all his effortlessly sexy Ethan Stanton glory. In contrast to my terrible sweaty existence. He waved at me with his coffee mugs, displaying that same old blood-boiling annoying ear-to-ear grin. And my world began to twirl in front of my eyes when unconsciously I waved back. Why the fuck am I waving at him?

Suddenly, Mrs. Jenkins gripped him in a bear-hug and I couldn't tell why I started losing grip on my vision. Blood rushed out of my head as nausea punched me in the guts. It was too much to take in a single moment that my mind got all puzzled up. I firmly grasped on the bags in my hands, clutching them for dear life.

I found it quite confusing as to why I commenced seeing two Stantons in front of my eyes suddenly? Everything felt so light as if I was floating in the air. My breath happened to be heavy, yet my body felt so light. I sensed the darkness starting to cloud my vision. I dropped the bags and clenched my head in denial and squeezed my eyes shut, but his grinning face continued to flash in front of my closed eyes.

"Starz." He called to me and my legs suddenly felt like jelly. Everything around me started to wobble, sensing him coming towards me like I was standing on the deck of some old ship stuck in a terrible storm. I tried to open my eyes, but my vision became hazy. I could no longer have a grip on my surroundings. And then my legs gave out.

I found myself floating in the air, only this time I was falling backward. I heard someone calling my name. Or maybe I was hallucinating. I was being sucked into a big black hole. My mind was repeating the same awful questions. 'Why did he come back?' 'How did he find me?' The last thing I remembered before my head hit the floor was his big blue eyes looming over me.

AM I DEAD?

A shooting pain swamped my head as I tried to move. Ouch! Definitely not dead. I squeezed my eyes even harder when my fingers traced the painful lump starting to develop on the back of my head. While at the same time, someone was shouting nearby, making me even dizzier.

Heaviness in my head was making it difficult to open my eyes, but I tried hard to slowly flutter them open. The first thing my eyes observed was a sexy ass swaying in front of me in worn-out ripped jeans. It made my head spin in confusion. *What is happening? Am I hallucinating?*

Squinting my eyes, I tried to focus on the person pacing around me anxiously. Was it really him?

"I don't know, man. I told you she just fainted and hit her head. You tell me you are the fuckin' emergency services…" It was definitely Ethan. He was shouting at someone on the phone. As he looked at me, opening my eyes, he immediately dropped his phone to rush by my side.

"Are you okay? What happened? Does it hurt?" I closed my eyes back again to clear my mind. *This can't be happening, right?*

"Starz?" He spoke rather gently this time.

Slowly I opened my eyes again, hoping it was all a big nightmare and I would wake up in my bed with Finn snuggling beside me. But to my utter disappointment, it was not my bed. It was not even my apartment. A wave of panic hit me at that realization, and I tried to stand up too fast. My head spun, and I fell back on a make-shift pillow made out of a towel, with a thud. This bed didn't even have a mattress.

"Easy, Starz! You might have a concussion." He said, touching his palm to my forehead, and my eyes fluttered open in alarm.

"Where the hell am I? Did you kidnap me? How did you find out where I live?" My body jumped right into defense mode, jerking upright on its own, like a reflex to get away from him.

"Relax. You are not kidnapped. You fainted in front of your apartment and I thought you wouldn't want me to barge into your place without an invitation, so I brought you to my apartment. I called 911. The ambulance is on its way." I managed to sit up a little against the headboard and winced in pain, rubbing the back of my head. I cringed away from him, folding my legs in, as my eyes studied him sitting at the edge of the bed.

But then, what he had just said finally registered in my mind and I shouted in shock, "Did you really call 911 on me?"

"What else was I supposed to do? You just fainted in front of my eyes!" Was he genuinely worried? No, it couldn't be. He was Ethan Stanton. Nothing about him was genuine.

"Cancel the ambulance, I am perfectly fine and..."

Before I could complete my sentence, Mrs. Jenkins appeared at the doorway, holding an ice pack. "Here, I brought some ice." I stretched my arm, but she handed the ice pack to Ethan, ignoring my presence altogether.

Ethan tilted my head forward with his left hand and placed the ice pack between me and the headboard with his right, and then gently rested my head against it. My head was still spinning with the slightest movement, and his proximity made me even dizzier. His cologne smelled like the morning mist after a rainy night mixed with peppermint. Maybe I did have a concussion.

"Do you guys already know each other?"

"I..." Before I could've said something, Stanton was by my side, his hand encircling my shoulders.

"We are childhood buddies, Mrs. Jenkins. We were inseparable once. Weren't we, Starz? But then life happened, and we grew apart, but now I am back." He squeezed my shoulder lightly, and I tilted my head up a little at him with a closed-lip smile. "Yeah!" I let out an uncomfortable chuckle.

"You will lose your hand, Stanton, if you do not remove it right now," I muttered underneath my breath, and then he quickly placed some space between us.

"Well, it's good to have old friends around, but don't hesitate to make new ones." She winked at him, and I almost gagged. She passed me a cold stare and quickly turned her seductive smile back at him.

"Of course, Mrs. Jenkins," Ethan responded rather chirpily.

"Oh, just call me Linda. After all, I am not much older than you," she replied, fluttering her eyelashes. Ethan excused himself to talk on the phone, which was apparently still connected to 911.

I tried to control the nausea building up in me and surveyed the place around me to divert my mind. I noticed the things that were lying in the corridor a minute ago were now scattered all over the place. The layout of the apartment was exactly like mine, and then it dawned on me.

He knows where I live.

He is shifting here.

He is my neighbor now.

My next-door neighbor.

"Oh, god! No!" I let out a disgruntled groan. Ethan and Mrs. Jenkins's heads jerked towards me instantly.

"What happened? Are you all right? Should I call the ambulance back?" He asked, crouching down at me with horror in his eyes.

I'm so screwed. You can't do this to me, God. I buried my face in my hands with an urge to kill the person who wrote my fate. I wanted to hit something or smash Stanton's face. Warning bells were ringing in my ears. And without thinking, I yanked a hand at him in madness and gripped his shirt. A gasp escaped Mrs. Jenkins's mouth. But she was the least of my concerns.

"Would you mind giving us some privacy, Mrs. Jenkins? I really need to talk to my new neighbor." I tried to sound as polite as I could, but maybe it came out as a threat. Her head bobbed between us and after palpating the urgency of the situation, she fled the place.

"Oh, I almost forgot. I have baked a pie for you, but it's too heavy to bring it here. So, feel free to come over anytime, Mr. Stewart." She called from the doorway. I rolled my eyes as she grinned at him, and then I heard the sound of the door closing at her back.

"You! Narcissist jackass!" I stood up and charged onto him as his feet sprinted out of the room. "Are you stalking me now?" I marched toward him until his back hit the kitchen counter, trapping him at the very place.

"I swear to God, Stanton, you'll regret this before you could comprehend the consequences. I thought maybe... just maybe, that night would have knocked some sense into you. But here you are, with the same stubborn, undefeated egotism. Why can't you just leave me alone?" I yelled at the top of my lungs while loosening my grip on his collar. And to my surprise, he ran off to stand at the other side of the kitchen counter, far away from where I could scratch his face. I could see he was scared. His pale face stared at me in utter disbelief while straightening his shirt.

"Is this how you welcome your new neighbor? Oh crap, where are my manners? I'm Ethan, your new neighbor, and you, Miss?" He extended his hand towards me and I clenched my teeth to subside the strong urge to scream. His mere presence was making me lose my shit.

"I'll tell you who I am." Picking up a pan from the kitchen counter, I stormed towards him. But anticipating my moves, his eyes widened and in the flash of a second, he was on another side of the counter. Ugh, I hate this cat-and-mouse chase game.

"Cool your jets, Starz! You can't just kill me in broad daylight. And if you didn't notice, you are the last person Mrs. Jenkins had seen me with. There are so many witnesses. Come on, you are too cute to be a murderer." He raised his hands in surrender in front of me, and all I could do was roll my eyes at his pathetic attempt at flirting.

"Why? Why have you followed me this far?" I asked, finally resigning as the adrenaline rush left my veins.

"Umm... because you forgot to say... goodbye?" He shrugged sheepishly, and I folded my hands on my chest in annoyance. This conversation was pointless, so I made up my mind to rather leave it right there.

"You will regret it, Stanton. Are you enjoying your little 'make her life a living hell' game? I'm warning you dude, pack your bags and leave, or I'll make you." I turned around, walking towards the door when I heard his voice once again.

"I hope you know CPR because you take my breath away, Starz! And please, don't scare me like that ever again. I thought you dropped dead from the ecstasy of seeing me. You almost gave me a heart attack." He grabbed my hand in his and let it rest over his chest, just as he let out a deep dramatic sigh.

My face screwed up in disgust, and I jerked my hand right away. I very likely wanted to punch him in the face. But instead, I let out a loud groan with anger consuming me and stormed towards the door. I was dwelling with utter bitterness. I yanked the door open to move out and slammed it shut at my back before I heard him one last time.

"It was nice meeting you, neighbor!"

Sprinting inside my apartment, I finally allowed the resentment to consume me entirely. Throwing myself on the bed, I buried my face in the pillow and screamed as loud as I could to let out the anger and frustration that built up inside me. I so wanted to pull his guts out and wrap it around his neck, so that he will eventually choke to death by his own useless self.

My body started to experience panicked restlessness, and I began to pace in the living room. Why did he follow me this far? *Why is he here? What is he trying to achieve by living in a small apartment in Florence, Alabama?* This was a ridiculously small town for a guy like him. This boy was so unpredictable.

God, I'd got a stalker, and I didn't even know it. I had no idea since when he had been preying on my neighborhood. *Oh, god! What should I do now? Should I call the police? But what am I going to tell them? That I've got a new annoying, creepy neighbor slash stalker. After all, he hasn't broken any laws. Yet! But then, I can't just let him have his ways. He just doesn't belong here.* It had only been ten minutes, and I had already begun to feel trapped in my own apartment.

He was never going to change. I was so foolish for indulging myself in the painful guilt of insulting him in front of my whole family. It had been bothering me for so long that for one moment I even thought about reaching out to him and apologize. But now, I absolutely agreed with dad, he freaking deserved it, or maybe worse.

They say if life gives you a lemon, make lemonade. But I wanted to cut those lemons, dip them in salt and pepper, and then squeeze them into his eyes. *Ugh! What's happening to me? Why do I keep losing my temper?*

I was so happy and content an hour ago, but look at me now. He has ruined my day off. Does he even know how difficult it was for a resident to get a day off, that too on a Saturday? I was so looking forward to having a day out with my girlfriends. Now I wanted to do nothing but bury myself deep in my bed and never leave the place. Else, I would accidentally encounter his dumb face in the hallway. I gulped down a huge glass of water and tried to calm down my haphazard nerves. He had tortured me enough on that island, not anymore. I reckoned to take a shower, as I was stinking like anything.

Just as the hot water caressed my skin, it worked like a tranquilizer on my stressed nerves. Nothing could be compared to a relaxing, steamy shower. Mere minutes in the shower melted away all my anxiety. I felt relaxed and composed. Stepping out of the shower, I wore the most comfortable superman shorts and a loose jumper. Finn was relaxing on the couch, so I carried my breakfast cereal and a perfect steaming cup of coffee towards the couch, and switching on the television I cuddled beside him, letting out a relaxing sigh.

"This is how life should be." I breathed in the addictive aroma of coffee and let it sink into my soul. Disturbing the lovely peaceful moment, my phone started to ring, and I jumped up in surprise on my seat. Rubbing the spilled coffee off my sweater, I stood up, frowning. Unknown number!

"Hello, this is Ethan Stanton. Are you the same Sarah Walter, who was looking hot like a barbecue sauce on her parent's wedding anniversary night and whose fiancé can kill anyone with his boredom?"

What the heck?

"Err... Nope." What on earth was he doing now? *Please don't tell me he is searching for my number by calling every Sarah Walter in town. Seriously, Stanton?* I cleared my throat a little while covering the phone to make my voice unrecognizable for him. Now he wants my number to torment me day and night with creepy calls and texts.

"Hello Ms., are you there?"

"Err… yes. I'm not your Sarah. And a little tip for you. If you are trying to find someone's number who is running away from you… you might not want to reveal your name first." *This dude is never going to leave my side, never going to let me take a breath of relief.* With my good advice, which came out more like a taunt, I went to hang up. But his voice on another side forced me to listen to him again.

"Well, that's a genuine thought. Thank you, 'not my Sarah'. Have a nice day."

"You too." And I was finally able to hang up. I increased the volume of the television and frowned when my phone began to buzz again.

"How did you know she is running away from me?" He blabbered as soon as I pressed the green button. Now I was frustrated.

"Geez! I don't know! Maybe your intro tipped me off."

"Really? Oh! I'm such a moron! That makes sense! Then what should I do now?" I almost growled at his question. *Is he seriously asking for tips for talking to me from me?* Let's say if I could travel from phone to phone, I would have strangled him right then and there.

"Hello? Are you there, 'not my Sarah', but still seem like a good person?" I puffed out a heavy breath, looking up. Seriously, God?

"Well… go milder on the intro. Don't straight away tell your name. Let her take the first move." Ugh, I can't believe I just said that. I hung up the phone without waiting for his reply. I was beyond frustrated. If I were in a movie, I would have thrown my phone out of the window a long time ago, but this is not a movie and phones are expensive. But the second I made up my mind to switch it off, it rang again. Seriously? And there I had the urge to launch a missile straight to his apartment; after all, there was only one wall between us. I picked it up again, ready to warn him to dare not ask for another tip.

"Hello. Is it my beautiful Starz, whom earthy people call Sarah Walter? Who has another earthy being as her fiancé, but totally deserves an as hot as sun boyfriend like me!" I stood up abruptly in shock, and then anger began to twirl inside me. How did he recognize me? Did he recognize my voice? But I made sure to change it. Maybe it wasn't enough?

I was cursing myself in my head when he said from the other end, "Did it sound good?"

"What?" I was confused.

"Your advice 'not my Sarah'. Does this one sound milder? Will this work on her?"

"Oh! Right!" So he didn't recognize my voice after all. I blew out a sigh of relief and cleared my throat again.

"Well, you might want to lose the last line," I replied in the most genuine-fake tone I could muster.

"Okay. Point noted, madam. Thanks again 'not my Sarah'." And the line went dead.

My eyes opened with the buzzing sound of my phone's vibration, but it stopped before I could locate it. My body felt a little numb as I blinked several times to place myself in the same century. Did I fall asleep watching television? My muscles ached as I pulled myself up from my cozy couch and Finn jumped off. Aww, I didn't know you were sleeping with me.

Rubbing my eyes to pull my body out of laziness, I checked the clock, and it was showing five in the evening. Wow, I took a hell of a long nap. I found the phone buried under the cushions and checked the missed call. It was Lucas. He was working on a high-profile case in Boston and had requested an early hearing. So that he would be able to take time off for our wedding and honeymoon, hopefully without any interruptions this time. I called him back.

"Hey!"

"Hi, Luc."

"Why didn't you pick it up? I thought you may have got a call from the hospital on your day off."

"No, I was just taking a nap."

"Oh! Sorry! Did I disturb your sleep, baby?"

"No, it's fine. It was a rather long nap, anyway. How are you? How's work coming along?"

"Oh, it's strenuous, but I am positive the judge will rule in our favor. So, in the end, it all pays off." There is always a surge of enthusiasm in his voice when he talks about his work.

"That's great." I liked his dedication toward work. It even inspired me to work harder and be a better doctor.

"Well, Sarah, I wanted to apologize. I won't be able to visit you next weekend either. There is this huge fundraising event next Saturday to which all the big shots are coming to. And Sam is finally looking forward to making me a Partner in his firm."

Well, I take back my words for the work dedication stuff. Sometimes it was just too much. He changes most of our plans for some or the other big events to further his career. I understand that work was important, but sometimes it feels like only work was important for him. I realize that even I was not able to give him much time due to my long shifts, but it hurts nonetheless.

"Oh! Great! I am so happy for you, Luc!" I congratulated him half-heartedly.

"Thanks, love. You will be the wife of a law firm Partner soon enough. Got to go. Are you visiting your parents tonight?"

"No. I have a shift tomorrow and I don't want to be late." In reality, I had too much of them on the island. I needed some time alone.

"Okay, love. Take care and see you soon."

"Bye, I love…" and the line disconnected before my sentence was complete.

I stared at the phone for a minute. Sometimes I wondered if he really loved me or I was just one of the stepping stones in his climb towards a successful life.

What the hell was I thinking? Obviously, he loved me. We would have been married and on our honeymoon right now if not for that fire incident. I smacked myself on the head and got up from the couch.

Making myself a steaming coffee, I put on some music and opened the balcony door, and went out to take in the evening breeze. I had a quiet neighborhood. Long, less crowded lanes surrounded by Tulip Poplar and Pink Dogwood trees. Enjoying the scenery, I watched kids playing in their backyards and couples chatting and laughing with each other. This was my type of life, peaceful and harmonious. I could never live in one of those big cities. Too crowded for me.

My eyes caught a glimpse of Mr. Tate, our watch-keeper, as he smiled up at me, bowing down his hat in a friendly gesture. I waved at him with a chuckle. He was an old man with sweetness and joy always tugged on his sleeves. I had liked him since the day he helped me move my luggage to my apartment when I moved in here, without even taking a single penny from me. He was like a second father to me; he even scolded me once for not visiting my parents often, regardless of living not so far away from them.

Taking a sip of my coffee, my eyes fell upon a tall guy in loose ripped blue jeans and a white shirt with a mattress tugged at his shoulder. He looked handsome with his muscles clenched. *And Dude, he had a sexy ass.* Either he was moving in or moving out of one of the apartments in the building. I smiled and moved my gaze elsewhere. But then I realized who he was and all the memories from this morning came rushing back in.

"Yo-ho, Starz?" I was at a loss of words when the familiar voice touched my ears. Quickly, I looked down to see Stanton's head staring up at me with a huge smile on his face.

"What are you doing?" I spoke with my gritted teeth as we had already attracted some eyes on us.

"Got a new mattress for my bed. Would you mind putting some food in this fire belly? I'm so ravenous that I could eat a horse." My cheeks burned with embarrassment as everyone around us started looking up at me. Well, there were also some cons of living in a small town.

"Just like you've purchased that mattress, go and buy your food, too. And if you need help, then why don't you ask your friend Willy at the strip club?" I shouted back at him, which attracted even more eyes. And after getting self-conscious under the watchful eyes, I rushed back in.

Closing my eyes, I was taking deep breaths to calm myself when the doorbell echoed in the house and I jumped out of my body. I somehow knew who it was and my legs refused to move towards the door. The ring buzzed again, and every nerve in my body was on high alert. *Sarah, just stay strong. He has just come here to annoy you more, just relax and don't stop yourself from slapping some sense into him.* I was consoling myself mentally.

I slowly walked towards the door. A shriek left my mouth when his face appeared three times bigger than its size when I checked him through the peephole. "Stanton, you have surpassed every freaking limit to get on my nerves! What do you want now?" I shouted from behind the door because I was not in the mood to face him again.

"Err... I need some help."

"Are you kidding me? I hate you and you should have mutual feelings. And enemies don't help each other. So, please disappear." I yelled again, praying mentally that he would go away.

"Okay, I won't bother you again. But just tell me how to make lemonade if you don't have lemons?" Argh, seriously, lemons again? I clenched my teeth tighter as my body trembled in anger.

"Add your balls in it, if you have any," I shouted at the top of my lungs and forcefully pushed open the door to shout some more at him, but he was nowhere to be seen.

Right then, I remembered that my apartment had only one problem. One big problem. Instead of inside, the front door opened outside, and I had pushed the door fiercely, forgetting Ethan was standing on my doormat. As a consequence, my eyes were now staring down at a dead Stanton. Well, not actually... 'Dead' dead.

He was lying shattered on the floor. Groaning in pain with both of his hands cupping his nose. I kneeled, a little worried, but when he looked up to meet my gaze, his eyes popped up with that same stupid smile plastered on his face as he spoke up.

"Is this how you felt when you fell from heaven?"

Fifteen

Sarah

DAY SEVENTEEN

You know your whole day is ruined when you wake up to the sound of hardcore punk blaring into your head.

"Stanton! I'm going to kill you!"

An annoyed groan left my mouth while trying to bury my head in the pillows. Why was he so determined to ruin my damn mornings? I had a shift starting this afternoon, and I didn't know when I would get the next chance to come back home to have a good sleep in my own bed. I needed to get as much sleep as possible before I head back to the hospital.

I tried to ignore the noise and go back to sleep. But it didn't work. I swear the walls were vibrating. I wasn't sure if this building was strong enough to handle his rock concert. This was not what I signed up for while buying this apartment. I rolled over, annoyed enough to murder someone, when Finn started barking, making everything worse.

Throwing the sheets off, I stomped outside. And before I could've stopped myself, I was at his door. Manically banging my fist at his door, with my eyes closed, like I really wanted to break it down.

The door opened unexpectedly, making me stumble forward and my fist met his sculpted, sweaty, bare chest. I regained my balance to glare at him, but my jaw must have gone slack and I must have lost control over my breathing when his post-workout body blinded my vision.

He was breathing hard, chest rising and falling with droplets of sweat trickling down his hard, tanned, naked torso. The teasing sweat drops had captured my attention as they were disappearing under the waistband of his lowers. I could appreciate every single ripped muscle in his body pumping from the exercise. And boy, there was a shamelessly strong urge buzzing in me to reach out and touch that finely sculpted art piece.

"Hey, neighbor! Are you checking me out?" I rolled my eyes and reluctantly retrieved my hand, and finally looked at his face. He had a Bandage across his nose that was making him look rather cute.

"In your dreams, Stanton. Just turn the damn volume down. This is not your mansion. There are people trying to sleep here." I tried to sound assertive, but my voice was a little muffled by all the hot muscles thumping in front of my eyes. Suddenly, I was aware of how little I was wearing. I came running directly out of bed in my Scooby-Doo shorts and a tank top.

"Oh, you don't want to know what happens in my dreams, darling." With a sharp intake of breath, I could practically see him making out with me in his mind. I couldn't help myself from imagining what goes in that dirty little head of his. I got lost in those seductive blue eyes. The moment was filled with sparks of very high sexual tension between us.

What the hell was happening to me? Don't fall for his cheap tricks, Sarah! I struck a note in my head and closed my eyes. Shaking my head vigorously, I felt a jolt of spark run down my spine. By the time I opened my eyes, he had turned on his heels and vanished back into his apartment. Within seconds, the music stopped.

The silence suddenly felt awkward. As I was going to take a step back towards my door, he reappeared and grabbed my hand. "Hey, not so soon, neighbor! It's a beautiful morning. At least have a cup of coffee with me."

His mere gesture retreated me back into my right mind. His touch somehow made everything real and had me jolt out of the trance. The morning haziness vanished from my mind and I once again saw Ethan for what he really was. I looked straight into his eyes and spoke, "Why the hell would I have anything with you? Just go away, Stanton, before you regret it." My voice didn't falter this time, and his reaction to my words confirmed that the message was delivered.

I yanked free my hand from his grip and headed back inside my apartment, slamming the door behind me. I could feel my heart racing in my ears. Finn came near, sensing the tension in the air, and I bent down to snuggle into his soft fur.

You cannot fall for him again, girl. Don't act so immaturely. It took you nine years to come out of the mess of a life he buried you into and left to die. He has not changed. He can never change. I kept repeating the words to let them imprint on my mind.

※

I had no idea how long I stayed there by the door hugging Finn. It might have been an hour or two or just a few minutes. My brain was not working properly. At some time, I decided to move into the bedroom and tried to go back to sleep, but it was of no use. Finally, I resolved to get out of this building to get some fresh air.

Pulling on a pair of track pants and a loose sweater over my tank top, I gathered my hair into a messy bun. As I was tying my shoelaces, Finn started jumping with excitement, wagging his tail so hard that I almost laughed at his enthusiasm. Putting a leash on his collar, I took him out for a walk.

After a long jog, I could feel the heat radiating from our bodies as we soon settled on a park bench. I forgot to bring my sipper and as a result, we both were panting for some water. I closed my eyes and tilted my head backward, feeling the morning breeze on my sweaty face. Once again, my mind started to drift off in the past when I felt a tug at my hand and the next second, I lost my grip on Finn's latch as he ran away.

By the time I opened my eyes and got a grip on my surroundings, he was nowhere to be seen. A sudden panic started to rise in my stomach. But soon the voice of his soft, friendly bark fell in my ears and I finally spotted him. He was some hundred meters down the jogging track, wagging his tail vigorously at some guy who was crotched down to fondle him.

Catching up to him, I noticed he was actually drinking water from that guy's bottle, who was caressing his ears as if it was his pet. A pang of jealousy hit me, as I had never seen Finn so friendly with anyone before. It would not be exaggerating to say that he hated Lucas's guts without any reason and there he was, being so friendly with a stranger.

Reaching up to them, I cleared my throat and both of them tilted their head up to face me. To my utter luck, he was in fact not a stranger. He was none other than Stanton. "What the hell? Are you following me now?"

"Hey, calm down. I just came out to jog because the music in the apartment was bothering you. I didn't even know you were here. Cross my heart and hope to die." Ethan uttered, standing up and making a cross over his heart with his right hand.

I rolled my eyes so hard it made me dizzy for a split second. Ethan extended his hands to hold me but thought better off with it at the last moment. "Hey, are you all right? You look exhausted. I would offer you water, but the little buddy here finished it all up."

"I will live, Stanton." Crouching down, I picked up Finn's lease and started to pull him away. Little betrayer.

Clearing his throat, Ethan started strolling along with us. "Oh, this is your dog, I had no idea. He really likes me, though. At least someone knows how to identify a genuine person." He ran a hand through his hair. The same old habit of flustering that I shamelessly remembered.

"Don't get your panties in a bunch, Stanton. He was just thirsty." I retorted, rather sarcastically.

He paused for a few seconds as I increased my pace, but then opened his mouth again. "I am fine, by the way. Thanks for asking." This time his voice was laced with sarcasm and I had to reluctantly turn my head towards him to catch the meaning. He was touching the bandage on his nose and I understood he was talking about the little mishap of last night.

"Well, it was your fault standing so near to my front door. I told you to leave me alone multiple times, haven't I?" I paced forward again, futilely trying to outrun him.

"Don't you think you should make it up to me, though?" His question stopped me in my tracks. Make it up to him? For hurting his nose? What about all the things he owed me? My face must have shown how angry I was because Ethan retreated two steps back, raising his hands in defense.

"Hey, no need to fire laser beams. I was just talking about catching some breakfast together. Neighbors occasionally do that, right?"

I was too angry to say anything and so he continued, "You know, there is a breakfast food truck down the lane which serves Belgian waffles, your favorite breakfast."

Of course, I knew that! It was one of the solid positive points to purchase this apartment. But I was not going to give him the pleasure of feeling proud of remembering my favorite breakfast after all these years. "That was nine years ago, Stanton. My taste has changed, and that too for the better. I don't fall for sweet delusions anymore."

His face fell with my last sentence, but instead of feeling triumphed, I somehow felt a little disappointed with myself. Also, my stomach was rumbling with the thought of warm waffles topped with sweet maple syrup. Argh, this was all so frustrating.

I love his company, but I hate him. A look at his smiling face makes me want to smile too, but I also want to slap that smile off his face at the same time. His body affects me so strongly that I feel like a teenage school girl ogling over hot college boys. Argh! My mind is a mess right now. Why the hell is he playing with me? What does he really want?

"What the hell do you want, Stanton? What exactly are you doing here?" My voice came out so harsh that I almost scared myself. Ethan took a step back and locked eyes with me. He just kept staring at me with such intensity that I started to feel a little self-conscious. I was on the edge of turning around and fleeing when he finally spoke.

"I have come to apologize, Sarah. I know I screwed up. There are not enough words in the world that could explain how sorry I am. I want to show you that I am really repenting of my actions. My feelings are not fake. And what happened on that island…" I held up my hand in front of him before he could say any more. I didn't want to listen to one more lie coming out of his mouth. My eyes were stinging with tears trying to make their way through.

"Please listen to me, Starz," he took a step forward, reaching for my hand. But I had enough of him. I snatched back my hand and shouted.

"Stop! Just stop!" But it came out more like a plea. I turned around and ran towards my building before he could spot my tears. Leaning back at the closed door, I sobbed into my hands.

॰

A nasty headache had set in by the time I was ready to leave for work. Before heading out, I pressed my ear to the door to check for any commotion in the hallway. I did not want to face Ethan after the dreadful encounter this morning. I couldn't hear anything, nor could I see anyone from the peephole. Thus, opening the door just by an inch, I peeked outside, and the coast was clear.

Gathering my belongings, I gave Finn a hug and cautiously moved out. Too scared to make a noise, as if Ethan would burst out of the walls any second. I locked the door behind me and was just passing by Mrs. Jenkins's door when Ethan opened his door, escorting her out. "Thank you for the pancakes, Mrs. Jenkins. I mean Linda."

It appeared like he was almost pushing her out while she was clearly reluctant to leave. Her eyes fell over me and she gave me a rather disgruntled roll of eyes. *What the hell have I ever done to you, lady?*

"So I was saying..." Mrs. Jenkins started turning back towards Ethan, completely ignoring my existence. But he didn't acknowledge her. His eyes were fixed on me.

"Where are you going?" Ethan asked, eying the duffle bag hanging by my shoulder. There was a hint of desperation in his voice.

"Well, good afternoon, Mrs. Jenkins, and good afternoon to you too annoying neighbor, who should totally mind his own business." I started to walk past them just as Mrs. Jenkins held on to his arm with both hands, trying to distract his attention from me.

"Wait!" He called out from behind when I reached the edge of the staircase. "Please don't run away again, Starz. It took me nine years to find you." What the hell? Did he think I was running away or something? I turned around to face him and found his face just inches away from mine.

"I am done running, Stanton. You don't scare me. I won't let you destroy my life anymore." I retorted, staring deep into his blue eyes and poking his chest with my finger at every word.

"Then why are you leaving, girl?" His voice was so low and desperate that he sounded like a child being left by her mom on the first day of school.

"Oh, for God's sake, Stanton! People like us need to work. Not everyone is born with a silver spoon in their mouth like you." For a split second, his eyes were dazed in confusion and then he let out a deep breath that he was holding in for so long. Giving him a tight-lipped smile, I turned on my heels and left him hanging there.

❦

Thank goodness my apartment was only a short drive away from the hospital. I couldn't explain how difficult it was to cover that short distance with my head pounding in my ears. Parking my Chevrolet Aveo in the staff parking lot, I pulled out the duffel bag from the backseat and realized I forgot to buy coffee on the way. Now I would have to drink that dirt from the vending machine in the hospital cafeteria. Argh! The day kept getting worse and worse.

Marking my attendance, I headed straight for the on-call room. Stuffing in the extra pair of clothes I had brought with me into my locker, my mind kept going back to the desperate look on Ethan's face when he thought I was running away. He said it took him nine years to find me. What does that even mean? Was he really looking for me all these years?

After we left the island, dad asked me why I didn't told him about Ethan sooner, instead of putting up with his façade. I didn't say anything and he dropped the subject but the thought never left my mind. Why exactly did I tolerated all his drama and even persuaded Ash to not say anything to my parents, telling her that he will get tiered and leave by himself much sooner than later.

Did I really thought he would leave or was I glad he was there? Did I really wanted him to see that I had moved on and was very happy with Lucas or was I just trying to make him jealous?

I slumped onto one of the bunk beds, holding my head in my hands. Why, God, why? Why are you doing this to me? First, you sent Ethan into my life to destroy me completely, and just when I was finally pulling myself together and was looking forward to a happy and safe life with Lucas; you sent him back to rage havoc in my life again.

The first few days after coming back from Hawaii, I kept on narrating the story of the fire at the wedding and how I was still unmarried, to everyone. But then someone asked me why didn't we get married the next day or even the next week since we were there for one whole extra week? Why postpone it for forty-five days? And I had no answer.

Thinking back, I realized that the thought didn't even cross my mind at that time. Seeing Ethan there, all thoughts of marriage actually skipped my brain. It even felt so weird being romantic with Lucas under Ethan's scrutinizing eyes as if I was cheating on him. I know it doesn't make any sense, but it still felt so weird.

To be honest, it actually felt comforting, thinking that I was still unmarried. The anxiety that was cutting me from inside before the wedding had just vanished and it felt refreshing. At that time, I thought it was just general anxiety about marriage. Everyone gets little cold feet before going to the altar. But now, it seems like it was much more.

I wasn't saying Lucas was not the right choice. In fact, he was much more than I could ever imagine deserving. But it just felt like we needed more time. I don't think we really knew each other properly yet. Although we had been dating for almost two years now, but in these two years we had actually spent less than two months in each other's company.

He has always treated me with respect and gave me full space. We didn't even have a single fight since we started dating. He was a perfect gentleman through and through.

When he proposed to me this past Valentine's Day, I had no reason to refuse. The first thought that crossed my mind was how happy mom would be and how she would now stop nagging me every time I visited her that it was time for me to find a proper man and settle down. So I said yes, and we started planning the wedding right away.

He endorsed my every suggestion, saying, "whatever you desire, dear". Destination wedding in Hawaii, 'no problem'. Honeymoon in Paris, 'of course, my dear'.

There was not much scope for him in Florence, so he asked me to get my residency transferred to Boston. We were supposed to stay in his apartment for a few days after our honeymoon and look for a house to start a life together. We had actually not even lived together yet, bar a few days every other month when he visited me or I visited him.

Thinking back, even Lucas didn't say anything about exchanging the vows the next whole week after the fire incident. He straight away agreed to postpone the wedding for forty-five days. Maybe even he was relieved that the wedding didn't actually happen. He might also not have been ready for the big change in his life. I believe we need to sit down and have a proper conversation on the matter.

I took out my phone from my pocket, checking for any messages from Lucas. There were none. I contemplated calling him and telling him about Ethan arriving out of nowhere and renting an apartment in my building. But then I discarded the idea. I knew what he would say. 'Call the cops. File for a restraining order. I have many criminal lawyer friends there who would help you.'

According to him, all the problems in life should be solved via enforcing one or the other law. We hardly managed to persuade him against filing a forgery case against Ethan regarding the incident in Maui. I believed the only thing that convinced him was the fact that he had hit Ethan first and he was scared that it could be used against him. He would take no risk against anything that could destroy his reputation.

So, I dropped a text instead.

'Reached hospital, will be on night shift tonight, so won't be able to call. Text me if anything comes up. Love, XOXO.'

I tried calling Ash, but it went straight to her voicemail. Looked like she was still traveling. Well, at least someone was enjoying her life. Leaving a short message for her to call me back, I popped a Tylenol in my mouth and headed towards the OB/GYN ward. No matter how messed up my own life was, I still needed to work hard to make other's better. To help people in need;

Even if I was the one who needed some help first.

Sixteen

Sarah

NINE YEARS AGO

I was sitting cross-legged on Ash's bed while she was rummaging through a fashion magazine, showing me some exquisite ball gowns and commenting on them like an expert. I must admit she had some serious fashion bones in her body, even though she herself dressed like an emo. We were having a girl's night as her parents were out of town for the weekend.

The past four weeks had been the best days of my life. Initially, I was afraid that the incident at the party would draw Ethan away from me, as all guys were alleged to lose interest after sex. And his reputation in school as a player was also one of the reasons for my skepticism. But once again, he proved everyone wrong.

He had been a complete gentleman to me after that night. I had never felt closer to him before. We had been spending every free minute of the day in each other's company. From studying together for the finals to walking home after school, we had become the lovebirds of the neighborhood. It was like our relationship had crossed the last hurdle that was stopping us from being one. He had started giving me so much attention as if his whole world revolved around me. Though I always respected his personal space, I would be lying if I said I didn't like the extra attention.

The only thing that bothered me, though, was that we hadn't talked about college yet. Every time I tried to bring up the matter, his mood got grim, and he somehow changed the subject. But we still had ample time for that, so I wasn't that much worried. I was sure we would work it out.

Since the day I introduced him to Aunt Rose, she had been bestowing her boundless love over Ethan. I was sure she had made it her mission to feed him all her recipes. I was also certain that she had been passing all the information of my love life to my Mother over long phone calls every night. Because, other than our routine weekend phone conversation, she called me in the middle of last week giving me all mother-daughter talk about safety and precautions. It was really embarrassing, and I was so swayed that the story of the party night was almost at the tip of my tongue ready to be spilled before her, but the rational part of my brain convinced me to save my dignity.

I hadn't shared the details, even with Ash, till date. To be honest, spending all my time with Ethan had put a little distance between me and Ash, and the fact that she still couldn't trust him an ounce didn't help the situation. Thus, this girl's weekend was a much-needed break for our friendship, but I still found myself zoning out on her and getting lost in Ethan's thoughts.

"Hey! Are you even listening to me? Earth to Sarah… knock-knock!" Ash's sharp voice jolted me out of yet another such daydream and I found myself reclined against the headboard of her bed in an odd position.

"I am listening, Ash," I said, twisting my neck to relieve the strain.

"Oh really? Then tell me what I just said?" She asked sarcastically, knowing all too well that I was lying.

"Okay, you got me. I zoned out for a while. Now get me something to eat. Your fashion talk has drained all my energy." I said, while standing up from the bed.

I guess I stood up way too quickly because just as my legs touched the floor; the room started spinning, and I slumped back on the mattress with a thud. With my eyes squeezed shut, my mind was having a moment of silence. Every muscle in my body relaxed, and I tried to clear my head.

"Are you all right?" Ash's voice made me open my eyes reluctantly, and I nodded in reassurance.

I had been feeling very weary lately. School exhausted me to the limits as if I wasn't coming home from sitting in classes all day but from a harsh punishment of standing under the hot, blaring sun for hours. I was so drained that I felt sweat building on my forehead. A voice at the back of my head was telling me I was soon going to get sick. I hated being ill. And being ill when graduation was around the corner was not doing any justice to it.

"I am telling you that Stanton is Satan in disguise and is draining all your precious energy." The seriousness in her voice made me laugh out loud. Ash had made it her mission to persuade me to stay away from Ethan.

I shook my head as Ash walked out to get something to eat while I leaned my head back on the headboard, trying to breathe through the weariness washing over me. It was quiet around the house. It somehow made me calm until my nostrils crinkled at the stink of chicken. And in the spur of the moment, I felt a lump in my throat. My hands shot up to my mouth when the awful feeling was back.

"I'm telling you, this whole dieting thing for graduation is going to pull you into deep waters." Ash's voice followed the disgusting smell. My stomach lurched at the sight of the food she was carrying.

"Are you okay? You appear like you are going to throw up any second." My hands brushed over my forehead, making me realize I was lathered in sweat. Her words worked like a charm on my already bad condition, and the waves of nausea overwhelmed me. Ash stared at me saucer-eyed as she had already palpated the possibility and the next moment I sprinted towards the toilet.

I was glad my legs worked faster than my brain. Hands wrapped around my stomach, I heaved until I felt nothing but a naked void in my gut. Soon I felt Ash's hands rubbing my back, offering some soothing words.

"Shit! You are sick, babe. I think we should see a doctor or something!" She handed me a cup of water and with my heavy eyelids, I vaguely nodded at her.

I missed prom because of a stupid stomach bug, and now I was going to miss my graduation. Why is fate playing such games with me? Why, God? Why?

I never thought I would be spending my precious Saturday evening sitting inside the sterile examination room of an ER. It was a busy night, voices slipping from outside were giving me a clue that there were patients that were in urgent need of care, unlike me and my nausea. It had been a while since I was waiting for any doctor or nurse to arrive. And thus it had given me enough free time to think about all the bad food choices I made last week that could have landed me and my stomach here in this scenario.

Ash wanted to call Aunt Rose, but I persuaded her not to because I was feeling just fine. Maybe it was just a one-time thing.

"Okay, what have we got here?" My back straightened up when a woman entered the room. The first thing I noticed about her was the light blue scrubs and the serious professional look on her face. Her face was deeply rooted into the notepad in her hands, eyes roaming over the form in which Ash had filled out some basic information about me. And once she was satisfied with that, she finally looked up at me with a smile.

"Hello, I'm Nurse Alice. How are you feeling now, Miss Walter? Would you mind informing me about your symptoms in detail? Like since when did they start occurring or anything you can add up?" I shrugged my shoulders, crossing my legs to feel less anxious in front of her.

"Well… it's been a few days, maybe a week. It started with low body aches. Mainly in the mornings. Like I'm exhausted without doing anything. And after a couple of days, I started feeling this strange thing at the back of my throat. Like I want to throw up after every heavy meal." She started writing down the words flowing through my lips.

"Any headaches? Diarrhea or muscle aches or cramping?"

"No muscle aches. But yeah, sometimes there are headaches. Not frequently, though." She gave me a habitual smile as I shifted in my place, and then she shook her head.

"Well, as I see it, there is nothing to worry about, Miss Walter. Your symptoms seem like you have some stomach flu or it might be food poisoning from the weird food and cocktail of drinks you teenagers have at parties. We can run some blood tests if you would like. One more thing: you forgot to fill the column of your last menstruation cycle. Here…" The sound of my phone ringing echoed in the room, stopping her mid-sentence. She gestured to me to go ahead and take the call as she turned around to file out some papers on the desk.

My face lit up seeing the name flashing on the screen, yet the haziness in my heart couldn't feel the happiness that should be there. "Hello!" I tried my best to conceal my quick breaths and sound less edgy.

"Hey, gorgeous. How are you? What were you doing?" I wished I could match the amount of vigor in his voice following through the phone.

"I'm okay. I'm at Ashley's. I told you we are spending the weekend together. We were just going to watch some movie or something." I glanced up at the nurse nervously. It was very nerve-wracking lying to him when she was listening to everything. I just didn't want him to worry.

"What were you doing, Ethan? Do you have any plans or something?"

"Yeah, about that..." The break in his voice made me realize he was sounding a little skittish. As if he was discerning to confess something to me.

"It's my father, Sarah. He has asked for my assistance. Well, it is more like a forced request that I can't deny. You know him and his judgments." My heart sank at the mention of his father. I could sense something bad was coming up. I was noticing changes in Ethan's day-to-day schedules from the past week. The school wasn't over yet; still, his dad had started keeping him busy. Making him climb the early ladders of their family business, sharing his knowledge and experience with him, gradually trying to mold him into his own version. Into a person, he wasn't.

"I'll be accompanying him on some business tours in the coming days. I don't know the full itinerary, but it looks like we are leaving tomorrow." There it was. And my breath got caught up in my throat. "But..."

"Sarah, I'm really sorry. Baby, there is nothing in my hands, you see."

"I'm sorry for intruding... but have you missed your period?" The nurse's voice forced me to pull out from whatever apology Ethan was throwing in my direction.

My head was muddled up with the reality that Ethan was going away from me. I would no longer be able to see him. To feel his touch or his breath over my skin. I was staring blankly at a distance, not sure why all of a sudden the light in the room was insanely bright. It was blinding me. Making a shooting headache threaten its way to my head.

But it wasn't all because of Ethan's leaving. The truth was something else. Something unavoidable. And I couldn't run from it. And the fact that I was shaking my head at the nurse's question was a plain denial of the truth that made me dizzy.

The truth, that I was screwed.

❧

The very next morning I was standing in the living room of the Stanton Mansion.

Coming out of the ER last night I insisted Ash to drop me off at Aunt Rose's, making an excuse of wanting to sleep in my own bed as I was feeling sick. She believed I was still a virgin, so the information of missing my periods by about two weeks didn't ring any alarm bells in her mind. After she dropped me off, I waited for Aunt Rose to fall asleep and then sneaked out of the back door to buy pregnancy test kits.

"Please make yourself comfortable, Miss," I nodded at the servitor of the mansion attending to me, giving him a brief smile when he assured me and walked away. Yet my gaze continued to follow him, till he closed the seamless double door and disappeared behind them.

The vast sitting area made me feel like I was nonexistent. My head lifted towards the art covering the walls. I was astonished by the mere scale of the room, capturing the magnificent beauty of the carvings embarked throughout the ceiling. The baroque art was something of a treat for the eyes. A smile stretched over my lips, glimpsing at the series of beautiful portraits hung over the walls. I was dying to have a closer look, but I held myself back.

It was my first time visiting Ethan's house. Although I already knew how rich he was, right at that moment, my eyes were actually witnessing the extravagant life he had for the first time. He was literally born with a silver spoon in his mouth or, in fact, a golden spoon. I mean, he had everything that could make anybody desperate enough to trade places with him. Yet, the beauty of the house was not helping the swelling ripples of anxiety inside me.

The fact that he was going to leave town today forced me to face him uninvited early in the morning. My eyes burned holes over that closed door, losing my patience with every passing second. I was counting every minute against the complete silence surrounding me. Nothing but my racing heart could be heard in my ears. My nervousness was obvious because I was squirming in my seat, dying to talk to Ethan and hoping he wouldn't freak out. I checked my watch one more time. It had been a while since I came here. Still, not a single soul could be acknowledged. I could feel my hands getting sweaty and I rubbed them once again over the fabric of my skirt.

The muffled sound of footsteps outside the door made unease creep into my chest, and I stood up. Straightening my back, I cleared my throat, trying my best to slacken the flabbiness out of my voice. My head replayed the scenarios that I had practiced as to how I was going to face him.

Minutes went by, but no one came through that door. And I stumbled back into the chair. Letting out a deep sigh, disappointingly. The tormenting wait was getting on my nerves. I was already dying with impatience, thinking about the outcome of telling him the truth, and yet; he was only making everything worse with all this delay.

As seconds ticked by, the line between my patience and curiosity started to reduce to ashes. I stood up and now my legs were showing the way on their own. My hand swirled the doorknob against the advice of my sensible mind, which was screaming at me to remain seated. My sight drifted from the enormous door at my back to the nerve-wracking massive stairways in the hallway.

"No, David, I want this deal in my hand today. I don't care what you have to do. Just get over with it!" My eyes noticed a tall figure storming down the staircase. He was over the phone while walking in my direction and my back stiffened. He was so occupied in the conversation that he didn't acknowledge my presence. Yet, my eyes clearly recognized him.

Mr. Stanton's personality elucidated the aura of dominance. The command he had over the business in the town exhibited his dynamism. Noticing his elegant posture with his one hand concealed in the pocket of one of the finest suits he always wore, I couldn't help but appreciate the similarities that were so apparent in Ethan.

"Hold on a second." Within the moment of him gliding by me and my eyes returning to the staircase, I sensed him restraining himself at the place. Taking some steps back, his eyes quickly acknowledged me, as he was now standing in front of me. And the first thing I noted about him was how tall he was.

"My apologies. I wasn't aware we have company." I nervously smiled at his sweet remark, trying my best to leave a good impression on him.

"Good morning, Mr. Stanton." He responded with an even warmer smile, for which he was well known in the whole town. He was one of the school board trustees and I could hardly recall any event that he'd missed in which Ethan was given an award. And now that I was seeing him up close, I could clearly see where his son had got those killing looks from.

They were one of the richest families in the town. Running a business of hotels and restaurants. And I believed the business was flourishing because lately, Ethan couldn't help bragging about some seaside hotel in Hawaii they were soon going to acquire.

"I'm sorry to bother you, Sir. I'm Sarah, your son's girl..."

"Schoolmate!" Our heads turned towards the voice. Firstly, my forehead furrowed, but then it all soon cleared up, after catching sight of Ethan rushing downstairs. In the flash of a moment, I found him standing beside me.

"This is Sarah, Dad. We go to school together." This was not the kind of introduction I was expecting from him. My perplexed gaze studied him. After waving a brief uneasy smile at me, he turned back to his dad, with beads of sweat covering his forehead.

"Well, you must be special. Because my son hardly brings any friends home." Ethan let out a snicker, and there was a feeling in my gut that told another story. He was imprisoned by something that I was unable to sense. His body language spoke of how uncomfortable he was at that moment. He seemed kind of jumpy. Maybe I was mistaken, but from where I was watching, he looked as if he was scared of his dad.

"We were just leaving, dad!" My smile dropped as I realized that he didn't cherish my presence in his house.

"Well, it was very nice meeting you, Sarah. If I were not in a hurry, I would love to have a chat with you. But you kids have fun." He told me with a smile and then turned towards Ethan.

"Come back soon, son. You know we have to leave in a couple of hours." Ethan nodded as Mr. Stanton moved along. He ran after him as they exchanged a couple of words that made him lower his gaze in disappointment. I wondered what his dad said to make him feel this way.

Mr. Stanton continued his phone conversation as I watched how the chauffeur ran to take his bag from one of the servitors and, in a couple of minutes they were off to the road. My eyes followed the car till Ethan appeared back in my sight with an anxious look etching his features.

"Hey, angel. I'm sorry about all that. My dad is something… You have no idea." He ran a hand through his hair. The same old habit of him when he was feeling nervous. "Anyway, why are you here? Did something happen?" He walked towards me with an anxious look consuming his face. I could feel how his father's presence had affected him, but now was not the time to focus on that.

"Ethan, I… I mean… we… we need to talk." I couldn't meet his eyes when I said those words. But only sensed him letting out a deep breath of anticipation.

"What? Are you okay, babe? Should we go somewhere?" My lips parted away, but my mind got clouded with blankness.

"A walk would be fine." He nodded, with a small smile on his lips. I could tell he had palpated that I was not feeling fine in his big house.

We were both quiet as we exited the big gates out of his driveway. The street was empty and so silent that our footsteps reverberated in the air. I could feel Ethan occasionally stealing glances at me. He was as nervous as I was. His hands were shoved in his pockets, just like his father's, as he was kicking a stone in the pathway. And then, letting out a deep breath, I turned towards him.

"Are you breaking up with me?"

"I'm pregnant."

My brows knitted together when we both spoke at the same time.

"What?" He was, as expected, shocked.

"No… What?" I was confused.

"I would never break up with you, Ethan. I've come to tell you that I'm pregnant." I repeated, to clear up the confusion. It felt like a huge burden had just been lifted off of my shoulder.

When he didn't say anything for a while, my eyes bored into him. I tried to study him. He simply stood there, silent and frozen in his spot. No words came out of his mouth like he had lost his voice. I struggled to search his face for any kind of emotion, but it remained blank. His dumbfounded eyes lingered over me, blinking rapidly, as it looked like his brain was still trying to process the news.

Maybe he was in shock. It was the exact reaction I was afraid I would get. I never wanted him to freak out, but the news was startling for me too. I mean, the moment those two lines appeared in front of my eyes in each of the four pregnancy tests I took last night, it knocked the living breath out of me. My world came crashing down in front of my eyes. The truth felt like a punch to my stomach. Or as if someone had tossed ice-freezing water over my face. I wanted to call Ethan right away but thought better of it and decided to do it face-to-face.

I already knew confronting him with the news won't be an easy task. That is why I didn't want to do it over the phone and came all the way to his house. Sooner or later, this had to be talked over. However, I was there for him and I knew he would always be there for me, too. Together we could certainly find a way to overcome this and move towards a brighter side. No matter what would happen next, we would stick together and stay by each other's side.

The very first thing that whacked my brain was the thought of my parents. Their disappointed faces, after realizing what I'd done with my future, were something I couldn't get out of my head. Putting my father's reputation in jeopardy was the last thing I ever wanted. He was my sunshine, the person who understood me very well; perhaps even better than my mother, and that was what I feared. This could break his heart.

Ethan remained tight-lipped at his spot, and I patiently waited for him to recover from the news.

"Ethan." I tried to pull him out of the trance, but he pointed a finger at me and quickly took some steps back. His hand moved towards the side pole, taking support from it as if he would fall without it.

"What did you say? I mean… are you sure? I mean… are you certain? Oh, Jesus Christ! My dad is going to kill me." I flinched at his disbelieving words.

"I'm sorry… I'm just babbling. It's just I don't know what to say right now." He racked a hand in his hair as he swallowed down his anxiety.

"Shit! This wasn't supposed to be happening. We used protection. We didn't plan for it. I mean, we are just kids. How can we handle another? I mean, this is going to change everything. Our lives. Our future plans. Our finances." His hand was stroking his forehead as he continued to shake his head in denial.

"How many times did you take the test, Sarah?"

"Four times!"

"Oh, my shitballs. We are so screwed." Looking at his troubled face, I slowly walked toward him. But another shout pierced through the air that halted me in my tracks.

"We are finished, babe. Our whole life is over. We've ruined our lives. Hell! What am I even going to say to my dad? He is definitely going to kill me!" At this point, my lips started to tremble. A tsunami of fearful emotions hit me, making my guts churn. That was the moment I wanted to run away from that place and never come back.

I was forced to believe that I was responsible for all this. It was embarrassing to even look at him. You could call me a coward, because I was not brave enough to argue with him right now, especially not in this situation.

"We messed up everything, Sarah." He almost yelled, holding my shoulders tight with both hands. I couldn't hold it anymore. My confidence broke down into pieces. Tears flooded my eyes. It made my vision blurry. The further his brutal retort echoed in my head, the further I shook in despair. I was astonished, trembling with a sharp sting in my heart.

Watching me tear up he started pacing in front of me, with resentment clouding his features. Maybe it was my blind faith that was still anticipating some compassion from him. A hug, at least. Because I knew my real Ethan. He was thoughtful and caring. And I believed I was the only one who could deal with him at this moment.

"I'm so sorry! Please, stay with me." I wondered what I was even apologizing for. Why was this happening to me? I did not do anything wrong. I couldn't be tagged as a bad guy alone. His cold shoulder caused more tears to shed from my eyes. I was bruised, physically as well as emotionally. A sob escaped my mouth when he turned towards me.

"Oh, my God. Please don't cry. I don't know what I'm saying. My head is a mess. Please, just stop crying." He grasped my face under his cold hands, but I just shook my head.

"I'm sorry." The strain in my voice conveyed the sheer strength I was left with. I was exhausted, restless, and too vulnerable to quarrel with him now.

"It's okay. We are okay. We can handle this. We have to think straight. We have to deal with it." I wasn't sure if he was talking to me or himself. But the softness in his voice convinced me that my Ethan was back. I could feel he had conquered his resentment. The person that was missing all this time was now standing in front of me. But then, I was still very scared of him. His lashing out was still ringing in my ear.

I shivered when the coldness of his fingers stroked my face, making me look into his eyes. I surveyed his face, and all I could find was concern written all over it.

"You know how precious you are to me." His voice was silvery. Just the perfect blend of velvety reassurance to comfort me. I wanted nothing at that time but to embrace him. And I acted on my desire and threw myself in his arms. I hugged him tightly, leaving no space between us. I felt like a drowning person gasping for air and he was the only one who could save me. More tears trickled down my eye, as I buried my face in his chest, deeper.

"Sarah?" I wanted to stay in his arms forever, but he slowly separated us and captured my attention with his comforting hands encircling my cheeks. I chuckled when he stroked my nose with his. I loved these little things. The touch was enough to get my senses back.

"Sarah, what have you thought about it? I want to know what is running through your head." His eyes were locked with mine, hope etched in them. He was searching for some answers on my face, and he soon earned them when I nodded.

"Yes, I mean, I know we can't keep it. I already have made up my mind." And for the first time since I'd come here, I saw a real smile on his face, the smile that reached his eyes. Straight away, he let out a deep breath of relief and pulled me into his arms, thanking me continuously.

"Perfect. This is for the best. Now, leave it to me. I'll take care of everything. You don't have to worry about anything. I'll make an appointment for tomorrow with the best OB/GYN in the city and we will see what happens next." I simply nodded, making myself believe it was indeed best for our futures.

"Tomorrow?" I separated from his embrace and glanced at him.

"Yeah, tomorrow. The sooner the better. Is there something wrong with that?" He inquired, taking out his phone.

"But the day after tomorrow is our graduation. Can't we wait for just a couple of days? It's not like something will happen in two days." It was our freaking graduation. I'd dreamed of this day since I stepped into high school. Mom and dad were especially coming to see their little girl graduate from high school. I couldn't take the risk. What if something would go wrong and my stay in the hospital would get extended for more than one day? There was no urgency now. We could do it any time after graduation.

"But you know my dad, Sarah. We are supposed to leave in an hour. I have no idea how I am going to convince him to postpone the meeting. And then canceling another tour would be like welcoming a storm. And besides, I'll get the best doctors for you and everything will be over in a matter of hours. You are thinking way too much. Just sit back and watch how everything goes smoothly. It will be over in just a blink of an eye. I'm sure they will discharge you within six hours. And don't worry about graduation. Your name would be the first our principal will be calling with a diploma and a medal in his hands."

I softly smiled, still not entirely convinced with his plan. The fear of getting admitted into the hospital itself started to make my skin hot. I looked back at Ethan, who had a comforting smile to cheer me up.

He closed the distance between us by giving me a bear hug. He cupped my cheeks in his hands and fulfilled me with an everlasting kiss; which would surely linger on my lips and mind for quite a long time.

However, the dismay that commenced to build inside my heart couldn't replenish me. The uncertain feelings at the back of my head kept disturbing my mind. My heart couldn't help but beat faster from anticipation that something wrong was going to happen.

The early rays of dawn were shimmering through my bedroom's window. I glanced at the clock and it showed 4:36 AM. It was supposed to be a peaceful moment where I could lay my head on a soft pillow and stare at the glints of sunrise through my flickering heavy eyelashes. But, today something was unusual. Today, I wasn't feeling like admiring the magnificence of morning sunrays. The desire to get lost in the beauty was missing. The uncomfortable, strange feeling had been trying to engulf me entirely. Maybe I was unhappy, or maybe the unreasonable feeling lingering around me was the work of pregnancy hormones.

It felt like something inside me shattered yesterday, in a thousand pieces that couldn't be glued back to the original. I didn't know if it was the truth. Or maybe it was just my imagination, and I was the same girl as I was a day before, but still, I never felt this distant from myself in my life.

Ethan had not called or texted me ever since we parted ways yesterday. I didn't even know if he was in town or not. He was supposed to leave with his father yesterday. Maybe he left and forgot all about me, or maybe he didn't. I had no idea what was going on in his mind. Hell, I didn't even know what exactly was going on in my own freaking head.

I wasn't filled with utter sadness. Instead, it was something that could be correlated with numbness. It might be something pertained to Ethan's fallout on the big news, or perhaps I was thinking too much. It was a lot to take-in, in a single day. And I knew my mind was unnecessarily making things up without any solid account. I supposed these conflicting emotions were not leaving me anytime soon. Squeezing my eyes shut, I rested my hand against my forehead and tried to empty my mind. I was waiting for sleep to overcome me again; when I sensed someone calling my name.

I promptly jerked up and found the most handsome face smiling at me from my window. Awestruck I stood up and witnessed him climbing in when I finally got cognizant of the fact that it wasn't a dream. Holy mother! I thought I was dreaming about him, but he was indeed sneaking into my bedroom. He just stood there with an awkward smile etching his face.

"Hi." He waved his hand at me and I looked over the window. It was quite a height to climb.

"Are you okay? What are you doing here?" Okay, that came out a little rude. But spare me the chivalry. I was sleepy as well as stunned. He looked down and seemed lost deep in thoughts.

"I couldn't sleep." He said, unexpectedly, taking me by surprise.

"Me neither," I muttered, walking over to him.

"I wanted to see you. And I...you know..." For instance, I was happy that I crossed his mind. He had been missing me, but the sad look on his face narrated a different story. Something was bothering him as he looked everywhere but me.

"Is everything all right? Something is bothering you. Tell me." I spoke, meaning every single word. My eyes noticed him moving closer, and then he held my hands. I didn't know why he was so quiet. He made me sit over in the chair and dropped to my level, letting out a deep sigh.

"I am so sorry for everything, babe. I shouldn't have acted like that. I'm ashamed of the things I put you through. I hope you can forgive me." He looked so fragile, shaking his head disappointingly, bowing down.

"But trust me, Sarah, the second you took off, I wished nothing else but to make you see how sorry I was. I freaked out, Sarah. You don't know my dad; he is so strict. That's why I don't invite any of my friends to my house. And then you appeared out of the blue. I panicked. I know I should've acted like a mature person, but everything happened so quickly that I wasn't able to think straight. Please..." I covered his mouth with my hand. I no longer had the strength to endure one more word. He was breaking down, like melting ice, and I couldn't see that.

"Please, don't apologize. It's my fault. I should've waited for you to come back from your trip." I was feeling bad for making him feel this low. Why was he even doing it? I parted my lips to protest again, but he hushed me with his finger on my trembling lips. He held both of my hands now as his eyes pierced deep down into my soul, which was making me anxious with every passing second.

"No, Sarah, not this time. You always concealed my mistakes, but I am not allowing you to do this today. Just give me one chance to apologize to you for my misdeeds. It was so wrong of me to shout at you. I'm so sorry, darling." I just nodded at his vulnerability as he stood up with his back facing me.

"Your tear-filled face didn't let me sleep; it was so unbearable." He turned around and closed the distance between us. Sparks flew by when he caressed my face with the back of his hand.

"Please forgive your man one last time. I promise I won't give you another chance to regret it." And I somehow knew he meant it. His eyes were etched with honesty and kindness.

I didn't know I had been crying until his fingers came up to rub off my tears. More tears flooded my eyes, and he too was on the verge of crying. It was the most delicate moment of our relationship. I rested my head over his heart, finding comfort in his heartbeat.

I did not know how I was ever going to live without him. I didn't have the courage to think about a life where he wouldn't be around me. My life had no purpose without him. I would just become a lifeless vessel if he ever thought of leaving me.

"You know, to make everything go smoothly, I made an appointment for 9 o'clock sharp this morning."

"Hmm." His hand rubbed my back, shooting down a sensation of serenity in my spirit.

"The doctor will be attending you first thing in the morning and you would be free to go home well before evening. Isn't it great?" My head yanked back, now looking into his eyes. Maybe he peeked through the fear in my eyes since he caressed my hair, planting a kiss on my forehead.

"Sarah, love, you don't have to worry about anything. She is one of the best OB/GYN in this town. I've already spoken to her about the matter. Everything will be handled anonymously following complete secrecy. You just have to go there and it will be over before you even feel a sting."

"You are not coming with me?" I abruptly babbled, already finding the answer in his eyes. He looked down briefly, letting out a sigh, and fear struck my heart.

"I so want to, but you know that everyone in town knows my dad. I somehow bailed out from the trip he was supposed to take me yesterday. But I could not be seen visiting a maternity clinic with you. People talk, you know. They will put two and two together in no time and God forbids if the word reached my father. He will make my life a living hell." I could see the sincerity in his eyes. But shouldn't being by my side be his first priority?

"I promise I'll not leave you alone. I'll be there on time. We just can't go together." My heart wanted to believe him, but fear engulfed my soul. I nodded in disappointment.

"I'll wait for you."

Seventeen

Ethan

DAY EIGHTEEN

Y ou know you're in love when you start to evolve into a completely new individual. One small feeling in your heart changes your whole life; brings so much positivity around that you begin to live unconditionally. You become a better version of yourself. Now that I finally understood it, I know why I'd been madly searching for her. It was not because of something I wanted to prove to her; it was because I wanted to find myself. The real Ethan, who had been lost without her.

A mere glimpse of her brings my whole world to a standstill. In fact, she herself had become my small world. I had started smiling just because of her presence in my life. Half the time, I didn't even know I was smiling. It was like some black magic spell had been cast on me. Her happiness meant more than anything to me. Little things about her made me wonder how much these years had changed her. Every single moment spent with her earned me a chance to learn a new thing about her. And all that rendered me to fall in love with her all over again.

The next morning when I regained consciousness on the island, after that fateful night, I went in search for her, but she had already vacated the hotel. I rushed to the airport, but she was nowhere to be found. I wanted to apologize. To her. To her family. I had betrayed each one of them. I wanted to beg on my knees for forgiveness, but fate took that chance away from me.

I raised havoc at the reception desk, seeking the contact details of Starz and her family. But they had explicitly instructed the staff not to disclose their information or they would sue the hotel. Tom dragged me away from the desk, telling me not to create a scene that could attract any paparazzi.

As I returned to my cottage, the hotel manager came down to hand me the keys of my Corvette, which Sarah's brother had blackmailed out of me. There was a small note with it.

'Don't make my sister cry again'.

I got a little agitated that even that little devil, who walked hotel corridors in his bathrobe with a different girl by his side every night, was giving me a chivalrous lesson now. But then an idea struck me. It was quite easy to get his number out of about a dozen girls he had dated on the island. But I didn't call him. As it turned out, finding out someone's address after you know their number was even easier.

So, I went to meet him in person and after a lot of convincing and bribing; I found out about Sarah's workplace from him. Discovering that she was a Doctor, a Resident at Eden Rose General Hospital in Florence, Alabama, filled my spirit with utter warmth. I knew she was a smart girl. Her dream of becoming a doctor and helping other people in need had finally come true. She had turned out to be a lifesaver, the utmost selfless human being.

Getting her address out from the hospital was a cakewalk for Tom. I told you he was a man of all means. I really wanted to congratulate her on pursuing her dream. She was the strongest woman I'd ever met in my life. Even after so many unexpected turns of events in her life, she never gave up and did mold her life in the best possible way.

Initially, I thought of just meeting her once to apologize, but then Tom asked me if I needed a place to stay in Florence and I thought, why not? To my great luck, we found an empty apartment just next to Starz's, and I believed that the Goddess above us was actually giving me a second chance to repent my sins. And I was not going to let it pass this time.

I was going to do my best to show her how I felt about her. How I'd actually changed myself for good. I knew there was no room for me in her heart, but I was ready to dig out my own private basement there. I wanted her to see that we could build a future together. It felt so good to imagine sharing a life with her. Waking up right next to her. Always be there for her in good as well as hard times.

Yesterday's encounter was quite a piece of work. I knew I was testing her patience. But then I also loved that at least things were progressing between us. Even if the progress was in the wrong direction, I was pleased that at least we were moving somewhere. I liked the way she shouted at me. The show of emotions on her face. The hint of tears in her eyes. All of that proved that she still had feelings for me.

I didn't want to stress her or make her feel that I was forcing myself on her, but I had no choice as there were less than thirty days left for her wedding. Shit!

Well, first of all, I needed to jump-start with a little friendship. I need to become a friend of hers and not the annoying jerk I'd been so far. I wished I had some magic so that I could see myself through her eyes, to get a hint of how my presence was affecting her.

I was pacing in my tiny living room for the past one hour, jumping toward the balcony at every slight noise in anticipation of finding Starz to walk up to the building. But she had gone AWOL. She didn't come home last night. I thought maybe she had a night shift and would turn up in the morning, but it was lunchtime already and she was nowhere to be seen. I was anxious after seeing her leave with a bag yesterday, but when she told me she was going to work, I believed her. What if it was a lie, and she had run away once again?

After much self-restraint, I finally dialed her number, ready to pretend again that I didn't recognize her, and address her as 'Not my Sarah'. I couldn't believe she really thought I would not recognize her voice. I could identify her voice in a crowd of million people screaming. I was building some excuse in my mind to talk to her, but the call went straight to voicemail.

That's it! I couldn't wait anymore. Pulling up a shirt over my t-shirt and doing my jeans, I headed downstairs and hailed a cab for the hospital. I was having terrible thoughts sitting in the back seat.

What if Starz was missing, and they were also looking for her?

What if she had resigned from her job and shifted to some faraway place and directed everyone not to disclose her location to me?

What if I could never find her again?

"We are here, sir! That will be twenty dollars." *Wait, what? Have we arrived already?* I was dragged out of my neurosis, observing the hospital building situated right across the street. I paid the driver and crossed the street on my shaking legs.

Better late than never, Ethan. Clearing my throat, I gathered all the nerves that were fidgeting inside me and pushed ajar the glass door. The first thing that struck me was the awful smell of the hospital. Well, what could I expect? Did I ever tell you I hate hospitals?

It really freaks me out seeing so many sick and miserable faces in one place. I even looked it up on the internet and it turned out they have a term for it. It's called Nosocomephobia, or the fear of hospitals. And surprisingly, it was a very common phobia. I always felt like anytime someone would grab me and jab a needle into my skin here. Long story short, I bloody hated hospitals.

I could feel the tingling sensations in my limbs as I went further inside. Rubbing my sweaty palms on my pants, I walked towards the reception and noticed a lady behind the desk arguing with someone on the phone.

"No, Mr. Fox, we haven't received your test results yet!" I plucked up the courage to gain her attention, but she shoved her hand flat at my face to shut my already dying morale.

"As I said before, there is no need to call us ten times a day, Mr. Fox. Ern... yes, sir, I understand that. But we do know how to do our job. Yes. Yes. I totally get that. Fine, I'll let you know the second it arrives. Have a nice day, sir." I jumped a little when she shoved the receiver down a little too harshly while letting out a deep sigh.

"Ma'am?" I attempted to ask her about Sarah's whereabouts when the phone rang once again. "Oh, God!" She exclaimed.

"Eden Rose General Hospital! Yes. Hmm... hmm. Yes, yes, absolutely ma'am. We can reschedule that. Just give me the date and let me check the availability. Yes, we have an 11 AM slot free that day. Okay, ma'am, I am confirming your appointment to be shifted. You need to come empty stomach for the test." Deciding she had no time to answer any of my questions, I turned around to find someone who could be of any help.

"Thank you for calling us. Have a nice day!"

"Yes, Sir, how may I help you?" I turned back as my ears perceived her voice. She wasn't even looking up at me as her eyes and hands were busy on the computer in front of her. But it was okay, as by now I was used to being ignored.

"Well… Good morning, ma'am. I am looking for Dr. Sarah Walter."

"Department?" She asked, still not looking at me and I got confused. She passed a printout to a man behind her and picked up another one when, at the same time, the phone buzzed up again. Oh, come on. I was a little pissed off now. She took off to pick up the receiver, but unexpectedly, I pushed her hand down, disconnecting the call, and, at last, gained her full attention.

She finally raised her eyes from the screen and I wished she hadn't because she was firing lasers from her eyeballs. Man, how can someone be so annoyed even before mid-day? Her one scary eyebrow heaved up to my action, and I stepped back, holding up my hands in peace. "Sorry! But this is urgent!"

"Which department?" She asked, so annoyed that I was glad of the two feet distance between us. The light bulb in my slow brain lit up finally and I answered.

"Oh! Obstet...trics and Gynecology." I stammered awkwardly.

"Second floor," she said, burying her face back into the screen and attending yet another phone call.

There was another reception on the second floor, but this one looked a little less busy. Waiting for my turn, I noticed numerous couples sitting in the waiting area. Ninety percent of them looked heavily pregnant. I could not have felt any more out of place in the midst of them. A couple of them looked up at me and I passed them my best grin of nervousness and in response, they nodded at me, a little confused by my weird expressions. I struggled to settle down, but it was too difficult, as I was still in fright.

People were disappearing and then reappearing from three doors across the hall, which were supposedly OB/GYN OPD. I looked around and observed a nameplate on one of the three doors furnishing a 'Dr. Walter'. Could it be Sarah? Tilting my head at weird angles, I strived to peek into the room whenever somebody walked in or out of the door. But unfortunately, I wasn't able to catch a glimpse of her, nor a tint of her voice. And it was getting on my nerves.

I was nervous, becoming anxious with every passing second. I could feel the panic-stricken formation of sweat in my clasped hands. My foot involuntarily tapped on the floor, eyes glued to that door. Suddenly a panic-ridden lady in blue scrubs walked rushing past me and yanked open 'Dr. Walter's' door and sprinted inside.

A moment later, she emerged from the room with Starz at her tail. My face lit up after seeing her. She was wearing the same clothes she left the house in yesterday, topped with a white lab coat. Hair tied in a messy bun, she looked tired, yet angelic.

"Yes, he is on his way, but I don't think he is going to make it on time. I don't know what to do. Her vitals are dropping, but she is not buzzing. She is just asking for you, Dr. Walter." The lady in scrubs was speed talking.

And then the voice was muffled down to become inaudible. I turned around, with uneasiness seeping into my skin. I tried to think of a possibility that I could be of any help to ease her stress. I didn't even know their condition, but Starz's worrisome face was hard to fade away from my subconscious and it left me even more troubled.

Starz halted at the reception and eyed the lady in the scrubs. "Nurse Polly, I need the labor room ready in five minutes and start the IV." Then she turned toward the woman at the counter. "Joanie, transfer all OPD patients to Dr. West and buzz Shelley," and they both fled out of there.

I was left bewildered. She didn't even notice me. I was standing right in her course, but her mind was too preoccupied with the patient that needed her at the moment. I didn't know why but it made me delighted beholding her all bossy and woman at the frontline attitude. Her aura screamed of power and an achiever temperament.

I tried to keep myself out of sight as I followed them from one door to the other. She was rushing towards her destination while passing friendly nods to fellow doctors and nurses, and I made sure to spot the one who turned around to check out her ass. Well, it's just that a man always knows what other men are thinking.

Anyway, not their fault. She was looking damn hot in that white coat. After endless passageways, we finally arrived outside a room that was tagged as the Maternity Ward. Wait, what? Starz and that nurse Polly rushed inside and I was left all by myself outside with my discomfort overwhelming me. I looked around and spotted some people in what looked like a waiting area and thought about settling back on a bench. It was strange to be seated there.

Well, it was not the room alone that bothered me, but a gang of five kids that were staring at me like I was their favorite ice cream flavor. I waved at them awkwardly and instantly a little girl stood up from her seat and walked toward me. She was maybe around two years old and was holding a worn-out teddy. She gazed up at me so intently that her big brown eyes were making me self-conscious.

"Hello, little human." I attempted to pass her a friendly smile, but she kept on gawking up at me, not even blinking for a second. She scooted too close to me, making my soul tremble in panic. And the minute she placed her head on my lap, I panicked. "Okay, that's too close, princess." Right at that moment, a nurse walked outside the room, allowing me to overhear some heated conversation coming from inside.

"No, Becky, we can't wait any longer. It's been hours since your water broke and I don't think you're understanding this properly, but I can already see baby's head in the birth canal." Starz's voice was filled with a great deal of impatience.

"But he will be here soon. I can keep the baby in. Ahh!" And I jumped out of my skin when a woman's blood-curdling scream fell into my ears. I believed my soul left my body for a second.

"Becky, don't be ridiculous. You are fully dilated. You will give birth any minute now. So, we are done talking here." And with that, another shriek filled the air. Instinctively, I covered the ears of the little girl till the door closed and silence fell upon us. The doors must have been soundproof.

"Is the woman in there your mother?" She nodded and offered me her teddy, whose one eye was missing.

"It's my turn. I'm going to sit next to Amy tomorrow on the bus."

"No, you're a liar. It's my turn tomorrow."

I flipped around and noticed two boys starting up a fight. They appeared to be in the same age group and when I looked closely; they looked like twins. Soon they were rolling on the floor, thrashing each other.

"Are those your big brothers?" The little girl once again nodded at me and then giggled when one landed a punch over the other's face. I stood up, watching one beating another as he was crouching over him and I made my mind to intervene. I rushed to separate them, feeling like the one who was being beaten up was me.

"Come on. How old are you guys? Five?" I grabbed both of them from their collars and separated them out from their little tussle. I shook my head in disappointment, discovering the poor beaten-up kid's torn shirt.

"We are almost six! And who the hell are you?" They both shouted at me at the same time and I was impressed with the synchronization they had.

"Well, I'm the only sane adult here, so you brats have to listen to me. This is not the time to fight. You guys are going to have a sibling soon." I tried my best to sound stern and clear.

"Whatever!" they spoke once again at the exact same time.

"Mr. Ethan?" I paused for a second. My mind was perplexed by the fact that someone called me. My eyes met the same nurse Polly who was having a nervous breakdown a few moments ago, but now she was standing in front of me all relaxed and holding up a smile that seemed forced.

However, my attention soon drifted off when I caught a glimpse of the screaming woman who was being transferred to another room. Oh, my

God. She was going to have a baby soon. I jumped in alarm, hearing her screaming in distress.

"Sir?" The nurse spoke again to me.

"Ahh. Yes, I am Ethan." I gulped down a huge lump that formed in my throat.

"Oh, thank goodness. Come on, sir, Dr. Walter has been waiting for you for ages. Let me escort you to the labor room." What? Where? But the next second, she grabbed me by my forearm and dragged me in. *What is happening?* Starz had been waiting for me! Did she know I was here?

I had a very bad feeling about all this. This was not going in the right direction, as I presumed while stepping inside this hospital. I couldn't quite understand how, but in a few moments I was thrust inside a scary-looking quiet room, and then sooner than I could comprehend what was happening, I was surrounded by people who wrapped me up in a green robe with gloves over my hands, a head cap and finally a face mask that began to suffocate me. I couldn't breathe. How the hell were you supposed to breathe in this?

The nurse shoved me along and my eyes sighted the words 'LABOR ROOM' printed in red as she dragged me in with her. Man, she had a firm grip. The second I placed my foot inside the room with bright light and odd-shaped chairs, I couldn't believe what was in front of my eyes.

"There she is!" The nurse politely whispered near me from behind, but I was frozen dead.

My eyes popped out of their sockets and my breakfast threatened to come out, witnessing the unimaginable scene unfurling in front of me. I don't think I would ever be able to erase it out of my mind in this lifetime. The image of that scene was burned into my retina.

It was a horrendous image of a woman lying on a half bed, with her legs wide open on some kind of stand and a crime scene filled with blood everywhere that made my eyes bleed. She was screaming her lungs out while grabbing her thighs and all the other people around were yelling at her to PUSH! PUSH! PUSH! And I think I felt lightheaded right there.

"Who the fuck is he?" The woman howled at me in pain and I flipped around, ready to flee the hell out of there.

"He is your husband, Mrs. Roland." The crazy nurse said what? *Please, someone, do me a favor and shut the hellhole of this nurse.* She once again grabbed my forearm and pulled me closer to that furious, violent woman. She was sweating profusely. Her face had turned into a big red tomato, ready to burst any second. She stared at me in confusion for a moment and then, all of a sudden, she took my shirt and yanked me too close to her face. I squeezed my eyes shut in fear and clasped my lips together while feeling her hot breath on my face.

"I know you are not my husband, but you are hot and I need somebody to condemn, so let's just pretend for a few seconds or I'll..." and she cried out once more, blasting my eardrums.

"Push, baby. Push! Come on, my cupcake. I'm here now!" I pronounced, caressing her hair. Everyone's head turned towards me in admiration, but I kept my focus.

"Okay, Becky, you are doing great. Now push a little harder." My head yanked towards that familiar voice that came from the person handling the crime scene, and I recognized Starz. I sighed, noticing her beautiful eyes concealed under the safety glasses. She was looking gorgeous even under a face mask.

"Yes! It's coming. The baby is coming. Would you like to witness this beautiful view, Mr. Roland?" Y*es, the baby is coming. This is good news.* I was grinning at Starz.

"Mr. Roland?" She repeated.

"She is calling you, idiot!" Wait, what? I looked down at Becky and she appeared pissed while all the other people in there had their eagerly awaiting eyes glued on me and I simply nodded in Starz's direction.

I was doomed. I had no idea what I was even doing in this room. But I needed to get this baby out. It was like I owed something to this screaming lady from my past life. I carried my dying tormented essence towards Starz. All this time striving to keep my eyes fixed on her beautiful face rather than the bloody mesh I was going to witness soon.

I could feel her smiling at me from behind her mask. Starz was encouraging me. But was it enough? If I die of a heart attack right now, will it be considered a murder or a suicide?

"Come on, Mr. Roland. This is a beautiful miracle." She once again tried to cheer me up, but my insides were screaming in terror. I wanted to jump out of the window if it could save me from a cardiac arrest. But I knew I was sentenced to be guillotine, as I looked beyond the green cloth and then I believe I was paralyzed.

"Oh. My. Fuckin' balls! You're going to die, woman." I screamed after witnessing an actual bloody nightmare. There was so much blood that I couldn't believe how she was still alive. The heaven in between the legs of a woman had been turned into hell.

The woman yelled while having another contraction, but I couldn't support her now because I was numb. My horror-stricken eyes had seen enough, and now they had gone blank. My brain did a backflip, and I blinked vigorously, struggling against the blackout that was threatening my sight. I was mortified to the soul.

"Are you okay, Mr. Roland?" Starz asked, but I gave her my 'talk to the hand' gesture and turned around.

"Where's the wastebasket?" I politely asked another doctor and the second she gestured towards it, I removed my mask and threw up. I spat my guts out. I was going to blackout any time now. My senses were getting softer and weaker. I accepted the support of the nearby wall to keep myself steady and calculated that I needed some IV for myself too.

But then the baby's cry filled the room and my head yanked straight back up to the site of the bloodbath. My senses spun back to attentiveness. The baby had arrived. I'd become a father. I rushed towards Starz, noticing her cutting the cord and handing the baby to the nurse.

"Congratulations, Mr. Roland. It's a boy!" I witnessed the nurse checking and cleaning the smallest human I had ever seen, and then she handed me the cleaned baby wrapped in a fresh cloth and my eyes became watery. I'd never been this happy. I was over the moon.

"I've become a father." I turned towards Starz, but she was busy with thread and needle doing something which I didn't want to see. I was crying in pure joy.

"We have become parents, Cupcake. It's a miracle." I sobbed while holding the baby closer to my face. Someone pulled at my jeans and I noticed Becky. Oh! She is here. It's her baby. Not mine and Sarah's. I was trying to wrap my head around the reality of the situation.

Just as I handed her the newborn, she pulled me into a deep, longing kiss. I grunted, struggling to pull back, but she took her time and when she finally loosened her grip on my shirt, I ran towards Starz to share my happiness.

"Congratulations, Mr. Roland." She drew out her hand for me to shake, but it froze mid-air for some reason. Grabbing her hand, I pulled her into a tight hug, leaving no place for air between us. God! That felt so right. I couldn't quite recall when I felt this good while hugging someone. I could feel her heart beating against my chest, and I sighed in relief. I sniffed into her hair, smelling lavender that left me a little dizzy. The moment right there felt so wrong, yet so true. I wanted to stay there forever.

She fitted perfectly in my arms. Her touch only made me want for more, but I sensed her struggle to get out of the hug and so I loosened my grip but ended the hug with a light peck on her cheek.

"I'm so lucky!" I exclaimed as she just nodded at me in disbelief, her mouth making a perfect 'O', confusion written all over her face, and then I ran off to hug the other medical staff. The atmosphere inside the room was so warm and joyful. However, shortly after that, we were interrupted by some commotion proceeding from outside the door. All heads turned towards the door when it was yanked open.

"You can't go inside, sir!"

"Please don't kill me, honey. I was stuck in traffic." An almost bald man came rushing in, begging for forgiveness on his knees. I took several steps back when panic crossed my heart as I noticed Starz perplexedly staring at the real Mr. Roland and then towards me. Towards my unmasked face. I could easily read when reality dawned in her staggered eyes.

"Well, here goes nothing!"

Eighteen

Sarah

DAY EIGHTEEN continues…

"I swear I have nothing to do with that lady!"

"I just wanted to see you, Starz! You didn't come home last night and there was a bag on your shoulder when you left yesterday. I just had to confirm that you didn't flee again. I was just about to leave when the nurse dragged me in. It wasn't even my fault."

"Okay. Fine! I'm sorry for kissing you. But I couldn't help it!"

"But, just so you know. After seeing you in those blue scrubs, I think you are my morphine because you're taking my pain away, baby!"

I was dashing out of the Labor Room and Ethan was at my heels shouting answers to unasked questions. His frantic voice echoed all around the maternity ward, forcing me to hide my face in my hands.

I was flustered, horrified, and tried to look anywhere but him. I couldn't believe what my eyes were witnessing. This was really happening to me. My nightmare had come true. I was indeed officially humiliated at my workplace and now I needed to pack my bags, change my identity, and leave this country.

I shot him a dirty look when he was grinning at me like a light bulb. Security guys were yanking him towards the exit, but he didn't miss a second to humiliate me further. For a moment I flinched in concern, watching him getting squashed between two well-built guards.

A flush crept up my cheeks, noticing the audience that had gathered to witness the drama. I tried to lay low and hide my face behind some reports I had in my hands, but it was a futile attempt against Ethan's circus. I was struggling hard to preserve whatever dignity I'd left with, seeing that even the senior doctors had joined us and were enjoying the little carnival.

"Just take him already! Please!" I screamed through clenched teeth. I was surviving the most embarrassing moment of my professional life. God, why do all the wrong things happen to me? I begged Mother Nature to open up and swallow me when people began to exchange curious stares between me and Ethan. No, Sir. I don't know this man. *Nope! Never seen him before.*

"Oh, my goodness! I love drama!" My back stiffened as a dangerously familiar voice caressed my ears. "Dude, bring out some soda and popcorn. I am busy capturing this art piece on my phone. Damn! Who is this, hotshot?" I already had a solid urge to roll my eyes, thinking about the aftermath of this event.

"What's going on here? What did I miss?" Another familiar voice came into the picture and I wished the Hospital had some kind of magic cabinet like Narnia from where I could escape from all this torment. It was absolute misery.

"Chill, man. I can walk on my own. No need for this hospitality." I smirked, watching him finally walking towards the exit in peace. Observing that the drama had concluded, I headed to the on-call room, letting out a deep sigh. My mind was already working on making up a cover-up story about all this chaos.

Just as I opened the door, I witnessed my fellow resident Shelly gathered around half a dozen staff members. "You guys won't believe what happened to us in the labor room. You know, the senior obstetrician had gone to St. Brooklyn hospital for some medical conference. And unfortunately, Sarah and I got stuck with this stubborn woman, who was in an advanced stage of labor but wanted to wait for her husband to come before birth. Long story short, this idiot appeared from nowhere and imposed himself as her husband during the whole procedure. Or maybe he was a baby stealer." I let out a deep breath of relief when Shelly got lost in her thoughts and opted out from sharing further details.

But, I had celebrated a little too early because the next second she shouted, "Holy cow, I almost forgot, he kissed Sarah." Shelley pushed her glasses further in, finally noticing me standing at the door just when she was done with her mind-blowing narration.

"Shut the door, Sarah! What happened next? Hurry up, spill the beans, you lucky girl!" She poked my shoulder and my nose wrinkled in disgust. I tried to avoid her strange smirk when I felt a firm grip on my forearm as Melissa, a resident from the Pediatrics department and my only true friend in the Hospital, whirled me towards her.

"Holy shit. Was it just a peck or a full-blown make-out session? Wait a second, aren't you engaged or married or something?" Shouted another resident. *Why is no one on duty right now?* Nodding my head while looking down, I stepped inside and tried to walk past those two overly enthusiastic girls, but they didn't budge an inch. I was desperately trying to avoid eye contact with any of them and walked in casually.

"Oh, it was just a misunderstanding. He just mistook me for someone else. Maybe he was there for you, Shelly." I tried to laugh it off, but none of them looked convinced. I folded my hands at my chest stubbornly and was ready to shove them out of the way when I got paged and so I escaped the little gossip party, excusing myself with a fake smile.

I attempted to get back to work, but it was really hard since my head was a mess. I was having a hard time concentrating. Maybe I was being paranoid, but the fear of what Ethan would do next wasn't leaving me alone. From the moment he had come back into my life, I'd been having a hard time finding any peace.

I was wrong to underestimate him. He was a cunning man with well-formed plans. And he was gradually making his way into my life. First my family, now my work. He wished to unsettle every aspect of my life. Not limiting himself at anything. I was sure something big was cooking in his empty brain and before it gets too late I had to find it out. I needed to be careful at every step.

I shook my head, struggling to come out of all these twisted apprehensions. Maybe I was just overthinking all this and nothing bad would happen. Checking the next person on my list, I entered the patient's room for a follow-up. "How have you been feeling, Mrs. Fisher?" I plastered a smile on my face despite the hurricane raising havoc in my head.

✧

DAY NINETEEN

I ditched going home again last night because I didn't want to face Ethan. I swear I wanted to kill him, but at the same time, there was this small part in my brain who wanted to see him every day.

The incident at my parents' anniversary had proved to be much more than what it looked like from outside. My mind kept going back again and again to all the anger outbursts at the dance floor. And I eventually deduced that it had provided me some kind of closure. I realized that I diverged all my emotions and rage from the past nine years in that slap and was now free from a very heavy burden that I didn't even know I was carrying around. I had actually forgiven him, not only for the sake of my mental peace but from my heart as well. I had been feeling so light and ready to happily move on with my life, finally forgetting the past. But then he showed up here and everything got messed up again.

So I decided it was better to stay hidden at the hospital for a while. I knew it was a stupid move. I couldn't avoid him forever and would have to face him, eventually. But right now I was not in the mood to confront him or, for that matter, my own confused feelings, to be precise.

And to make matters worse, Lucas had not called or texted or even responded to my texts in the past 48 hours. I knew he must be busy with his work, but I was his fiancée, for God's sake. This was not the first time he had ghosted me, but it was hitting differently for the first time. Maybe it was because of the fact that we were supposed to be married by now or because of Ethan's presence. I didn't really know, and I was not sure I even wanted to know.

So, taking the safe side, I decided to camp at the Doctor's lounge and asked Mrs. Jenkins to take care of Finn like I usually did when I had a busy week at the hospital. She might hate my guts, but her kids loved Finn and were more than happy to earn some extra bucks I gave them for their help.

Thankfully, the day passed without any embarrassing event like yesterday. After a couple of hours of routine rounds on my patients, I called off the day. It was already six in the evening and I needed nothing from this day but to have a nice warm shower and a welcoming, cozy bed. I wrote the last entry in the record book at the nurses' station while stroking my neck, feeling my aching muscles stinging gravely.

After that, I entered the locker room, and just as I noticed Melissa sitting on the bench, reading some fashion magazine, I turned around, trying to dodge the inevitable talk. But I realized it was too late as she said, "Well, you can't keep avoiding the only sane person at your workplace." I grimaced, already regretting the decision of coming here instead of heading home for a shower. I squeezed my eyes shut and gritted my teeth, trying to come up with a better comeback.

"Melissa, I promise it was all just a misunderstanding. I'll tell you everything tomorrow. I just don't have the energy for all this right now." I tried not to blink in order to avoid being caught in my lie. Her skeptical eyeballs examined me and I felt like I had failed a test and was now being evaluated by my strict mother.

"Okay, call it what you want, but it looks like the lover boy is in no mood to leave you quite yet." My eyebrows drew in, puzzled. What? She gestured towards the window with her head and I cursed under my breath.

"No way in hell!"

"Tell me about it, girl." Her eyes never left the magazine as I rushed towards the window, while mentally praying this was not happening to me. He just couldn't be here again after all the humiliation of yesterday!

But, I was proved wrong yet again. He was right there, standing on the main street, savoring a burger whilst looking like a lost tourist. I stared in uncertainty as he held out his half-eaten burger and started having a conversation with it. I was certain he even blew out a kiss towards the sky. Might be thanking whoever uncovered the paradox of discovering burgers. He had completely lost his marbles. *Good, now I can prove to the police that a psychopath is living next door.*

"I'm going to exorcise the love shit out of him," I murmured and then turned around, promptly throwing my things into the locker, before dashing out.

"Don't forget to mention my name to Sugar-Lips!" Melissa's voice echoed behind me.

Pushing open the front door, I marched straight towards him, tugging my handbag back on my shoulder. But he was gone. My eyes searched the neighborhood, but he was nowhere to be found. It seemed like he had disappeared into thin air. My brows snapped together in annoyance. What the hell? A while ago, he was gobbling down food, like he hadn't eaten for centuries, and the next second he just vanished. Maybe God finally heard my prayers.

"If I were you, I would go right." My head snapped up at the voice and witnessed the self-proclaimed only sane person in my workplace hanging out from the window with her hand signaling me to go right.

God, I'm surrounded by buffoons. Pulling my handbag closer to my shoulder, I started on the sidewalk. I was not sure where I was heading in particular. There was a cafe only a few meters away from my hospital. I thought to ditch the plan of finding that moron and get a coffee for my migraine instead. But then I noticed him trying to hide behind a tiny menu.

"So invading my house was not enough that you have started stalking me at my workplace, too?" A line appeared between my brows as I waited for the wonderful response he was about to come up with. My eyes drifted off towards his moves just as he put down the menu on the table and let out a sheepish chuckle. Rubbing the back of his head, he stood up, and I folded my hands on my chest, still waiting for his reply.

"Stalking is such a wrong word, Miss. I'd prefer one human being carrying out a passionate study of another." There it was, the perfect Ethan Stanton reply. He took some steps towards me and was about to open his mouth again when I held up my palm and twirled around; already feeling annoyed by his presence. Letting out a deep sigh, I started to march back towards the hospital parking.

Shaking my head in denial about his reparative dim attempts, I dug my hand in my handbag searching for my car keys. I tried my best to engulf my anger and not lash out at him in the middle of the street. I struggled hard to divert my mind from him, but it was difficult when he kept on babbling gibberish all along, walking next to me.

"If you are searching for your keys in there, then let me give you a quick recall, doctor. You took a favor from your concierge this morning to take your car to the garage, since you were having trouble with the engine." Oh crap! My shoulders slumped in realization as I grasped my forehead in displeasure.

"Not that I'm complaining, but I could've easily fixed it for you with my strong and skilled arms." My eyes went round when he ran his hand into his hair and then kissed his biceps, making a terrible effort to show his muscles.

Shit, how could I forget to pick up my car in the afternoon? I checked my watch and let out a groan as it was showing quarter past six. Great, the garage must be closed by now. *You are responsible for it, Sarah. Now live with it!*

Wait! I suddenly halted my steps and turned around. "How do you know that? How long have you been stalking me?" I was beyond angry now. Had he been keeping an eye on me in the hospital all day? *What a creep!*

"Hey, it's not like what you are thinking. I saw someone taking your car and thought he might be stealing it. So when I confronted him he told me that he works with you and you have asked him for a favor." All of a sudden, his tone became defensive, washing away that annoying smirk off his face.

"Starz, you have to listen to me." I shook my head as he approached me and I backed up.

"You didn't give me one chance to explain myself yesterday and didn't come home again last night. So, I had no alternative but to come here to check on you. I was just hoping to get a chance to have a normal chat with you." I was annoyed to the limit by then.

"Yeah? Okay, you want to talk? Then talk." I lifted an eyebrow and glared at him when all of a sudden, his face turned all serious.

"Starz, I know you won't believe me, but I am really sorry for crossing the line. I know I gave you enough reasons to hate me. But believe me when I say I've realized what an idiot I can be sometimes, and I swear I have no funny business this time."

He searched my face for some kind of response, but discerning he was not going to get one; he continued. "I'm so proud of you, Starz. You really did it. You've become a doctor and have your own apartment. You have made a place for yourself in the world like you always used to say you will".

"Umm… Thank you!" I was kind of stunned that he remembered my future plans from High School.

"I'm sorry if I'm rushing in. But, Starz, I think I really am falling for you. Or in fact, I never ever got over you." I flinched at that, but he continued speaking as if trying to rush all the words out before he couldn't speak anymore.

"I know you don't feel anything for me and Romano is way better a person than I can ever be. I am not expecting anything from you. I just wanted to apologize and I know you have forgiven me, but I know you still loath me and that's something I can't make peace with." My head shot up and my mind went blank.

"I know I don't deserve you, Starz. Not now, not ever. I was a total jerk back then and I can't tell you how sorry I am for what I have done. But I want to amend things. I just want to be a part of your life. To be friends with you..." I raised my hand up, cutting his monologue. My head started spinning, and I had to close my eyes to make it stop. I couldn't listen anymore. None of it made any sense.

Shaking my head, I turned around, looked at both sides, and sprinted to cross the street. I heard him calling after me, but I paid no attention. I needed to stay far away from him to keep my sanity intact. His words were echoing in my head. I was still grasping at the fact that he had been here the whole freaking day.

"Starz? Starz! Sarah Rose Walter!"

"What?" I barked, whipping my head back, looking straight into his eyes. I was trying hard not to let the tears spill from my eyes.

He must have seen something on my face that made him decide not to say anything. So I ignored him and hailed a cab home.

❧

DAY TWENTY

By the time I reached home last night, my head was throbbing and my breath was coming out ragged. But seeing Finn wagging his tail as soon as I climbed up the stairs calmed me a little. I fed him and warmed some canned soup for myself. After finishing our meals in silence, we turned in for the night.

It felt like Finn somehow understood my state of mind and was cuddling me for comfort. But despite the comfort of his warm fur, sleep was difficult to come. I slept in short spells each time, waking up with a startle. The memories from the past were haunting me. Memories that I had buried all those years ago and promised myself to never visit again.

My eyes opened with the sound of doorbell and I observed the sun peeking from behind the curtains. I was in no mood to rise and contemplated calling sick for work when the bell rang again. Half-heartedly, I left the comfort of my bed and opened the door.

Ethan was standing in front of me, a good three feet away from the front door, with the same lopsided grin on his face that I fell in love with in high school but had started to hate now.

"What part of 'NO' you don't understand, Stanton? I don't want to see you. Period! You know, it's never too late to shut up and mind your own business." I was so tired. I didn't even have the energy to be angry with him.

"Do you have any idea how adorable you look when you come in all mama bear's form?" Out of nowhere, he came forward and pinched my cheeks. I squeezed my eyes shut as pain crept up my face, and I slapped his hands away to get him out of my personal space.

"Oh, God! What will it take for you to leave me alone?" He was acting as if yesterday's conversation had never happened.

"We can start with a meal. After all, a neighbor is like a second family and family should eat together! And I am really sick of take-outs." I glared at him, but he averted his eyes away, admiring the wall next to me.

"Fine!" I blurted out and for a split second, I didn't know who was more surprised by my answer. Him or me?

"Wow! I hadn't expected you to agree so easily. I came prepared to get down on my knees and beg."

"Well, here is the deal; I'll help you get your shit together, like buying some real food, teaching you a little bit about cooking, and, most importantly, how to be less annoying to your neighbors. But you have to promise me that you will stop tormenting my innocent soul the very second after that!"

Our cynical stares held each other at the place. As if daring each other to back out of the deal with our eyes. We were leaning on each other, trying to create a hard stare. To find out how serious the other person was. Trying to read each other's minds.

"We have a deal, Miss Walter."

"Very well, Mr. Stanton, it's done, then!" He extended a hand at me and I certainly shook it with a firm grip. Staring deep into his blue eyes all along, surveying carefully his masked face to find any kind of mischievous plans.

"I need to go to work. Meet me outside the hospital at around 6 in the evening, and order some pizza till then." And I slammed the door in his face.

❦

To say that the day passed in a blur would be a big lie. I found myself checking time on the clock every hour or so in the beginning and every fifteen minutes after lunch. By the time it was five in the evening, I was trembling with anxiety. What the hell had I agreed for? What was I thinking?

I called Lucas to tell him all about Ethan, but we ended up talking about his work and then he had to end the call abruptly as his client arrived for a meeting. So the topic of Ethan never came up. He did apologize for not responding to my calls and texts the past couple of days. He was busy with this high-profile case, which would confirm his place as a partner in the firm.

I headed to take a shower to calm my nerves, but by the time I logged out for the day, I was sweating again with fear and anticipation. I was praying hard that Ethan wouldn't show up. I even considered slipping out of the backdoor through the emergency exit and hailing a cab home. My car was still in the garage as the guy who took it was on leave today and I couldn't escape my shift to go pick it up myself.

At six in the evening, I peeked down from the window, hoping against all odds that Ethan would not be there. But he was already waiting on the sidewalk by the exit door with a small bouquet of flowers. Seeing the flowers, I realized what a bad idea it was, and I decided to head down and tell him to stay away.

But when I reached him, the flowers were gone. He was standing there with both hands shoved in the pockets of his khaki shorts. His black shirt looked so crisp as if he ironed it just minutes ago. He looked quite nervous.

"Good evening, neighbor." He said with so much sincerity in his voice that all my anxiety washed off.

"Hey, my car is still in the garage, so we will have to take a cab to the supermarket."

"Okay. But just so you know, I'm a little short on cash. Would you mind if we share the cab fare?" An involuntary laugh escaped my mouth before I could stop it. I surveyed his face to find the amusement. But when I noticed him scratching his head in embarrassment, my eyebrows rose. He was not kidding at all; the chatterbox was actually serious and felt ashamed about asking for financial aid.

A chuckle left my mouth, experiencing the opportunity where a millionaire or maybe billionaire was asking for money from a person like me. My bottom lip was pulled back between my teeth, seeing him wincing in awkwardness. He shoved his hands deep in the pockets and, after a while, greeted my eyes with an adorable crease at the bridge of his nose. I tried my best to suppress a smile and not to get affected by him. Putting on my straight face to not make fun of him, I replied.

"Well then, I guess, you would be indebted to me till the end of this world, Mr. Stanton." I winked at him just as a cab halted in front of us. As the cab rolled down the road, I saw a beautiful bunch of white lilies in the hands of a little girl playing down the lane.

By the time we reached the store, I already felt worn out. The place was jam-packed at this hour. Children were running in the aisles, perhaps playing some type of hide and seek. We witnessed more than one toddler lying flat on the floor, whining to buy something in particular, and embarrassed parents apologizing to everyone. But I was somehow relieved that our trolley was almost filled with every essential item that could keep him alive for almost a month.

"You know, Starz, I keep on thinking about you and just a thought of you make these strange bubbles blow up in my stomach. Do you know what I've been going through?" I looked back, the corner of my mouth turning up. Was he trying to flirt with me? He better not. I shook my head, watching him leaning over the trolley with one hand underneath his chin. The same stupid cheesy grin furnished his face, which I was foolish enough to fall for back in high school.

"Stomach gas. It can be a symptom of colon cancer. You should definitely consult a doctor or maybe just wait for the agonizing, brutal death." I replied with the most serious expressions I could muster. His hand slipped off his chin as he straightened up, composing himself.

"Or I should just stop drinking so much soda."

"Well, carbonated drinks only damage the liver. Try poison. Guaranteed effect!" I nodded with pursed lips at him and turned to the next aisle.

I couldn't believe that he really thought I would fall into his trap all over again. His cheap sweet talks and gestures were just an entertainment show for me now and nothing more. I wished sooner or later he would open his eyes and see the real world, rather than living in his fantasyland.

I walked towards the dairy products section and while searching over the items, my eyes fell over a cheese jar, and I leaped over to take it. *Short girl problem 101, when you can't reach the top shelf in the supermarket and it gets really embarrassing.* But before I would've taken another jump, a tanned muscular arm came next to my face and grabbed the item that I had been struggling to attain. I settled back on my feet and looked over at the person with my brows snapping together.

"Here, beautiful." A fine piece of dreamy eyes encountered mine as I saw how handsome my savior was. His big torso was engulfing me completely. He scratched his beard, keeping good eye contact, and I couldn't help but put on a goofy smile. My eyes drifted towards his hand as he extended the jar.

"Thank you!"

"Oh, no need for that. It's my pleasure. I just saw you struggling there…" But before he could've completed his sentence, a heavy trolley hit him from the side. And I realized it was my trolley. My head tilted to the right, shooting daggers at Ethan. He pulled back his hands from the handle of the trolley and looked everywhere but us when the handsome guy gave him a stern look.

"Anyway, I'm Ben, and you?"

"She is leaving!" My gaping face closed up when Stanton pulled me away. I frowned, feeling utterly displeased. *What does he think of himself?* I shot him a dirty look, which he totally misunderstood, as he pushed the trolley forward, tugging me along with him, and I was dragged away from Mr. Darcy.

"Stanton, we are forgetting the fresh apples." I tugged at him to slow down.

"I don't eat apples!" He affirmed, and my frown deepened.

"What? Why?"

"Because an apple a day keeps the doctor away!" He winced back in pain when I gave him a hard shove in the stomach with my purse.

"That's the worst joke I've ever heard, Stanton." We finally reached the billing counter. The lady behind the counter shook her head, fighting back a smile.

As soon as Ethan left my hand so that he could pull items out of the trolley, I stormed outside the store with my arms folded around me. I felt a flick of irritation and resentment grew inside me when I caught him stealing glances at my way.

"Shit! Global warming is real!" He said, coming out with his hands full.

I shot him a side glare, and he shrugged his shoulders in defense. But fortunately, a cab pooled in by our side and I let out a breath of relief. As Ethan placed the groceries in the trunk, I opened the door and climbed in. I relaxed my back in the back seat when I took in the sight of Stanton climbing into the passenger seat. Thank goodness.

When the next couple of minutes went smoothly, I closed my eyes, relaxing back on the headrest. The quiet surrounding diffused peace throughout my body and I smiled, feeling the gentle movement of the cab loosening up my aching muscles. I could feel the softness dwelling in my chest and if someone had not spoken up, I would've definitely drifted into a dreamless sleep.

"Man, you look miserable. What happened?" Ethan's voice pulled me out of peace and I peeped towards the front row with one eye.

"Nothing, pal. It's just my wife. She thinks I'm having an affair. I did everything to make her believe me, but she just doesn't want to hear anything. I love her, man."

"Dude, let me give you some advice. Call off tonight's shift. Go home early to surprise your girl and make love to her, like the first night."

"Thanks, brother." They half hugged each other and my eyes bored into them. My jaw went slack as I was stupidly gawking at them. What the fuck did I just witness? I couldn't believe what was going on in front of my eyes. Throughout the ride, my eyes swapped from Ethan to the cab driver. Capturing Ethan's amusing expressions in the rearview mirror, I stumbled back, folding my hand over my chest and averting my eyes outside the window.

"Oh, let me tell you a joke to brighten your mood, dude. A wife complains to her husband 'Just look at the couple down the road, how lovely they are. He keeps holding her hand, kissing her, opening the door for her. Why can't you do the same?'" I rolled my eyes when Ethan's mimicking voice sounded nothing like a woman but some choking cat.

"Then the husband replied, 'Are you mad? I barely know that woman!'" They burst out laughing like it was the funniest joke on this planet. And I couldn't hold back the smile that was furnishing my lips now. Well, a smile is contagious, and seeing their hysterical snickering, I was struggling hard to hold back mine. The joke wasn't half bad. It was all bad. *Someone shoot me, already.*

Soon enough, our car ride came to an end, and after paying the driver, I turned towards Stanton, who was struggling to hold all the bags together. While taking some sacks from his hand, we started heading upstairs but didn't exchange any words, yet the amused look on both of our faces was certainly telling us that we were tolerable until the next encounter.

Climbing up the last stair, I moaned out of exhaustion. He passed me and unlocked his door while balancing all the items in one hand. A line appeared between my brows, seeing him scratching his head while giving me a sheepish look at the same time.

"What?" *I swear if he has his underpants hanging in the living room, I'm leaving.*

"I don't have much in here. But soon I'll get some things done." I walked past him and found myself standing inside an almost empty apartment. I'd been here before but I was appreciating his apartment properly for the first time now, which seemed just like mine but more empty.

My eyes drifted from one old worn-out couch to a small coffee table overflowing with stacks of empty pizza boxes. Moving towards the kitchen, I noticed a kettle on the stove. I didn't bother to even check the fridge and turned around to appreciate Ethan's anxious face.

"Wow! Please tell me at least the gas stove works."

"Yeah, I just got it fixed!" The thrilling tone in his voice was certainly telling me how much he was proud of it. Placing the packets in my hand on the kitchen counter unfurled a cloud of dust in the air and I wrinkled my nose.

"This place really needs some work, mate!" I could tell he was actually embarrassed and even if he was here to make my life hell, I felt bad at that moment for making him feel ashamed. Thus, letting out a deep breath, I walked toward him and placed both my hands over his shoulder. Saying he was surprised by my action would be an understatement.

"Don't get your hopes up. I just want to say if you want to eat home-cooked dinner, then put on some great music and pour a glass of wine for me." And with that, I swirled around and got to work.

After cleaning the countertop first, I hurried to wash my hands and then started to unpack the grocery bag. A chuckle escaped my lips when soothing jazz music floated in the air, caressing my ears with its elegance. I looked over and found Ethan cleaning up the table and packing the trash bag with all disposable boxes. My face lit up when he opened the balcony gate and ginger-colored brightness filled the room and a comforting breeze struck my hair.

"Okay, tell me what should I do next?" I looked up as he handed me a glass of wine. I didn't notice when he changed his clothes and was now wearing a striped t-shirt and pajama shorts. He was looking nice and comfortable.

"You can slice the tomatoes. But please don't dismember your fingers. I don't want to ruin my sweet tomatoes." I handed him the tomatoes and knife and he bowed, accepting my command. I placed the pasta to boil on the stove and started preparing the sauce. Unknowingly, we settled into a friendly chatter. Seeing the weird faces he was making while handling the knife with utter concentration, I was having a hard time hiding my smile.

After he diced the tomatoes, I showed him how to make the batter to dip chicken wings before frying. The oil sizzled in the pan as I placed chicken wings in it, and Ethan jumped two feet out of fear. I couldn't hold back myself and laughed out loud, bending double.

I didn't realize where the time flew by, among his stupid jokes and my frowning. And at last, I was almost done with the pasta and chicken wings. I leaned over the stove, sniffing the mouth-watering aroma of food, and a low moan escaped my throat. God, I was hungry.

"Now, go freshen up chef de cuisine. This server will set the table." Shaking my head on his overdramatic action, I headed for the washroom to freshen up a little. I couldn't emphasis more: a few splashes of cold water can do wonders on a deadbeat body.

Strolling back towards the living room, I was wiping my face with a towel when I noticed something weird. The lights were dimmer than before. And my eyes narrowed when they landed on the decoration on the coffee table. Candles were burning in the middle of the food and empty plates with cutlery surrounded it.

"Stanton, please don't tell me this is a date?" My screeching voice smacked him and he jumped up from the couch. His startled eyes met mine and then they shifted towards the table. A muscle in my jaw twitched as I felt a flash of irritation.

"Oh! No! No! No! No! This is not what it looks like." He quickly switched on the light and blew out the candles and then rushed toward me, but I held out my hand to stop him midway.

"I swear; I didn't mean that! It's just a stupid thing I read in some lifestyle magazine. It was supposed to relieve stress. I swear, Starz!" My eyes bored into him, surveying his face sharply.

"Okay, fine. It's just that I'm so starving that I can't even fight right now. But tell me, were you really trying to be romantic?" I uttered, settling down on the couch and filling my plate with everything present on the table.

"Occasionally, I'm romantic." He shrugged like it was not a big deal and landed on the couch, but fortunately at the far corner.

"So, tell me, Stanton, what are you really doing here?" Crossing my legs up and placing my plate in my lap, I turned towards him, who was busy devouring the pasta like he hadn't eaten in centuries.

"What?" He barely uttered a word with his stuffed mouth. He had already gobbled down half of the food on his plate and it seemed like my question intruded on his luscious moment. Struggling to gulp down the pasta in his mouth, he took a sip of wine and turned toward me.

"Well, you won't believe me even if I tell you the truth, so let's play a game."

"You have my attention."

"Two truths and a lie. If I win, I'll tell you my main purpose of coming here, but if you lose, you will have to promise a real date with me." My eyes narrowed at him as he raised his one brow, waiting for a response.

"You know I am engaged." I gave him an obvious gaze.

"Oh yes, I am well aware of that. Don't worry, I will not harass you. If you don't want to call it a date, fine, call it just a simple dinner at some restaurant with a neighbor."

I had this feeling that he was challenging me with something that I could win easily. Thus I nodded.

"Okay, I'll go first." I put down the plate on the table and, after taking a sip of the wine, I clenched my hands together in excitement.

"I can play guitar. I collect fuzzy socks. One of my cousins is a porn star!" I took in the sight of his grim, serious face as he narrowed his eyes at me. We were having a strong, no-blinking competition. The lines on my forehead hardened when I turned a blank face.

"First and second are truths, and third is definitely a lie." He replied confidently and yanked his collar up, looking too cocky.

"Ha! Wrong. I truly have a porn star cousin, and I wish I had collections of fuzzy socks." His face dulled as all of his cocky expressions faded away at my victory.

"Wow, it must be that blondie giving me weird eyes in Hawaii, the one your brother was shaking."

"I won't agree or disagree, but I won that one." I jumped in excitement. I guess the wine was gaining on me.

"Oh, don't be so pleased, Starz. My turn hasn't come yet!" He countered, trying to put up a stern face, but his eyes were smiling. I shrugged him off while flipping my hair with a smirk plastering my lips.

"Okay! I once rode a horse to a bar. I still live with my Nanna. And I am a vegetarian." He took a mouthful of drink and then settled back in his place, giving me a smile that was waiting for my answer.

"Hmm, it's simple. We are having chicken wings, so that clearly means the third is a lie." I screamed at his face and stood up on the couch, doing a happy dance that I'd won this game.

"Well, it was the first one, Starz." I frowned at my place, as my eyes landed on his wincing face. What? He would've told me if he was a vegetarian. I settled back in my place and stared at him intensely.

"Crazyhead, why didn't you tell me before? I was teaching you all the while how to fry chicken. Wait, you rode a horse to the pub? No, you still live with your Nanna? Shit, you are hilarious Stanton." I crackled up, giving him an encouraging pat on the shoulder.

"Okay, okay, enough embarrassment for one day. Now that we are equal, it's your chance to break the tie." After enjoying a great laugh, I composed myself and began to think of what I should say to him. Looking at the ceiling with squinting eyes, I rubbed my jaw and in that instant, a question popped in my brain.

"I've got a tattoo on one of my jugs. Once, I had sex with a pizza delivery guy. And Ash scratched your car the day you two broke out in an official combat!"

"What the fuck! I'm so going to kill that bitc… big, beautiful brunette. What's with you and pizza guys? Please, I don't even want to hear the answer. Not another word, you win!" He threw his hands in surrender when a big grin furnished my face.

"Now come with me!" He spoke standing up, and a line appeared between my brows when he held out his hand. He smiled, noticing my intense stare jumping from his hand to his face.

"I won't bite. I promise!" He grinned. Shaking my head in disbelief, I took his hand standing up to his level. We walked towards the balcony sitting area and then stopped at a chair lying in the middle of it. I didn't know what we were precisely doing there, but I waited patiently.

"Close your eyes!" And as expected, totally conflicting to his request, my eyes widened up, welcoming a chuckle from him. "Just trust me on this! Please!"

"Just remember, I'll kill you if you try any funny business!" And I closed my eyes. A smile stayed on my face, with my heart racing up at the thought of him around me. A strange feeling overtook me for a second. I sensed him standing too close to me, a brush of hot breath, and then it faded away. I felt bare.

"I love it when you give me death threats. It makes me like you even more." His voice sounded distant, and I let out a breath of relief. It was just a false alarm.

"When one door closes, another opens, just like when you let go of something, something else holds you back!" My brows narrowed together at his strange words and when I opened my eyes, an expression of surprise fluttered me. He was standing there with a guitar in his hands.

"Are you kidding me?" I shook my head with a blush veiling my face. Why was I blushing?

"Come on, you just accepted that you can play!" And with that, he shoved the guitar in my hands. For a good minute, I just stood there, not sure whether I should storm off from his apartment or jump off from that balcony.

My eyes averted away from his as I replied with a bashful smile, "I can't!"

I tried to hand him back the guitar, but he just ignored it. Settling down on the floor and then wrapping his hands around his folded legs, he just gazed up at me.

"You got this, girl!" He nodded at me and I let out a hard breath, closing my eyes for a moment. Rearranging the instrument in my hands, I stepped back and then sat on the chair.

I ran a hand over the board. It was a heavy, promising wood. The smooth touch sent a wave of satisfaction to my nerves. It was one fine piece he owned. Though it had been ages since I played something, I knew every chord of my favorite song. Yet, I was scared. My heart pounding in my chest like it was going to explode. I felt my palms getting wet with a flicker of sweat covering my forehead.

I played the strings, letting the music flow through my nerves, and decided to let my mind get lost in the melody. The music felt like my soul flowing through my body and getting melted in the surroundings. And then the lyrics started flowing automatically through my mouth. 'Willow by Taylor Swift' floated out of my heart. Every word of that song felt like it was telling my story. The sensation was so strong that I let my voice touch the higher notes.

My voice broke a little when I came close to the end of the song. The music was swimming through my heart, making me so relaxed that I totally forgot where I was until I opened my eyes. I bit my lower lip when suddenly all that enclosed us was silence. Our eyes met, and I smiled from within.

Ethan didn't even blink. He was staring at me like a kid looking at the moon.

"You don't know how precious you are, girl!" Ethan said, breaking the silence but not breaking eye contact. And I could see in his eyes that he really meant what he was saying. I kept staring at him. Drawn in by his allure. It was like our eyes had their own language and were talking without words.

Before I could've said anything, my eyebrows snapped together as a familiar tune filled the apartment. It was my phone ringing. I rushed back into the living room searching for my bag and, after finally gripping it up in my hand; I froze at my place.

"My dad is calling. Make a noise and I'll write you a death certificate myself!" Signaling him to zip up his mouth, I picked up my phone.

"Hey, dad. What a surprise!"

"It's mom, and where are you? What's the music?" My shoulders jolted upright as my nose crinkled at her noticing power.

"Music? What music, Mom?" I waved a hand at him, giving a sign to slap the music off. I watched as he climbed the couch in an attempt to dash towards his phone when he tripped and landed flat on his face, with the couch forthcoming over him.

"What was that noise?"

"Huh? I don't know, maybe rats." I couldn't decide what was more important at that time, my mother's interrogation or wincing Ethan crying for help.

"Anyway, by what time will you reach home tomorrow?" This was the second time I was speechless. Two minutes and my mom already had complete control over my body. And then it hit me. Holy cow, I meant to meet my parents tomorrow. I totally forgot! I didn't even have a car.

"Mom! The thing is, my car is in the garage. I don't think…" I was cut mid-sentence when the doorbell rang. A line appeared between my brows, thinking who it could be. Averting my eyes to Ethan, I noticed he had the same expression. The doorbell rang again and my mother's endless questions started with it while Ethan opened the door.

"Good evening, Mr. Stanton. Your car and other necessities are here!" Tilting my head, I noticed a well-dressed man in a suit past Ethan.

"Finally, man!" Ethan said way too loudly, and I slapped my hand over the phone. I raised my eyebrows in exaggeration, giving him an annoyed look when he shoved his hands over his mouth.

"Mr. Stanton? What's that voice? What's going on there, young lady?" Mom was shouting on the phone. I was helpless, speechless. I shrugged when I didn't have anything to say.

"Mom, you'll see me tomorrow. Okay, bye." I disconnected the call with a glare fixed on Ethan. He quietly nudged the door close, giving me a sheepish smile.

"Stanton, I need your car."

Ninteen

Ethan

DAY TWENTY-ONE

Trying to disguise my nervousness behind a big smile, I knocked at Starz's door. My hands lurked around my neck just as I adjusted my favorite blue shirt one last time and sighed. The anticipation was killing me. I couldn't sleep all night thinking about the morning. I had spent the longest time setting my hair today and made sure my cologne was concealing my nervous sweating. The door creaked open just as I peeked at my watch. 7:01 AM.

"You are late!" In a matter of seconds, she gave me a sideways glance and walked past me, with Finn following her.

"Good morning to you too, buzzkill!" I mumbled a little too sarcastically, hiding the thumping of my heart seeing her in a pale-blue dress, just as the locks of her golden hair were flowing over her shoulders. My forehead creased when I noticed her going for the door of that crazy lady.

"Thank you so much, Mrs. Jenkins! You don't know how much you've helped me. You're a lifesaver."

"Oh, you're embarrassing me, Sarah! It's the least I can do. But don't forget about our little deal, dear." Patting Finn on the back, she gave him a go, and he ran inside the house, looking unduly excited to play with those noisy kids.

"I won't, ma'am!" My eyes narrowed at Starz, as she winked at Mrs. Jenkins with a grin endowing her lovely lips.

Shoot!

Focus Ethan!

"Hey! What was that?" I asked as soon as Mrs. Jenkins's door closed. My voice echoed in the corridor just as she passed me a half-smile.

"Nothing to be bothered about, Mr. Stanton!" She replied, spreading her right hand towards me, palm up.

I hesitated at first but then held her hand with mine. Her skin was so soft; a warm sensation ran down my whole body. My eyes almost closed with satisfaction, but then I felt a jerk as she threw off my hand.

"What are you doing? Give me the keys, idiot."

"What?" I was disoriented for a second. My cheeks burned up with embarrassment as I realized my mistake. Fixing my eyes to the floor, I started patting my pockets for the keys but suddenly got my senses back.

"You need not bother, dear. I'll drive you anywhere you want," I announced, trying to build my crushed confidence back up.

"What? Who said you are coming?" She asked, raising her eyebrows and placing her hands on her hips.

I was stunned for the second time in a span of few minutes. Thinking back, I comprehended that she had only asked to borrow my car, not me. I just assumed that I would be accompanying her.

Oh Shit!

But the ball had already been rolled, and I was not going to back down now.

"Every deal comes with the 'conditions apply' clause, dear. And my car comes with me. Take it or leave it." I held my breath, second-guessing my bold move. What if she canceled the plan? But I knew that her car was still in the garage and she promised to visit her parents.

She kept staring at me. As if daring me to backtrack. But I stood my ground and stared back with equal intensity.

"Fine, suit yourself." Suddenly, she shrugged her shoulders and turned around. At first, I thought she would walk back inside her apartment, but she started heading toward the stairs. Maybe she was planning to take a bus.

"Are you coming or not?" Her voice echoed in the stairways and I let out a breath that had been stuck in my throat. Trying my best to hold back the smile which was threatening to break free, I ran behind her.

Nonetheless, arriving in the driveway, I scratched the back of my head when I saw her pouting while noticing the black Cabriolet parked in front of the gate. Narrowing her eyes, she looked over at my restless face and shook her head.

I could tell that she was assuming I was flaunting my money to impress her. But it was not like that. Though no doubt I wanted to make an impression on her, but not by all these fake things. She might have believed that my upbringing had taught me that these materialistic things could win anyone's heart, but what I really believed was that money couldn't impress the ones who had real essence.

However, I was pulled out of my thoughts when I saw her walking toward the car, and I rushed to open the door for her. But I got the wrong door.

"I'm driving!" My jaw hung open, watching her stealing her way towards the driver's side. I unlocked the car and placed my ass in the passenger seat before handing over the keys to her. I was too afraid she would just drive away, leaving me standing there. Meanwhile, she put on the seat belt and concealed her sexy eyes behind sunglasses.

"Bon voyage!" I shouted as we rolled off.

Shortly after cruising down the freeway, traveling south, I got bored to tears. Given that Starz already knew the directions to her parent's house, there was complete silence engulfing us. I felt like I was sitting inside a torture room where I had no permission to utter a single word. Although now and then, I stole glances at my girl, but her eyes were glued to the road, with an expressionless face.

"Starz?" I looked at her, but she just ignored me altogether. I yawned, stretching my arms out and brushing them against her face. I acted aloof all along as she shrieked, trying to toss my hands away from her face.

"Eww! What are you doing? Keep your dirty hands off of me!" She shouted, throwing tickling slaps on my upper arm, and I suddenly felt so alive. I straightened up in my seat and turned toward her with a big smile on my face.

"I'm sorry. I was just stretching my big muscular arms. It's been weeks since I properly worked out." I cockily spoke as she rolled her eyes, and I smirked further.

"Oh, really? And here I've been thinking, what were those uneven tumor-like swellings in your arms! You should get them checked for malignancy." What? I pressed my lips together and stumbled back into my seat and turned on the stereo.

"But seriously, Stanton. Aren't you a little overdressed with this shirt and a tie?" I couldn't hold back a chuckle that left my mouth, appreciating the fact that she actually noticed me, but then I looked down, feeling overly uncertain about my clothes now. Shit! I knew that. I should never have listened to Tom.

"Oh, come on. I'm not looking that bad. Haven't you heard of the famous saying, first impression is the last impression? I don't want your parents to hate me forever."

"Yeah? Right! Wait, what?" Her sunglasses slid up into her hair as she shot me a goggle-eyed glare. I noticed her letting out sharp breaths as her forehead creased.

"Stanton, you're not coming to my parents' house!" Turning right, she parked outside a gas station, focusing all her attention on me. Her fuming eyes bored into me and all I wanted was to stare into them until she would start falling for me.

"Sometimes, you creep me out, Stanton." She slapped my forehead and after being dragged back to the earth, I stumbled back to my place as she continued.

"Is that why you wanted to come? Do you really think they would forgive you?" Scratching my stubble, I bowed my head just as her shoulders slumped.

"Oh, come on! My dad hates your guts, Stanton. Is it so hard to catch?" She yelled, rushing out of the car. She threw her hands in the air just as I walked toward her to calm her down.

"He will rip out your guts and throw a barbecue in his backyard the moment he sees you." Color drained out of my face and I gawked at the seriousness in her voice. My hands instinctively snapped down to cover my torso while she shrugged and headed towards the 7-Eleven.

Well, to some extent, she was right. He knew my true identity and was aware of our crazy past. So his hate for me was obvious. Though I didn't tell Starz that I had already visited her parents last week before coming to Florence. They live in a small suburb just outside Montgomery. I had apologized repeatedly until they got tired of me and accepted the apology, while almost pushing me out of the door.

Yet I knew they had not forgiven me. How could they, after all the pain I had caused to the family? I still wished I could change their perspective for me. In their eyes, I was nothing but a spoiled brat who wanted to hurt her daughter for entertainment. I was not afraid of them, but their hatred was something that could come between me and Sarah. And I needed to work hard on that. After all, they were her parents and my future mother and father-in-law. Fingers crossed.

My eyes darted towards Starz, noticing her coming out of the store, and I rushed to open the gate for her. Her mouth was stuffed with chips, and after noticing my beaming face, her eyes narrowed at me. The corners of my mouth turned up and, leaning over the door frame, I noticed her raising an eyebrow. I bent further over and she leaned back.

"Father-in-laws are just like eggs. Firm from the outside, but soft from the inside. You just need to know the right recipe to make a frittata, mio amore." I tucked a lock of her hair behind her ear and turned around with a smirk, not before seizing the car keys from her hands.

"I'm driving!"

"In your dreams, Stanton!"

She ran after me, and in no time, she blocked my way to the driver's side. A mischievous smile etched my face, noticing her jumping in the air to snatch the keys from my hands. She was a possum in front of me.

"Stanton! Give… Me… The… Keys!"

The moment she let out a growl, I smiled in defeat, and once again we were back on the road. I put on some hard-core punk music and settled back in the passenger seat. Putting on my sunglasses, I leaned back, resting my head on my hands. The weather was perfect, and I was feeling cheerful, but my happy time was cut short when all of a sudden she turned down the music.

"My ears are bleeding, Stanton!" She switched my jam to some country music. A cowboy singing about how blessed he is to have the girl of his dreams and automatically a grin tucked at my face beholding Starz singing along.

She was lost in her little happy place and I couldn't help but ogle shamelessly at that beauty. I wanted to steal that moment and maybe I did it by recording her lovely voice on my cell phone. *Man, I love this girl!*

"Wow!" I couldn't hold back but regretted it as soon as the word came out of my mouth because she stopped singing. Suddenly remembering she had company. But before the pause could turn into an uncomfortable silence, I spoke up.

"So, what's your most embarrassing childhood memory, Starz? Mine is so humiliating that you will never want to talk to me again!" I let out a chuckle, remembering the shameful incident.

"I already don't, so shoot away!" She tilted her head towards me, giving me a sarcastic smile.

"Well... I once peed on myself in front of my crush in elementary school. She never talked to me again from that day forth."

"What a lucky girl! I wish it was me."

"Then you would have been my first kiss, too." I passed her a wink and her nose crinkled in disgust. I couldn't tell what was I enjoying more, her pissed-off looks or her suppressed smile, which she was struggling hard to hide. Sometimes, it gets so hard to guess what's going around in this woman's head.

"Come on, Starz! Spill the beans! Did you have any childhood crush, or maybe a little adventure?" My brows waggled in excitement.

"Well, there is this one incident. One time in summer!" Heat rose onto her cheeks and I could already tell this was going to be an amazing conversation.

"I kissed a boy when I was eight or something. But instead of kissing me back, he started crying, frantic wailing if I may describe!" I laughed as she looked down for a second, looking a little flustered.

"Oh, it was so embarrassing. His mother came to our house the very next day, complaining to my dad how I ruined their family tradition of no kissing before kissing the bride at the altar. I was so ashamed when she grumbled for a whole half an hour to my dad about me being a bad influence on neighborhood kids!" She snickered, looking straight as if remembering the incident that still mortified her.

"But my dad was dandy! He just showed the lady the door and asked the boy to man up!" She laughed once again and in that smile, I witnessed that angels do exist.

I was lost in her face when suddenly she pressed down on the brakes, making my body almost smack into the windshield. My forehead furrowed just as I jerked my head in her direction.

"What's wrong?" My heartbeat was racing in my ears.

"I'm so sorry. I noticed a couple down the road. I think... they might need our help."

I respected her concern, but still shook my head in denial. It was not a practical decision. We just couldn't let anybody ride with us and, above all, I had Starz with me. Her safety was my priority at that moment.

"Well, I couldn't agree more, but I don't think we should help some hitchhikers. They could be robbers, stoners, or even worse, porn stars!" Her mouth set in a hard line, and she sniggered at my serious face.

"Don't you think they are a little too old for that?" My eyes darted towards the rearview mirror and I surveyed the couple who were staring at us. They looked maybe in their late sixties and somehow harmless. But I still had my doubts. I had this feeling in the pit of my stomach that it was not a good idea. Or perhaps it was just my mind, taking it too seriously on account of Starz's presence with me.

"I'm letting them in!" She declared, and my brows drew together, watching her shift the reverse gear. I blew out my cheeks, accepting my defeat by her exorbitant beauty. Her foot pressed the gas pedal gently and just as the vehicle came to a smooth halt, my suspicious eyes sized the strangers.

"Are you guys okay?" Starz asked, leaning over me, as the window rolled down, giving them a warm smile and all I could do was to speculate why were they standing in the middle of nowhere carrying so much luggage.

"Oh dear, thank goodness. We were returning from camping, but then we got lost on our way back and now we just can't find our parked car." The lady uttered with a big smile on her face. I observed her sharing a look with her partner and then her eyes averted towards me.

"Oh, looks like you guys are off on a honeymoon or something. We should not disturb you, young birds." At the next instant, Starz's face yanked towards me and a flush crept up her face. I scratched my head, winking at her, and she turned around, trying her best to hide that blush.

"Oh, no, no! We are just... friends!" She stole a quick glance at me and a big grin crept up my face.

"Oh yeah, Madam! Friends with great benefits!" I declared and witnessed her face turning red. She shot me a death glare in addition to a playful punch on my arm and then turned back towards the couple.

"We will be glad if we could be of any help!" Starz asked and all I could think of was that she used 'we'. *Wow! I can clearly see progress here.* There wasn't any slip of the tongue or anything. *Yup, she is really into it.*

"Oh, thank you so much. Just give us a ride down to the next service station. I'm sure we would find some aid there." Just as the old man finished talking, Starz turned to me, and my eyebrows raised in confusion. She stared at me intimately and all I could do was stare back at her, even more puzzled.

"Help them with the luggage, genius." She uttered with gritted teeth, and with realization hitting me, I rushed for their help.

Putting the heavy bags in the trunk, I noticed the old man helping his lady get into the car. She gave him the sweetest smile anyone would die for. Starz also exited that car, closing their door for them. And when they settled down, the old lady placed her head on his shoulder. Time slowed down right there, as my eyes froze over the love they were reciprocating. I wondered if I would ever be that lucky. They must have seen so many ups and downs in life to make them inseparable. Tucking a silly smile on my face, I went back to take my seat, now driving.

"If you don't mind me asking, how long have you guys been together?" Starz was beaming while leaning back in her seat. I noticed the couple in the rearview mirror exchanging longing looks. They had started making me uncomfortable, and I shifted in my seat.

"Oh dear, we just completed forty-five years together. We were high school sweethearts!" The woman responded, and the old man kissed her on the forehead.

"Aww, that's so romantic." Starz appreciated while leaning even further and her eyes sparkled with excitement.

"But I still don't get it. Why are you guys carrying so much luggage while camping?" The seconds the words left my mouth I received a raw pinch on my arm and man that hurt!

"Are you all right, my love? Why are you getting so pale?" The old man's voice made me jolt upright in my seat. A line appeared between my brows, noticing the lady getting dizzy under his man's arms. Starz and I exchanged an anxious look as she offered water to her. But the lady just shook her head.

"Stop the car, please. I think she might throw up." I jumped on the brakes and the car came to a screeching halt. Our eyes dashed towards the old lady as she rushed out of the car. Darting towards the side of the road, she started throwing up, and my nose crinkled in disgust. Starz soon followed her and lent a hand, rubbing the woman's back and holding her hair back.

"Is she all right? Should I call a doctor?" I asked the old man, getting apprehensive about his wife. She was throwing her guts out and I had no idea what to do.

"Bring some water, Stanton!" Starz's screech bellowed in my ears and I dashed towards her. I passed her the bottle and noticed the woman's sweating face. She was soaking wet. Her face had turned even paler, while her eyes were getting drizzly. She threw splashes of water on her face and then gulped down the rest. I slowly shifted closer to Starz, a little uneasy about all this.

"Is she going to die?" I whispered in her ear but held up my hands in surrender as Starz shot me a death glare. *What? I am seriously concerned, woman.*

"I can't thank you enough for helping me. I just want to say how grateful I am that you guys came for my help." She clubbed our hands and kissed them one by one and I looked away, feeling uneasy. The touch of her lips made me cringe. And before I could've pulled my hand back in disgust, I found myself handcuffed with Starz. My face went blank, seeing the old sack stepping back.

"Oh, my! You people are so foolish, it's almost adorable. God bless your poor souls." The way she said it made me question if she was robbing us or blessing us?

Saying I was stunned would be the understatement of the century. For a few seconds, my body froze at the spot as my mind was unable to wrap itself around what was actually happening. And the old witch took advantage of those precious moments to place a good distance between us and dashed towards the car.

"Don't you dare think about it, lady!" I finally got my senses back and tried to scare her, but my nose scrunched up when she mockingly started laughing at my face.

"Have a nice day, losers!" And she sat in the passenger's seat of the car, which was now being driven by her old hag husband. Without thinking, I swung my legs in action, darting towards her in quick motion, but my hand tugged back and I was hauled back with the same pace, making me stumble straight to the ground, taking Starz with me.

"Oh, my hand!" Starz whined.

"Oh, my car!" I moaned, witnessing the increasing distance between us. I was screaming from inside, sitting by the empty road with my head in my hands. *Why am I losing my cars since I met Starz?* My baby just got abducted and I couldn't do anything.

"At least we are alive." Starz's voice fell in my ears and I shot up daggers at her when she smiled down at me sheepishly.

I stretched out my hand and observed Starz's hand entwined with mine. Well, it's not like I was complaining about the company, but I still didn't like to be handcuffed in the middle of nowhere.

"Come on, stop weeping like a five-year-old kid and get up. Those bloody crooks got my purse." I slowly looked up at her, noticing she had put her free hand on her hips in resentment.

"Are you freaking kidding me? I just lost my baby and all you care about is a few bucks in your damn purse?" I stood up, pulling her up with me, rubbing off the dirt from my pants.

"Can you ever think beyond money? My purse had my phone, my Hospital ID, my driving license, and a family pic I always carry with me. Last time I checked, a billionaire like you can go buy whatever car he likes, but no amount of money can buy my things." She placed her free hand onto her hip, turning her face away from me.

Okay, she had a point, but I was mad and stubborn enough to keep throwing glares at her. I took out my phone, trying to call for assistance, but it had no service. I tried in vain to gain access to any network by stretching my hand in the air and moving here and there.

"Or maybe, you know, if you hadn't left the keys in the ignition, we…" My piercing gaze darted towards her as her voice trailed off. *Don't you dare go there, woman!* "I'm just saying." She shrugged her shoulders at me casually.

"I told you it was a bad idea to engage with hitchhikers in the middle of nowhere. Maybe I should've bargained you against my baby!" But inside, I knew it was not her fault. She was the soft-hearted helping type who saw goodness in everyone. But I should have been smarter than being fooled by those old hogs. I was frustrated and wanted to hit something, but taking a few deep breaths, I shoved the useless waste of space phone into my pocket and looked at her in defeat.

"No signal"

"Whatever! They are not coming back, so let's move now. I'm hungry!" I was amazed at how calm she was at handling the situation. I half expected her to start crying, but I couldn't be proved more wrong. We started walking side to side, eagerly waiting for some vehicle to pull up for help.

We were pulling at each other's hands while walking and I was afraid of hurting her wrist, so I grabbed her hand. "What the hell?" She shouted and started trying to squeeze her hand out of the handcuff.

"Stop it, you are going to hurt yourself," I yelled before I could restrain myself. She looked frightened, staring into my eyes.

"I am not going to hurt you, Starz. Just trust me for once," I said in a soft tone now. I didn't want to scare her. She looked at me bewildered, but then finally gave up harassing herself and noticed the redness of her hand. After a few seconds of hesitation, she held my hand again, and we started our march again in silence.

After an hour long stroll, hand in hand, we were drained of all our energy and were thirsty beyond limits. My smile had been replaced with worry watching Starz in a bad shape. She was getting paler, with her skin blanching in the sun. I was sweating like a pig. Loosening my tie, I rolled up my sleeves to send some ease to my burning core.

"We are in the middle of nowhere. How are we going to reach home? Oh, God, it's so hot out here." With the back of her hand, she cleared the droplets off her forehead. I wanted to hold her, to shield her from the sun, to take her to a safe place.

Hardly any vehicle hustled off on that freeway. And the one which appeared drove off as hurriedly as they came first. No one was willing to come forward and lend us a hand. "Guess what? People don't believe in giving rides to hitchhikers in the middle of nowhere." I told her sarcastically, and she rolled her eyes in response.

Another half an hour passed when we noticed a public bus approaching us. We stood in the middle of the road, determined not to let the bus pass without taking us with them. The driver got skeptical about seeing the handcuffs, but when we narrated our story, he almost laughed at our faces.

I paid for the tickets and settled in the back. We were exhausted, hungry, and, above all, thirsty. I could see the restlessness on Starz's face. There was still no network on my phone and we could do nothing but wait until our destination arrived.

The whole bus ride passed quietly. Starz dozed off, resting her head on my shoulder while I admired her beauty. I was relieved she was safe in my arms. Behind all her toughness, she was the same Sarah with kindness and tenderness in her heart, and she deserves to be protected all the time. She was still holding my hand and her hot breaths around my neck were sending tingling sensations throughout my body. At that moment, I found myself thanking the heavens for bringing this day into my life.

As our stop approached, I dared to clear some hair strands off her face and explore her tired features closely before waking her up. I appreciated Starz opening her sleepy eyes and noticing how close her face was to mine. She pulled back and looked the other way, but couldn't hide the blush rising on her cheeks, which was hard to ignore. My body drew forward, with the bus coming to a halt, signaling that our stop had arrived.

Getting down, we both ran towards a convenience store looking for water. Handing her a bottle I pulled out another for myself. Water never tasted better than at that moment. Starz started choking, and I had to pat her back, telling her to take it slow. Taking some granola bars and chips for munching, we called for a cab.

As it turned out, Starz knew the cab driver. I guess everybody knew everybody in a suburb like this. I called Tom and asked him to contact the lawyers and register a complaint about the theft, while Starz narrated our story to the cab driver. We were surrounded by stunning landscapes, and I found myself captivated by the magnificence of the nature surrounding us.

The mishaps of the day had turned the three-hour journey into a six-hour one. By the time we reached our destination, it was already past lunchtime.

As we entered the driveway, a large house came into view. It was an ideal white house with a white picket fence, as shown in county farm-state advertisements. I could make out a big barn in the backdrop adjoined by a stable. Although I had visited the same place just a week ago, somehow it looked more mesmerizing with Starz by my side.

"I can't promise anything, but if you find my father with a shotgun, I would advise you to just make a run for your life!" Starz turned around with a worried look on her face as we climbed the front porch and the corners of my mouth turned up. This sure looked like she had started caring for me, after all. And then, with the second knock, someone opened the door.

"Sarah! Where have you been? We have been trying to call you for the past two hours." Mrs. Walter opened the door and the next second, she pulled her into a bear hug. But unfortunately, I was also tagged along.

"Choking! Mom!" The moment her mother let go of her, Starz shifted from one foot to the other. Her mother's eyes drifted to our handcuffed hands and then back to our faces.

"Good evening, Mrs. Walter," I said, stealing glances between the two ladies.

I noticed as her mother smiled shyly and then gestured us to come inside and my heart started to beat faster. Why didn't she ask anything? Was she expecting me? Had Starz informed her parents that I was tagging along? I struggled to hide my fidgeting just as we settled down in the living room. I was on the edge, anxiously looking around with a puzzled mind.

"Oh, my baby girl! I missed you, Ray." A familiar tough voice echoed from somewhere down the hallway and soon enough Mr. Walter entered our line of sight. But his welcome grin fell off midway when his eyes landed on me and I reciprocated the welcome with a nervous closed-lip smile. All my imagination that Starz's parents were already expecting me flew out of the window. They were just not acknowledging my presence altogether. Maybe they hated me even more than before. Good progress, Ethan.

"Dad! You look old." Starz ran towards him, forgetting the major part that I was linked with her. She hugged him with pure excitement, and I couldn't do anything but stare at the ceiling when Mr. Walter's face was too close to me, with his wide scary eyes shooting deadly daggers at me. And then his eyes landed on our interlocked hands.

"What is this? What is happening here? What is this bastard doing in my house? And why are you handcuffed?" His scream bounced off the walls and my jaw hung open. I knew now where Starz's anger issues had come from.

I opened my mouth to speak, but words betrayed me. I was too frightened to speak. But Starz came to my rescue and narrated the whole story while portraying me as some kind of hero who saved the day.

Mr. Walter eyed me intently as if analyzing the scenario in his mind and then suddenly he broke a snigger, pulling me into a bone-crushing hug, patting my shoulder with a little too heavy tight slaps. I mouthed 'Thank You' to Starz, who gave me a wink. But the victory was short-lived as Mr. Walter muttered in my ear, "Don't try anything that would make me kill you," low enough so that only I could hear it and my heart sank back into my stomach.

"Honey, I think that would be enough!" On Mrs. Walter's call, I was finally able to free myself.

"Jane, dear, please take out my hatchet. I can't see my kids suffering anymore." Mr. Walter spoke in a politely hazardous manner to his wife and color drained out of my face. He was undoubtedly going to chop my arm off.

"Oh dear, why bring out the launchers when I have a handgun." My fear-stuck eyes drifted towards Mrs. Walter when she drew out a hairpin from her neatly formed bun while heading our way, and I let out a breath of relief. We settled down on the couch together just as she began to decode the lock.

With every wrong twirl of that pin, Mr. Walter's patience was thinning and my heart was tumbling down my body. His pacing in the room was giving me panic attacks.

"Get a hold on yourself, Stanton. You're sweating like a pig." Starz whispered, and I pressed my free hand on my forehead and found myself dripping wet.

"Oh, fuck it!" Our stunned faces shot up towards Mr. Walter, comprehending his falling patience. And then, after giving us a hard glare, he disappeared somewhere inside the house. I couldn't think straight. I was crying from inside.

"Ah-ha!" My head yanked upright with the sound of metal clanking. "You two are free now." Mrs. Walter declared, just as the lock came undone and I yanked my hand far away from those handcuffs. "Now, who's hungry?"

"Found it." Right at that moment, Mr. Walter re-entered, holding a chain-saw and my jaw fell to the floor.

He was going to chop me into pieces.

By God's grace and Starz's intervention, all my appendages were intact, and I was sitting at the kitchen table with Mrs. Walter. My eyes drifted towards the large window with Mrs. Walter's gaze where the father-daughter duo stood and seemed deep in conversation. It forced me to adore her face, which was showing a thousand emotions with every word they were exchanging. She was smiling wholeheartedly and not even a slight amount of hesitation was palpable between them.

Light-reflecting from the glass was magnifying her freckles. I felt vested, grateful for the time allowing me to admire her raw beauty. She wasn't just beautiful; she made everything around her lively too. That made everyone admire beauty in all the little things. My heart filled with warmth by just a glimpse of her. I knew I was crossing the line by literally gawking at her, but I couldn't help that she had captured every single stroke of my heart. I was spellbound by her dark magic.

The sound of metal clattering made me turn around, and I noticed Mrs. Walter preparing the dinner table and I rushed to assist her. "Please let me help you!" I laid out the plates and bowls on the table while all along I could feel her eyes on me as she was arranging the cutlery.

But my eyes wandered back on Starz as if they had a mind of their own. I wished I could be a part of their conversation. Like a family who shares every little detail of their lives with each other. I could tell how close they were. It was like they were always real to each other, deeply bonded to share everything. Anyone could easily guess by just looking at them that Starz was a daddy's girl.

"Ethan?" A soft voice fell into my ears, but I ignored it.

"Hmmm..."

"Ethan?" The voice came a little louder this time, and I had to avert my eyes from Starz.

"Huh? What? I am sorry... yo… you were saying something, Mrs. Walter?" I stammered, turning my whole body towards her with a jolt.

"You know my daughter is engaged, right?" I scratched my head at her question with a mortified expression furnishing my face.

"You're a nice guy, kid! But if you try to break my daughter's heart all over again, I'll cut your balls off." My head yanked towards her, catching sight of a scary reassuring smile on her face just as she finished laying out the napkins.

"Supper is served!" She called out and walked inside the kitchen, but not before tapping my shoulder in a gesture of letting me know how serious she was.

"Oh, and, please call me Jane. Mrs. Walter makes me feel so old." And yet again, blood had drained out of my face. *This family is loaded with psychopaths.* Not a single person could be declared mentally stable here. One was ready to chop my arm off, and another was after my balls. *Oh, God. I don't know if I'm ever going to come out alive in my quest to make Starz fall in love with me.*

Soon after a near-death experience and an intimate fatal warning, we were ready to have an early supper. I thought I had a big escape from her father's deadly glares but little did I know Starz would make me sit right next to him, with his wife following me. I was trapped between two psychos. I could do anything just to avoid their deadly grimaces. My pleading eyes drifted towards my only chum when she sat down right in front of me, giving me a look that clearly said, *'I warned you, dude.'*

"So, Mr. Stewart, how come we are having this pleasure of meeting you? Again!" Before I could've devoured my first bite, another fatal question was launched in my direction by Mr. Walter and I put down my fork, closing my mouth altogether.

"Sir, please call me Ethan!" I insisted when he gave out a bitter laugh.

"Oh, my bad. How foolish of me to be wrong all over again. I should apologize to you for calling you by your phony name, Mr. Stanton. Old man's memory, you know!" I nodded, looking over Starz, whose face was buried in her plate. *Someone save me, please.*

He was roasting me exceptionally tenderly and I could do nothing but deflect every sharp arrow being flung in my direction with a weak smile. I was injured, but I still had some breaths left. My eyes witnessed as he was about to open his mouth once again to shoot me down when all of a sudden Starz spoke up.

"Stanton, pass me the potatoes!" She tried to rescue me. I could appreciate the weak smug on her dad's face when she called me by my last name instead of my first name. But I was not a weak competitor.

"Here you go, Starz." As I passed the dish, I realized my mistake of calling her by her nickname in front of her parents. I bowed my head and fluttered my eyes towards my plate as it was my time to smirk. However, I earned a kick from my girl from under the table as she gave me a cute, innocent glare.

I could feel Mr. Walter's eyes exchanging looks between us just as I felt the temperature in the room start to rise.

"Starz?" Mr. Walter's questionable eyes settled on his daughter, and I smirked even further.

"Umm…" She was speechless and uncomfortable with her dad's hard gaze on her.

"So, who is ready for dessert?" Mrs. Walter once again jumped into the situation, saving her daughter's ass while Mr. Walter was fuming from inside when he noticed her daughter blushing at my assertion.

"Oh, I almost forgot. This is for you, Mrs. Walter! I mean Jane!" Starz's forehead furrowed at my statement, witnessing me slipping out a small box from my pocket.

"Oh, dear. You shouldn't have!" A smile etched my face when Mrs. Walter's eyes gleamed with joy seeing the pendant I had bought for her. I didn't have much time to plan out everything, but I could see she liked my gift. Yet, I couldn't help but notice Mr. Walter's skeptical eyes on me. I cleared my throat as I was convinced he wasn't appreciating the moment.

His piercing gaze was getting darker on me, and then he spoke, "Ladies, if you will excuse us, I need to have a man-to-man talk with our guest. We will enjoy the desert in my study. After all, we hardly got any time to get familiar with each other. Right, Mr. Stanton?" My head yanked towards Starz, who was exchanging looks between her dad and me. My face scrunched up in fear, mentally screaming for her to save me, but she just shrugged her shoulders at me. Traitor!

"Sure, Sir!" Starz gave me thumbs up, and I hardened my glare at her. If I was going to get murdered in that dark bloody room, I was so going to haunt her ass till eternity.

The short walk to his office was silent and absolutely unsettling. I couldn't remember the last time I felt such a chill crawling into my soul. Like a lost puppy, I followed him inside the room. My frightened little soul jumped up in alarm when the door creaked on its hinges while it closed behind my back.

"Please take a seat, Mr. Stanton!" I scanned the dimly lit old room. The expensive-looking furniture was furnishing every single corner while a few pieces of landscape art were hung over the walls. Concealing the slight edginess stroking my body, I settled down on a chair. My eyes floated back to him, noticing him pouring some fine liquor into two crystal glasses, and then he handed me one.

"So, Mr. Stanton, how long have you known my daughter?" Settling the glass on my sweaty palm, I gulped down the nervous lump in my throat and made an effort to appear comfortable under his deadly glare.

"Well technically, Sir, she already knew me when we started the freshmen year, but I didn't exactly know her till I asked her to be my girlfriend at some random party. You know… umm... I should shut up now!" I cringed at my words, mentally hitting myself on the face with a baseball bat for babbling nonsense. I think I officially made Mr. Walter hate me even more. He poured another drink for himself and gulped it down the very next second.

"I'm a man of my words, Mr. Stanton." *Okay, here it comes.* "I don't play with words nor do with people. I say what I think. And right now I want to tell you that you're one selfish bastard whom I have the pleasure to meet and greet in my house. My daughter was imbecile for letting you be a part of her life."

Well, that hit my self-esteem. This was the moment when I swallowed the whole glass in one shot. The bitterness of liquid burned my throat, but it was nothing near to his bitter words that hurt my pride. He was Sarah's dad and he might have achieved great success in his life and I respected that, but I never gave him the authority to insult me so relentlessly.

A humorless chuckle left my mouth when I lifted my glass for him to pack it up again. His gaze remained glued to me as he walked over me, swelled with disgust and hatred. But unfortunately, he didn't know his resentment wasn't strong enough to thrash me down from my trail to his daughter's heart. His loathing was nothing comparable to my love for Starz. Man's pride is his most prized possession, but only till it doesn't come between him and his woman.

"Mr. Walter. I don't know what you've heard of me and I believe it can't be any worse than what I really was. But I'm no longer the man I used to be. Just like your daughter, who's no longer the girl who dated this moron. She is smart, strong and the most kind-hearted person I've ever had the pleasure of meeting. You can't label someone's kindness as foolishness." I stood up and walked towards the nearby wall. My eyes shined with passion, witnessing the stamp collection of Mr. Walter.

"This collection is a real treasure, Mr. Walter." My fingers ached to feel the craving for stamps, but I believed he was not the man to let some stranger have a closer look at his possessions.

"You can have this treasure if you can assure me that you'll disappear from my daughter's life." My head yanked towards him, once again noticing the aversion sharply written on his face. "Oh, I almost forgot. You're a billionaire or something who can buy anything." Letting out a dry laugh, he gulped down his drink and placed the glass at the table with a little too much force.

"But your daughter is not a thing to be traded, Mr. Walter. I know I'm nowhere near perfect for her, but I am in love with your daughter and I would stop at nothing to win her back. Even if I lose myself in the course." I walked forward and stood just ten inches apart from his face, staring deep into his hate-filled eyes, daring him to retort.

When he didn't bother to say anything, I continued. "And even if I lose, Sir, at least, you'll have a story to laugh about a halfwit who was after your daughter and she rejected him for his father's pride. Because, believe it or not, that girl outside this door never stopped loving me for a second in all these nine years." I placed my glass on the table, making no sound, and nodded my head in a gesture of taking my leave.

"But don't forget that heartache and betrayal, kid, just like the one you gave her, have a strong persuasive power to even overwhelm the little emotion that you call love and convert it into hate." My head leaned further, with his voice stroking my ear and I spoke back.

"Then I'll count on that hate, Mr. Walter. Because the bottom of the story is to be courageous enough to take the risk of rejection." I tried my best to swallow down my annoyance.

"And I am nothing if not a risk-taker."

Twenty

Sarah

NINE YEARS AGO

It was quarter past eight in the morning and I was sitting on a bus surrounded by strangers. I had memorized every word written on the paper Ethan had handed me regarding my appointment with an OB/GYN. A woman in her late fifties stumbled onto the seat beside me. A reassuring smile came through her as my eyes shifted over the notebook she was clutching.

"She is beautiful," I said, with my eyes glancing over at the photograph of a little girl. For a moment, she seemed confused, but then she looked down over the picture, creasing out of her notebook with some letters and her face lit up like a thousand roses.

"Oh. Yes. Yes, she is, indeed. She is the best granddaughter one can ask for. Isn't she perfect?" Her eyes were beholding so much love that it somehow made me feel so alone. How had I landed myself in this situation where I was all alone when I needed my loved ones the most?

"She is a beauty." I replied, trying to meet the enthusiasm in her voice. She was beaming like anything. Her fingers caressed the face of the little girl in the picture and I chuckled hearing the whole story behind that picture. I noticed her beautiful freckles, and they compelled me to shrink back my mind toward yet another beautiful soul on this earth, my mother.

I plunged deeper into the recollections of my lucid childhood with my mother and began to miss her badly at that delicate moment. I wished nothing more than her presence at this arduous time.

I needed nothing but her love to comfort my terrified soul. I wanted her. I needed her as a supporting pillar, or maybe just as a friend, to listen to my problems without judging me. To reassure me that whatever I was doing was the right thing to do; that everything was going to be okay.

I nodded in between the conversation, trying my best to listen to her words, but I couldn't. The fake smile I had been carrying was screaming at the fact that the woman was making me feel miserable rather than happy.

I saw as the woman clasped the photograph closer to her heart and stared outside the window. At that moment, my phone vibrated, jolting me back to reality. Quickly unlocking the screen, my eyes read the message Ethan had to send me.

'Are you on your way?'

At first, I presumed to answer him back by a text, but then, I considered calling him and confessing how scared I was at that point.

The phone rang for a long time and then ended up on voicemail. I frowned at that unfortunate circumstance and grimaced at the phone screen. Shoving the phone back into my pocket, I noticed the lady beside me standing up.

"This is my stop. It was very nice talking to you." I nodded with a half-smile.

It was hard to concentrate on my surroundings when my mind was still glued to him. I knew he was not ignoring me or something, but the strange feeling in my gut shouted, something was definitely up.

It could be some random meeting he was still stuck in and had put his phone on silent, or it could just be the network. There were so many possibilities that I decided to brush the justification off and rather leave a voicemail instead. So I dialed again. The phone rang once more until it went to voicemail and I cleared my throat before the beeping sound.

"Good morning! It's me, Sarah. Guess who went missing again? Yeah, it's you..., Ethan. Aha... anyway, I wanted to remind you about the appointment. Yeah, I know, I know, I don't have to remind you, you obviously remember, but you know me. Scared, nervous, and alone. Right now, a little support would be of much help. Please come on time. I love you. Bye."

And with that awkward snicker, I hung up the phone. Shaking my head to clear the cloudy thoughts of my brain, I started to look outside the window. Once again, fidgeting, getting anxious over crazy thoughts that my mind was building.

While battling with a dreadful feeling in my gut, my stop had arrived, and this was it. No chickening out now. Stepping down from the last step, I pulled out the paper from my pocket that Ethan had handled me last night. Though I already know the contents by heart, I read the names engraved on it once again.

'Dr. Beanie Hobbes'
'Heartstone Hospital', 548, Falcon Street.

Lifting my eyes to scan my surroundings, I assessed the street names stamped on the signboards and then followed the direction to my destination.

I was exhausted. I had crossed only five blocks, and it felt like my legs were going to give up with each step. It was a rather cold morning, and I could clearly see the mist escaping my mouth, yet I was sweating like I had run a marathon. Just when I was thinking of turning back and making a run for my life, a colossal building came into view.

My eyes took in the sight of the hospital as my head lifted, noticing the huge plus sign on the top of the structure. From outside the structure looked nothing less than a grand hotel, because of the crystal glass panels wrapping it entirely. It was a multi-story building, and I sighed, gazing at the number of people rushing in and out of it. Perhaps it was one of the major hospitals in the town, still; I was totally unfamiliar with this side of the city.

Looking over the building, I started fidgeting again when an unexplainable thought crisis hit me. An inner battle ran in my heart for a whole fifteen minutes, jumping between the thoughts of moving forward or reverting and dropping the entire plan. But, eventually, I blew out a sharp breath and walked inside.

As the entry gates slid open, a draft of warm air hit my face, filled with a tincture of disinfectant, enough to welcome a migraine. I wish I was fabricating it, but there were quite a large number of people in there. I instantly got scared that Aunt Rose or one of her book-club friends would find me there, so I bowed my head down and pulled up the hood up of my jumper. The sound of people chatting and the clatter of metal and glass all around made my head sway in all directions. And then, my eyes averted toward an enormous clock hanging over the middle of the hallway, and I realized that I was about to miss my appointment.

I had to make it quick. So, while people on the other side of the reception table were busy attending calls and providing information to people standing in a queue, I strolled towards a nearby wall, discovering the map of the whole building glued on it. I wondered if the map was pretty hard to read or my mind was not working properly, as nothing was making sense to me.

At that time, I made up my mind to relax in a nearby chair and wait for Ethan. He must be on his way or could storm in any second from the entrance. Thus, walking towards the nearby empty bench, I settled down.

Ethan had explained that he had already booked an appointment for me on a priority basis and had personally talked to the doctor so that I wouldn't have to waste my time in inquiry and could go straight to the fourth floor, but right then, I had no idea where I should go. Or maybe I didn't want to go alone.

Impatiently, I started tapping my foot. The butterflies fluttered in my stomach restlessly, with the abrasiveness of the bleach assaulting my nostrils. Resting my chin against my palm, my shoulders slumped. My eyes only rolled back and forth between the main entrance and the inquiry counter. Waiting for that one face to appear. After an entire half an hour, I was still sitting alone, breathing the air of disappointment, and Ethan was nowhere to be found. I tried calling him, but his phone was off.

At first, I considered heading toward the exit, but the voice inside me didn't let me take that option, therefore I was forced to go to the second alternative. Clenching the paper securely in my sweaty hand, I marched towards the inquiry, four people were sitting for assistance and out of them, three were already busy on the phone and I was certain, I listened to one of them talking about how much she had fun last night.

After wasting a sum of fifteen minutes in the queue, all I got from enquiring about Dr. Hobbes was the 'fourth floor', which I already knew. Shaking my head in displeasure, I tried to swallow down my irritation and searched for the stairs.

By the time I reached the second floor, I was totally ragged and finally decided to take the elevator. The minute the elevator door opened, I hurried to get in. But the second I saw a person leaning in the corner wearing blue scrubs, looking as if just coming out of surgery, I was ready to run on my heels.

An encounter like that just before having my appointment was the last thing I wanted at that moment. I saw him giving me a bemused smirk, and I turned around on my heels. I looked to my right and then left to contemplate where I should go when I heard the door of the elevator sliding shut and I sighed.

"Aren't you coming in, Miss?" My back straightened up against the voice that appeared from right behind me, and I somehow connected the dots, that he had been holding the door for me. Twirling around, I let out a sheepish chuckle and entered the elevator.

I stood as far away from him as was practically possible, almost touching the sliding door. With my back facing him, I could feel his eyes burning a hole in the back of my head. But, I tried my best to retain a hold on myself. Impatiently, I pushed the button again and again, suffocating in that small space.

"Are you all right?"

"What? Yes. No. I mean yes. Do you know where I could find Dr. Hobbes?" I was so unguarded that even my voice betrayed me. My body guarded up when I witnessed him taking a step towards me, but then I relaxed back when he took the paper from my hand.

"Oh, go straight to the fourth floor and ask anybody from there. The whole floor is the OB/GYN Ward. She may be handling today's OPD. But, why do...?" He was cut short on his risky question when I seized the paper from his hand and walked out just as the elevator doors opened on the fourth floor.

I observed the OB-GYN ward, which was like the rest of the hospital, with the walls unadorned in white, except for the enormous pictures of mothers and newborns staring at me from all directions. My head stirred with unusual emotion with each tense breath. I forced myself forward. Pacing towards the end of the hallway, a big glass door came into my view and at last, the doctor's name imprinted on it in bold letters and I let out a breath of relief. Thank Goodness!

There were plenty of chairs on either side of the hall, but regrettably, most of them were already occupied. However, the only out of the ordinary thing in there was me; the second I stepped into that waiting area, I could sense several eyes on me full of judgment, and right there, panic shot up inside me.

Almost everyone had their forehead furrowed. Some had a puzzled look, while others might have already figured out my problem, as they were at a juncture where their staring soon turned into repugnance looks. Their behavior screamed how much I didn't belong in that room.

The pounding in my chest accelerated when I had to walk in front of everyone to the nurse's station, who notified me that I missed my appointment and now I had to wait for my turn until my name was announced. And then I turned back, moving towards the last vacant chair in the corner.

I sat down letting out a deep sigh when the person next to me turned her head. I awkwardly smiled at her, but my smile dropped, noticing her rolling her eyes at me. Wow, just five seconds and my face was already pissing people off.

I bowed my head to the floor, dropping my eyes to admire the plain tiles of the floor. One way or another, I felt imprisoned by their piercing gazes, judging me without even being aware of my side of the story. It felt like they were grazing holes in my body.

I made a strong effort to hide my anxiety. Settling down on my chair, I began to tap my foot impatiently. I felt like if I kept on moving my limbs, I would feel less apprehensive, less uncomfortable, but it only earned more glances, this time glares, shooting straight towards me and, unfortunately, I had to sit still. On the other hand, my eyes never left the front door; eagerly waiting for his arrival.

I struggled to control my emotions; but by not being able to move a muscle, I felt trapped, paralyzed. I was near demise. The heaviness inside that small waiting area was increasing with every tickle of the hands of the clock.

I was immensely alarmed. The pit of my stomach deepened against the trickling drops of sweat seeping down from my temple. The clacking sound of the receptionist's pen and the constant boring commercials on the Television were driving me insane. I could feel tension and dread building up inside me. I rubbed my hands in order to calm down my screaming nerves, but after finding them sweaty, I rubbed them against my jeans.

What was happening to me? I'd been experiencing hot flashes and my heart was pounding manically. My forehead was flooded with sweat like I'd been running miles and above all my breath was so shallow that I felt like someone was strangling me. My hands shot up to my throat, trying to make the suffocation go away.

Maybe it was because of the emotions that I had been facing, seeing that everyone in that room was accompanied by someone, and here I was, sitting all alone by myself. Was it loneliness or just insecurity of my heart?

With every passing second, the uneasiness within me was consuming my spirit. My mouth felt arid, and I licked my dry cracked lips, feeling thirsty. I walked over to the water dispenser and picked up a disposable cup, filling it in, and quickly gulped down the water to send some ease to my parched throat, not for a moment letting my eyes meet with anyone. I licked my dry lips again and walked back over to my seat, yet again, sitting on the edge of the chair.

I was twitching from inside, still; I did my best to mask my fear. I didn't let them see what was happening underneath my essence. I pulled out my cell phone from the bag and started to dial his number again. He should have come here by now. My lame, sweaty hands clouded the screen of my phone. Rubbing the screen against my jeans, my eyes caught hold of a woman who was, for my discomfort, peering at me.

My eyes drifted to her tummy, observing that she was quite far along in her pregnancy as her tummy looked really huge. Sensing that she wouldn't stop staring at me anytime soon, I managed to pass a weak comforting smile at her, but her nose suddenly wrinkled up in disgust, and then she turned around, muttering something to the man sitting next to her.

My smile dropped, feeling horrified by the way she grasped her belly and turned away from my gaze as if protecting her baby from me. It made me feel pathetic; feeling low on myself, like I was some wicked witch who could cause harm to her baby.

I felt like a wandering ghost. Loneliness was squeezing my heart to produce constant pain, letting me be aware of my mistake. I tried to hold myself together before fear could devour me alive. I began to breathe in and out rigorously to calm down my mind, but then I felt a tap on my shoulder. My head lifted, and a line appeared between my brows, looking over a tall figure hovering over me like a dark shadow.

"Stop staring at my wife. You're giving her undue stress." My forehead furrowed at the man's request. I glimpsed behind him, getting familiar with the fact he was talking about the same woman with the huge belly. Putting the information together rather slowly, I straightened my back against the bench and responded.

"I'm so sorry... if... if I made you guys feel… I mean... I had no intention of making her uncomfortable." My head held high, staring at his annoyed face. But, as if my answer poked his ego, he tossed my bag on the floor and leaned further closer, scaring the living shit out of me by the sudden outburst.

"Listen to me, whore. I'm very much familiar with bimbos like you. Quit staring at her or I'll call the security." By this time, tears had welled up at the back of my eyes. Hair at the nape of my neck bristled and my blurry vision skimmed my surroundings. Everyone was already gaping at us, hungry to find out about the affair.

Grasping the arm of the chair, my shrunken watery eyes stared back at his face, which was burning with rage. I was failing poorly to stop my body from shaking in terror.

"What's going on there?" The nurse's call made him settle back on his bench. Not before giving me a hard gaze.

I wiped my eyes with the back of my hands, but no matter how much I tried, the tears refused to fade away. I hurried to pick up my bag, and without wasting another second, I tried to call Ethan. My shaking hands struggled to unlock the now crazed screen of my phone. I was begging my phone to find his number. I knew that his number was the only one I dialed today. Still, my aghast spirit took a whole minute to reach him.

My mind was distorted. I couldn't think straight. But, once his name flashed in front of my eyes, I pressed the dial button, but then someone called my name, consequently, the phone slipped out of my hands.

The second my cell phone landed on the floor, it shattered into several pieces. Losing the last odds of contacting him, an agonizing whimper escaped my lips, making my whole body shudder in disbelief. I struggled to breathe. My chest rose and fell, trying to find oxygen for my frantic lungs.

This was the moment when the frail wall that was holding me up finally collapsed. I needed him by my side. I couldn't take this all alone. I wasn't strong enough. I knew my world was crumbling down into pieces without him. Kneeling to gather all the chunks, my ears were assaulted once again.

"Sarah Walter!" Perceiving my name for the second time, my head jolted up. My foggy vision regretfully strived to find the source of the voice. And they finally settled on an unduly slender woman, wearing a blue scrub with a stethoscope around her neck.

She seemed pretty annoyed, but first I had to put together my phone so that I could speak to him. I knew he was on his way, but I wanted to inform him to come as early as possible. It was an urgent situation.

"Didn't you hear me, schoolgirl?" The voice came right from above me and I shuddered. I wondered, how on earth did she recognize me in this crowd? Did Ethan give them my profile, too?

For a few seconds, I couldn't move from my spot. I felt like a deer trapped under the headlights. I was trembling with panic. I didn't want to face her or anybody in that room. I just wanted to run far away from all those judgmental faces.

"What's the matter with you? Come on, you already missed your appointment. Pick up your mess and follow me." Maybe I was getting on her nerves. But, I couldn't help it. I needed to talk to him. He might have gotten lost in this building, just like me.

I knew I was no longer caved in by the shadow of that nurse, but time was running out. Sobering in with each sniffle, I began to join back all the pieces of my phone. Tears were soaking my face, trickling freely onto the floor. I couldn't stop myself from shaking. Even as I pressed my hand against my heart, it wouldn't stop pounding.

I stood up and hurried to turn on my phone, but I failed. I tried once again, but still, it didn't show any sign of working. My heart dropped in my stomach. It felt like, with every passing second, it plunged deeper into my guilt.

"Come on, child, we don't have a whole day for this." My skin crawled and my body jumped with that unexpected warning. My head yanked toward her, witnessing her standing near the door. I could feel people judging me once more. My surroundings were compressed with shameless sniggers and indistinct gossip. The commotions rebounded with three-fold intensity. My skin felt blotched, and I bit on my bottom lip, enough to fill my mouth with the metallic taste of blood.

Immediately, every nerve in my body started screaming at me not to go after her. Begging me to run as far away as possible from this terrible place and never look back, to just disappear. The air inside my lungs felt way too shallow to breathe naturally. I began to hyperventilate. It felt like someone was digging their claws into my throat, strangling me. Someone was trying to choke me and I couldn't do anything. My legs started to give up. Anytime, they would make me collapse on the floor.

My mind began to create distorted images. I was getting uncertain of my vicinity. My head played the game of anticipation, producing laughing faces insulting me, and I found myself even more wretched. I squeezed my eyes shut in a desperate attempt to block out all the taunting images. But with each chuckle, a new wave of agony shook my body.

"This way, girl!" My head shot up, and I stepped back. My vicinity had started to float, making my vision cloudy. I grasped my stomach when the feeling of nausea hit me.

My mind had surpassed the sniggers and was now concentrating on my shallow breaths. My head spun towards the loud siren of the ambulance coming from outside of the window and my heart began to hammer inside my chest like it was going to explode anytime. Adrenaline shot through my veins with a fight-or-flight instinct. And I made up my mind.

I had to sprint away, fast. I was no longer struggling to keep my sobs quiet. And, in no time, I turned around to dash away from that awful place. Grabbing my bag closer to my heart, I sprinted towards the glass doors. I knew I needed to get out of that place if I wanted to survive.

"Where the hell are you going?"

The adrenaline might have overpowered me, as I felt entirely sturdy now. I could hear my heartbeats in my head. I wiped my soaked face and kept on running through the corridor. With every ounce of energy I had left with, I tried to push my body forward. I couldn't stop now, not until I reach somewhere safe. A shooting pain eloped from my head and I grasped it, trying to prevent any chance of getting wobbly.

I put on a great effort to inhale some air into my lungs, but it was not working. By now, I realized that the only certain way to live was to jump into this storm. As long as I had air in my lungs, I would get plenty of time to think about this baby and my future. The distance was all that mattered at that instance. The safety of my unborn child was the only thing in my mind at that time.

As I finally reached the stairs and a burst of fresh air hit my sweaty face, my lips lifted into a smile. But then I tumbled.

Time seems to freeze when you are falling to death. A squeal left my mouth, pronouncing that my body was floating forward in obscurity. Blood drained out of my horrified face, witnessing the gushing wind thrashing my body. I had lost all control and was plunging into a deep void that I couldn't do anything about.

Everything seemed to cloud into a blur that swirled around my remains. My hands fought violently to grip anything that could save my life. But unfortunately, I found nothing. I saw myself falling into the darkness from where there was no turning back. The air left my lungs, and I closed my eyes, waiting for my inevitable demise. Everything slowed down until I hit my head.

Excruciating pain filled my forehead. The impact was so strong that for a second, my vision went black. A tinkling noise rang in my ear. Acute pain crept up my legs, and I could feel my ragged body rolling down the stairs at a callous pace. I screeched in agony when the clatter of my breaking bones echoed in the surrounding. Unbearable pain spurted out from every part of my body. I could perceive the noise of people screaming, but slowly they were fading away. And in the blink of an eye, I was lying in a heap on the floor.

I landed flat on my stomach. Every part of my body screamed in pain. I might have bitten my tongue as my mouth began to fill up with metallic taste. Blood began to seep out from my head, blurring my sight further. The pain overpowered all my senses, and I felt my body going numb. I blinked several times, struggling to stay awake. I could no longer feel my heart beating. I was slowly entering into an enthralling realm and I didn't want to turn back.

The intensity of light began to reduce as my eyes became heavier with time. I could feel the life draining out of me. A tear ran down from the corner of my eye as I surrendered myself to the darkness. I lay there on the floor barely breathing and the last thought that crossed my mind was...

Why didn't he come?

Twenty-one

Sarah

DAY TWENTY-NINE

Dawn started to break the darkness of the night and with the slight unfolding of curtains, I could appreciate sunshine peeking into the on-call room in the hospital. I sighed, breathing in the fresh air after completing yet another night shift. Autumn mornings in this town had different kinds of vibes in them. There would always be a little chill surrounding the dawn, perfect to have an early coffee.

Heading back to my small desk, my eyes dropped to the bunk beds, and I smiled, witnessing my three favorite girls in deep sleep. Not willing to disturb their precious sleep, I slowly tip-toed towards my locker and after taking out my stuff, I closed the door as quietly as I could.

My shift was over and so was the vigor inside my body. The sleepless night had an unfavorable effect on my brain as it was shutting down and I couldn't quite tell if my eyes were becoming clouded or it was just the gloominess of the weather.

Signing out on the duty register, my eyes drifted from the papers in my hand to the poster on the wall portraying a grinning fake doctor cradling a newborn, and right then, Stanton's face flooded my mind and my cheeks started to feel hot. He sure looked adorable with the baby in his arms that day. He would surely become a loving father one day.

"What's happening to me?" The nurse at the counter gave me a strange look, and I smiled at her, shaking my head to come out of my creepy imagination.

It had been a whole week since I last saw him. I knew driving him to my parents' house was a mistake, but I never thought my dad would leave such an impression on him with his threats that he would vanish overnight unannounced. I still can't quite erase the image of that evil grin on my dad's face when we found the guest room empty in the morning.

He left a note saying something urgent came up but had not tried to contact me ever since. Maybe his little male ego got hurt that night and now he wanted me to beg for forgiveness for my parents' mistreatment. If that was the case, then I guess he was better off alone. I knew he didn't want to say goodbye or show any kind of courtesy, but he could've at least given an honest bow to the queen, acknowledging that I finally won the war. I was beaming in delight, feeling the sensation of satisfaction overwhelming me, leaving me totally restored.

Yet there was a weird feeling in the pit of my stomach. Every morning I half expected him to show up at my door. I kept on peeking in the corridor now and then, anticipating that he could be right next door and still not talking to me. I was a little ashamed to admit it, but I suppose I kind of had been missing him.

I had to stop myself many times from knocking at his door just for the sake of knowing he was not dead in there, but I stopped myself out of self-respect. Maybe he didn't want to be bothered, or perhaps he was not even in there. What if he had already left for good to go back to his previous perfect life?

Walking out of the hospital gates, my head lifted to the sky, and I thanked God for tossing him out of my life. Because people like Stanton need to understand that everything you desire in the world can't always become yours.

Tucking in my coat close to my body, I started walking towards my car when my phone started ringing. Instant hope engulfed me, anticipating it was Ethan. I mentally slapped myself for thinking that. Fetching the phone out of the purse, I beamed seeing my other half's name flashing.

"Hey señorita, kissing you is like drinking salty water. The more I drink, the thirstier I get." I cracked up and shook my head at Ash's chirping voice.

"Shut up! Where the hell are you?"

"Madrid, babe." I was stunned as I started to walk on the sidewalk. Last time I checked, she was heading to Rome from Australia. What was this girl up to? I mean, I was happy for her as she was living the best days of her life, but what was with the frequent change of places.

"Now listen to the important part. Ryan has been giving these signs lately that I think he is going to propose!" We screamed just as she finished her sentence. I felt a tint of embarrassment flowing through me when I noticed I had captured quite a few eyes on me. But who cares when my best friend is being proposed to. I was freaking happy for my girl. It was finally happening. After all these years of experiencing downfall by her doomed love life, at last, she had found a true man who was ready for commitment.

"Oh, I want to meet you guys so badly. When are you coming back, Ash?" My words were full of hope. Oh, I was dying to know the whole story. The days they spent falling for each other even more and the nights with love. All the awaited girls' talk was making butterflies flutter inside my stomach.

"Soon, babe! After all, only two weeks are left until your grand wedding ceremony. Time flies so fast when you're with the right person." My smile dropped. A strange, unsettling feeling stroked me, leaving my mind troubled. Suddenly, the chill in the air around me felt uncomfortable.

I had tried talking to Lucas on several occasions in the past week, but he had been really busy and somehow words never left my mouth, even when I got a chance. His busy schedule never bothered me before. After all, even I sometimes pulled thirty hours shifts totally cut-off from the outside world. But off-late I had started feeling a kind of void inside my chest.

I had no idea what had changed inside me for making me feel this uneasy with the thought of my upcoming wedding. Perhaps I was having cold feet with the wedding day coming closer and it was really frightening me. Or maybe I was just too tired to feel the comfort in the air. After all, I was the same girl who was standing at the altar just last month, filled with contentment in her heart and a smile on her face.

"Hello, are you there?" Ash's voice pulled me out of my inner contemplations.

"Of course, Ash, you are so going to plan an exotic honeymoon for me this time." I heard giggles on the other side of the line as I started to unlock my car.

"Are we going somewhere?" And with that sound, the breeze changed its fragrance with Ethan's breath.

My head turned to the voice. My heart discerned a strange kind of ease upon perceiving the familiar sound that had been missing for a while now. And before I could hide it, a smile came wandering to my lips, witnessing the face whose features had been quite the reason for unrest in my mind. It took me quite a while to appreciate that the cell phone was still lying against my ear when the line had already gone dead, and thus I put my phone back in my pocket.

Why was I nervous? With my eyes darting towards the satchel he was holding and then back at his deep sapphire eyes, words left my mouth before I could've held them back.

"Look who came back to life. Hi! I was just going to file a missing report of my brainless, annoying neighbor." He tilted his head towards the ground with a sheepish smile and my smile only deepened, staring back at his bashful features. He shoved his free hand deep in his jeans pocket, looking embarrassed and somehow cute.

Oh, kill me already for calling my enemy cute.

"Wow, today you said 'hi' and my heart almost stopped beating." He was right back to his old self, and a giggle left my mouth. This boy was never going to settle back.

"Starz, I believe I owe you an apology for disappearing like that from your parent's house. I bet your dad had plans for me to make me feel further welcomed in his house in the morning." I shook my head at his pathetic humor.

"But it was an emergency, Starz. Not to sound cocky, but you know I run a freaking company?" I battered my lashes while nodding my head in acknowledgment. He let out a chuckle while looking down in recognition that I was not the right person who could get impressed with him flaunting his money and power.

"Well, I wasn't…" My words were cut short when a fleeting chime of a text message intruded on our conversation. My eyes narrowed at him when he hastily pulled out his cell phone and his lips curved up in a pleased smile while reading the message. He appeared genuinely happy while shaking his head and shoving his phone back in his pocket.

"If you don't mind, it's quite chilly out here. Can we go someplace warmer?" My eyebrows rose at his question.

"Oh, no, no! I'm not flirting with you, nor am I asking you out for a coffee! I was just worried that you might catch a cold. Uh… I mean a coffee would be great at this time! Shit, I sound so sloppy." A smile crept on my face as I found myself admiring how uncomfortable he was, just as his eyes met mine.

"Dude, where is my creepy, self-obsessed neighbor, and what did you do to him? Since when did you start sounding so cheesy, Stanton?" The corners of his mouth turned up and out of the blue, he circled his hands around my shoulder.

"Roses are red, violets are blue. Is it the rain or am I falling in love with you?" And we were back on track. There he was. The same old devil who was born to make my life hell.

"Roses are red, violets are blue. If I had a brick, I would throw it at you." My head turned towards him with a threatening closed-lip smile and he slipped his arm off my shoulders before I could get any chance to break it.

"Well, I don't do breakfast dates with strangers, but now that you've officially taken over my morning peace. I guess you owe me a coffee, at least." And we started walking on the almost empty street lane. Did I just say date? My body trembled when the cold breeze around us howled wildly. It was enough to make a chill run down my spine.

My cheeks flushed, and I pulled my coat closer to my worn out body when my eyes drifted towards his serious features. He seemed lost in his own world, sinking deep in his thoughts. I wanted to know what was running through his mind. Or maybe what was bothering him? But then I looked away when he almost caught my eyes on him. Maybe he was planning his next move to embarrass me with something worse.

In a little while, one of my favorite buildings in the neighborhood came into view. And just then, a tiny raindrop fell on my cheek. My face lifted to the sky, and I smiled, feeling the droplet on my fingertip. Our heads turned towards each other and we exchanged a grin and the next second I knew we were running towards the cafe. My eyes drifted towards my hand and I noticed it interlocked with Ethan's and a strange sensation trailed through his skin against mine. A flush crept over my face when my eyes darted towards Ethan, who was beaming like a thousand candles, just as he was stealing glances at me.

"Wow, your hand fits so perfectly in mine." He said, raising our joined hands.

"Yeah right!" I laughed at his silly attempt of flirting, and we reached the building, quite too soon. He bowed and opened the door for me, and I chuckled shyly at his small gesture.

Just a step inside the room and my nostrils were ambushed by the intoxicating aroma of freshly baked cookies and caramel. I drank in the tang of coffee beans as I found myself under the spell of my love for caffeine. The hostess glanced over us when the doorbell tinkled on our arrival. Passing her a smile my eyes roamed over the seats, noticing the place wasn't too crowded. She escorted us towards my favorite window seats from where the street could be appreciated, which appeared all gray because of the pouring.

We got comfortable on the sofa in front of each other. I was feeling a little twitchy making eye contact with him. He could read everything going in my mind and I was uncomfortable, feeling a little exposed. I stretched out my legs in front of me and shuddered when our knees brushed under the narrow table. I looked away, resting a hand on my lips, assessing his reaction. He was already enjoying a good smile at the expense of my nervousness.

"So, how was your day, or should I say night, Starz?" I was thankful to him for breaking the awkward silence that started to engulf us. I smiled and took in the sight of him as he took off his jacket and leaned back, stretching out his hand on the edge of his settee.

"It was good. You know, no embarrassing encounters, no stupid nicknames, and above all, no one to get on my nerves." He titled his head, bowing down while at the same time I gave him a small smile as he shook his head in amusement. He looked too frivolous at that instant.

Shoot! What was happening to me? Maybe the lack of sleep had melted my brain.

My head lifted when I noticed the waitress arriving with our orders. When did we even order? Oh, I remember now! Ethan ordered coffees when I was busy ogling him.

She rested the hot cup of coffee in front of me and I closed my eyes, inhaling the great aroma. I wrapped my fingers around it, enjoying the heat that spreads through my hands. Taking in a big sip, I let the warm liquid sit on my tongue for a while before gulping it in. Warmth spread through my body and I felt less weary. But then a line appeared between my brows when I felt Ethan's eyes on me. My forehead creased, watching his usual steady gaze flickering from my hands to my face.

"I'd marry your dog just to see you every single day." My mouth twitched and before I could anticipate that he wasn't joking, I had a big grin on my face. Shaking my head at his remark, I rubbed my palms together.

"So, how did you and Romano meet?" My back straightened at his abrupt question just as my left eyebrow rose in surprise at his straightforwardness.

"Digging into the wrong side of the street. Aren't we?" He shrugged, looking down while stirring the spoon in his coffee.

"Well, technically, we first met at a stupid Christmas party. Our mothers are high school friends and therefore, we had a chance to be present at the same place when they introduced us to each other. We still laugh at the fact that we both never wanted to go to that party in the first place. We completely ignored each other at that party and forgot about that encounter altogether. But then after a few months, we met again at a hotel in Boston where I went for a medical conference and thought it must be destiny making us meet like this again and so we eventually started dating." A smile etched my face, making me recollect the moment when we spent the whole evening trying to be less awkward with each other.

"I wish I could be the reason for that smile on your lips." His words brought me back to reality. My forehead furrowed at the tenderness painted all over his features, and my shoulders slumped.

"Tell me, what will it take to get you convinced that I'm not going to fall for your charm once again, Mr. Stanton?" I inched forward, letting him read the emotions that were flashing in my eyes. A chuckle left his mouth as he licked his lips and leaned closer, resting his interlocked hands on the table.

"Well, I would love to take you on a proper date, Miss Walter." I loomed even closer to his face just as his eyes rested on my lips. I could sense the inner battle he was going through when his eyes drifted between my eyes and my lips. He was struggling to maintain proper eye contact. Whereas I was trying my best to hold back the emotions that were struggling to escape.

"Not in this lifetime, lover boy!" With a flicker of my index finger, I nudged his forehead, and he recoiled in disappointment. He looked disheartened as he stumbled back on his seat, averting his eyes toward his coffee. Did he really think I was making a move on his irresistible personality?

"You know you never answered my question, Stanton!" My eyes were settled on my hot coffee and when I looked up, I found him looking at me intensively, with a raised eyebrow.

"Why are you here? It can't be about forgiveness anymore, is it?" I perceived he was nervous when he took in a deep breath, running his hands through his hair. He looked everywhere but me.

He suddenly disappeared under the table and then appeared back with my missing handbag which I lost with his car last week. What?

"Oh, my God! How did you find it?" I snatched my bag from his hands and rushed to check my belongings inside. My eyes gleamed in astonishment, as every single thing in there appeared untouched. A blush crept on my face when my fingertips brushed against that nine-year-old carnival ticket that held some unforgettable memories of our first date. I have no idea why I still kept it. Maybe it was symbolic of the good times I wanted to relive. I just hoped he hadn't seen it to make me feel embarrassed.

"So, you went in search of your beloved car. That is why you were missing for a whole week?"

"Yeah. You can say that." Suddenly I gasped in fear. "Please tell me you didn't hurt that old woman for stealing your car?" I still had been having a hard time forgetting the bewildered look on his face when they drove off with his Cabriolet.

"Well!" He shrugged his shoulders and the mischievous smile on his face narrated the whole story when his cell phone buzzed once again, dropping my smile.

I wished I could read whatever was written in those texts. Because every single message was making him smile in a way like a new couple flirting with each other. This time I couldn't hold back the strange feeling stirring in my heart when instead of avoiding the text, he texted back and got a reply within a few seconds.

"Seems like someone found a new friend." I joked, averting my eyes towards my cup.

"What?" He looked up and studied my not-so amused face. "Oh, it's nothing. Oh, my goodness, my cookies are finally here! The cookie monster is coming right away. Run for your life!" He rushed to get the order, and I shook my head, once again disappointed with his behavior.

He had avoided my question altogether and I started to wonder if he was ever going to answer me in this lifetime. Relaxing in my seat, I undid my ponytail and shook my head, relaxing my hair. I could feel the sting in my scalp as I let my fingertips massage my head.

I let out a humorless chuckle, thinking about how foolish I was for thinking I was going to get an answer from him today. What else could have been expected from him? He was the same person who dodges himself from all kinds of liabilities and emotions. I knew that he was not a sensitive type of guy. But he also didn't have the right to play with someone else's emotions.

Digging my fingers deeper into my hair, my head tilted backward, glancing around the now busy tables. I noticed a young couple sitting in the corner, kissing each other. And I diverted my eyes away in haste.

They landed over three familiar faces beaming at me from the doorway, and my jaw went slack. They waved at me all at the same time, and I found myself waving back with my bewildered face. What the hell were they doing here? They were all fast asleep when I left a little while ago. Why did they have to come here of all the places? And I was thunderstruck when I watched them heading towards me.

"Great we caught you here!" Gemma declared, just as the three ladies enclosed my table from every angle. I bowed my head, hiding my face in the safe haven of my hands. I didn't have the willpower to even meet their gazes. But the next second, I received a hard shove, when the two girls settled down next to me with Gemma taking the front seat where a while ago Stanton was sitting.

"Are you on a date?"

"He is so handsome!"

"Girl, I never knew you would come out as a dark horse one day!" I was attacked by their never-ending interrogation and before I could've answered any of them, Ethan was standing in front of us with cookies in hand and an awkward look etching his face.

"Um... looks like you are busy, Starz. I guess I should just take my leave!" He was about to turn around when Gem grabbed his hand and pulled him down on the spot next to her. She shifted a little too close to him with a flirty smile just as he tried to move away to the farthest corner. I shrugged my shoulders when he passed me a scared look. I believed he would've fallen flat on his ass if he would shift even an inch further. They ordered their drinks and diverted their interrogation toward Ethan.

"Hi! What's your name, sweetheart? Oh, you've got some fine biceps, sugar lips." Stanton mouthed '*sugar lips*' to me and I slapped my hand over my forehead. He appeared distressed sitting next to her, and she was doing her best to not leave any air between them, while her hand roamed over his forearm. His body jerked up a little as if her touch burned his skin. He took hold of her hand and settled it back on the table.

I should never have agreed to come here with him. He raised an eyebrow toward me, and I couldn't do much but force a smile on my face. "We are Sarah's colleagues. I'm Shelley, she is Melissa, and right next to you is Gemma!" He returned a nervous smile and bowed his head at them.

"I'm Ethan! Starz's... Sarah's neighbor." And it was yet another facepalm moment. Why did you do that, dude? You literally wrote your own death certificate. I noticed as Gemma's face lit up with excitement at the mention of the word neighbor as she leaned on the table, tucking me along.

"Oh, I'm going to move in with you, babe!" I rolled my eyes at her use of words and Stanton chuckled in anxiety, exhaling a deep breath.

"Isn't he the same guy from the labor room the other day? He is so cute. Where have you been hiding him? Do you have his number?" Mel continued to mumble silly questions in my ear, and all I wanted to do was to smack my head on the table.

"So, do you have a girlfriend, Ethan?" Mel turned her face towards me when she received a smack from my shoes on her leg. I looked away when she yelped in pain, delivering a death glare.

"Oh, my God. Look what I found in my fortune cookie."

'You will go on a date at the end of the week.'

All heads turned towards Shelley, just as we witnessed her bouncing on her seat. She was beaming when a flush crept on her cheek. She tugged the piece of paper closer to her heart and I felt happy seeing her so pleased.

"Why are they even serving fortune cookies with coffee?" I scolded the place as a good morning was turning into a disaster.

"Mine says."

'You will have a busy day at work'.

"As if I don't already know it." Mel frowned and tore the paper into endless pieces, ignoring my question altogether.

"Well, it's better than just *'better luck next time'*!" I could not hold back the chortle escaping my lips when Gemma spoke up. She was scowling badly when, for a brief moment, my stare drifted towards Stanton and my eyes halted at him. It's like when you glance at him, only to find out he was already staring at you. He was watching me so intensely that I couldn't hold back my smile and had to look down to hide my face.

"They offer them with the morning coffee, as a daily horoscope," Ethan replied to my long-forgotten question.

"Your turn, babe. Tell us what's written in your fortune!" Gemma turned her face at him and my eyes bored into him. He seemed on edge, as his fingers slowly unfolded the piece of paper and then his head shot up to me.

"The love of your life is right in front of you!"

The second those words left his mouth, I was shoved against the window as Mel took my place just in front of him.

🌿

"You think you're a charmer, don't you?" I inquired, unlocking my apartment door.

"Yeah, can't help it. I was born with it, darling." Stanton quickly followed me, heading towards my kitchen. Shoving my shoes off, I stumbled onto the couch, resting my legs up on the table. Finn rushed towards me and settled down, his head on my lap. I smiled and started to caress him.

"By the way, it was nice meeting your friends. I never thought doctors could be so attractive!" My eyes shot open just as a smile crept on my face. Did he just accept that he checked out my friends? Putting my legs down, I turned back on my couch, resting one hand on the headrest with a smirk furnishing my lips.

"Yeah, right! And here I almost believed that you were having panic attacks between those ladies." He handed me a glass of orange juice and went back into the kitchen.

"Seriously, Ethan! You were hilarious today. The whole time your face was like 'Starz, please help me! They are going to eat me alive.' I feared you would piss your pants." I threw my head back and laughed hysterically. I looked over to witness an angry pout on his face and I cackled even more.

"I think you are forgetting the part where your wild friend was eye-raping me! I had no idea I was this irresistible." He settled down next to me as I rolled my eyes at him. He is so self-absorbed.

"But trust me, Starz. You've got some nasty friends. She even whispered into my ears that our proximity was making her wet." I spat out the juice, taken aback by his words. I felt a flush creeping onto my cheeks as he dabbed my lips with a tissue, but the moment was brought to an end when his phone rang. The call forced him to flee the room as he strolled toward the kitchen.

I hid my irritation behind my pursed lips when he started giggling like a timid teenage girl. He had been reluctant this whole morning to tell me who his newfound infatuation was. And I felt a tint of annoyance filling me. I knew it was wrong on so many levels, but my undue interest in the call made me eavesdrop on the conversation.

"No, girl. I'm okay! You just take care of yourself. I don't want to come back home and see you in bed. Now I got to go, I'm busy doing my laundry. Bye!"

Hastily, I stumbled back onto the couch when he ended the call. My temper sparkled. I curled my palms into fists, shaking my head at how flawlessly he just lied to that girl. Attempting to swallow down the irritation after grasping the fact that he was once again playing with somebody's heart, my body shook with repugnance. It sickened me to recall that I believed in this guy even for a second.

"So, where were we?" He settled back on the couch, but I just crawled away in disgust. The closeness was sickening me, and I was glad he noticed the sudden change in my body language. He was no longer welcome in my house.

"Are you all right?" Shifting his body completely towards me, his eyes surveyed me when I just continued to stare at the wall in front of us, fighting hard to control my temper and not lash out at him. He wasn't worth anything.

"I need to sleep, Stanton! You should go. Somebody is waiting for you at home." Yet again I refused to meet his eyes, but I could feel his puzzled gaze on me. What was he confused about? The level of stupidity that made me trust him for a while.

"What? I don't understand!" And right at that instant, I smoldered with resentment when his innocent act made me loath his mere shadow. I stood up on my bare feet and turned towards him.

"You are such a great actor, Stanton! I just heard you lying to some innocent soul about being here. You never stop being an asshole. Nine years back, it was me and now you have found a new prey to play around with and then leave her broken and dead. You're such a sadistic, self-centered prick." Fury roared through his eyes as he was on his feet now. My eyes fluttered in anger when our height difference made me feel a little defensive.

"What the hell are you talking about?" He roared. I turned my eyes away, folding my hands on my chest. "I was on the phone with my Nanna."

I let out a dry chuckle at his pathetic attempt to save his ass. "Yeah, right! You have been texting your Nanna this whole morning." I air quoted the Nanna part, which made him rake his fingers in his hair in annoyance.

"Well, yes, woman! You can call her up if you desire!" He forced my hand open and slammed his phone on my palm. "But you're right about the lying part. I'm sorry, but yeah, I lied to you about my disappearance. Nanna was ill, okay? So, that night when I got the call, I had no time to wake you up and explain the whole scenario. I had to leave. I flew to San Francisco on the first flight and in the meantime, Tom found those criminals and your belongings. I just came here after dropping Nanna at my parents' in Fairhope last night." I swung around and clenched my teeth when my stubborn attitude was brought to my senses. His eyes narrating the truth, and I felt embarrassment flooding my spirit. I was ashamed.

"I... I am sorry. I didn't know..." His gaze was glued to the floor while misery featured his face. I felt bad for making him feel this low.

"There's no other girl, Starz. Not have been in the past nine years." He spoke with his eyes still fixed on the floor, and then he looked up. His eyes gazed into mine when he held my face in his hands. I felt warmth flowing through his touch. The tenderness in his eyes made my heart loosen up from my agitated mind.

"You're the only girl..." I closed my eyes when his thumb caressed my cheek. "I would love to torture day and night." And the instant his words made actual sense to my rational mind, I punched him in the stomach, running away towards the kitchen.

"Just accept it, baby, you got jealous." I was horrified. My face must have turned red, with embarrassment flowing through me. I wanted to punch that smirk off his face.

I tried to compose my body but failed badly. Something inside me sparkled, and I shuddered with that strange feeling. It wasn't only my face, but my whole body was on fire. I felt like my blood was raging in shame. Butterflies swirled in my stomach and I found myself drowning in humiliation. I looked away, desperately finding a distraction from his face, when he rushed to stand on the other side of the kitchen counter, resting his chin over his palm. I could sense a smile escaping his lips while enjoying the view of my pathetic condition and before my mind could've put some rational thought in my subconscious, I emptied a glass of water onto his face.

"I bet this was the amount of wetness you were talking about with Gemma!" My eyebrows snapped together as he let out a gasp. I had no idea why I did that. I couldn't believe he was now soaking wet, but I felt pretty much relieved by diverting the topic. My silly act had faded the awkwardness in the air and I was very much glad of that.

"What the hell was that for, you green-eyed monster?" I yelped when I witnessed him launching forward with a jug full of water and I ran for my life. Finn barked at Ethan, but he didn't stop, nor did he get scared with Finn growling in rage.

My waist was already under seize of his strong arms when Finn grasped a good hold of his jeans to tuck him back. I squealed and struggled to get away from his grip, and in the middle of that chaos we witnessed the whole jug of water getting emptied on top of Finn. We gasped in shock when he whined loudly and ran outside the house, knocking Ethan down in the process, and I felt bad for my little friend. But then I looked down and just as Ethan's eyes met mine we burst out into a manic laughter.

But soon we were cut short when I heard a familiar voice at the door.

"Sarah?"

Twenty-two

Sarah

DAY TWENTY-NINE continues…

I couldn't believe my eyes. A man was standing at my front door, and I couldn't help but stare at him with a bewildered look. I couldn't move, nor could utter a single word. I was literally gawking at him. His puzzled dark crystal Hazel eyes met mine, and I blinked several times, trying to reason out why was I so startled.

"Lucas!" I was star-struck. It took a minute or two for the new information to sink in.

"Hi!" I flashed a brief nervous smile, waving my hand at him. But then he surveyed my face, with his forehead creased.

"Hi, Sarah! I had a meeting with a client in your town. So, I thought maybe I would give you a surprise visit." His voice contained a hint of unevenness. Well, what could I say, I surely was surprised. In fact, I was pretty much shocked, so much so that my mind was still trying to comprehend his presence in my house.

He was still standing at the door, waiting for some kind of acknowledgment. I could sense he was nervous or may be anxious about coming here unannounced and perhaps I was increasing his uneasiness when I remained quiet.

"Oh, that's so thoughtful of you. Please, come on in!" I finally managed to speak some sensible words.

"Sarah, I found Finn in the corridor. Why is he all wet? Wait! Why are you wet?" He was confused, which was understandable. As Finn made his way inside, Luc patted his back lovingly. But Finn rushed towards me as if he couldn't wait to get away from him. He was kind of a little too friendly dog, despite that, he never seemed to like Lucas very much from the beginning.

"It's been raining since morning, you know! I got soaked driving myself back home. This is just rainwater." This was one of my stupidest habits. I babble nonsense when I get nervous. I found myself shifting from one foot to the other when his presence started giving me tension. I couldn't think straight. But then an abrupt noise made a line appear between my brows, and before I knew it, I was staring down at Ethan Stanton.

Oh. My. God! He was still inside my house. How the heck did I forget that? Luckily, the couch was facing the other way, so he was concealed from Luc's view. My pupils dilated, and I shot him a glare as he was still lying on the floor. *Don't you dare to move a bit, dude!*

I needed to get rid of him, but unfortunately, there was only one way out of this apartment!

"You all right, Sarah?" My head yanked up, and I saw a bemused look on Luc's face that made me appreciate how disoriented he was. But then, my senses breathed on fire when I saw Luc walking towards me and at that instant, I secretly started fluttering my hands towards Stanton to move his ass.

I struggled to let him know that Luc was heading straight toward us. I took some steps back, making a weak attempt to hide him behind me. My heart was racing fast and my mind had started visualizing all the bad outcomes of this situation. But then, the corners of my eyes crinkled when I saw Stanton crawling towards the other side of the couch and I took a breath of relief.

"Oh, I'm good! Absolutely fine!" I shrugged, giving a dismissive wave of my hand. "Still on the right side of the grass!" I managed to shoot a glare when Ethan slapped his hand on his forehead on my answer. I let out a nervous chuckle when I noticed Luc coming closer to me. He settled down his briefcase and my eyes drifted towards his hands, which were holding a bundle of red roses.

"This is for you. You're beautiful, as always." Handing me the bouquet, he planted a quick kiss on my lips and heat rose to my face, as I could sense Ethan's eyes on me. His touch always had an unusual effect on my body. The touch felt comforting, yet too unfamiliar.

A heavy silence settled between us, and we found ourselves stealing eyes from each other. I placed a hand on my heart, trying to find some words that could end this awkward silence. And then I went into completely paralyzed mode when I saw Crazyhead standing right behind Luc. Slightly tilting my head, I gestured to him to exit the house from my eyes. Because I didn't want these two people to come face to face ever again in my life.

Stanton started to give me some silly hand gestures. He pointed his finger at Luc and then towards the door, making me comprehend that he wanted Luc to leave the house rather than him. Stanton imitated an expression of nausea, seeing the flowers in my hand, and I risked an eye roll at him. But unfortunately, Luc caught it and abruptly half turned to inspect why I was peeking behind him.

"These are gorgeous. It's just that I just came out of a night shift, so I'm a little offbeat today." I tried to capture Luc's attention by putting my hand on his face to make him face me as Ethan ducked down.

"Oh! I am so sorry. I should have called before showing up at your door unannounced." Luc was really looking guilty, and that made me feel mortified.

"Oh no, it's absolutely all right. Just give me a hug and I'll be fantastic." I grasped his shoulders and pulled him in to wrap myself around him. But my eyes widened when I observed Stanton charging at him with my baseball bat. *Are you freaking kidding me?* I quickly pulled away and settled back at my place.

"I'll put them in a vase!" I gestured towards the flowers and turned around to run off towards the kitchen. I honestly didn't know what to do. Out of the blue, Luc grabbed my wrist and pulled me back into his arms, taking me by surprise. My torso recoiled at his chest just as my eyes captured his hard, profound gaze. My breath quickened when he tucked a lock of hair behind my ear. Everything happened so fast that my heart almost skipped a beat. His hot breaths caressed my face, and I shuddered beneath him.

"Let me see you properly first. I've planned a lunch date for us and then a movie night. I can't stay over, but I can make this day count." His husky voice compelled me to stay in his arms. He was staring hard as if looking for something in my eyes, and I felt extremely vulnerable in his embrace. My lower lip trembled as we breathed the same air and I found myself nodding my head in acceptance, and he flashed a dazzling smile.

I couldn't believe the person in front of me was my bashful fiancé. I never knew he could take such moves. As much as I knew him, he was not the type of guy who would take the first step. I can't remember when was the last time I found him comfortable around me, let alone taking a romantic turn in our relationship. Something had definitely gotten into him because he was sort of too good to be true. I had great respect for him for this. And then the moment ended when the front door slammed shut.

"Who was that?" Luc turned towards the voice, alarmed.

"Umm… Wind?"

After a hot shower and two espressos, I was ready in a bottle green fit and flare dress that covered my knees and an off-white cardigan to keep the cold away. Carrying my purse from the table, I headed towards the living room. A smile etched my face when my eyes landed on Luc relaxing on the couch, with his loosened tie resting on his wrinkled white shirt. He appeared exhausted and, above all, too innocent while sleeping. I didn't want to disturb him. The corner of my mouth quirked up. I found myself settling down next to him and closed my eyes too when I sensed him shifting in his place.

"Oh, shit! Did I just doze off?" My mouth twitched just as I looked over at him. He was rubbing his eyes while yawning, and I just nodded.

"You know, it's not a big deal. We can stay in and order some takeout." I suggested, but in that instant, he stood up, shaking his head in denial.

"No, we are definitely not doing that. I really want this day to be special." My forehead creased at his comment. There was nothing unique about this day. What was he talking about?

"I'm really sorry to keep you waiting. I'll just go and freshen up." He dashed toward the bathroom and I shook my head at his nervousness. I couldn't come up with a single day in our relationship when he hadn't apologized to me.

It didn't take him long and the next minute he came back straightening his shirt sleeves. Grabbing the suit jacket from the back of the couch, he tucked it back on. I noticed him racking his fingers through his hair, making a few water droplets stumble on his face, and then they trickled down to his shirt. He curtailed his steps just in front of me while adjusting his tie, and I stood up.

Brushing off the water droplets that were resting on his nose, I couldn't help but giggle, noticing him turning crimson. And before the moment could've turned into an uncomfortable quietness, we exited the house.

Luc had rented a car for the day and just as the wheels of the car came to a smooth halt, asserting that we had reached the planned venue, he rushed to open my side of my door. I gave him a genuine smile for his courtesy. Although once again his touch had a peculiar effect on my skin, I found myself staring into his eyes to determine what was running into his mind. But soon, my attention was diverted to the place in front of me and I decided not to get prejudiced at his preference, before experiencing it.

Honestly speaking, I always thought Luc to be a fancy, expensive restaurant type of guy. But saying that the sight before me was unexpected would be a huge understatement. We were at the Aquarium. I never pegged Luc to be a nature lover. It was kind of sad though because it proved how little I knew about him.

We walked through the gates of the aquarium and soon a lady dressed in a pencil skirt escorted us inside. My eyes were wide open, taking in the pleasure of the magnificence surrounding us. I was lost in the gracefulness of that place. The place was huge and everything was too blue, which had a calming effect on my soul. We were the only people present there, and I allowed myself to fall into a rabbit hole and rediscovered myself in dreamland. It was an otherworldly experience. Everything appeared glitzy through the reflection of the water and my eyes sparkled, perceiving all the splendor.

"Sarah!" Luc called my name, making my gaze shift towards a mahogany table settled in the middle of a long passage. My eyes noticed the details on the tables, the upside-down plates, the burning candles, and the beautiful flowers in the vase. It didn't take me too long to comprehend it was a date table and the whole aquarium had been booked only for us for the day. A familiar soft tone pulled me back into reality and I noticed Luc waiting for me to join him at the table and I quickly rushed towards him.

Soon, a waiter joined us and filled up our champagne glasses. However, yet again, I couldn't keep my eyes settled on the table and they began beholding the magnificence of a thousand distinct fishes around us. It wasn't that I was visiting the aquarium for the first time, but the magnificence of it was hitting me differently when we were the only two people there and there was a champagne glass in my hand.

"Thank you for brining me here. Everything is just so pure and captivating." A stupid grin was tugging on my lips and I couldn't help it.

"Thank you for coming into my life." I blushed at his remark and unfolded the napkin on my lap while looking down to hide my flustered face. A piece of soothing classical music was playing in the background, and I doubted I ever felt so calm in my life. I perceived I was really starving when soon the food was served and my eyes shined, noticing the delicious dishes that seemed too many for two people.

"Bon appétit!" Luc declared, and I shoved my fork into the lasagna. I opened my mouth, but before I could've tasted the mouth-watering slice, my eyes fell over an aquarium diver who was waving at me. He was swimming with the fish right behind Luc. My eyebrows snapped together. I turned around to check if anyone was standing behind me, but indeed, he was staring at me and I waved back, confusingly.

After a few seconds, I started to feel a little uncomfortable. I tried to look away, but from the corner of my eyes, I couldn't help but feel the aquarium diver's gaze at me. And then my jaw went slack when the person struck me with a heart hand gesture and my eyes narrowed at him. This time it hit me and I couldn't believe what my eyes were witnessing. *What the heck is Ethan doing here?*

My hand snapped to my forehead, and I struggled to hide my face. It was him; I was super sure. I had no idea he would stoop to this level to torture me. My heartbeat started to race when I noticed it had captured my date's attention and he turned around to have a look.

I winced when Stanton gave him a thumbs up, and Luc nodded in return. And suddenly he disappeared somewhere with a backflip. I looked both ways, but he was nowhere in sight and right there I noticed him on the glass ceiling with a big cardboard note in his hand.

'I'm taller than him!'

My eyes rolled back at the note. I didn't know why he was doing it. Why was he making it so hard for me to just sit there and eat? And then once more he disappeared into the water. The place was not soothing to me anymore, and I wanted to run far away from him. I just couldn't afford the encounter between these two people.

'Hanging out with my enemy is not good.'

He emerged once again with another note, right behind Luc. He pulled out his goggles and winked at me, whirling backward, intending to deliver an impression on me. I scowled, rolling my eyes, but then Luc once again turned around, making Ethan instantly dash behind a big rock.

"Are you okay? Aren't you enjoying the food?" My gaze fell on Luc, startled and struggling to concentrate on his face while, all this time, Ethan was blowing kisses at me from behind him. And it was making me annoyed. I wanted to dive in there and strangle him to death.

"No, it's really good," I said, pointing toward my plate and starting to stuff my mouth with food, trying to make him believe I was really enjoying it. While my eyes kept on tossing death glares at Ethan. I was losing my patience bit by bit, and it was getting really hard to hide my annoyance from Luc. I could feel the irritation radiating from me just as I was strangling him in my head.

Around thirty excruciating minutes later, the lunch drew to an end, and I took out a breath of relief. We stood up, Luc wrapped his hand around my waist, thanking the assistant for the great service and food.

Having a private tour of the aquarium was next on Luc's agenda, but I declined, making an excuse for being exhausted due to the night shift. We turned around, ready to take our leave when I extended my middle finger behind my back toward Ethan, who was still hanging around to torment my sanity.

Just as we quickly exited the exquisite place and made our way inside the car, it started pouring. Making our way through the heavy traffic, I could feel the chill in the air. I realized I was shaking when Luc rested his hand on mine, holding it to send a wave of warmth flow through my body. My eyes drifted towards his face, noticing the disarming smile on his lips. There was no doubt that my fiancé was handsome as hell. Not only his hazel eyes were breath-taking, but the liveliness in them was also hard to overlook.

The vehicle halted at a red light, and I started enduring the mesmerizing beauty of my neighborhood. My eyes rested on the gloomy sky, and I blew out a breath on the glass to draw a heart on the window glass. The rain fell like it wanted to let go of everything that had been holding it back. I tilted my head upward and watched the darkness that had overpowered the daylight. I grimaced when a guy blocked my view. He halted his mountain bike just in front of me and I couldn't help but notice that he was dripping wet. The hood of his sweatshirt was concealing his face and soon enough he drifted off when the lights turned green.

As we headed downtown, Luc revealed that he had booked seats for us for the latest Rom-Com playing in the theater. It was such a sweet gesture because I knew he hated such movies. The rain had finally run its course and had turned into a light drizzle. I imagined what it would feel like to stand underneath the rain and feel the tiny droplets on my skin.

"Let's just skip the movie and go someplace close to nature?" I suggested, turning around looking straight into Luc's eyes.

A grateful smile flashed on his face, and then he turned the car towards the central park. The rain-soaked streets sparkled in joy and I rolled down my window, permitting the chilling breeze to pervade the air inside the vehicle. A drop of water landed on my cheek and my mouth curved into a smile.

In a little while, we were walking down the long pathway surrounded by greenery. I smiled, observing the perfect sound of the earth's voice, singing a compelling song. Everything was so alive around us that a silly smile kept on furnishing my lips. The trees, the grass, the nurturing flowers, all radiated such liveliness that I was no longer annoyed by Stanton's mischief. In fact, I'd completely forgotten about him.

The breeze passed through my loosened hair and my eyes squeezed shut, inhaling the perfect earthly smell of the wet soil. There were vendors of candies, hotdogs, and popcorn at the side, and we bought cotton candy to savor our taste buds. I encircled my arms around my body, enjoying the perfect bitter coldness in the air, feeling like a teenager once again. But, the blissful feeling lasted only so long before I was snapped back to reality when I felt strong arms around me. I looked back, noticing Luc's jacket resting on my shoulder. He passed me the same dazzling brief smile as we walked further along.

A light fog had settled down around us, engulfing every object in the distance. My eyes traveled towards the edge of the garden, and I noticed the diminishing daylight, making me stand still, taking in the serenity of the moment.

"You know, I was hell nervous about all this. I thought you would get mad at me for showing up unannounced. Thanks for not giving me a heart attack." I flashed a smile, glimpsing up just as he passed me a sheepish look.

"Well, sometimes we, ladies, like surprises." I teased.

"Do you believe in fate, Luc?" Before I knew it, those words had left my mouth. I mentally cursed myself for even asking that. What was I even thinking?

"Fate is something you could hardly put a bet on. I'll just say if you endeavor for something, then you ought to work your ass off to have it, regardless of what others believe." There was this strange tint in his voice that made me stare at him a little longer than usual. And I couldn't hold back what escaped my mouth next.

"Why are you marrying me, Luc?" He turned around, glancing back at my fragile soul. Halting just in front of me, he bowed his head for a moment and then stared into my eyes with an innocent smile.

"Because it's the right thing to do, Sarah. We have been dating so long and it's the right time to get settled." He sighed and then grasped my hands.

"The day I let my heart touch by yours, I knew you're the right girl for me. I know we don't know each other that well and I also know I'm neither a romantic guy nor good at the kind of stuff women like, such as plucking stars from the sky and bringing flowers on every date. But it's obvious what my heart feels for you. I've fallen for you, Sarah. Fallen for you hard."

I was dumbstruck. I couldn't move. It felt like my body had lost all sensations. My dazed eyes bored into his innocent ones. My surroundings had fallen into complete tranquility. His words were loud and clear, but despite everything, I was still trying to comprehend their meaning. For a little while, he dared to maintain eye contact with me, and then he bowed down to the ground. He was embarrassed; ashamed of letting his feelings known.

I knew we were not a typical romantic lovey-dovey couple. There was more of an arrangement in our relationship rather than passion. For months, I thought he was marrying me just because our parents were very good friends and he didn't want to let them down. But today, I was blown away by his confession of love.

I was at a loss for words, and I knew it was only making the situation worse. I stared into his bright eyes, and my heart fell still. Everything was slow and subtle. My hands squeezed the hem of my dress into fists and I let my eyes follow the path of his hands. He rested his cold hands on my cheek, and I felt him leaning into me.

Our warm lips pressed against each other, and I felt my mind drifting elsewhere. I was no longer in my body. It felt like I was looking at two strangers kissing in the rain from outside. I could feel his racing heart against mine. My eyes fluttered open as I felt his lips smiling against mine. I blinked several times, feeling the drizzle on my face.

"You are so perfect that I think I'm dreaming." And then he gave me a smile that could melt a thousand swords, but my heart was still frozen cold. And before I could have reciprocated his warmth, my eyes found Ethan standing at a distance looking right at us with a cold stare.

⚘

My hands slid down to the sides after our bodies shared one last hug as Luc took his leave. We were standing underneath the front porch of my building and I noticed how his eyes flicked and his shoulders slumped in deep dejection as the day came to an end and we exchanged goodbyes. He glanced at me one last time and then kissed the back of my hand and I shivered under his touch. He headed towards his vehicle and I finally let out a breath of relief I didn't realize I was holding.

Luc rushed towards his car in a haste, holding up an umbrella over his head since the downpour had regained its potential. My dress was half soaked, and I so wanted to get out of it as soon as possible before I catch a cold. Hurriedly settling in, he rolled down the window and waved his goodbye just as the wheels rolled down the street. My eyes remained fixed on him till he faded away from my sight. I blinked several times, still trying to wrap my head around the whirlpool of feelings swirling in my mind.

But the day was over and so was the energy from my body. All I wanted now was to sleep for twenty-four hours straight. I turned around and climbed the stairs to reach the front door of the building when, out of the blue, someone yanked open the door, taking me by surprise. The person came like a shooting star and crossed me before I could've read his face. My eyes trailed behind him as he shoved the trash in the bin and closed the lid a little too harshly. My forehead creased, noticing the same sweatshirt I had seen a little while ago on the biker in the rain, and realization crossed my face when he turned to face me.

Ethan had been following me all day, and right now his face had a grim expression as if I had killed his cat. I opened my mouth to utter some sarcastic remark, but he simply walked past me, heading straight back into the building without sparing a second glance. I couldn't understand what had just happened. Did he just shun me?

His attitude bothered my self-esteem and before I knew it, my legs were following him.

"Thanks for giving us a little visit at the aquarium. I couldn't have asked for a better surprise." I teased at his back, yet he remained quiet. A line appeared between my brows at his silence as he climbed further away. Tagging along, I struggled to catch his pace, but it was like I didn't even exist for him at that moment.

But I wasn't in the mood to back out and allow him to feel proud of his dirty deeds. Before he could've entered his apartment and slammed the door in my face, I rushed to block his way. I stubbornly crammed myself between his scowl and his apartment's door, standing tall and determined.

My eyes narrowed at him when I surveyed his face and noticed him rolling his eyes at me. I wanted to hit his head for that, but I held myself back. He glanced everywhere but at me. I crossed my hands on my chest and gawked at him till he got annoyed enough to look me in the eye. What was wrong with this guy?

"Sarah! Move!" My face dropped and my hands fell on either side of my body in shock. He called me Sarah! Though I hate that stupid nickname he had given me, it didn't feel right when he called me by my name. His voice was calm, yet threatening. However, I couldn't ascertain what was the reason behind his annoyance, or maybe I knew it and wasn't ready to accept it yet.

"Look, dude, you are overreacting. You can't get mad at me for kissing my fiancé!" His eyes lingered on me with a tender look for a moment, but then abruptly, the cold stare was back.

"I'm telling you one last time, girl. Get… out… of… my… freaking… way."

A tint of irritation flashed on my face, and I stubbornly stomped my foot on the floor. He wanted to make things complicated that let them be. I had made up my mind that I wasn't going to move my ass until he would learn to get over his uninvited temper. But what I didn't realize was that he had already made up his mind to not tolerate my stubbornness and take the wheels under his control.

A surprised squeal left my lips with my eyes bulged out in shock when he scooped me up from the ground in a flash like a ragged doll and carried me on his shoulder into his apartment. My stupidity had landed me in this embarrassing situation as I struggled to get away from his strong arms wrapped around my waist, although it all went in vain under his firm grip. The awareness of my dress sliding up with every step he took turned my cheeks crimson.

"You knucklehead! Put me down, right now!" I screamed, but it was worthless against his brooding. I grimaced and started landing some punches on his back, but it appeared like I was just tickling him.

At that moment, my eyes shamelessly darted towards his back pockets, noticing his jeans hanging dangerously low. Before long, I was gawking at his lovely ass with a smirk etched on my face. I should be honest to admit that I wanted to trail down my hands and feel that fine art. Wait, what? No! You're bloody engaged, girl!

But the next second, every bit of my nasty imagination flew out the window when I was roughly tossed down on the couch. My body bounced back up against the cushions with the same intensity that I was thrown down with and my head yanked towards him, noticing him just leaving me in my condition. Anger stirred within me and I shot him a glare. *What does he think of himself?* I felt insulted by being dragged against my will. He was treating me like I was some fly who he wanted to crush down with a rolled magazine. But I wasn't going to tolerate his shit and allow him to treat me like I was nothing. Maybe he had forgotten, but I was no longer that girl who allowed him to treat her like trash. Thus, blowing out a harsh breath, I headed toward him.

"What's wrong with you, dude? Would you even care to explain what has gotten into you? You were missing without any news for seven whole days and now all of a sudden you're showing me this attitude as if I owe you something. I'm sorry, but last time I checked a coffee doesn't mean anything more than a casual moment between two strangers." I swallowed down my frustration, trying to control my shaking breath.

"Whoa! We really made great progress!" His sarcastic remark spurred the irritation inside me even further.

"If I'm a mere stranger to you, how did you know I was gone for exactly seven days and not more or less? Don't lie to yourself, Starz. We affect each other in an exceptional way. You can't expect me to stand here and do nothing when you are out there kissing some random guy." Resentment clouded my thoughts when his sharp words troubled me, just as I noticed how his body trembled with the flares of annoyance that started to engulf him.

"That random guy is my fiancé!"

"Fuckin' bullshit!" He sneered as I gazed at him with rage. I couldn't believe he was acting so bitterly to me. *What has happened to him? I* let out a bitter chuckle when I finally realized why he seemed so upset. It was all a dirty act all along and now that he was fed up playing the sweet guy act, he was showing his true colors. And his selfishness wasn't able to digest the happiness in my life. Anger rose in me like a tide and I strolled toward him.

"What did you just say? Huh? Fuckin' bullshit?" With every word my finger harshly poked his chest causing him to fall several steps back. "I'll tell you what bullshit in my life is. It's fuckin' you!" He held up his hands in front of me, bowing his head towards the floor, and my anger doubled at seeing his insulting laughter.

"Oh, come on, you can't fight me. You are like a possum in front of me."

"Or maybe your male ego is too scared to get beaten-up by a girl."

"Yeah, right! I'm terrified, woman." And the next moment he took hold of both of my arms and caused me to sink down at my spot, leaving me trapped underneath him. I struggled to get away from his grasp, only for him to pull me further in so that he could stare into my eyes and find out the truth behind my words.

"You don't love him, Starz. Then why bother marrying him, anyway?" Despite my attempts to conceal my eyes, he deepened his gaze into my soul, and my only recourse to prevent him from getting too close to my heart was to be sarcastic. I let out a humorless chuckle, looking everywhere but at him.

"Oh, a man whore is giving me a lesson on love? What an irony! You are in no position to tell me what I should or shouldn't do. So, let go of me!" He acted on my threat and let me go. I could no longer feel his warmth and it felt a little strange with cold engulfing me. I turned around, already regretting that I even bothered myself to have a talk with him today.

"Is it, Starz? Then why did you take off his ring?" His words halted me in my tracks. I was glad he couldn't see the startled look on my face.

"Doctors don't wear jewelry. I could lose it. And besides, I'm... allergic to gold!" I uttered quickly. But the brief pause in my words made a mocking sneer escape his lips. He walked back a few steps and his loud mocking laugh echoed in the room.

"Another hogwash! You can babble whatever story you want, but I know the truth, girl! You never loved him and you never will. Because you never did stop loving me, Sarah Walter!" His words made a fit of anger beat at my heart and I turned around to face him.

"Ha- Ha! Stanton, in which disturbing model of fantasy world are you still living in? News flash! The world doesn't revolve around you, dude. The thing is, you are just a jealous two-faced bastard who can't see anyone being happy over your selfish, sick soul." I said, pointing a finger at him. I was shaking in fury. *How dare he say something like that to me?* I knew from the first day, letting him back in my life was not a good idea. I never wanted to let him affect me in this way.

"You know nothing about me, darling! I'm much more than just a two-faced bastard." He threatened his way toward me and I stepped back, daring to meet his piercing eyes. He had a cold stare featuring his stern face, just as a muscle in his jaw twitched. My eyes drifted towards his hands, which were now clenched tightly into fists. My lower lip trembled, witnessing him decreasing the distance between us, and then my shoulder tensed up when my back hit the wall.

I was trapped, and before I could've managed to escape his ambush, he yanked both my hands on either side of my head against the wall. My pupils dilated, perceiving the shuddering muscles in his forearm, and then he leaned into me. I was scared. Scared to feel the emotion that I wasn't allowed to feel. The feeling that I had buried into the deepest core of my spirit. I had promised myself never to feel this vulnerable ever again in my life.

"Starz, I'm aware that you want me to believe that you don't fancy me, but your eyes are painting a whole different picture that you're too afraid to peer into." My eyes wandered toward his mouth and I took a sharp breath in when his tongue slithered out, moistening the aridness of his lips.

"Yes, I'm jealous, darling." Towering over me with his enormous shadow, he let go of my hands, but his hands stretched out on the wall on either side of my head, making me imprisoned underneath his gaze. I offered him a disgruntled look when his smug look savored the helplessness I was feeling.

He leaned in and whispered in my ear, "I'm so jealous right now that I just want to kiss you, to taste you so passionately that it would leave you begging for more. I'm jealous that I want to tear off your little soaked dress, which is tempting me since you've placed a foot in my apartment. This jealousy is driving me insane. And you know what, Starz? No matter how much you deny it, I know that you're enjoying this jealous part of me." His lips brushed against my ear and a chill ran down my spine, making me tremble underneath him.

I hated myself at that moment for giving him the satisfaction of how badly his touch was affecting my body. But before he could've taken another step, his phone started buzzing against his pocket and my body relaxed a bit. His face screwed while checking the name on the screen and he turned around with a disgruntled look, finally setting me free. And I thanked the person on the other side of the line for cutting the dangerous moment short.

Because I hated him for being right all along.

Twenty-three

Sarah

DAY THIRTY

The incessant clouds gave out the impression of a painted canvas with diverse colors and I couldn't help but compare it with my life at that moment. As the sun was rising from the horizon, my surroundings were at a complete standstill and I knew it was the calm before a storm. My hands fidgeted on my lap and one last time my eyes surveyed the colors spread across the sky and I bowed down, not feeling like enjoying the breathless beauty of sunrays spread across the clouds.

I shook my head in refusal when the flight attendant requested to refill my glass. She smiled at me and then disappeared at the back of the curtains and my eyes drifted towards Ethan. On the outside, he was calm and composed, with one foot resting over the thigh of the other, but his furrowed forehead was narrating a whole different story of chaos in his spirit. He was looking out of the window as if appreciating the beautiful morning sky, but only I knew his mind was occupied by something entirely different.

It was one bunch of bloody mess. My expression dulled, witnessing the clouds of sadness engulfing him completely. And though hours had passed since we got the news, it still felt like we're struck by lightning just a while ago.

As his phone started buzzing, his piercing gaze left my vulnerable sight, and I composed myself back. He took several steps back, but his eyes lingered on me before curling down on the floor. My chest rose and fell with rapid breaths when I finally got my senses back. I could hardly build up the courage to accept reality. I never felt so vulnerable in my life. It was like he had overpowered me in every way; mind, body, and soul.

He turned his back towards me, and I settled down, rearranging my dress to its proper position. I couldn't help but notice after pulling out the phone from his pocket, he muttered a curse, noticing the name on the screen. He wasn't grateful to the person who had called him. And I wondered who could make him more enraged than me.

"Hey, how's it going, mom? You good?" My eyes drifted towards the floor as I made my mind to leave the house at that moment and not intervene in the conversation.

"What's going on, mom? Why the hell are you crying?" My brows snapped together, sensing the quick change of tone in his voice. Setting my eyes on him, I noticed his stern face, and I could sense the turmoil in the atmosphere. Something was clearly wrong.

"Mom, is everything all right? Mom! Talk to me!" I flinched at the sudden rise of his voice. My body tensed up when he continued to try to talk to his mom, but it felt like she was not in a position to form her words properly.

My hand rested on my chest when I feared the worst. Is she okay? Has anything happened to his father? A thousand thoughts ran into my mind and I silently prayed everything was okay. A long, thick, painful silence engulfed us when I appraised that she was finally able to utter something. My eyes landed on his hand gripping the back of a chair and his knuckles turning white just as his expressions hardened with the continuation of the conversation. I wanted to know what the cause of the grimness on his face was. The silence was eating me from inside and I wished I could hear the voice from the other side of the line.

"Mom, everything is going to be okay! Have faith! I'll be there as soon as I can!" The serenity in his tone made me stare at him even harder. His expression was narrating a different story, contrary to the way he was expressing it. There was something wrong with his way of talking to his mother and the next moment I was proved right when he cut the call and hurled the cell phone on the floor with immense force.

I jumped in fear at his sudden outburst with my eyes noticing the metal piece, which now happened to be broken in half. And just as my eyes drifted back at him, he was clenching his hair while his eyes turned bloodshot and the muscles along his jaw clenched. The look on his face was masked with terror. As if his whole world had fallen apart.

"Sarah, go home!" His voice was cold and dry. The edge of caution in his tone made me uneasy, yet I didn't stir an inch from my place. I held up my guards and was *about to ask about the call when I witnessed him dashing inside the bedroom, without even giving me a second glance.*

I followed him inside and found him packing his bag haphazardly. My eyes were having a hard time matching his pace. He yanked open the bedside drawer to take out his wallet and another phone. Gliding past me, he went outside to pick up his broken phone and took out his sim card to put in the new phone.

"Ethan, what happened?" My mind was slowly joining all the pieces together; his family was in need of him because something terrible must have happened and he had to reach there shortly. But I still needed answers. I couldn't live with all these unanswered questions burning inside my soul.

He moved along once again as I watched him dashing out of the room while carrying up the bag on his shoulder and typing something on his cell phone. I witnessed him stomping towards the main door, and just as he was about to leave without answering my question, I tightly took hold of his forearm, halting his steps right there.

I could feel his tensed muscles against my touch, but I brushed it away. Slowly, resting the bag on the floor, he turned around, and there I noticed the pain gripping his face. My soul shuddered at seeing his heart-rending eyes. He tried his best to not meet my eyes, and I could feel the tension building between us.

"Nanna is in the hospital, Starz. She met with an accident. I need to be there. Please go home and be safe." I wanted to hug him tight but held myself back. Releasing himself out of my grasp, he walked ahead. But before he could've put his foot out of the house, I couldn't stop myself from asking if I could join him.

I was dragged back to the present when the pilot announced that we were going to land soon. My eyes went back towards Ethan and noticed the same old scowl on his face. He hadn't uttered a single word throughout the journey. Every time I tried to have a conversation with him, he gave a straight short reply, voluntarily ending the conversation. It was clear that he didn't want anyone around him right now. But I was scared that if I left him alone he would plunge deeper into despair and go completely numb.

Walking down the steps of the aircraft, a cold breeze stroked me and I shuddered, pulling my coat closer to my body. Ethan approached me from behind and wrapped his arm around my waist, guiding me towards a car parked on the runway. Greetings of the chauffeur died down because of the screeching voice of the engine in the background, and we settled down inside the vehicle.

"How far is the hospital, Manfred?" My eyes followed Ethan and then finally rested on the person who was taking us to our destination. The person hesitated a bit, and I sensed he was somehow closer to Ethan's family.

"Ten minutes, Sir!" Ethan settled back on his seat, with annoyance gripping his body. I didn't know how to make the situation less tense when all I could think of was what would we find at the hospital. A distressing silence fell between us as he continued to stare outside the window. I couldn't help but notice that he was blocking all the emotions by hiding his heart behind a wall. Part of me wanted to feel his despair, so I wouldn't feel so cut off from him, but there was another part of me who was scared to let the emotions in.

As we reached the hospital, Tom's familiar face received us, and Ethan nodded at him before rushing inside the hospital. Heading towards the designated room, I trailed along with them and in no time, my eyes met with plenty of people waiting outside the room. A woman came running towards us and buried herself in Ethan's arms. She was crying bitterly and I could easily feel the pain radiating from her soul.

"Mom, I'm here now. Don't worry. Calm down." I looked up and witnessed him clenching his jaw in helplessness as he was struggling to console his mother. But she broke down even harder, drenching his shirt with her tears of sorrow.

"The best team of doctors have performed a two-hour surgery, but they fear she might go into an incessant coma!" Tom informed us and right there I saw a sudden change of expression on Ethan's face. He turned his back to us and slammed his fist into the wall, making me jump with shock.

"I want that motherfucker as soon as possible, Tom." His threatening voice made me witness the anger gushing out of him. Tom placed a hand on his shoulder and lightly squeezed it. It was like they were exchanging words without saying anything. And the next second, Ethan rushed inside the critical care room. My legs followed him without giving a second thought and found him frozen at the door. My eyes averted towards the patient lying on the bed and straight away I could perceive the matter was serious.

I turned around and left the room, as I was getting impatient with the lack of information. His family members eyed me curiously, but stealing my eyes from them, I made my way towards the nearest reception counter. The on-duty nurse provided me with the name of the doctors that had operated on her and shortly I seized the opportunity to talk to one of them.

It was a hit-and-run case and her condition was bad. A car crashed her into the sidewalk when she was having a stroll after dinner just outside her house. Her skull was fractured, which resulted in a serious intracerebral hemorrhage. She had lost a lot of blood and that coupled with her old age, painted a weak picture of recovery at this stage.

'I am afraid she is not going to make it.' The surgeon's words replayed in my head again and again, and I found myself suffocating in that big corridor. I was breathing hard and felt my eyes suddenly getting swamped with tears. The feeling was strange as I didn't even know the person lying on her deathbed. But I knew this news would break Ethan apart, and it pained my heart.

Turning around, I ran outside the hospital because the place was choking me. The surrounding pain wasn't letting my body breathe normally. The air outside was freezing, but it soothed the scorching heat burning inside my chest. But then I felt a touch on my shoulder and I quickly straightened my back, knowing who this person was. Wiping my tears away, I twirled around, trying to bring a fake smile to my lips.

"Are you okay, Starz?" His fragile voice made me look at his face and I came across a tired man. It looked like he had aged ten years in the past few minutes. The wrinkles on his forehead were displaying how worried he was about me. Me? While it was his family member who was not going to see another daylight.

"I'm fine! Go inside, please. Your mother needs you the most right now!" I tried to send him away before I could've lost control over my body. I was weak and his presence was only making it worse.

"I'm sorry for my careless behavior last night. I lost control of my temper, Starz." My head shot up, and they met his eyes that were shimmering with tears. For the first time in my life, I witnessed Ethan Stanton helpless. He was so fragile right now, and he clearly hated the fact of being so exposed. "I'm also sorry for dragging you into this. I shouldn't have brought you with me." He was struggling hard not to let his tears fall.

"I came of my own free will, Ethan." Staring down, I grabbed his hand in mine and smiled, rummaging through my thoughts for something reasonable to say. But, the words that left my mouth surprised even me.

"We are not capable of regulating everything in our lives, Ethan. Sometimes we have to endure something terrible with the hope that this shall soon come to pass." I squeezed his hand and looked straight into his eyes.

"I'm here for you, Ethan." I tried to put on a brave front for his sake but internally cursed myself for being so weak. I wanted to tell him the truth which I had been curbing in my heart from setting free. I craved for him to know that I would be there by his side, no matter what happened. I wanted him to be aware of the fact that even if I endeavored to be away from him, my heart would never allow me to leave.

We headed back inside, still holding hands for support. I couldn't help but sense the dread in the air. Everything was so quiet. I stumbled in my seat, unreasonably afraid that something bad was soon going to permeate us. My eyes drifted towards Tom and Ethan when they began to offer coffee to everyone. He settled the cup in his mother's weak hands and then gave her a soft kiss on her head. He was trying hard to hold his family together.

But then a line appeared between my brows when I noticed a strange tension between Ethan and a man leaning against a wall. Ethan held out a cup for him, but he simply looked away, not even withstanding to spare a glance in his way. My heart stirred as Ethan's face fell and he turned around to leave the man alone.

I could feel a frown etching my features at his rude behavior. I couldn't understand why the man reacted in this way and moreover who the man was. My eyes bored into him and recognition flashed in front of my eyes.

He was Mr. Stanton, Ethan's father. But what I couldn't get was the reason for uneasiness between them.

❦

Minutes turned into hours, and we still had not received any news from the doctors. Though the doctor had proclaimed his conclusion, we still had some hope. And nothing could be more vital than hope in that fragile moment.

The day had given way to darkness, and I noticed almost everyone dozing off in their seats. Mr. Stanton was supporting his wife, who was resting her head on his shoulder while his head was leaning back on the wall. Tom was also passed out in one of the corners. Slowly, taking out my shawl from the bag, I wrapped it around my freezing body and strolled away from that area in search of Ethan.

I found Ethan sitting in the stairways, lost in his own world. I doubted he noticed me when I took a seat next to him and sighed, feeling the weariness flowing through him. Scooting closer, I wrapped one end of the shawl around his shoulders, trying to warm the frozen muscles of his body. I noticed him filching lightly when my touch pulled him out of his little reverie all of a sudden. He looked at me, confused and vulnerable.

"She is the only real family I am left with, Starz. A beautiful soul. After getting abandoned by my parents, she gave me the love and support of both a mother and a father. She never asked for anything in return. Her selfless love was the only thing that kept me sane in my dark days, mad in search of something unattainable. She knew there was something that was bothering me all these years, but she never pushed me for answers. And now, I might have to live with the regret that I couldn't even manage to have the last words with her. I don't know what I'll do without her, Sarah!"

There were so many emotions playing on his face right now, but fear was overpowering them all. The fear of losing someone he loved. I leaned my head on his shoulder while holding his hand in mine. His fingers were freezing, yet they spread a strange kind of warmth in my body.

"This town is doomed. It steals away everyone I love the most in this world. I should never have agreed to bring her here in the first place. It's all my fault. I should just have stayed with her in San Francisco." He buried his face in his hands, sobbing into his palms.

"Nothing is your fault, Ethan! Never ever think like that." I said while pulling his hands from his face. Intertwining our fingers, I held his eyes. All I could do was stare at his vulnerable features, filling up my heart with his pain. This was the guy I had fallen in love with in my adolescence. My first love. And maybe my only love. Inhaling a sharp breath of air, I shivered with an inner conflict. I wanted to hold back, yet desired to walk down the forbidden path.

"Mr. Stanton, can I have a word with you?" I blinked several times as we were intruded by an unfamiliar voice. We stood up, and it was then that I noticed some men in police uniforms. He squeezed my hand slightly before taking his leave and then the police officer and Ethan headed towards a far corner.

"We have caught the guy, Mr. Stanton. He is totally wasted and even the vehicle is also not his own. But it's a clear hit-and-run case. Though the lad seems in his early teens and will come under juvenile justice, still we will not let him go away easily. Shall we make it appear as a custodial suicide?" My hand snapped over my mouth, listening to the words of the officer. He was waiting for Ethan's approval and when my eyes drifted toward him, I found him falling deeply in remorse. I knew that he was having an inner battle between his vengeance and morals.

"Put him in juvenile incarceration. And let me know about his family's conditions!" Ethan quickly dismissed them and strolled back inside the hospital. There was an edge of irritation in his voice that made me notice he was not entirely happy with his decision. Following his movement, I noticed him quickly hurrying inside the restroom. There was so much to handle in a single night that I guessed he needed some alone time. He didn't want to show his weaker side to me and I accepted that. At least, he was not in denial of his emotions.

My legs followed my heart, and I found myself staring through the thick glass of the room into the essence of the beautiful lady on the bed. Her chest rose and fell with each struggled breath and somehow I found myself attached to her. I wished I had the pleasure of knowing her and hearing her sweet voice. She raised Ethan and I could now appreciate the gentleman she had converted him into. Her skin looked so fragile that I was certain it could melt anyone's heart. Her gray, lustrous hair doubled her striking beauty. And I couldn't help but grieve at the misfortune of not meeting her in person.

"This is not the end. It's just the beginning of the next phase of your better life." I whispered through my trembling lips, and as if on cue the monitors started to beep loudly. I pushed my hands to my ears, trying to stifle the deafening sound of beeping. I knew what was happening. Doctors came rushing inside the room and I stepped back. They kept on trying to stabilize her, but I knew she was fading away with every passing second.

Within seconds, the family gathered outside the room and Ethan's mom broke down once again. Her cries echoed in the area, and I felt like I was fading away in the background. Shaking my head, I was just backing away when my back bumped into the wall. My legs were numb and I could feel the thumping of my heart in my ear.

Tears swelled in the back of my eyes when I witnessed Ethan running inside the room, desperate to hold her hand while it still had life. Her soul was slowly drifting away from her body. The doctors stepped back and noted the time of death just as Ethan started shouting at them.

At that moment, time froze around me, and everything appeared to be happening in slow motion. Ethan grabbed hold of the collar of one of the doctors as Tom struggled to separate them. Anger radiated from his body when he was barking at the medical staff. He thrust his fist into the nearby wall, and a tear escaped my eye, suffering through the enormous amount of agony scorching through him.

I rushed towards him when I noticed blood seeping out his knuckles. But then I found myself frozen on the doorstep. I couldn't go any further. I was scared. I was terrified of the thought that I would lose myself if I took one more step toward him. There was this thin thread that was lurking between us. And it had been holding me back at a safe distance.

However, when he turned around and his eyes met mine, I shuddered. He was crying. His bloodshot eyes were concealing so much pain in them that I winced. His pain made me so vulnerable that tears started to run down my cheeks till I was immersed in agony. I stormed in his direction and halted just an inch from his face. His body suddenly became lax, noticing me and Tom let go of him. I could feel the throbbing ache his heart had been going through. He was breaking from inside and I couldn't do anything.

"She is... she is gone, Sarah!" His vulnerable heartbreaking voice tore away the weak thread holding me back and the next second, I crushed my body into his. My hands encircled his neck just as I buried his face in the crook of my neck. I was holding him so tight as if I dreaded he might disappear.

I feared that my heart will explode with the amount of love I could no longer hold back.

Twenty-four

Sarah

NINE YEARS AGO

Every favorite song has an untold story behind it. Somedays we get enchanted by its melody, while on others we listen to the lyrics, understanding each and every word and feeling it deep in our hearts. It all depends on what your heart has been going through at that time. And right now, I was lost in the sweet melody of an unknown song.

It feels so good to experience early morning sunrays warming up your face. Gentle heat stirring your whole body on a wintry morning, taking away every ounce of weariness with it and leaving behind a long trail of serenity. It was so pure to indulge. The warmth of a thousand emotions spread through my body and I felt fulfilled. Perhaps nothing could be so satisfying than this awareness. Every string of my muscles loosened up while lying flat on my back on fresh frosty grass. I just wanted to let go of everything.

Last night's heavy pours must have filled this place with life. The soothing bird songs were causing a tranquilizing effect on my soul. A smile crept on my lips when I felt tiny water droplets dripping on my face. Nevertheless, I kept my eyes tightly closed. I didn't want to know how I got here or where this exactly was. All I cared about was the ultimate feeling that carried extreme peace to my very core.

"Wake up, Ray!" A woman's voice whispered in my ear. The murmur was so calm and inviting that it made me open my eyes.

The first thing my sight caught hold of was the sunrays filtering out of white clouds. I heaved up slightly on my elbows and looked down to my right to acknowledge damp grass squeezed up in my palm. My face lit up, noticing the wonderful scene in front of my eyes. Subtle sunrays were kissing the dew on the grass, making them sparkle like a thousand diamonds.

Gently, I stood up on my feet, afraid to disturb the serenity of the place, and before I knew it, I was lost in the splendor. I never imagined this type of place could exist. Maybe it was some hidden world I had accidentally stumbled upon, leaving behind every desolation of my life.

My eyes couldn't hold so much perfection in one sight. Though it was swallowed by dense mist, I could still appreciate the beautiful meadow right in front of my eyes. It was a captivating luxury. Daisies were nurturing the place, enveloping the land like a bride's veil. The grass was rustling gently in the breeze and I closed my eyes, devouring the exceptional earthly scent of freshly drenched mud and flowers.

Out of the blue, I felt a tap on my shoulder and I turned around. Ethan's blue shimmering eyes welcomed me with a bewitching smirk that spread warmth inside my body. Tenderness crept to the bottom of my heart when he crossed his arms on his chest and passed me the most beautiful, heart-melting grin. He had the kind of appearance that could stop any girl in her tracks.

"Come with me." His bewitching voice made me follow him.

He proceeded towards the meadow and, without thinking, I tagged along. I beamed in delight when he looked back at me. A corner of his mouth lifted up and then he started to run. Slowly, my legs began to keep pace with him. We were sprinting in that field, surrounded by endless flora. I was so happy that my whole body was aroused with excitement. I was full of hope and joy. Just like a free bird, I darted in whatever direction I wanted to. There was no barrier that could stop me. I had never felt so liberated in my entire lifetime.

But soon I was exhausted. "Hey, slow down. I can't run any faster." My body jerked to a stop just as a scarcity of breath kicked in. I leaned forward to send some ease to my burning lungs while resting my hands on my knees. I tried to catch some oxygen, but the air just wouldn't get in my lungs. Sweat rolled down my forehead, and I squeezed my eyes, noticing Ethan heading towards an enormous tree.

"Come on. Don't you love me, Sarah?" I frowned at his remark and then noticed him moving forward to climb the tree.

Of course, I loved him. I'd always love him. I nodded in dare and then followed his grueling pace. It felt like he had challenged my love and I dashed forward without complaining about my burning body. The heat was scorching out of my soul and I sprinted farther, ready to join him. My chest heaved up and down as I was running out of air.

Yet, I was grinning like a crazy, over-enthusiastic person when my feet came to a halt just underneath the tree, and looking at his lively soul, made my body elope towards him on its own. And then a sharp shooting pain transpired from my right leg. A short squeal left my mouth, feeling the sting that was consuming me. I tilted my head in agony and found him still mounting higher up the tree.

"What are you still doing down there? You are going to miss the view." His voice echoed in my head and I took in a sharp breath and pursued to climb the tree. My chest rose and fell with rapid breaths, but I concentrated on my destination, on him. Just a few more steps and I would be there by his side. I raised my chin and noticed him settling on one of the highest branches. He had already reached the perfect position. The adrenaline rush was pushing me forward. Urging me to do what I couldn't. I climbed further and further. I couldn't deny being scared, but somehow, the excitement was overpowering the fear. Just as my eyes evaluated the joy behind his closed eyes, I pushed myself even more.

As I took my last leap, I scraped my knee. The pain seared through my leg and was increasing in waves. I gritted my teeth just as blood began to seep out of the wound. It was burning, making me stop my endeavor. I tried to move my leg to reach my aim, but just as the muscle stretched, the pain shot up like thousands of needles stabbing me all at the same time.

"Ethan, help me. I'm hurt. I can't go any further." His head tilted forward, examining my condition. Taking the support of the branches, he slowly rambled down and ended up beside me in no time. My cheeks turned pink, seeing him caressing my knee. I shuddered, just as he blew out his hot breath over the cut. He shook his head while his eyes were trained on the wound and my brows snapped together in confusion. What was he thinking? He shoved his hair back away from his face and looked up as his lips curved into a smile.

"Sarah, you know how precious you are to me?" I nodded, and my eyes twinkled while he held out his hands. I placed both my palms on his.

"Since the day you caught my attention, I wanted to have you by my side. I wanted to live every second with you and now that you are with me, I can finally confess my dark fears to you." His words left me puzzled. I struggled to read his face, but it was all blank.

Suddenly, he closed his eyes and ducked his head down as if struggling to get the words out of his mouth. But when he looked up, his eyes were blazing with hatred.

"I never loved you, foolish girl." And then he pushed me off the tree.

✿

Noooooo…

My eyes fluttered open but then closed shut again within a fraction of a second as the scorching sunrays blinded me. The beam pierced my vision, resulting in a sharp shooting pain penetrating my temples. I sensed someone rushing towards the windows to mask the source of light, and I felt a little relieved.

"Call the doctor! She is awake!"

My head started spinning against the consciousness of the nightmare I had just experienced. Despite realizing the fact that it was just a dream, born out of my imagination, I kept my eyes closed, letting the fear linger around me like a mist. I was left terrified and was struggling to find an escape from that elusive world, a world that almost felt real.

"Sarah! Dear! Can you hear me?"

Reluctantly, I flicked open my eyes once again; only to discover my mother hovering over me. Her big brown eyes were gazing up at me while soft snuffles escaped her lips. Her tired face reflected the pain she had been enduring. But then, her eyes were filled with hope.

"Oh. Thank God! You are all right, dear! I am right here with you!" She reassured me while lightly patting my hair. However, it looked like she needed reassurance more than I did.

At first, I thought I was in yet another dream. My vision was vague, but I pushed my mind to perceive things clearly. Everything surrounding me was covered in white and it made me uneasy. My eyes averted toward a beeping monitor at my left, and then to a bunch of daisies in a beautiful vase sitting at the side table. I closed my eyes, striving to inhale the aroma, and the moment the scent hit me, my brain took me back to my dream, where the flowers were rustling freely in the breeze. Maybe my head was tricking me and I was still dreaming. But then, it didn't take me long to figure out the matter. Evidently, I was lying on a hospital bed.

A doctor and a nurse came rushing into the room, followed by my father. The nurse escorted my mother and father outside while the doctor looked at me as if I was a miracle.

"Hello, dear! I am Dr. Benson. Could you tell me your name?"

"Sarah. Sarah Walter." My voice sounded so scratchy. Like I had been screaming all night. My throat hurt. Instinctively, my hand tried to reach toward my throat to ease the pain. It is then that I noticed needles piercing my skin. I took in the sight of the tubes connecting me to various machines.

"Very good, Sarah! Do you know what day it is?"

"Hmm... yes! It's Thursday, 16th May." What did he think? I lost my memory or something. I wanted to roll my eyes at him, but I was too tired for it.

The doctor scribbled something on his notepad in a hurry and then smiled at me. "Actually, it's Friday, 31st May. You had a terrible fall in a hospital in Fairhope and hit your head pretty hard. You have been in a medically induced coma for more than two weeks, child."

Two weeks! Two weeks! I had been out for more than two weeks! My head jerked up, meeting his eyes, and then I looked at the nurse. She was staring at the doctor as if checking the rationality of his words. For a few seconds, I prayed that it was merely a joke. But when the doctor's eyes remained glued to mine with the same sad expression for my depressing fate, I realized the truth in his words.

"Where exactly am I?" I asked as I realized I was perhaps not in Fairhope anymore.

"You are in Montgomery State Hospital. You were transferred here in a very critical condition." I closed my eyes, trying hard to stop my head from spinning from all the information.

"I know it's too much to take in, dear, but the good news is that you are completely out of danger now. Well, technicality, you also had a shoulder separation and a twisted right ankle, but they are almost healed now. You will be good to go home in a couple of weeks."

His words hit me like a sharp blow to my guts. My hand instinctively covered my belly. "My baby! What about my baby?" I almost shouted, as much as my scratched-up voice would allow me to. I tried to tilt up my body on my elbows, but then I noticed the big dressing encircling my right elbow. With the slender movement, I could feel a sharp shooting ache radiating from my whole arm and my head started spinning.

I shivered faintly when my cold fingers touched my forehead and I sensed a large bandage on it. The nurse put his hands on my shoulders and eased me back on the pillow.

"I'm sorry, but we couldn't save the fetus. You had lost so much blood that it was an impossible task." I stared at her blankly, still trying to comprehend her words. I let out a harsh breath, staring down at my hands. In principle, I shouldn't be sad as I was going to abort the child anyway, but still, for some unknown reason, I felt awful. My eyes filled up with tears on their own as I felt a sharp void inside me.

"But your entire family is here, dear, and they all love you so much. Would you like to meet them now?" The doctor interjected with clear fake enthusiasm.

"Maybe. But first I want to sleep a few more hours." I didn't want to face anyone right now. I needed some time to process everything.

"Certainly, Sarah." The nurse injected something into the tube connected to my arm, which eased me back to sleep.

"Hello, Sarah. How are you feeling today?"

My head swirled with the voice and out of nowhere, I felt a sharp string of pain crawling through my head. It felt weird to hear my name. I turned my head in the direction of that voice and found two people in white coats. I guessed they were the doctors who had been treating me. I recognized one of them from yesterday as he smiled at me while simultaneously cleansing his hands with the sanitizer.

Soon, two nurses entered the room and proceeded to remove the needles from my forearm. My jaw clenched when pain shot up to my arm. I had to bite my tongue to obstruct the scream that was about to escape. It hurt badly.

Subsequently, they helped me to straighten up my back; assisting me into a partial sitting position, steadily. It felt like my body was denying any kind of movement. Every muscle of my body was stiff and aching and all I wanted was to lie down and descend deep into slumber. The woman doctor slowly came closer to my bed and flashed light from her tiny torch straight into my weak orbs and I squinted.

"What would you like to do today, Sarah?" She asked, whilst the other one started to scribble something on his writing pad, I began to explore my body carefully.

"Can I get some water?" My scratchy voice indicated how rough and dry my throat was.

The doctor gestured to the nurse, who helped me gulp down a few sips of water. After making a few more notes on my vitals and commenting on how well I was doing, the doctors left and my mother entered the room.

"I missed my graduation!" That was the first thing that came out of my mouth seeing her. My whole world came crashing down like a house of cards. I started sobbing as panic rose in the deepest core of my heart and I felt wretched.

The one day that could've been the best day of my life had slipped by from my hand. My mother and I were planning for it for the whole month. She was so excited to finally meet Ethan. I rolled up in a ball of self-loathing and pain. I missed the day about which I had been dreaming almost my whole high school life.

I wanted to talk to her about the baby, but couldn't make the words come out of my mouth. Somewhere deep down, I knew that I was the one who was responsible for all this. The guilt was eating me alive. It was my own fault that I was in this position. I knew I should be thankful for being alive at the least. This was a punishment I had received for not confiding in my family. I deserved it very well.

"Ray!" My father's voice startled my senses as if pulling me out of a limbo. I no doubt loved my mother a lot, but I had always felt closer to my father.

I was mortified as well as disheartened facing him. Filled with humiliation, I dropped my eyes and then squeezed them shut. Sadness clouded my features, and I felt utter remorse. My body flinched in alarm when he crouched next to me and I opened my eyes. He took my hand in his and squeezed it lightly; as if ensuring me that he was always going to be present by my side, no matter what.

But I was too ashamed to even look into his eyes. I had let him down. I had disgraced him, my whole family. I had proved myself as a terrible daughter. He had trusted me and I did nothing but shatter his faith. Nothing was comparable to the guilt I was feeling at that moment. My eyes were fixed on our interlocked hands and I didn't know when, but tears flooded my eyes. He called my name once again, and I snuffled, trying to hold back the water in my eyes.

I never felt so much disgust and bitterness for myself. I had no strength to face his eyes. I just couldn't. I wanted to run far away from them, where I wouldn't have to face anyone. My heart was just too weak to perceive pity in everyone's eyes.

"Ray, baby girl, don't you want to greet your dad?" I shook my head harder when tears trickled down from my eyes. And then I couldn't hold myself any longer as I flung myself into his arms. I just sobbed harder and harder under his shelter.

"I'm sorry, dad. I'm so, so sorry." I pleaded, with my breaking voice. I was on the verge of losing my senses and blacking out at any moment now.

I struggled to breathe as if my mind had lost control over my body. Grief was consuming me, and I doubted if I could survive one more second. I was sinking deeper and deeper into the enormity of my misery. I didn't care about people who were witnessing me in that pathetic condition, because I had him now. I just wanted to let go of everything. I was completely hollowed from inside. No feelings were left, but sorrow. My breathing was ragged, gasping for air with every sob. I was shaking so badly that I wanted to give up. I cried until no more tears fell.

"Ray, Ray, I'm here. Your father is here. You don't have to fear anything now." His comforting words made me break down even further. I missed him so much. After all this, he still cared about his daughter.

"I'll protect you now. I promise, Ray! I promise!" His words penetrated my heart. How could he still love me? I didn't deserve his love at all. My grip loosened up on his shirt as I leaned back, my eyes boring into his.

Those green orbs were shimmering with tears. He looked so vulnerable that it made my heart clench. Quickly wiping off his tears with the back of his hands, he managed to uphold a smile that was slipping away with every passing second. He was barely controlling his emotions. But, I found a safe haven by his side. My lower lip trembled and tears tumbled down my eyes when I noticed the fear in his eyes; the fear of losing me. And I embraced him all over again.

"Sir, she needs to rest. She is still too weak to have a proper conversation." Unexpectedly, a nurse interrupted us. But I didn't care about her advice. I still had so many things to say to my dad. But when I sensed him shifting back, I tightened my grip around him like a five-year-old.

"Baby girl! She is right. We can talk later. Your health is the priority." With his words caressing my ears, I groaned stubbornly. I just shook my head, as I was not in the mood to leave my dad's side just yet. I hugged him even more securely. But he ended the hug and clubbed my face to look at him straight.

"Now you're going to lie down and sleep. I want my daughter to get healthy soon and for this, you need to rest. I promise I'll be right outside the door. Call me anytime you need me."

He wiped my tears one last time and then passed me a smile that failed to reach his eyes. I watched as everybody started to make their way to exit one by one. For the first time, I noticed that Aunt Rose was also there in the room. My dad was the first one who made his way outside hastily. I knew he was just trying to look strong in front of me while deep down he was broken seeing me like this.

I was sure the moment he would step outside; he would cry like a baby. My mother kissed my forehead and then turned around to leave the room. I witnessed as she held on to my aunt's hand to maintain her stance. I stared at them as Aunt Rose looked back at me, giving me an assuring smile, and then I was left alone with the nurse.

The nurse eased me onto my pillow and I closed my eyes. Two weeks of my life had passed in a blur. So many things would have happened in these two weeks and I doubted if anyone in my school was aware of my condition. But then there was one person who might be losing his mind in concern at this moment. He might have been awfully sad too, too absorbed by the guilt.

I couldn't imagine how many times he must have visited me to catch a glimpse of my bruised face. He must have come to see me every day. Dad must have given him a hard time. I found myself surrounded by sadness when I thought of how terrible he would be feeling about my condition. I was certain he would be blaming himself day and night for this misfortune. I couldn't dare to imagine his pain. I was not that strong enough. I was so deeply lost in my thoughts that I couldn't tell when slumber overpowered me.

The next day, following the early morning visit of the doctors and nurses, I was left with some additional instructions and cautions.

As my breakfast arrived on the table, I requested my parents to leave the room and get some rest, which they clearly very much needed. Taking a bite from my apple, my eyes roamed over the magazine that was there to help burn my free time. I frowned, finding so many ridiculous pieces of relationship advice, and before I could've scooped over to the next column, my head snapped up when someone barged in. I witnessed the door becoming a victim of my best friend's over-enthusiasm.

My jaw went slack when I saw her standing at the door, trying to catch her breath. The corners of her mouth turned up as she gave me a lopsided grin. My body recoiled in fear, seeing her running towards me and in the end, she engulfed my tiny frame in a bear hug.

My whole face lit up just as I tried my best not to die of suffocation and the pain shooting in my arm. I tapped my hand on the back of her shoulder, and luckily, she stepped back, wiping the sweat from her forehead. I chuckled at her heroic entrance.

"Did you come running all the way from Fairhope?" I asked, astonished. Pointing her index finger at me, she gulped down a whole bottle of water, and in the end, she breathed out a small burp before uttering some words.

"Huh? No, I took the bus. But it was the elevator that was taking an eternity to reach your floor. And then once again I got lost in the corridors." She tried to calm herself and then spoke again.

"Every time I come here, I somehow always fail to remember your room number. Oh, I'm so stupid, I should've asked at the reception." She kept on babbling.

Only one minute had passed since she arrived, and I was already grinning from ear to ear. I was lucky to have a friend like her. She was the person who could see my spark and faults at the same time. Every time I took my worry to her, she had an answer for it. It was like she had a solution for every problem in my life. I believed I loved her too much to call her just my friend; she was my soul sister.

"Your Mom told me yesterday that you were finally awake but no one except the immediate family was allowed to visit. So I had to wait, but I couldn't wait any longer. Now tell me, how have you been handling things?" My forehead creased, sensing the change of character in her voice.

I tried to shift in my place, and I noticed her rushing toward me for assistance. I settled back comfortably as she added one more pillow for my back. She seemed uncomfortable and my confusion amplified when she settled on the bed near my legs, not meeting my eyes.

"I'm feeling good. Just a little achy and dizzy at times, nothing more. Doc said I can go home in a week or two. But you need to tell me why there are no flowers addressed by Ethan? Has my dad already misunderstood him and thrown them away?" I feared this most. I knew my dad very well. He could cross every limit to save her daughter from any perceived harm.

Ash's shoulders slumped at the mention of Ethan's name, and my smile dropped. I noticed her blowing out her cheeks just as she raised her chin. "I know it's a hard time for you. But you are stronger than this, babe. You can skip these crappy formalities and tell me honestly how you are actually feeling from the inside." I looked at her, puzzled. What was she talking about? What was I missing?

"Is something wrong?" I asked, trying to read her face.

"I see you are still not aware of the truth!"

She stood up and started pacing in the room. "Hey, what's the matter? You're scaring me, Ash." I asked and she stopped to stare at me with a stern look.

"He never did come to see you, Sarah. Not even once. He doesn't care if you're dead or alive. He is nothing but a selfish bastard." I couldn't help but compare her words with my own state of mind. They were harsh and muddled up. What had gotten into her?

She must have made a mistake. She was once again misinterpreting him. I was unmistakably positive that she was not here when he had come to see me and my parents might have turned him away.

"Now you don't believe me, right?" She tamped down her irritation. I shook my head to try to convince her, but I knew she had measured the truthfulness in my body gesture.

"No, it's not like that, Ash. Maybe you missed him by seconds. I mean you can..."

"Seriously, babe? Are we seriously doing it? First of all, I can't believe you hid your pregnancy from me. And now, you are still defending him. I suspect you are truly blinded by his cheap tricks. You foolish girl!" I strived to swallow down the frustration as anger stirred within me. She repeated the words Ethan had said to me in my disturbing dream.

"I never left your side in those critical days, Sarah. I was always here." My eyes bored into her, trying to gain some strength by grasping the sheets tightly in my small hands. I felt so vulnerable that I could crumble at any point.

"He never showed up, Sarah. But you know what, I still gave him a chance. I thought maybe, just maybe, for the sake of humanity, he would like to see you. I thought for once, I could be wrong about him, and somehow he, in reality, didn't know about your condition, so I went to his house. And you know what? He said he didn't know who I was. He refused to even recognize me in front of his parents. I should've learned from the experiences. I should've known his true nature." She was burning with hatred. I was too stunned to speak.

"I was right. This whole time, I was absolutely right. He is just a manipulative bastard who doesn't give a fuck about anything or anyone but himself. I hate myself for trusting him even for one second." My head started to spin at her words. I was almost choking on the rage. How could she say such things about Ethan? With every painful word, she was just taking a huge step back from my life. I always doubted that she hated him, but now it was clearly visible on her face. She was in total disgust. But I knew she had been flawed.

"I can't believe it, Ash. Maybe it was all a big misunderstanding between you two. You know how he looks at me, with so much love and tenderness." I tried to brush off her prejudice with a light comment, but at the same time, my body was trembling with fear.

"For God's sake, shut up! For once in your life, try to come out of your imaginary bubble and perceive reality. The fact is that he never loved you. He was just using your stupid fairy tale imagination to get into your pants." I felt insulted by her words. My eyes were fixed on her, just as anger boiled deep in my body. She had overstepped every damn threshold.

My heart began to beat faster as I started to feel a headache slowly creeping in. I closed my eyes and leaned my head back on the pillow, struggling to subside my fury, but I failed.

"Get out! Please. I don't want to hear any more bitter lies from your awful mouth." I tried my best to control my anger, but inside, I was smoking with resentment. She was no longer my friend.

"Are you for real? You've fuckin' lost your mind!" She almost yelled, and I pressed my lips together, looking over her. We stared into each other's eyes. Her eyes were pleading with mine to believe her.

"What's going on here? Young lady, this is a hospital. Are you yelling at the patient? You need to leave now." The nurse came bursting into the room. Fury vibrated between us as we traded a hard gaze. My body was trembling with bitterness, and I felt the vigor draining from my body with every passing second.

"I never wanted to discuss this with you in this condition. But, I had no choice. The sooner you realize the truth, the better it will be for you." Ash strode over to the door and turned around for the one last time before leaving.

"Sometimes, someone has to play the role of a bad guy to make everything right in the end."

❦

Without giving a fair warning, depression can come crawling into your heart. Moving slowly. In no time, it can entrench your mind like you were always surrounded by it. It follows you around like a black shadow, encircling you, engulfing you, eating you alive from inside. Nothing seems to matter in the world after it overpowers you completely.

I'd always loved the feeling of the morning breeze touching the leaves, creating a soft rustling sound that has the power to calm any spirit. But not anymore. The bitter truth that had plunged over my heart gave birth to a wound that had been festering my soul with suffering day after day.

Sorrow had crept down in my spirit, which was previously the residence of love and joy. But that seemed like a story of past life now. Heaviness had embraced my remains, and even after hours of sleep, I still always felt exhausted, both physically and mentally. It seemed like it had become a routine to carry around this weight on my shoulders.

The floating dust in the air made a prominent appearance as the streams of sunrays struck my face in that quiet room. Two weeks had gone by since I was discharged from the hospital and subsequently returned to my parent's house in Montgomery. I had barely left my room ever since. It would be wrong to say that I was surrounded by darkness, but it was my mind that had been converted into a gloomy, empty cell. All day long I just kept my eyes focused on the ever-changing colors of the sky with every passing minute.

Doctors had confirmed that I was fairly healed, to the extent that I could return to my normal life; the normal life that was heading towards a dead end. They also concluded that my body was restored as if the accident never happened, but what they didn't see were the wounds that were permanently carved onto my soul.

Hours of early daybreak had long passed, but I was still lying in my bed among the warm sheets that were covering my body. Strangely, it made me feel protected. I was lying on my left side, focusing on the things my bedroom window was revealing to me. It was another new day, yet, not the one that could make me feel less miserable.

My brows knitted upon hearing footsteps heading towards my room. Someone was coming to see me and I covered my face, pretending to be asleep. I didn't want to face anybody, let alone have a conversation at that moment. The wooden door opened, and a shudder ran down my spine with its creaking sound. My parents have removed the lock from my room's door, maybe afraid that I would lock myself up and attempt suicide or something.

"Hey! Honey?" It was my mother, again. Her voice sounded fragile as if she was struggling to hold her guards up. I sensed her approaching and then she stopped just next to my bed.

"Look, what a beautiful day it is. I bet you can't afford to miss it." Silence stretched around us and I could hear her shallow breaths, showing how close she was to losing her patience. Nevertheless, my stubbornness had overpowered me and I just refused to budge an inch from my place. My mind didn't want to go anywhere; it felt safe in the dark silence of these sheets. The brightness inside me had died, leaving no room for happiness. The numbness was the only thing my heart could feel now.

"Oh, I see you are still asleep. No worries. Take some rest, honey. I love you." She whispered with disappointment because she very well knew that I was awake. Weighing my stubbornness, she closed the door and left me alone to myself. Something swirled in my heart, and before I knew it, a tear rolled down my eyes. I was so overwhelmed by the pain that my body shuddered. But I didn't let it overpower me. My face never showed any sign of misery that my soul was going through. I was slowly turning into a lifeless toy.

I knew I was causing great pain to my family. My behavior was affecting everybody's life, but I was tired of pretending. I was hurt, shattered, broken to the extent that everything just stopped making sense to me. The whole world had started feeling dull and unworthy.

My appetite was diminished to negligence, and so was my existence. Everyone had noticed my deteriorating health. Every morning I promised myself that I would at least try to handle my poor condition, but by the end of the day, the pain overpowered me, making me go to my bed with tear-filled eyes.

Something had broken inside me, something so unrepairable. My heart was shattered in so many pieces that it was impossible to even locate them, let alone fix them.

After a few more hours of inner battle, I finally convinced my mind to take a shower and head downstairs. Avoiding all the eyes that had lit up seeing me coming out of my room, I walked out of the back door and settled back on the small steps facing our backyard.

It was a usual afternoon, and I engaged myself, staring back at the dry leaves that were fluttering away by the fairly gushing wind. I was so engrossed in contrasting my life to the dead vegetation around me that I didn't notice when a person settled down next to me.

Mom's warm hands pressed against my forehead. I flinched a little when she replaced the old bandage with a new one, with a sheepish, reassuring smile playing on her face.

"Lovely. The wound is almost healed. You're all fine, baby girl." Observing the promising words, I couldn't do anything but force a smile and then drop my vision towards our interlocked hands. But she had been mistaken. I wasn't completely healed. There was still a deep cut in my heart and it was infected, spreading the poison throughout my body.

"Now tell me, where are we going to celebrate?" Dad's overexcited voice touched our ears, and I followed Mom inside the house. I found Aunt

Rose sitting on the couch. She had been living with us since the accident. Angus was nowhere to be seen. He must have gone to school. I couldn't even remember what day or date it was. Dad suddenly appeared out of nowhere and twirled me around.

"Celebrate?" My brows snapped together as his words left my mind muddled. He exchanged a look between my aunt and my mother, who were now standing next to me with smiles on their lips.

"Oh, dear. You forgot, didn't you? We've got to celebrate your acceptance in the Johns Hopkins pre-med program that you had always dreamed about." My mom spoke and when I looked over at my aunt, she had tears beaming in her eyes. They were all looking at me, expecting an answer, and I panicked. I couldn't go anywhere, I simply couldn't. I didn't have the strength to bear all this.

"I don't want to celebrate. I am not sure I am even going to college. And perhaps you guys can't see it, but I'm not quite feeling well." I said with a calm voice and started heading upstairs, back to my safe haven.

"Is this only about your health, Sarah? Or you just want to be left alone, so that you can keep on living your sorrowful life with your head buried in a hole?" My head shot up to my mother. Her eyes glanced into my soul, daring me to lie to her face.

"Jane!" My body jumped at the low threatening voice of Dad.

"What, Mark? Can't you see how she is torturing herself? For goodness' sake, look at her, and tell me, does she look normal to you? She is dying a slow death, starving herself, turning into nothing but bare-bones." I glanced up at the ceiling, struggling to hold back the tears that were threatening to spill out of my eyes.

"She doesn't want to talk to anyone, doesn't want to leave her depressing room, and doesn't even want to take therapy. She just wants to be left alone all the freaking time. Yesterday, when that poor child, Ashley, came to pay a visit, she refused to even see her face. Can you believe it, Rose? I don't know about you Mark, but I can't see my daughter like this!" From the corner of my eyes, I peeked at her, stumbling over the couch with her face hidden in her palms. My heart stirred, listening to her cries, and I found my eyes welling up again.

"Jane, I understand. But this is not the right time to discuss this." Dad tried to calm her down. He kneeled in front of her and attempted to hold her hands, but she just shrugged him off. My tear-filled eyes were fixed on them, witnessing them breaking down because of me.

"The right time will never come, Mark. Tell me, when was the last time you saw her smile? Her condition is deteriorating, Mark. Day after day, she is breaking apart and we are doing nothing. But I can't let this happen in front of my eyes. I'm her mother. She is my flesh and blood, for God's sake." And then she started crying. Dad leaped up, now sitting beside her, when she collapsed into his arms.

My heart was throbbing with pain as if someone was clenching it in an iron fist. I couldn't see them like that. Dad quickly wiped his tears away while trying his best to comfort her. They could no longer hide their emotions that had been welling up for a while now. I stormed towards them. Getting down on my knees, I secured her hands in mine, feeling remorseful.

"Mom! Mom? Please don't cry. I am so sorry for everything I put you through. Please, I can't see you like this. I promise you I will go to that therapy." But she never stopped crying. I turned towards my father, who was sitting there with his head between his hands. What have I done? What have I turned my family into?

That was the day I decided that enough is enough! My parents didn't deserve this. Hell! I didn't deserve this. I would never forgive you for this, Ethan! All I ever did was love you more than anything in my life!

"Yet, you did nothing but shatter me, Stanton."

Twenty-five

Sarah

DAY THIRTY-FOUR

I had already expected some chaos when I made up my mind to follow Ethan back to the town where we grew up and fell apart. But the memories that were engraved on every street corner were too painful to recollect. Since Aunt Rose had left the town several years ago, I never had any reason to revisit after that incident nine years ago.

I thought of having a trip to my old school and meeting up with some high school friends, but I was too scared to relive those memories, and to be honest, I didn't even have any true friends back then except Ash. So I had spent the past three days almost cooped up in a hotel room, leaving only to meet Ash's parents. Ethan had also rented a room here, along with his friend, Thomas. He could have stayed at his home but didn't. I guess there was some type of feud going on between him and his father.

I was grateful to Ash's Mom for lending me this dress for the funeral, but it was certainly a piece of work to place in order. My hands had started to ache, with blood leaving my fingers as I tried once again. Struggling to place the lock right into the metallic link at the nape of my neck.

I was about to give up on that dress when my body shuddered at an abrupt sensation of a soft graze on my skin. Lifting my head, I gazed back through the mirror to find Ethan's handsome face clouded with a gloomy expression. I had rarely seen him in these past three days, as he was busy in preparations for the funeral, or maybe he was just hiding from me. I contemplated many a time to go back, thinking maybe my presence was making him uncomfortable in front of his family, but I just couldn't leave without paying my respects to his Nanna.

"I knocked, but you didn't answer and the door was open." He said with his eyes glued to the back of my dress. The line amid his brows was narrating the amount of agitation his mind was going through. My stare only deepened, noticing every single detail of his face when he just concentrated on the latch of the dress. For some strange reason, the stroke of his fingers against my skin felt welcoming. It fluttered something deep down in my stomach.

"Done!" Just as his voice stroked my ears, I shook my head, coming out of the little reverie I was just about to get lost into. Turning around, I smiled nervously, murmuring a small thank you in return. I noticed his bloodshot eyes, which he was trying his best to hide. He looked tired, crushing under the weight of despair and grief. Yet he was not ready to let anyone in, to share the weight on his shoulders. Taking a step forward, I adjusted the collar of his shirt and tugged at his loosened tie, adjusting the knot in its proper position.

"I know you are scared, Ethan. But you have your whole family standing beside you. And you have me by your side. Just hold on to me. I promise I won't disappear." I said, holding his hands in mine and squeezing them for support.

"I'm exhausted, Starz!" He said with a deep sigh. I had never seen this vulnerable side of Ethan. I was only familiar with the cocky and overconfident part of him. But right now he was looking so exposed that I wanted to hide him from the world. I didn't know for how long we stared into each other's eyes. There was a peculiar depth in those sapphire orbs, making me plunge deeper into them.

His eyes held an emotion that made me feel safe around him. They had something to say to me, like a long-lost affection that was buried for years, but somehow he succeeded in holding it all back. Our eyes parted away with a knock at the door. We turned towards Thomas standing at the door, who informed us that it was time for us to leave.

⚘

The gloominess surrounding us was suffocating me. I wasn't letting it show on my face, but God knew how much I was scared to face the funeral. My lungs never felt heavier when we climbed out of the car and I found myself standing in front of the church. I wished I could turn back right there and never come back.

But I was there for Ethan, to support him. I couldn't just put myself first and leave him alone in that gloom. Living with the grief of losing a family member was too much to handle for him right now. That man who had been struggling hard to hold his family together needed me to support him. And that was exactly what I was going to do.

With every step towards the front door, knots in my stomach twisted harder. Grief embraced us as we stepped inside. Wrapping my hands around myself, I perceived Ethan taking hold of his mother's hands and supporting her throughout the way. It pained me to witness her falling apart, and I wished I could do something to make her feel less miserable.

As the eternal aroma of flowers stoked my nostrils, my head started feeling fuzzy. The pain deepened in my heart as we were slowly heading toward her. It was an open casket. The coffin was placed on the catafalque, painted beautifully with wildflowers. The solemn sadness of the music stretched throughout the room. And strangely enough, it had an incredibly calming effect on my burning soul.

But then my eyes landed on her divine face and I feared I would lose my sanity. There were so many emotions whelming up in my chest that I found myself choking on them. My face remained blank while all the chaos in my mind wasn't letting me breathe.

A sniffle stroked my ears when we settled down in the front row. Turning my head to the right, I noticed the silent weeping of Mrs. Stanton, as she was trying her best not to lose control of herself. Her futile attempts to conceal her sobs only intensified the heaviness in my chest. She held onto the woman sitting right next to her. Their features resembled to some extent that I wondered if she was her sister. As she kept murmuring soothing words to Mrs. Stanton while rubbing her back. I wanted to be of some help, but I hardly knew her and she most certainly wouldn't like the company of a complete stranger at that delicate hour of suffering.

I shook my head and straightened my back when I observed people beginning to join us. The hall was soon packed with a plentiful crowd as voices filled the hollow stretches of the place. I rubbed my sweaty hands against the soft fabric of my dress and concentrated on my breaths.

"Thank you, ladies and gentlemen, for joining us today. We are gathered here today to show our love and respect to Clara Beth McGill. She was not only a dear person who was loved by everyone but a treasured soul that we've lost. She was a daughter, a sister, a mother, a grandmother, and a friend to many. She played every single role in her life with complete compassion, loving everybody with all her heart." My head tilted upward at the realization of seeing Ethan at the podium.

"But for me, she was everything; the light of my life, the first ray of sunlight. She had that tint of warmth that drew out good in me even when I had lost every belief in my life." There was a pause in his eulogy, and I bit my lips. He looked down for a few seconds and then sucked in a deep breath.

"She was my best friend, my strength, my supporter in every way a person could be. There are a lot of things I want to say, but then, if she were here today, she would've given me a fine earful about how sloppy I am being." A soft chuckle left my lips, clenching my hands together over my heart.

"However, she was nosy in so many ways, like let's take her rattling about my uneven schedule or even my love life." He paused and shook his head, smiling sadly. "She bore with me throughout the ups and downs of my life. I could hardly think of a day when she forgot to remind me that I should be thankful for things God has provided me." He took a long pause and I could clearly see how hard he was fighting with the tears filled in his eyes.

"I know nothing will ever be the same and there will always be a distant emptiness in our hearts without her. And she will be missed more than anything. But she always cared about others' happiness more than herself and I hope we will keep that legacy alive in our hearts forever. Thank you." My eyes followed the trail when he descended the stage.

His bowed head and a blank expression couldn't tell anything, but when his eyes met mine, I looked through his soul. He let me see his vulnerable side. I could read in those sad orbs that he was breaking apart. Though we held each other's gaze for mere seconds, it was enough for me to see all the emotions he was struggling to hide from everyone.

The memorial lasted for a while, as almost everyone had some fond memory to share about Clara. She was indeed an incredible human being who loved everyone unconditionally and so was loved by everyone.

As we entered the graveyard, Mr. Stanton came forward to the rescue of his wife as she was barely holding herself up. The sorrow radiating from her settled into my chest and the despair grew like a blizzard, sweeping off my senses. I wished I could do something to take away all the pain from this family. Her husband didn't seem like a man who would have anything comforting to say to her. Yet he continued to stand alongside her, supporting her in that painful moment. His uniformed blank feature only reflected the sadness he had been feeling.

I glanced over to Ethan and my heart broke witnessing a teardrop rolling down his cheek as the casket was being lowered into the ground. I gripped the hem of my dress when a twitching ache stroked my chest. And before I could've rationalized my behavior, I strode towards him. My steps got arrested just beside him until our hands were brushing against each other. I looked up towards him, but he looked away, wiping his tears with the back of his hand, trying to hide his feeble side from me.

"Goodbye, Nanna. I wish we had met earlier so that I would've been honored to feel the love that you have shared to make everyone so happy. You will be greatly missed." I could feel Ethan's tender gaze over me while I was saying all those words, and I smiled weakly, feeling the love that I felt from saying something true to her.

My breath got caught up in my throat when I felt Ethan's fingers interlacing mine. He firmly held my hand, like he needed my support to save himself from drowning. And I shared the same support, interlocking our hands even more tightly.

"I'll always miss you, Nanna!" He whispered and I could feel the love stretching out from each word. He squeezed my hand like he was thanking me. The touch sparked a strange tension in my body.

Never had I imagined I would be setting foot in this house ever again in this lifetime. The place was filled with some of the most painful memories of my life, which came back alive as soon as I placed my first step in Stanton's mansion. Tranquility had settled into the house in contrast to the turmoil in my soul, restraining my thoughts as I took another weary breath.

The reception was extravagant, and I was ready to hit the sack as soon as the food entered my belly. Exertion of the day struck me all of a sudden. My eyes wandered around and a smile etched my face, seeing Ethan greeting the guests with the utmost warm smile he could ever fake. My legs followed him as he headed for the backyard to serve drinks.

But my steps ceased at the spot, noticing him coming face to face with Mr. Stanton. There was visible tension in the air when Ethan was having an inner battle to either turn around or face him. And it surprised me when he sat down next to him and offered a glass of whiskey to his dad. He took the drink without acknowledging Ethan at all. In that neglected fleeting moment, Ethan stared at his dad for a few painful seconds, and then his eyes dropped to the floor in disappointment. The way he squeezed his eyes and shook his head made me hate Mr. Stanton.

"Why do you hate me so much, dad?" Hands covered my mouth when my heart stirred at the amount of repugnance his question was loaded with. His eyes were boring into him, but Mr. Stanton never for once looked at him.

"Because you disgraced our family name. Nine years ago, you broke my trust, son. I never thought my own blood would do something like that. You should have just denied being part of anything that happened to that girl, but you disobeyed me. You kept on searching for that stupid girl like some maniac and made a fool of me in front of the whole town. You not only destroyed that girl's dreams but also mine. That girl created a rift between a father and his son and you couldn't think better of it. To be honest, I don't think I am disappointed in you. Had I raised you well, you would have been smarter. And I don't think I will ever come to terms with forgetting the humiliation I felt because of you. A father could never hate his child, son; he can just protect his child by not acknowledging his presence and his mistakes."

A tear rolled down my eyes when he simply stood up and walked away from his son. Leaving Ethan broken and crumbling. Mr. Stanton's words echoed in my head, forcing out a sob from my mouth. My tear-filled eyes fell upon Ethan. He had buried his face in his hands, and the amount of anguish flowing through him made me shudder. He was breaking apart and so was I.

"Sarah? Right?"

My attention was captured by a strange call. And when I turned to the voice, my eyes fell over Mrs. Stanton. I nodded as she gave me a weak smile with her tear-filled eyes.

"Thank you for sticking with my son, Sarah! You have no idea how much your support is helping him in coping with his loss." She paused for a second, taking a look at Ethan's fragile state, and then continued.

"He is hanging by a thread, Sarah. And I know he would rather fall than ask for any help. Just like his father, too stubborn to let somebody in and see his weaker side. But deep down, my heart knows he is scared. After all, she was his everything. She provided him with the unconditional love that I could no longer give him after... after that incident." She suddenly choked at her words. I couldn't help but conclude there was some unspeakable incident in the family that separated Ethan from his parents. My fingers squeezed her trembling hands in an attempt to reassure her. Her head lifted at me, bestowing me a weak smile as her eyes shifted to the side again, gazing at Ethan.

"You seem like a good friend. Please hold on to him, Sarah. He is alone, and this loneliness will eat him alive if we don't take care of him." Out of the blue, she caressed my face, and I was startled as it forced me to look into her eyes.

"His father loves him, Sarah! But he was just swayed by the brutal words of that godforsaken girl. How could he believe that our son could ruin an innocent life or leave someone alone to die? I have never resented someone as much as I resent that girl who dared to come to our house and stole everything from us. Her false accusation ruined our family after that night. She not only separated a son from his father, but she also took away the right of a mother to show her love to his son."

"I'm sorry, I don't understand!" I whispered with my trembling lips, feeling the fidgeting of my clasped hands.

"I don't remember her name, but her face is still very much alive in my mind. I might be getting old, but I'm not senile. Her words still echo in my head, Sarah! She claimed Ethan, my son, got a girl pregnant, and then he forced her to abort the child. He was barely seventeen years old, Sarah. And, God knows if that's true and as she alleged, that poor girl met with an accident and lost her child all because of him. Nonsense!"

I flinched at her disgust for Ashely when my eyes streamed with tears. I could never have guessed this was the reason he was all alone all this time. He was deprived of his parents' love at adolescence. He had nobody when he needed them the most. I feared I would lose consciousness with the truth tearing open my heart. The realization and pain were devastatingly hard to bear, and I started to breathe heavily.

My lungs felt like they were ruptured when the pain was too much to endure. It felt like someone was strangling me, digging his claws deeper into my throat. And without thinking of anything, I ran outside as fast as I could because I knew the best thing to do at that moment was to preserve my sanity.

I was getting breathless with every passing second. I couldn't tell if it was the weather that had its coldness piercing my skin or the perception of shame. My head swirled at every strange thought that crossed my mind. My soul burned with realization. I could join all the missing pieces together now. I was the reason behind all that pain. I was the person who made his family abandon him. This was all because of me. His father hated him so much that he was disgusted with even meeting his son's eyes.

My heart was racing against my nerves as if I had been running for hours. The coldness around me tried to smother the warmth in my heart, the truth that had just washed over me turned me numb. My brain shut down for a moment. I was not able to think properly. Ethan's mother's words were the only thing that continued to ring in my ears. The callous wave of guilt and sorrow washed over me. And before I knew it, my head started to flashback all the dreadful moments. The painful events that I believed I had gotten rid of at some point in my life. But I was so wrong. The dark, looming shadow of my past was hovering in front of me, ready to engulf me in darkness once again.

"You all right? Funerals make me want to puke too!" An unfamiliar female voice struck me and I turned my head towards the sound. My eyes focused on a girl who was quite younger than me. Her one hand was folded on her chest and the other was busy holding a cigarette butt between her fingers.

"I'm... Okay. Thank you!" Before she would have reacted to my condition, my phone began to ring loudly, and without checking the name, I pushed it on my ear with my shaking hand. Because the piercing sound almost gave me a migraine.

"Hello? Sarah? Hi. Hello? Are... are you there?" Ash's voice reverberated into my ears and my forehead furrowed in confusion. She sounded on the verge of crying and panic stung my heart.

"Ash?"

"Sarah! Oh. God!" I was right. She was sobbing. Her cries sent a scary jolt down my spine, and I feared the worst.

"Yes, I'm here! What happened? Why are you crying? Are you okay, girl?" My shaking hands gripped the phone like my life was dependent on it. I started to pace in nervousness when nothing but her snivels echoed from the other end.

"Oh, for God's sake, talk to me, girl!" I almost screamed in between my panic attacks. Her silence was making the moment so dreadful that I thought I would collapse with a panic attack.

"Everything was a lie, Sarah! Every fuckin' thing! He said he would marry me. He said we will get old together and no one can separate us till our last breath. But he had to ruin everything. Every fuckin' thing!"

"Shhh! Calm down, girl. Tell me what happened exactly? What did he say?"

"He cheated on me, Sarah. I don't understand. We were so happy together. Our lives were perfect, then I don't know what happened. One day it was all amazing and the next day everything turned into one bloody giant intangible mess. I don't know what to do, Sarah! I'm so..." Her voice broke again, and I cursed the douchebag who was responsible for her condition.

"First you listen to me. Nothing is finished until we choose it to be. And second, you are stronger than this. You just can't let some jerk stir you up like this. Ash, this is not you!" She was drunk and angry and I didn't think my words were doing any good at the moment. She continued to weep like a child.

"I don't understand. How could somebody cheat on me like that? He was using me all along. He just wanted me to be there to make his father believe he is no longer a brat! I feel so used, Sarah."

"Shut up! Nobody gave you the right to talk shit about yourself."

"Sarah, where are you? I'm coming over with the next flight. I don't think I can handle this all alone!" She broke down once again, but this time there was a need that reflected in her voice. On the other hand, I didn't know my life would give me bolts of shock one after the other like this. I hesitated for a whole minute and I knew Ash would sense something fishy in the situation.

"Sarah!"

"I'm in Fairhope, at Ethan's parents' house. A tragedy struck his family. A close one passed away in an accident! And... Well, he needed me by his side." I had lost control over my choice of words at that critical time. I didn't know why my mind struggled to reason out my actions for being with him. Like I wanted Ash to believe I didn't want to be here, but the odd state of affairs forced me to come here. I hated myself for even establishing that fact.

"What? Why? I mean how? Are you all right?" She sounded confused between her sobs.

"I'm okay. But Ash, I need to ask you something right now. I know you're in no condition to give me answers and I'm being a selfish bitch here, but for the sake of my sanity, please listen to me. It's killing me to be aware of the fact that I have been the reason behind the separation of a mother from her son all through these years!" I leaned against the nearby wall and pressed my head on it.

"What are you talking about? I don't get it?"

"Did you happen to tell Ethan's family about everything that took place all those years ago? Did you blame him in front of his parents? Did he really deny being part of everything? Did his family abandon him because of me?" A painful silence echoed from the other side of the line. I gripped the phone so tightly to my ears. I feared I would lose myself if I missed even a single word.

"Ashley?"

"Yes! But it was so long ago." She said with some uncertainty in her voice.

"But you told me that he denied being ever involved with me and refused to even recognize you. But it seems like his parents knew the truth and he kept on searching for me for days." I was panting by now. I wanted to know the truth. Was I fooled by my own best friend?

There was a long pause that I thought the line got disconnected but then she spoke with a very stern voice, "I just did what was supposed to be done by karma. You know he deserved it!" I closed my eyes when my fear was confirmed.

"Nobody deserves to be torn apart from his family, Ash! We are nobody to decide if a kid deserves his mother's love or not." I barely managed to whisper with my head in my hands.

"I don't believe it. Are you even hearing yourself? If you are having a hard time recalling something, then I would be honored to take you to meet the ghost of your past. He ruined your life, girl. He left you dying in cold blood. What I did was nothing compared to the amount of damage he had caused to you! I don't get it. Why, all of a sudden, you're defending Stanton?"

"I'm not defending anyone!"

"Well, it looks like you are! Sarah, please, after all these years, you just can't go back to being that same stupid girl who trusted that monster. He is the same selfish jerk, babe."

"I don't know, Ash. Maybe that girl never left me!"

If you believe overthinking is a deadly weapon that has the power to mess up with your head, then I believe you've never met guilt.

Guilt is like a parasite that could leave you rotten from inside till there is nothing left except a complete eerie hollowness. You would feel like an empty shell, deprived of any emotion that could help you to live again. You can't change what you have done and guilt would be your closest ally, who would walk you to your ruin.

It seemed like my heart had been ripped out of my chest, leaving behind numbness in its trail. The fact that I was responsible for his estrangement from his parents. The fact that all these years, he was deprived of his family's love because of me, felt like a dagger in my chest. I felt betrayed. Because I believed it was only my right to punish him for the things he did to me and no one else's.

But the susceptibility in his mother's eyes revealed how she was bound with invisible chains of hopelessness, forbidding her to love her own son. The manner in which she was begging me to never leave his side when I was the sole reason she had been deprived of his son's presence around her. And this bitter truth dragged me deeper into the hellfire of my own guilt.

Or maybe Ash was right! And I was indeed blinded by his ploys, which were making me neglect the red flags, that he was the same boy who broke my heart and left me to crumble. Ignoring all the things about my past was like walking on the pathway made of thorns that had already cut me deep once.

And I couldn't quite see if it was just a sting of guilt that was not letting me see clearly or something had changed inside me. Perhaps I was overlooking all the facts and viewing my life only from the perspective of a guy who had been living next door to me. And somehow, at that moment of my life, it made me undoubtedly certain of three things.

One: I was not the same Sarah anymore who hated him with all her heart.

Second: Before he stumbled back into my life, I was broken and was still trying to heal from the damage he had gifted to me, despite pretending to be strong and brave. I'd been living someone else's life all through these years. I was afraid to accept that when he came back he made me act like myself, the same little bashful yet a courageous girl who knew her worth.

And third...

A tap on my shoulder jolted me out of my thoughts and made me clear my tears away.

"Hello, neighbor! What are you doing here? I had been searching for you all over the house. I thought you left without even saying goodbye." I looked at Ethan, but my mind could not form any response to his questions. Guilt was swallowing my soul.

"What's wrong, Starz? Are you okay?" He asked again, holding my shoulders. I could not hold my tears and started weeping like a lost kid. Ethan hugged me and caressed my head to console me.

"Everything is okay, Sarah. I am here with you. I am sorry I dragged you here. I shouldn't have brought you to this mournful place." He spoke calmly, stroking my hair. He was thinking that I was sad because of the funeral, while I was struggling to breathe because of the pain I had caused in his life all these years. I still couldn't bring myself to say anything. I just kept sobbing into his chest.

It took a while for my hysteria to die down. "I am sorry, Ethan," I murmured into his chest and he just hugged me tighter.

"Would you come with me? I want to show you something, Starz." Before I had an opportunity to ask him any further questions, he seized a tight hold of my hand and rose to drag us in the direction of the house. I looked around shyly, but luckily no one, in particular, was looking at us.

"Slow down, I'm wearing heels," I whined when we were rushing through the stairs.

"Don't worry; I'll catch you if you fall down. Or do you want me to pick you up in my arms?"

"In your dreams, Stanton!" He threw his head back as he placed his one hand over my back to hold me still, but his slight act of compassion was enough for me to feel all woozy.

We soon reached a closed door. I didn't know why, but my heart was racing like some teenage kid who was about to have her first adventure.

Ethan twirled the doorknob, revealing a giant bedroom in front of me, and my forehead creased at the unfamiliar place. I had been to his house before but had never been to this part of the structure.

"Whose room is this?" I glanced around, thoroughly examining the place. It seemed like the place belonged to a teenage boy. The walls were painted gray with occasional posters of cars and rock bands. A bed in the middle of the place with a jersey hung up on the bedpost. And my eyes roamed all over the place, catching every single detail of Pirates' recollections. And in the end, they landed on Ethan, whose soft gaze was stuck on the wall, which was decorated with numerous trophies and awards.

I sauntered close to him and without making a single sound, began to closely monitor the honors. They mainly included athletic awards. My eyes roamed from those shelves to Ethan. I noticed him brushing his fingers over the trophy that was labeled 'football player of the year' and a distant memory ran through my head. They were all souvenirs of his high school football life and some unforgettable memories of our time together.

"You were really great back then," I spoke weakly, trying to read his face that contained traces of lost memories he was trying to remember at that time. He quickly looked up, while settling down the trophy and shaking his head, smiling innocently. He was struggling to hide so many memories playing on his face.

"Maybe! Now forget about all these stupid things. My motive for inviting you here is something far better." He quickly rushed towards the drawers that were situated near the windows and started fidgeting through each section. Casually glancing over the whole room, I settled back on the bed, with my hands feeling the softness of the sheets. There was no doubt that the room belonged to Ethan. But the seventeen years old Ethan.

"I have not been home in the past nine years. But my mother kept everything exactly as I left it nine years ago." He said, still looking through the drawers.

"Aa... ha! Found it!" My head lifted towards him, with a line appearing between my eyes. His back was facing me, but I could feel the proud smirk he was enjoying at that moment. And then he turned around, hiding something at his back. My head stirred to the left, struggling to catch a glimpse of whatever he was hiding. And then he revealed a giant book in front of my face.

At first, my mind couldn't comprehend what he was trying to convey to me. But when I saw the name of the school and the big title 'Yearbook', my eyes sparkled with excitement.

"Oh my God, after all these years, you still have it? I never got the chance to see it back then!" He gave me a proud lopsided grin and then tossed the book towards me while landing on the mattress beside me. Without wasting a second, I quickly opened the hardcover. And the first thing my eyes jumped onto was our group photo from that science fair, which almost took my sanity away. My eyes roamed over the small group and the memories of the hard work washed over me.

"The guy with glasses had a huge crush on you." Ethan tried to tease me and I lightly shoved his shoulder, shaking my head mischievously.

"No, he did not! He was just a sweet regular guy. I'm forgetting his name!"

"Oliver Hart!" Ethan pointed toward our names mentioned at the bottom of the photograph. "Yeah, such a regular guy that I had to threaten him to stay away from you when you people started to have after-school project classes." Ethan leaned back, with his elbows supporting all his weight.

"It was you? And here I thought my aunt's peculiar baking skills made him run away from me!" I dramatically threw my hands in the air, puffing out some air while shaking my head in disappointment.

I again shuffled through the pages when my attention was pretty much occupied with the prom dance column. I frowned, remembering how I got a stomach bug just before the dance, making me miss that night. I had been that kind of unlucky person. I dragged my finger to witness beautiful people in beautiful dresses and suits when my eyes ceased on Ethan's picture.

"What on earth?" The corners of my lips curved up and in the next second I knew I had the biggest smile on my face. It was a picture of Ethan at the entrance of the prom venue, where usually couples get their pictures taken. But Ethan was just standing there with one hand shoved in the suit's pocket while the other around his imaginary prom date.

"I told you I would go dancing and have fun, with or without you!" His one eyebrow arched up in arrogance and my mouth hung open.

"But nobody told me you had fun with your imaginary girlfriend!" The caption was speaking the truth, *'Ethan Stanton, captain of the football team and his hot, mysterious girl'*. We laughed talking about old school couples and funny stories behind every person. And then arrived at the part of our last semester. I quickly hid my picture behind my hands, feeling embarrassed at how stupid my curls were looking. It was like somebody had poured hot noodles over my head. While on the other hand, Ethan was Ethan, looking the same hot and gorgeous as he always did. Wait, did I just call him hot?

"Come on, it's not that bad. Umm... okay, it is a terrible picture!" Feeling greatly offended, I started to hit Ethan with the book. He cried out, faking being injured, rubbing his forearm and chest. My eyes beamed as I felt my face warming up from our proximity.

"Aww... I'm injured, Starz!" His eyes lit up with amusement while his lips tried hard to hide the smile that was threatening to break free.

"Stop it, you will tear the yearbook!" I halted my assault and started to skim the book for any damage. "Let me show you something interesting!" I looked at him skeptically for a few seconds and then slowly handed him back the book. I noticed him shifting from one page to another and then finally stopping at something that made his eyes gleam in utter glee. He swirled the page towards me and my eyes landed on a group photo of the whole football team and the large banner of 'CONGRATS PIRATES' behind them. And stapled across the next page was a picture of me and Ethan kissing deeply.

He had lifted me in the air with his arms around my waist as we were swayed by a heavy breeze. My one hand was caressing his face while the other was holding down my skirt in place. I remember being so embarrassed at the moment that I never bothered to look around to see people's expressions around us. While on the other hand, Ethan was deviously enjoying the moment to the fullest. His full grin against my lips narrated everything.

I caressed our happy faces in the picture, not being able to hide the smile from my face. My eyes flicked with beautiful happy memories of my past and I turned the page and my happy moment cut short to the end right there. My eyebrows lifted as they landed on a picture of Ethan posing with the cheerleaders. His hand was around the waist of the head cheerleader, who was whispering something in his ear. My eyes looked up from the picture, with a glare etching my face, and the next second Ethan snatched away the book from my hands.

"You weren't supposed to see that! Shit!" He tore out that picture from the book and ate the piece the very next second. He looked so mortified that his eyeballs were ready to pop out any second and the sound of my laughter vibrated in the whole room.

I threw back my head, laughing deeply at his self-conscious act. He literally gulped down the whole paper and I couldn't do anything but grasp my stomach and crack even more.

"Okay, I was a jerk, a terrible lousy human being!" But I was nowhere near stopping my chortle. My back laid straight on the bed while I cackled, still clenching my stomach. By then, my eyes were watery and my stomach hurt with all the hysterical laughter.

"Finally! The truth has been told! Now I can die in peace!" I joked between my snorts. But then in the middle of all this, I spotted a photograph of a lady glued to the ceiling. A line appeared between my brows just as I tilted my head to study the image further.

"Is that our gym teacher, Mrs. Herbert?" I gestured towards it with a finger and cocked my head further. If I was not mistaken, the face was indeed too familiar to ignore. I looked over at Ethan. Not a single reaction came from his side for one whole minute and then I witnessed a horror-filled look furnishing his face.

At first, his blank expression puzzled me. And then the next second I saw him stuffing pillows over his face, hiding his embarrassed features completely from me.

"And here I thought inviting you to my room was a good idea. Mom should at least have removed that!" He grunted under the pillow and I busted out once again. This time my imagination went wild, picturing a seventeen years old boy in the bed, taking pleasure from our busty gym teacher.

"My dignity is guillotined. Just take me already, God!" I was breathing hard between all that laughing. Happy tears started to flow freely as my heart rate increased threefold.

"You know I'll have to kill you, now that you know my biggest secret?" Ethan joked, and I shoved his arm, begging him to stop saying anything. My jaw started hurting, and I was struggling to breathe. His stupid replies were cracking me so much that for a moment I felt I would die laughing.

And after a whole minute of laughing and convulsing on the bed, my head turned towards him and noticed him staring at me intensely. By then, my fits of laughter had turned into more nervous and silly giggles when I couldn't blink, noticing the tenderness in his eyes.

We were lying on the bed. Staring into each other like he had found something new in my orbs. While my eyes struggled to find what had caused him to exploit me with that piercing gaze. I was really dumbfounded. I couldn't take my eyes away from his ravishing face.

I shivered when he tucked a lock of hair behind my ear. Our closeness allowed me to feel the hot breath rushing from his shivering lips.

"I'm scared, Starz. I'm really very scared." His eyebrows waggled as he let down his guards.

"It feels like instead of winning your heart, I'm losing you all over again. Like... fuck, I can't even explain it in words... I... believe I'm waiting for something that is never going to happen." His hot breath assaulted my face, and I struggled to catch a breath.

"I'm scared too, Ethan!" I melted away with so much warmth in his eyes that I believed I would disappear. My hand proceeded to caress his face. This time, my hands didn't tremble, nor did I have any cynical thoughts. I only wanted to dwell on the warmth of the moment. I couldn't believe my wild thoughts that wanted so much from this man.

Just looking into his moistened eyes made me wonder whether his lips would taste the same as, to my astonishment, I remembered so vividly from nine years ago. My chest rose and fell with rapid breaths and I took in a sharp breath of air when his eyes roamed over my lips. My brain was electrified, and every nerve in my body was burning. It was like he had ignited back some deep down buried flame in my heart.

"I missed you, Sarah. I am really…" Before his trembling lips would have finished the sentence, I pressed my lips onto him. At first, he remained frozen with shock. But soon I could feel his warm lips moving against mine. Slowly and cautiously, as if he was still trying to distinguish between reality and imagination.

As the kiss deepened, he held my face in his warm hands and pulled me in intensely. The kiss was so passionate that I thought I would faint under the touch. Almost immediately, he hovered over, deepening the kiss. His tongue savored every part of my mouth, leaving nothing untouched. It felt like he was thirsty for ages and I was the last drop of water on the face of the earth.

I knew this was wrong, so wrong that the inner voice inside me begged for me to pull away, but my body was responding oppositely. I had lost control over every rational thought at that moment. Ethan had burned down every nerve in my body that had the capacity to think reasonably. My senses had been seduced by the man with whom I happened to fall in love all over again.

His hands ran down my back, pulling me closer until there was no space left between us. I could feel the beating of his heart against my chest; the touch spread warmth to every single cell of my body.

My mind traveled back to the moment when I was sure of three things in my life after today's encounter. The third was the most treacherous one: the fact that this man had made me believe it was okay to trust someone all over again. He made me believe in second chances. And we both knew that this kiss was the beginning of something that I was most afraid of.

When we broke apart to catch some air, a strange feeling had already engulfed me; a feeling which was soundly blended with solace and serenity. I knew this was totally wrong. Even the very first part where I decided to join him on this journey was against my morals. I never thought I would spend so much time with a man who broke me into a thousand pieces. But yet again, here I was. Shamelessly kissing him without having a second thought that I might be repeating the same mistake that could ruin me forever.

My eyes were closed with relentless thoughts running through every neuron of my brain. He rested his forehead against mine, breathing softly as we gathered some much-needed oxygen. But then I couldn't overlook the thoughts strewing up in my head and my eyes dashed open. I was taken aback, gathering the jumbled emotions that had washed over me. I felt exposed. As if I laid bare in front of him.

"I need to go. I just..." I knew his eyes were struggling to catch a glimpse of mine, but I didn't look up even for a second. As a matter of choice, I stood up and promptly turned around, squirming to look for the door.

"Sarah! I'm sorry... It was… Please." He spoke so powerlessly that his broken words froze me in my place for a moment. He was standing so close to me that once again, I sensed his masculine scent washing over me. His eyes bored holes at the back of my head and my hand quickly rubbed my forearm, trying to soothe my nerves.

The silence fell between us as the only voice that echoed in the room was our uneasy breaths. It felt like he was measuring his every word before saying anything.

"Sarah!" I squeezed my eyes shut when he said my name with such tenderness. But I couldn't look back because I knew if I did, I would be running into his arms all over again.

"Goodbye, Ethan!" I barely whispered and without daring to look back,

I fled the room.

Twenty-six

Sarah

DAY THIRTY-SIX

Good morning, Starz,
I know you want nothing to do with me. But hear me out for once,
please. I'm ashamed of the things I did to you. I truly am sorry,
Starz. Please, pick up my call and let me explain.
Ethan

DAY THIRTY-SEVEN

Starz,
Please, it's been days since I saw your face. I'm so sorry for crossing
the line. I don't know what took over me. I'm a total knucklehead. I
should never have kissed you! I made a big mistake. Please forgive
me. I am begging you.
Ethan

DAY THIRTY-EIGHT

Sarah, girl
There is no easy way to say this, but trust me when I say that I am
dying of resentment here. I'm missing your voice, Starz. You can
bloody well yell at me all day, but please talk to me. Your silence is

more agonizing than those nine years I had spent without you. It's blisteringly insane how I am holding on here. Because all that I am left with in my life is you.

Ethan

PS: You know I won't leave you alone until you really forgive me.

DAY FORTY-ONE

It had been days since I had seen Ethan. I had been practically living at the hospital this past week in order to avoid an awkward encounter with him. I knew he was back because he had been slipping these stupid notes to me. The fact that I was terrified to face him and had been spending all my time daydreaming about that unbelievable breath-stealing kiss instead of preparing for my finals was petrifying. That kiss was something exceptional. It ignited something in me that had been missing for a while now. And it made me scared to the core.

I couldn't decide what was more offensive about his notes. For him to accept that he didn't want to kiss me and it was all a big mistake or the thing that I finally let him overpower me. Because, in truth, I kissed him first. I gave him an upper hand to defeat my guards and eventually win this game of ruining my life once again. I let him do that to me. I hated myself for giving him this control over me.

While there was something about Ethan's words that never let me tear those notes into a thousand pieces or burn them to ashes. Rather, I found myself staring at them again and again, no matter how mad or hurt I had been.

He left the first note two days after I fled back. Under my doormat, where I had hidden my apartment keys whenever I went for the morning run. And it somehow made me wonder why was I so happy that he knew my routine?

The second one was not a surprise either when I found it taped inside the sun visor of my car. But I was mad about the third one.

He had no right to go overboard with his stupid apologies. I still couldn't get over the fact that he somehow had information about my patients and he chose the sweetest old lady to pass over his note to me. He bloody well knew that I would never yell at that sweet woman or tear down his note right then and there. I could sense somebody from inside was involved in helping him.

Avoiding Ethan was a kind of passive-aggressive behavior to avoid the truth. The reality that I was possibly still absolutely, positively, and madly in love with him after all these years. It was happening to me all over again! And I wanted it to stop, but I didn't know how.

The past was repeating itself all over again. Because the sensation was weirdly too intense and somehow unfairly familiar to me. Let's just say, I had been feeling like the same stupid seventeen years old girl, who was so blindly in love with him that she couldn't wait to marry him and have his babies.

The feeling was insane, and I had no idea how to stop it from overpowering my senses. I just couldn't fall for that guy! Again! That arrogant, deviously dripping Greek God of a man! Every time I saw him, it turned me on! Whoa! Where did that shameless, filthy thought come from? Argh! Just kill me already. Would you, God?

He wasn't lying when he said he was going to make me fall head over heels for him. His threatening words echoed in every sensible corner of my head, repeating a thousand times with every passing second.

'You never loved him and you never will. Because you never did stop loving me, Sarah Walter!'

I was so screwed. I'd been going nuts about him since that kiss, or maybe just going insane. Yup, I was definitely going crazy, because only a fool would ever fall for a man like that! Yet again, I'd already fallen for that prick! *Yup, I'm that fool!*

But I wasn't up to the terms with letting him become aware of my pathetic condition. I just couldn't give him that satisfaction. Should I just pack my bags and run as far away as possible from him? Yes, indeed, it was time to change my phone number, my address, hell, even my name.

Even though it was safest to take a quick exit from this situation, I could not help but think, would I ever be the same loving person whom I had lost years ago? This might sound cliché, but I was feeling like I'd really started living again. He made me so comfortable in his presence that I could be whatever I wanted to be in front of him. I felt secure.

I had begun to feel much lighter nowadays. As if a heavyweight had been lifted off my heart and I could live freely once again. An emotional warmth had encircled my soul, which was once engulfed in darkness. It was similar to coming back to a place you can call home; where you could be yourself without being afraid of being judged.

I didn't care anymore if he really had changed and his feelings were true or if I had fallen for his tricks all over again. But admitting to myself that I had been feeling this way for this man was the hardest thing I had ever done in my life and I couldn't back down now.

The passion was insanely unsettling. No one had ever made me feel like that. It was like he made me feel vulnerable, made me let down my guard, yet wouldn't let me feel exposed. He made me feel safe.

On the other hand, I sensed this constant nudge in the back of my mind that I was about to get hurt again. I was stepping on a dangerous stone, a stone that was floating in the muddy bog. One missed step and I would be dragged down to the pits of hell.

The fear that it was all a game for him, a mere practical joke to satisfy his ego that no woman could ever reject Ethan Stanton, was still prominent. Maybe he had just been waiting for the day when I would admit my feelings to him so that he could reject me and laugh in my face.

This constant nagging in my head was not letting me abide by the feelings in my heart. My cynical thoughts were filled with scenarios of every possible dangerous aftermath. It was the same belief that made me freak out that night. I simply couldn't take it anymore. His ocean-deep eyes held so much compassion that I had to get out of there before I could've collapsed in his arms completely.

I had to do something to protect myself from another heartbreak that would kill me. I just couldn't let him be my downfall all over again. I was stronger than before and I would stand my guard to hide the feelings overpowering me. His presence had done enough damage to my senses. Thus, staying away from him and getting over these stupid feelings were my prime objective till I marry Lucas and get away from here for good. Perhaps this was the best favor I could do for myself.

After all, he was not the kind of guy who could spend his life with a single person. *Players don't settle down, period! They are only interested in two things: casual fling and moving on.*

I was scared of ruining my life. Afraid of everything that he had been making me feel. My mind just wanted to assume that it was all a big lie and sooner or later he would leave me at the same edge where I found myself nine years ago. And this time, I was sure I would not survive the fall. My brain was sure that I was falling into a well-laid-out trap. And much sooner than later, he would rip out the dreamy red carpet from right under my feet and give me a strong reality slap.

My heart, on the other hand, wanted me to believe him, to trust him one last time. The strong warmth in my chest begged me to see the righteousness in those eyes. I'd heard somewhere that eyes speak louder than any words ever could. And I shuddered once again, remembering that strange fear I'd seen in those deep blue eyes. That night, he made me see the vulnerability of losing someone you love. I couldn't imagine hurting him when he was already suffering. It was funny to believe we were tangible human beings with collateral damages.

But the million-dollar question was, was it just sexual tension, or I had really fallen for him? I slapped myself to drag myself out of the sinful mouth watery daydream of Ethan in his same old ripped jeans with a naked torso, as I encountered him on the day he moved next door. I huffed out a deep sigh when I recollected his hot breath on my cheek. It was the hottest tease I'd ever suffered.

"You okay there, babe?" I shook my head, blinking several times as if I'd awoken from the dead. My eyes quickly looked around to catch a glimpse of my surroundings. I was having a hard time recalling where exactly I was.

We were in Gemma's car parked outside Shelley's apartment and finally, my eyes noticed Melissa's face peeking in the rear-view mirror from the back seat while she applied the brightest scarlet shade of lipstick.

It was my last day at work before flying back to Hawaii for the wedding. My flight was scheduled for the day after tomorrow and so we decided to have a small recap of my bachelorette bash, combined with a breakup party for Gemma. I knew it was lame, but I kind of needed a distraction and welcomed the offer.

"Yeah, I am fine! It's just... a mosquito bit me on the face!" I mentally slapped myself at my lame excuse and quickly looked away.

"See, what did I tell you? This new air freshener of yours is so bad that only mosquitoes could survive in your car." Gemma turned to face Mell as they broke into a deep argument. While I looked outside the window of the car with a frown.

It had been two days since I had heard anything from his side. No note. No call. Not even a slight hustling on the other side of the wall. I checked my phone for the hundredth time, still nothing; not a single text. I wondered if he had totally abandoned me at last. My fingers quickly stroked my lips, contemplating if I was that bad a kisser that he had clearly dropped his plan to win me back.

I couldn't quite understand why I fought with Ash over Ethan, that too, when she needed me the most. I was too ashamed of myself. She flew back to her parents and only agreed to come to my wedding after repeated pleading and begging. After all, she was my maid of honor. She was clearly upset about my attachment with Ethan. I knew she was being protective, and I loved her for that.

"Sorry! My cat got stuck in the toilet. I had to give her CPR." Suddenly Shelley joined us, settling back on the seat beside Mell. I gave her a half-hearted smile just as her attention got captured by two dimwits who were still arguing over damn mosquitoes.

"Mell, Gemma, let's go before mosquitoes eat us alive here. I've heard they crave young and beautiful girls." Shelley tried to cut the conversation.

"She is talking about me!"

"In your dreams, girl." They continued to argue just as Gemma pressed the pedal and we drove off to our destination.

"I'm so going to get drunk tonight. I don't even remember when was the last time I felt this free." Gemma was the first one who broke the silence as the cold breeze stroked my hair on that slightly chilly night.

"That's why people call such relationships toxic, sweetheart. I'm glad you ditched that worthless piece of shit!" Mell placed her hands around Gemma's shoulder with a persuading smile just as she tilted her head to caress Melissa's hand with her cheek, letting out a deep sigh.

I smiled, looking at them, feeling the bond between them. Though I was thrilled to have a rousing blowout night with my girls after an endless busy schedule of hospital and studies, I somehow also wanted to have an escape. Where I could lose myself and just drift away in the ear-piercing music. I wanted to forget all the worries tonight that were holding me down for a while now. I just needed to let go of all the restraints and drown in absurdity till my skin would tingle and my lungs could take no more.

We perceived the long queue outside the club and the music coming from inside. Making me believe the atmosphere was all hyped up; fully equipped to give us our best night. As we stepped outside the car, a cold breeze grazed my skin, making me shiver at the spot. My hands automatically encircled me, already regretting my decision of choosing such a revealing dress.

"Whoa, it's really cold outside," Shelley exclaimed as if reading my mind.

"Soon you'll sweat your balls, sweetheart." Gemma's wide smile clearly told us how happy and unbound she was feeling at that moment. She was as excited as I was and without any delay, we jumped off towards the entrance. One of the bouncers gave us a charming grin and, without wasting a second, removed the barricade belt.

My eyes burned with ecstasy. While my head swayed with the music, which was so exhilarating that I had to close my eyes for a second to make myself get lost in the intoxicating ambiance of the club.

The night was young, just like a newly risen full moon; already bewitching everyone with its dark magic. The crowd was so maddening that I could feel my lips spreading into a wide smile, feeling the overwhelming ecstasy. The dry ice smoke swirled all around, making me feel like I had come to an alternate reality where worries didn't exist. I hadn't felt this enthralled in a long while. Goosebumps flared up my body just by indulging in the aura of that room. Shortly, we settled at our reserved table, calling the server in between.

"Drinks are on me since I am the one who caught his cheating ass," Gemma shouted at that loud music. And we all nodded, with big smiles furnishing our stupid faces.

Melissa gestured to us, and we gathered behind her, clicking lots of pictures. I laughed when we made silly faces and acted like teenagers. My head twirled towards the dance floor where everyone was having the best time of their lives. People were literally bouncing on the tune, and I started to sway in my seat when Shelley poked me on the shoulder. My attention diverted towards her with a raised eyebrow, when she signaled me towards Gemma. Sneaking a glance at her, I caught her scowling at her phone.

We observed her frown and murmuring nasty words to herself. Shelly and I exchanged a look while concluding that Gemma was reliving her past while deleting his ex's picture with every scroll.

"Babe, if you keep scraping your past, you will never be able to live fully in your present." I didn't know what overtook me when I said those words, but at that moment I shook my head and blinked several times to contemplate what I just said. Maybe it was my heart that longed for that peace in my present, irrespective of my past.

"Holy cow! It's been so long since I've heard such strong words. Way to go, doc!" Everybody nodded, and I smiled uneasily.

"To friendship and loyalty!"

"To friendship and loyalty!" We all toasted together with a big smile and gulped down our third round of tequila shots. My throat burned with the nasty metallic taste in my mouth as I slammed my hands on the table.

"Whoa! That was sick!" I declared just when Mell ordered another round.

Soon the drinks turned into a game of 'Truth or Drink' and we totally forgot about all the worries and concerns in our lives. Shelly had drawn the short straw today. So she was the one driving us all back home and thus sulking, with OJ in her hand.

I could already feel alcohol running in my blood. Pumping my heart like it was going to explode any minute. I happened to feel lighter and lighter with every drink. My fingers began to tingle and my brain stopped sending any kind of signals that could stop me from floating in the air.

"Burn in hell, jackass!" Gemma screamed her lungs out and I stood up, thrusting my drink up in the air to celebrate the night to the fullest! The night seemed to devour us with more and more toxicities in our blood, just as we laughed and enjoyed every second of it.

"So, how's your smoking hot neighbor? Is he still eyeing to win you back?" I struggled to glare at Shelley when she touched the forbidden topic. But there was something odd happening around me, as I couldn't get mad at her, nor could I scowl. But still, my smile dropped at her words. Why was I feeling bad about that?

"I don't know. Sometimes he treats me like I'm his life and sunshine and blah-blah-blah and the next second he totally ignores me. He has gone AWOL for the past two days as if he has given up on me. I don't understand him at all. Men are confusing." My expression dulled as I rested my chin on the table in defeat. My eyes roamed over my girls when they sighed, one after another.

"Maybe he already knows that you feel something for him!" Mell suggested.

"Or maybe he is keeping himself safe from the damage of being rejected by Sarah." My eyes racked between Mell and Gemma, and my eyebrows waggled in their contrasting opinions.

"Well, the way I see it, I think you should just ask him directly." Mell jumped off her chair and walked around the table, now facing me. At first, I was puzzled when she came too close to me. My head lightly jerked backward while my blurry vision tried to focus on her face. She grabbed my shoulders a little too tightly as I looked at her with wide eyes. What was she up to?

"Just go straight to him, grab his shoulders, and after taking a deep breath, look into his eyes." She was being damn serious.

"Eye contact scares the living shit out of guys!" Gemma's voice interjected us and I nodded as Mell let out a dry chuckle and the next second her face turned back serious when she once again looked into my eyes.

"Then say, listen, dude. I don't know what you are up to, but I kind of like you. So, you should rather tell me that you feel the same way or hold your silence at my wedding." She let go of me and then gave me a big grin as I let my face drop dead on the table in disappointment.

"Mell, have a drink and settle down. I have a better option for her problem." Just when Gemma overpowered the situation, Mell shrugged her shoulders and went back to her seat. But then my confusion increased when I noticed Gemma rummaging through my clutch.

"What are you doing?"

"Ha! Found it!" My eyes settled over her hand, which was now carrying my cell phone, and horror washed over me. Whatever she was thinking, her evil smirk clearly told me it was bad.

"Text him! Tell him that you are thinking about him right now! Trust me, his reply will give you a straight answer to your puzzled feelings." My disconcerted expression clearly told her that I was not convinced. My eyes roamed from my phone to her confident, beaming face when she sighed dramatically. I was having a hard time getting myself convinced.

"I'm not doing that!" The next second, my eyes almost popped out of my skull when I saw her typing on my phone.

'Hey, pumpkin!! Long-time no see!'

And the damage was done. She handed me my cell phone, and I quickly settled it down on the table like it was burning my skin. My forehead was covered in beads of sweat when our curious eyes were drilling the phone. Lying lifeless on the table while we frantically waited for it to light up. Did he just ignore me once again? The time tickled like we were living in a slow-motion era when all of a sudden Mell screamed.

"Oh, come on. Give me the damn phone!" I jumped up in dread when my eyes witnessed her typing hastily on the phone. I had to wrestle the phone out of her grip and read what she had typed but thankfully not sent.

'I can't stop thinking about you, hot stuff! I miss you so much it hurts; I need you so badly that I can hardly breathe!'

I rolled my eyes at her stupid phrase. "I don't talk like that and thank you, but I can breathe just fine! He will never..." My breath got caught in my throat when my phone chimed with a notification. The dingle sound echoed in my head and I slid the screen to unlock it. And the next thing I knew, I was frowning at his reply.

'Are you DRUNK, Starz?'

I chuckled and placed the phone back on the table. When all of a sudden all the girls screamed, jumping off their stools, almost giving me a heart attack. All because my phone started ringing, flashing Ethan's name.

"Pick up the damn phone!" Gemma shoved the phone in my hand and I almost jumped out of my skin when the severity of the situation hit me. My head started to swirl seeing his name flashing on the screen. A sudden wave of heat radiated over my body, making my palms sweaty. My hand began to tremble while holding that buzzing device. The phone continued to ring as my eyes roamed over all the girls who were giving me a boost to pick up the call and not to chicken out. But I was too afraid to face my fears. I pushed the phone onto Mell's chest and turned around, already prepared to run far away from this place.

"Starz? Shit! I mean, Sarah? Hello?" I squeezed shut my eyes cowardly when I heard a familiar voice on the speaker at my back. I sluggishly turned around with my eyes falling over Mell's smirking face and then onto her hand, which was holding the damn device.

"Say something, idiot." She softly hissed at me, and my shoulders slumped in defeat and I took the phone in my hands.

"Hey, neighbor?" I shrugged uneasily when everyone rolled their eyes at my response. Come on, I wasn't prepared for any of it.

"Is that you, Sarah? Wait, what's all that noise in the back?"

"Hey. I was..."

"Damn! Are you okay? Are you in some kind of trouble? Where exactly are you right now? Do you want me to pick you up?" I clenched my teeth when I heard a rumbling sound on the other side of the line and then a loud thud as if someone fell face flat on the floor.

"I'm fine. I'm fine! Hello? Please tell me you're safe, woman?" Aww! My face softened when he continued to shout through the phone and all I could do was admire the concern in his voice. *Dear heart, why him?*

"It's getting so hot in this downtown bar, babe! Check out the man at 9 o'clock. He is so hot! His flaming golden eyes are totally checking you out, Sarah!" A line appeared on my forehead when Shelley's uncertain yell reached my ears. *What man?*

"Where is this 9 o'clock?" Gemma turned around to look for the direction she was talking about when all of sudden Shelley snatched the phone from my hands and hung up the call. And I frowned at her rude behavior.

"If he is not here in the next fifteen minutes, you should completely forget about him." She opened my palm and jammed my cell phone back on it with a mysterious, evil grin. I couldn't quite get her way of handling the complexities of my life. My puzzled eyes wandered over her as she walked away, leaving me scratching my head in confusion.

Gemma exclaimed at Shelley's performance, like it was a matter of fact, and signaled the server for more drinks. But I needed to pee. I grabbed Mell's hand and headed to the ladies' room.

I didn't know about her, but I was definitely having a hard time walking straight. Either that or the room had started spinning around me on the axis.

"What if he doesn't show up on time? What if he doesn't get the hint and doesn't show up at all? Or just get stuck in traffic?" Before she would have answered me, someone tapped on my back, making me turn around and notice an unfamiliar face. As much as the mist enveloping my head was preventing me from thinking straight, I was certain I had never met this girl. And her frantic behavior of suddenly grabbing my shoulder and shaking me violently made it also certain that I didn't like her.

"Trust me, sugar, you deserve to be treated like a queen! If he gets late, dump his ass!" I tilted my head, trying to comprehend her words. Why was she shouting at me? Who on earth was she? Her lips continued to move, but my mind was too hazy to understand anything. Her red-painted lips were the only thing that my dull senses were able to focus on.

Mell started to push me towards the door when that strange lady continued to give me life advice, but sadly, I couldn't gather much out of what she was saying.

"Every girl on this planet deserves to be treated like a freaking queen!" I threw my hands up in the air when she yelled at my back.

"Hell yeah!" We all screamed at the top of our lungs while coming out of the restroom when my head crashed into a wall. My feeble body recoiled back from the impact. My already wobbling head quivered at the collision, making me clench my head. I scowled at the dark shadow hovering over me when I realized it was not actually a wall.

"What the hell! If you love your life, then clear the pathway for the queen, peasant." We laughed at my silly joke as I shook my head with my almost buttoned-up eyes.

"Starz?" A faint, distressed call brushed my ears, and I groaned because now I had to open my eyes and peer up at the person who was still blocking my way. As I lifted my head, my eyes clashed with the most mysterious stirring blue eyes in the whole wide world. Like a lightning striking a tree, my mind came to its senses with a jolt. My whole world sparkled in that smoky environment as I smiled. He came for me.

"Hey pumpkin, I missed you!" I was thrilled that I was finally getting the chance to meet him. And I surrendered myself in his arms. My hands automatically wrapped around his waist as I rested my head on his chest, feeling his heart against my ear. I knew that the smile on my lips didn't want to leave anytime sooner.

"Are you all right, Sarah!"

"I'm now!" I mumbled under my breath while still hugging him tightly. My heart was overwhelmed by this proximity. But the feeling didn't last long as he grabbed my arms and pushed me back at an arm's length. I groaned at the loss of his touch.

"Say something! Did anything happen to you?" My eyes were still folded when he yelled at my face. He clubbed my jaw underneath his heated skin and turned my face in every direction as if checking for some injury. He even tiled my face, exposing my neck to confirm if I had any vampire bite marks, and I giggled. I was feeling a little ticklish when he made me twirl at my place.

"How many drinks did you have? Shit! Do you even know who I am?" I could appreciate him muttering some nasty words underneath his breath while we reached our table. He seemed a little enraged. But why was he mad?

"Sir, only members are allowed in this club! You need to leave right now!" My eyes drifted towards two well-built men who had appeared out of nowhere and now standing behind Ethan. They seemed pretty furious at Ethan. *Why is everybody mad right now?*

"Shove up your membership in your ass!" Burying my mouth into my hands, I attempted to suppress my giggle when Ethan threw a wad of cash at their faces.

"Yeah, take that, fat-ass!" Mell screamed at them as they turned around with flat faces and quickly exited the area.

"By the way, I'm Gemma. Do you remember me?"

"I'm Shelley!" Gemma and Shelley introduced themselves, extending their hands while my face fell grim, as I witnessed Mell jumping into his arms. She landed a kiss on his cheek and I grasped the hem of my dress in a deadly grip. I wanted to strangle her right there. I never knew this jealous part of me existed.

"You remember me, right?" He nodded at her sternly and then turned towards me with a soft expression. And I took out my tongue at Mell. Take that girl. He was not going to get affected by some cheap flirting!

"What are you doing here, Starz? And what the hell are you wearing?" Ethan tried to grab hold of my hand once again when I pushed him away. He was such a mood killer.

"Is this prick bothering you, sweetheart?" My head jerked up towards a tall guy who was smirking down at me with a little too much cockiness. I opened my mouth and was ready to say something to him when Ethan intervened in the conversation.

"This prick is her boyfriend and you are going to turn around and mind your own business in five seconds or he'll seriously bother you!" I smiled and nodded proudly when the cocky guy quickly turned around and faded away into the crowd.

"We are going home now! Say goodbye to your friends." He hastily pulled out his jacket and tucked it around my shoulder, taking me in his arms. I smiled, snuggling into him, inhaling his intoxicating scent when he rubbed his arms around my back. But wait, did he just say we were leaving? Hell no! I quickly pulled away, pushing at his chest when his hands securely wrapped around my waist.

"We are not leaving so soon! It's Gemma's breakup bash! Come have a drink with us!" I felt so strong and dominant at the moment when I dragged him to the nearest counter and gestured toward the bartender. Or maybe he let me drag him. The bartender quickly filled two glasses, and I pushed one on Ethan's face.

"No, thank you. I'm good, Sarah!" I frowned when he took the glass from my hand and placed it back on the counter.

"Oh, come on. Just one drink! Why are you so mad?" I whined.

"I'm not mad!"

"Yes, you are! Mad! Mad! Mad!"

"Fine, I'm a little mad! Happy? Can we please go home now?" A bead of irritation was scratched all over his body, and I knew how to calm him down. The overwhelming desire to taste him washed over me. And I did what had to be done at that moment. I lifted myself up on my toes, encircled my arms around his neck, and finally pressed my lips to his. At first, I thought we were going to fall back. But he grabbed hold of my waist with one hand while the other one settled on the counter, giving us enough support to carry our weight.

Maybe I took him by surprise because at the beginning he didn't respond to my kiss. Hell, he stood there like a frozen statue. But short after I felt his both arms wrapping around my waistline, picking me up in the air as he loosened his jaw and brought out the tongue in the business. It was all so mushy and unbelievable that I felt like fainting in his arms. I sensed his tensed muscles relaxing. Just as his temper started to recede, and right there my work was done and I pulled away, with a broad smile etching over my face.

"There! Now you can't stay mad at me any longer!" I couldn't decipher the features on his face when his head remained bowed and body motionless and tense. I jumped up with a jolt when I heard him let out a grunt underneath his breath. What? Did I do something wrong?

"I'm taking you home, lady!" And before I could've comprehended what he was about to do, he grabbed my left arm and tossed me on his shoulder as if I weighed nothing. With my body sliding over his back like a sack of rice, I let out a squeal when he slapped my butt.

"This is my card. If you guys need any help, just give me a call!" I overheard him talking to my girls and the next second, we started to head towards the door.

"Ethan, I can't leave now! I want to pole dance!"

"Yeah, right! Like I want to marry you, girl! But none of us are getting our wishes fulfilled tonight."

Twenty-seven

Ethan

DAY FORTY-ONE continues...

"Bye, Sarah! Don't forget to use protection, baby!" I almost blushed when her friends screamed at our back and she gave them a thumbs up.

These girls are on fire!

It was almost one in the morning and soon the music faded into the background as we were approaching the exit. I wrapped my hands tightly around her waist, afraid she was falling asleep on my shoulder. She rested her head on my back and started drifting off like a little baby.

Her body laid still on mine, and the warmth spreading from her made a smile creep on my face. Her actions clearly stated that she was not in her senses. She had no idea who or where she was or what she was doing, but instinctively her little acts gave peace to my heart. I would cherish these last moments with her and would forever keep them as an unforgettable memory in my heart.

I never knew she could drink this much, but ironically, it was me who was intoxicated at that moment. I had been swept away the second she kissed me. My senses were totally whisked away by this crazy girl. It ignited a passion in my nerves. I could still hear my heart pounding in my ears from that fatal act. It felt like I was drowning in an ocean of love for her. Whenever I tried to swim out of it, she pulled me back with double force. Still, no matter what I did, it would never be enough to win back her trust.

"I hate you, Stanton!" All of a sudden, I heard her murmur, and I smiled, clenching her securely in my arms. At least I was running through her mind.

"Yes. You do, love!"

"Ethan, why...are...you...like...this? I want to... understand you." She was struggling with every word, making me smile even more.

"I hate you, Ethan. You are going to break my heart once again!" My smile fell as I stopped dead in my tracks, contemplating if I heard her right. A gush of cold breeze struck my hair, and I shivered, realizing two facts about my life.

First, she had still not forgiven me for my past deeds.

Second, even after everything, she still had feelings for me, to be able to think that way, or maybe it was only the alcohol talking.

Soon, we reached my car and after carefully balancing Starz I opened the door and settled her down on the passenger seat. Her face reflected so much innocence that I didn't know how I fought back the urge to kiss her when I proceeded to put her seatbelt on. I gawked at her, trying to savor every single feature on her face. Hell, I wanted to taste her and remember that taste until my last breath.

I wondered how someone could seduce you without even batting an eyelid. Leaning onto her, my eyes studied her beautiful features as we were just an inch apart when her eyes fluttered open.

My body jerked away in surprise as my head hit the car's roof and all the blood drained away from my face. It felt like I was caught in the act. I rubbed the back of my head and smiled uneasily.

"Hi!" She said the world's most innocent 'hi' to me and my heart almost stopped.

"I really like you, Ethan!" The earth stopped spinning at her confession. But then I shook my head and took a deep breath. Because it proved that she was just drunk talking. Feeling pity for myself, I lowered my head and looked up into her eyes.

"I know you're not going to remember any of this, but I want to apologize, darling. I've caused so much distress in your life that I wish with all my heart we could start all over again. But... never mind; I promise, I won't be a trouble anymore! And I also promise I will never stop loving you, no matter what." My heart clenched saying all that. As if I was buried under boulders.

"But I like your nose! I don't want it to go away!" She tapped my nose, and I chuckled, helplessly.

"Oh, God, please help me. Please give me strength!" I whispered, not meeting her peering eyes glued on me.

"Are we home yet?" My forehead creased as I shook my head. Is she joking to tempt me or just being out of her rockers?

"I'm afraid we haven't, yet, your highness." And I gave her a bow in respect of the power she held over me.

Closing her door, I walked around to the driver's side with a silly smile plastering my face. "You know, just for the information, your friend Melissa creeps me out," I told her while settling down. A line appeared between my brows when she didn't reply and when my head turned toward her, I found the seat empty and the door wide open. I panicked for a second, but then my eyes drifted towards a drunk figure strolling down the street, struggling to keep her balance.

"Really, woman?" I shook my head at her silliness and quickly locked the car before hurrying after her. "Where do you think you're going?" I chuckled when I perceived her increasing her pace after hearing my voice. Her determined self never looked back while she struggled to run on her wobbly legs in heels.

"I'm hungry!" I narrowed my eyes as I was now utterly confused. Did I hear her right?

"But it's way past midnight!" She looked back, giving me a noticeably annoying look, and then resumed her march forward. I observed our vicinity and noticed some wild spirits giving her looks, and I smiled sheepishly. I was helpless and had no option but to run after her.

"Starz, hold on!" She stopped abruptly in her tracks and turned around hastily, only to have her head collide against my chest.

"Ouch!" She rubbed her forehead, and I quickly took her face in my hands as she breathed hot breaths on my face. I smiled and shook my head, struggling to stay conscious when she was so close to me.

"You hurt me!" I couldn't understand why, but her words poked me right in the middle of my heart.

"I wish I could erase all the stupid things I've done to you. But unfortunately, this is the reality and I can't do anything but ask for your forgiveness." I just wanted to hold her close and never let go. She was special, and she deserved to be treated like a queen. She leaned into me and my thoughts went haywire, thinking about all the bad things she could do right now, when all of a sudden she undid the straps of her heels and shoved them in my chest.

"Stupid stilettos!" Right away, she grabbed my hand and began to drag me onto an empty street. Her stomach let out a funny sound, and I chuckled, but quickly covered my face when she gave me the deadliest glare I've ever seen on a drunk girl.

"Turn around!" A line appeared on my forehead when I didn't quite get what she was saying.

"What?"

"I said turn around!" She whined like a baby, and I let out a chuckle before turning around. My eyes popped out and my hands automatically went to grasp her before I could've assessed what was happening, as she was already enjoying the piggyback ride.

"Whoa! Enjoying the view, darling?" She nodded frantically, and I started walking.

"Hey! Look at that bloody gorgeous theater. They show classics. It's such a waste that their tickets are sold out for the entire weekend!" I glanced at the old building and then nodded.

"Anyway, tell me something about yourself, Mr. Stanton! How was your day?" Before I could've said something, she shot me another question, and God, how much I was enjoying her babbling.

I closed my eyes when her hot breaths at the nape of my neck sent shivers down my spine. The warmth that was spreading from her ignited a strong desire in me.

Oh, God. How long would I've to endure this torture?

"Well, it was going great until I heard a drunk girl's voice on my phone in the middle of the night!" We were walking in the opposite direction to the car, well I was walking to be specific. "You know, I almost had a panic attack over that call. Do you have any idea how many clubs are there in this downtown?"

"But you still found me! Aren't we destined?" She wrapped her hands tightly around my neck and life was sucked out of my soul. My one hand quickly rushed up to save my life when she began to strangulate me with a real bone-crushing hug.

"Sarah, your friend posted a story about your girl's night out on her social media account and tagged me! That's how I found you!" At that moment, I let out a deep breath when her grasp loosened over my throat.

"Is that so? And here I thought we have a spiritual connection like soulmate telepathy!" My legs halted at that moment, and I swear I was dumbfounded to my deepest core. What did this girl just say?

"So, tell me if you could be someone else for a day, who would you want to be?" Before I could think straight, she abruptly changed the subject, and I started walking again. *What's with this girl today?*

Her hot breath assaulted my ear and I could feel goosebumps erupting all over my body. I closed my eyes, inhaling her intoxicating aroma. She had no idea what damage her little acts were doing to my body. My heart somersaulted when I imagined the moment of us walking down the empty alley to be like any normal couple madly in love with each other.

"Ethan?" I was dragged back to reality when she slapped my back.

"Well, I would love to be you, so that you would go out on a date with me!" She went silent all of a sudden and my smile dropped, fearing I had pushed my luck too far and said something I shouldn't have.

"What's your biggest fear, Ethan?" My head lifted as she looked down at me and I got caught up in that intimidating look.

"I... I am scared. I am scared of falling for something that will never happen!"

"Then make it happen, Ethan!" She jumped down and turned me around with both hands on my arms, her eyes burning holes in my soul. I couldn't blink, nor could I breathe, because she was staring into that part of my heart, which I had secured with a wall of despair. But her eyes were tearing down that wall with that look which I would never forget.

"Promise me you will never stop fighting for us, Ethan!" She took my hands into hers and intertwined her fingers with mine. I almost shivered at the touch but was too baffled to react. "Promise me you will make my heart trust you again." And then her body lifted on her toes as she collapsed in my arms. She wrapped me in her arms like a rose holds its thorns because I had no right to touch her.

"Ice cream!" She screamed all of a sudden and ran away.

"What?" I could only whisper when my stare drifted off with her. I watched her running towards an ice cream parlor. I rested a hand on my heart when a smile crept over my face, feeling how vulnerable she made me feel just now.

"Darling, you are going to kill me."

Reaching the place, I was at first greeted by a grumpy man on the other side of the counter. And then by two girls who were engaged on their phones while having their treats. *Why on earth is an ice cream parlor open at this wee hour of the night?*

"I want chocolate chip cookie dough ice cream! With extra double chocolate chips!" I laughed at Starz's innocence and then nodded at the server. I couldn't help but notice he was giving Starz some noticeable frown.

"You heard the lady. And one strawberry milkshake for me!" We quickly settled down on one of the tables and waited for our orders. She rested her chin on the table, staring at me with a smile that could cure any pain in the world.

As soon as the order was served, Starz started munching on her ice cream like it was the last ice cream left in the universe. She got so engorged that I didn't think she would notice if the roof collapsed on my head right then. I stifled a chuckle when ice cream painted her nose. She seemed like she could eat a horse right there. Soon, the enjoyable view turned into torture when she took out her tongue to lick her lower lip smeared with chocolate.

Those pretty seductive lips sent my mind into a sensual hellhole. I shifted in my chair uncomfortably, trying to control the solid urge to reach over the table and wipe off that chocolate by kissing her deeply. Darling, stop this torment before I do something I would regret. I wanted her so bad, to feel those lips against mine; conquer them till they scream my name.

My resistance was crumbling with passing every second. I felt like a hungry vampire, craving for one drop of blood that could save him.

"Ethan?" It felt like someone was calling out to me for a while now, and just now I got my senses back that it was Starz who was now staring at me with a frown. Her lips pursed as lines appeared on her forehead, giving me a hard stare. I scratched the back of my neck, smiling sheepishly. Did she really catch me ogling at her?

"Did you say something?" My head leaned to the right, praying she was not mad at me.

"I said he forgot to add extra chocolate chips to my ice cream!" And with that, I huffed out a sigh of relief. I quickly changed my expression into a serious mad one and stormed off towards the counter, with Starz following me.

"Mister!" I tried to make my voice sound deep and husky at that person whose back was facing us.

"Hey!" My confidence faltered when he didn't turn around and I looked down at Starz, who was staring at me with so much hope. *Not now, man!*

"Excuse me, Sir!" I almost begged, but then got startled when Starz slammed a hand on the counter, making everyone in that shop jump in shock. The loud sound made me cringe so badly that my hand quickly went for my heart to stop it from jumping out of my mouth.

"Dude! Are you deaf or something?" My eyes traveled from Starz and then back to the now turned guy, who seemed even madder than Starz. Well, this was not a good sign.

"I said you didn't add extra chocolate chips to my ice cream!"

"We ran out of it!" Starz looked shocked as well as a little taken aback by that response.

"What? Then you should have told us when we gave out the order!"

"Whatever!" He almost rolled his eyes at Starz and turned around. But right then she did something that I never in a million years could have expected from her. She launched her ice cream cone towards him.

Oh… No! And in that slow, painful moment, I watched aghast the cone landing on top of that guy's freshly shaved head. I stifled a hard laugh and turned it into a cough when he turned around. The cream was dripping off his face just as he glared at Starz.

"Never, and I quote never, turn your back to a lady when she is talking!" Starz had a quick glance at me and I nodded, giving serious looks to that server. "Never!" I nodded and Starz turned back to him.

"I want you two to leave before I call the cops!" Is this guy joking or what? Because as much as I knew Starz, leaving the place like a coward was the last thing she would ever do before the apocalypse.

"Or what? Did you think you'll get away with this? Ethan, honey, call the cops. I'll tell them about this lowly man's rip-off!" What? I stopped listening after honey.

"Sarah, darling, scamming chocolate chips is not a crime yet!" I tried to calm her down. But her one death glare clearly signaled me that I should shut my cakehole. And that was exactly what I did, placing one finger on my mouth.

"That's it! Control your chick, dude! Or I'm definitely calling the cops!" I shrugged when he gave me one hard stare.

"Starz! I think we should get going now! I know a place that serves even tastier ice cream than here!"

"With extra chocolate chips?" Starz spoke, looking up at me with wide sparkling eyes and I was completely dazzled. The smile she gave me was the loveliest smile I had ever seen, and I was sure I would've cut out my heart for her if she had asked at that moment.

"Yeah! With extra chocolate chips!" I could barely let out the words when she wrapped her arms around mine and the next moment we were walking towards the door when a harsh voice nabbed us.

"Hey, crackheads, where do you think you are going?" I squeezed my eyes shut when Starz turned back with an even madder expression on her face.

"What did you just call us?" It was a threat, and I tried to hold Starz back when her smile faded and her expression turned grim. I could guess what was about to come, as I feared becoming victim of the collateral damage.

"You forgot to pay, genius!"

"Oh, my bad!" I nodded at him as my hands went for my wallet in my back pocket when a nervous laugh escaped my mouth. Two things happened at the same time. First, I realized my back pocket was empty because I forgot my wallet in the car. And second, Starz jumped over the counter over him for calling us crackheads.

"You- never- should- call -a -lady a crackhead!" I ran around the counter only to witness Starz sitting over his chest and strangling him. He was shrieking in pain and I bit my nails nervously because I was sure he was going to be dead soon.

"Take her off of me, dude!" He screamed for help and hesitantly I moved towards them. I gripped Starz by her waist and yanked her away from him before she could've choked him to death. "Take her away from me. I don't want any bloody money!"

"I'll teach you some manners, you crackhead!" She was fluttering in the air as I hauled her away by her waist. Her hands still called out to strangle him as she yelled at him some really bad but cute names. I scot her up on my shoulder and we were almost out of the door when I heard something that made my blood boil.

"Dumb whore!"

❧

"You shouldn't have punched him." My head swung towards her with a death glare when she gave me a toothy smile. "I mean, cutting off his tongue would have been enough!" I rolled my eyes and stood up, walking away from her.

"I'm sorry, your highness! Perhaps you could've given me a hint before going on a killing spree so that we wouldn't be behind bars right now!" My fingers wrapped around the bar with my stare fixed on the keys hanging on a distant wall.

"Well, he asked for it!" I shook my head when she just shrugged at me. Looking too innocent to believe that she was going to murder someone a minute ago for some freaking chocolate chips.

Soon, our luck played out when my eyes landed on one of the officers coming our way. "Time to leave this cage, Miss Hunter." I rushed towards her and taking her purse in my hand, I made her stand up. Though I could feel the alcohol was still running through her blood but luckily she obliged.

"We apologize, Mr. Stanton. We didn't know it was you!" They handed me my things, and I nodded in acceptance.

"It's fine!" I replied, as just a phone call to my lawyer bailed us out in less than thirty minutes. I grasped Starz's hands tightly and made it outside the police station before she could have done something stupider that would land us in grave danger.

"I don't feel good!" She muttered and my head jerked towards her when I knew what was about to come. In a matter of seconds, she started throwing up, when her stomach could no longer hold back those hard drinks. I held her hair back while she emptied her stomach. Rubbing her back, I smiled, shaking my head when she was regretting her decision of partying hard.

"Sir!" Someone shouted at my back and I noticed one of the officers running toward us with a register in his hand. "I'm sorry, Mr. Stanton, we need your signature here," I nodded and took the papers from his hand while at the same time holding Starz steady on her legs. After signing the formality, I noticed my car was already parked at the front and we took our seats.

"Now, we are going straight home!" I exclaimed in a thick voice to sound serious and rigid. I lifted an eyebrow when Starz didn't fight back. My head shot up when I heard loud snores. A chuckle left my mouth when I noticed her giggling in her sleep while mumbling something.

"Mmmmm... I'm so hungry! I want a pizza and a... a chocolate chip cookie dough ice cream!"

In a short time, we reached our building, and I carried her up to my apartment and settled her in my bed. She was fast asleep and shaking my head at her deadly deeds I smiled and left the room.

I went for a glass of water when my eyes drifted outside the window into the peaceful night sky. A thousand stars were shining brightly, just like my Starz. Remembering just how her eyes had lit up noticing me in that club, I rested my fingers on my lips. Still, a little shaken by that tingling sensation she had left on them.

I practically spit out my water when I sensed someone standing just behind me. I quickly turned around and held my heart. "Shit, Starz! You almost gave me a heart attack!"

"I'm terrified, Ethan!" She spoke with glistening eyes. "I'm here, baby girl! You are tired, you need some sleep!" I wrapped my arms around her as we walked toward the bedroom. We made it to the door when, all of a sudden, she pushed me back.

"Why do you do this? First, you give me hope only to take it away the next minute?" I was bewildered, my confused eyes trying to study her when all of a sudden a tear dropped from her eyes.

"I don't understand!" I tried to hold her back, but she pushed me away.

"You promised you would never leave, but then you left me broken!" She started crying hysterically and embarrassment washed over me when I became aware of the situation.

"You never loved me. I should never have trusted you!" She mumbled in her palms with a broken voice, and I could no longer meet her eyes.

"I loved you, Ethan. I loved you with all my heart. And I still fuckin' love you." She shouted, looking straight into my eyes while poking my chest with her finger. I was too dumbfounded to say anything.

"You're a fuckin' liar, Ethan Stanton! A manipulative scumbag." My eyes bored into her when she turned scarlet with all the crying. My heart broke seeing her like that. I wanted to hold her, console her, but she continued to hurl my hands away as if my touch burned her. Then she let out a humorless laugh.

"Starz?"

"Don't call me that! I told you, I hate that stupid name! And I hate your father for calling me your victim." She screamed at me, making me freeze. My father? What the fuck she was talking about?

She was now trembling with anger, and my hands squeezed into fists. I couldn't do anything. I couldn't make her believe how much I loved her or how much I suffered without her. Tongue-tied, I witnessed her stepping back as her legs stumbled. I feared she would fall. But she raised her hand at me when I tried to support her. Her legs collided with the couch and her body stumbled on it. Her eyes closed and with her drifting deeper into the slumber she muttered,

"Let's be strangers again, Ethan!"

Twenty-eight

Sarah

DAY FORTY-TWO

Everything seemed fuzzy as I drifted out of a disturbed sleep. I was lying on my stomach, with my cheek pasted over the pillow and dry mouth stuck with thick saliva. I had a disgusting metallic taste in my mouth and the sunrays coming from the window were blinding me. Trying to shift under the sheets, a loud painful grunt left my mouth as every single bone in my body ached and I could sense a bad migraine crawling in.

I retreated under the duvet, hoping to gallop far away from every single sound around me. I had yet to process why I was feeling this awful. But luckily the sheets smelled amazing, and I smiled, feeling snuggly.

But it didn't last long when my phone proceeded to buzz with notification after notification. And my stabbing headache was back. "Really, dude?" I sneaked out my hand in search of that annoying device but unfortunately couldn't find anything matching my desire. Squinting to my left, I finally found it and quickly turned it silent and noticed the time. It was almost noon. I groaned with frustration, but then my eyes fell over a note at the bedside and I lifted my head to read it.

"Good morning, darling!"

I groaned in utmost displeasure and turned my head away when another note caught my eyes.

"I'm starving! So, get your ass up... sleepyhead!"

My body jerked up in an instant as if a thunderbolt struck my senses. I sat up too fast and had to grip my head in my hands when it spun terribly.

"What on earth?" Aiming to understand those creepy messages, I shook my head. I knew the person who was notorious enough for leaving these strange notes in my bed, but how did he get in? And it made me focus on my surroundings and then down at me, with my brain still struggling to join all the jumbled pieces together. Thank goodness! I was still breathing, and above all, fully dressed. Well, this hooker dress could be considered a dress at that fragile moment.

The room felt strangely familiar, but I was definitely not in my apartment. My legs felt like jelly when I tried to stand up. Once my bare feet touched the cold floor, the room swayed painfully, causing me to lose balance. I reached out for the nearby wall for support while my other hand was still clenching my aching head.

My rational senses flickered with some recollections from last night and I squinted my eyes. I still couldn't recall with certainty how much had I drunk in a single night. Still, I had to conclude that I truly had a wild girl's night out to earn this terrible hangover.

With my brain still battling to recover from the previous night's trauma, I sauntered outside the room. Only to discover Ethan passed out on the couch. I was in his apartment! Sleeping in his bed with his sweet-smelling sheets! I gave him a weird look when I found him sleep-talking.

"Girl, come on. Can't you wait till we get home?" I was already feeling muddled and woozy. And listening to him talking gibberish made everything even more ambiguous about what the hell was going around here.

The funny smile on his face and his hands wrapped around the pillow, squeezing the life out of it like it was the most beloved thing of his life, made me gape at him with wonder. My eyes drifted towards Finn, who rushed in, wagging his tail, and then started licking Ethan's face as he erupted into another round of giggles. "Oh, stop it. Will you?"

So it wasn't only me, even my dog was crashing at the neighbor's place now. Shaking my head at my half-witted neighbor, I swiveled towards the kitchen. My eyes desperately searched for some coffee. Without a proper warning, my eyes fell over the mirror hanging in the hallway, and the next instant a wild, frantic shriek left my mouth.

"What? I swear I didn't eat your ice cream." Ethan shouted in response and fell face-first onto the floor. But then he quickly gathered his senses, and my eyes turned back at my reflection. I couldn't believe what I was seeing.

I looked nothing less than Medusa. My hair was an utter mess, spiraling out like thousands of snakes. I leaned into the mirror to have a look at my eyes. Because I was having a hard time finding them underneath my scary smokey eye makeup inspired only by the pandas. I cringed at a rotten smell surging out of my clothes. It was enough to make me feel fuzzy. Did I puke on myself?

"Did you just get scared of your own reflection?" It was a rhetorical question and, as predicted, Ethan cracked up in a burst of hysterical laughter the next second. I rolled my eyes at him when he fell with a thud on the couch, bending double with a burst of deep, loud, hearty laughter.

"You look like a truck mowed you down; over and over again!" My pounding head wanted to strangulate him already. However, every part of my body hurt with even the slightest movement, so I just dropped the idea of killing him today. *Go, live your life for one more day, Ethan Stanton.* I had no energy to engage in a banter with him right now.

I stumbled on the couch beside him, still holding my head down in my hands, while drowning in self-pity as to why on the earth, did I drink so much? I sensed Ethan turning towards me. But before he could've hurled another insult at me, I warned him, "I swear I'll choke you with your own sock if you crack one more joke on my face?"

I closed my eyes while Finn snuggled in my lap, soothing my nerves. Soon, I sensed someone hovering over me and I looked up, only to find Ethan staring down at me. My eyebrows waggled when I noticed him holding a cup.

"Trust me, I won't poison you with the only thing I'm good at!" Still staring at his fake hurt look, I took the cup, giving him my best cynical face. He bent down, placing a bowl of water for Finn and caressing his ears.

My eyes clipped on their own, by just inhaling the aroma of the tea. The first sip from the chamomile tea felt like someone lifted tons of weight from my head. I moaned in delight, feeling my body getting relaxed.

"So, was I just strangling you in your sleep, or was it much worse?" I asked, smirking, still deep down enjoying the tea. This guy knew how to brew a mean hangover tea.

"Well, it was nothing close to what you did last night!" I spit out my tea when his words hit me. I bet my eyes almost popped out of the socket when they filled with horror. My head jerked up towards him. Noticing him leaning against the kitchen counter, crossing his arms over his chest, purposely flexing his muscles. He turned around and walked away when I opened my mouth, ready to ask some serious dignity-saving questions.

"What do you mean? What did I do?" I shouted behind his back. My decent mood from drinking the tea was long gone now. A thousand questions were running through my mind and I stormed toward him. Settling down on the kitchen stool, I watched him slowly filling his coffee mug. He was certainly enjoying tormenting me.

"Oh, nothing serious, darling. You just got us arrested!" I was sure my jaw dropped to the floor gazing at him, filling his plate with scrambled eggs. I wouldn't deny I had been having a gut feeling since I'd woken up that something went out of control last night. But then I looked at him doubtfully when he passed a mischievous smile.

"Ha-Ha! What a joke!" I followed him when he relaxed on the couch with his breakfast.

"You are kidding! Right?"

He switched on the television, getting comfortable, placing his legs up on the coffee table as he relaxed back. A tint of irritation consumed me and the next moment, I tossed off his legs and cupped his jaw in a tight grip, catching his attention.

"Right?"

"Relax, they didn't put us up in the record." The edge of annoyance in his voice made me recoil. He straightened up on his feet as the coffee was spilled on his shirt and he had to take it off to stop his skin from burning. I felt heat creeping up my cheeks, glancing at his firm abs and I acted upon my survival instinct. Almost immediately, I flung water from Finn's water bowl at him.

"Thank... you!" He let out a sarcastic remark while lifting his hands in the air.

The hangover acted on its own and I felt annoyed. Why was he mad at me when I was the one who was having a terrible migraine? I crossed my arms over my chest and leaned back on the couch. Turning my face away from him, I tried to look mad while at the same time feeling guilty for burning him. For a few seconds, he didn't do anything, and I had to sneak glances at him. I almost let out a groan, discovering him smiling at me. He was making me more annoyed.

He patted his sexy body dry with his shirt and I was having a hard time diverting my eyes. He was half-naked and let me quote this 'he had a rather nice body'. Okay, fine, much more than just nice. He was devilishly hot! A person being this ripped should be banned from taking his clothes off! My eyes shamelessly studied every single muscle of his body, making muscles clench in my lower abdomen.

A strange yet familiar memory crossed my mind when my eyes fell over the scar on his shoulder. There was a long story behind that game injury. I didn't know how many girls in the school he had shared that story with, but I was one of them who knew why he used to flaunt it. It was a victory mark from his football days.

"Like what you see?" I swear every visible part of my body turned crimson with embarrassment. I noticed him giving me a smirk with a raised brow and I smiled rather bashfully.

"Put on a damn shirt!" I threw his shirt on his face and closed my eyes.

I shifted in my place when he took a seat beside me and then encircled his arms around my shoulders.

"I know there are many ways to say it, but I won't beat around the bush. Your apartment is just next door, but if you want, you could use mine as well." I turned towards him, confused at what he was trying to say. I couldn't hold back the blush when he held my hands in his and looked into my orbs. I was terrified thinking about what he was about to say, but it was certainly not what he actually said.

"You really stink, Sarah Walter."

I shot up, gawking at him, feeling infuriated, as well as a little hurt. And then turned around, storming towards the exit. Thankfully, the corridor was empty. Reaching my door, I remembered I neither had my keys nor my phone or purse. Hell, I was even bare feet.

"What? Am I too distracting?" He yelled at my back, as I sensed him following me with my belongings.

"No, my heart just aches seeing so much malnourishment in the world!" Before he would have reacted to my solid come back, I snatched everything from his hands and slammed the door in his face.

Looking at my reflection in my bathroom mirror, I noticed I was still wearing his jacket. But it was now totally ruined. I quickly stripped it off and made up my mind to wash it later and never give it back. It was too warm and comfortable to part ways with.

"Starz?" I groaned when my long, hot, peaceful shower was disturbed by his enchanting voice once again. Oh, Shoot! I forgot to lock the front door.

"I want to make it clear that I am not trespassing. It's just that Finn is biting my head off searching for you, so I am letting him and myself in." He shouted from what I believe to be my living room.

"Yeah?" I reached for my toothbrush while making an effort to understand what on earth he wanted from me.

"Starz?" He sounded much closer now. Was he leaning against the bathroom door? Suddenly, my hands wrapped around my body and my head turned towards the closed door. A feeling of embarrassment crossed over me, fearing him peeking at me. And then I sighed; 'Thank goodness the door doesn't have a keyhole'.

"Hmm," I mumbled, with my mouth full of toothpaste.

"I want to confess something to you! Would you please care to listen?" He said in a pleading tone and I wondered what could he possibly be talking about?

"Could you wait for me to come out?" I managed to say after rinsing my mouth.

"No! I think it is better this way! I don't think I would be able to get all the words out while facing you." I was confused and curious now.

"First of all," he started, when I remained silent.

"I owe you an apology for dragging you in that mess last week. I could only imagine how hard it was for you to meet my family, let alone attend a funeral out of the blue! I'm sorry, Starz." Ethan's awkward, nervous tone exhibited how embarrassed he was.

"No, I wanted to come! The only regret I carried back with me was not ever getting the chance to meet in person the great soul your Nanna was! I wish I knew her before!"

"Then why did you disappear that night? It was because of me, right? I did something wrong, didn't I?" I turned around as if Ethan was standing just behind me and bit my lower lip when the memories of the kiss flashed in my head. My hands caressed my lips, remembering how I lost myself under his touch. I had never felt such a strong pull towards anyone in my whole life.

"No, I... I was just called up for some urgent work. Why would it be something you did? The world doesn't revolve around you, Mr. Stanton." My face scrunched up when I stammered. I bet he could tell I was lying. But then I was thankful for not being face to face with him right now. I could not meet his eyes at this trembling moment. *Every door of my rational thinking shuts when he is close to me.*

"By the way, Ethan, did I say something stupid last night? I am having a hard time recalling anything!" I chuckled, aiming to lighten the mood. But inside, I really wanted to know where all this was coming from. Did I say something to him while I was drunk out of my mind?

"It's all my fault, Sarah! I should never have left you alone for my father to poison your thoughts. How stupid and thoughtless of me for thinking he would forgive me at some point in life. He hates me and I'm okay with it, but he has no fuckin' right to cross the line and insult you. Pardon me for his behavior."

The vulnerability in his voice made me remember the conversation I had with Mr. Stanton as I darted out of Ethan's room after that kiss. I bumped into him running down the stairs and I could right away sense he was drunk. He asked me where I was running to and tried to help me find my way, but stopped talking as tears started rolling down my face.

I couldn't understand how, but he recognized me. We had a brief encounter nine years ago, and I never thought he would remember me. He asked if I was the same girl from nine years ago. The same fateful girl who was responsible for ruining their family name in the town. And getting no reply, he asked me the most infuriating question. Was it even true or did I fake being a victim just to get back at Ethan for something stupid he did?

I was enraged and wanted to scream at him for abandoning his only son for all these years, but couldn't. I just fled the town. Hell, I didn't even return the dress to Mrs. Ellsworth. But I never thought it was Ethan's fault. I never mentioned that encounter to anyone. Had I said something last night?

"Please forgive me for what type of person I was. You never deserved the type of jerk I was to you." His words ran in a loop in my head, believing he was begging for forgiveness. And I wondered, haven't we already come a long way past forgiving each other?

"You deserved a man who would have proudly yelled at the top of his lungs, 'Hell yeah, she is my woman', for the whole world to listen." A smile broke from my face when he actually yelled his words.

"You deserved to feel loved when you let down your guards for me and loved me with all your being. Instead, all I ever made you feel was being cheated and abandoned." In a matter of seconds, a sense of annoyance washed over me and I wanted him to stop right there. It was the feeling of being torn apart after years of being patched up by a thousand different pieces.

"You deserved respect; you were worthy of every ounce of trust and honesty from me! I was a fool for taking your love for granted." A tear rolled down my eyes when I leaned back at the door and placed a hand on my chest, feeling my heart squeezing painfully.

"I know you're thinking, why am I saying all this today? Why now? It must be a long gone past for you, Sarah, but for me, it is still present. I have been living in a hell of regret and shame ever since. I could never let you go." His voice was deep and raspy.

The conversation had reached the point where I wanted to face him. Wrapping the robe around my body, I exited the bathroom and found him sitting on the floor, leaning against the wall while hugging his legs. I took in a sharp breath of air when he stood up and looked down, hardly managing to meet my eyes.

"I was scared, Starz, and still am!" He paused for a few seconds! "But I can't take it anymore! I need your forgiveness" I was feeling conflicted. I craved to crash into his arms, yet wanted to stay far away. My heart ached to comfort him, but my soul was too ripped apart to give any solace.

He looked up hesitantly and cupped my face in his trembling hands, making me stare into those piercing blue eyes. He held a sharp gaze that had the charm to pull out even the deepest buried secrets from my heart. He bored a hole into my soul and I evaluated the chances of ever going to survive under his stare. His eyes were asking me something, something that he was having a hard time framing in words. And I remained quiet when he continued.

"They say that everyone deserves a second chance. So I am begging you to give me one! I am begging you to forgive me one last time, Sarah!" He took my hand in his and squeezed it lightly as if asking me to hold on to him.

"I know you want nothing to do with me, and I absolutely don't deserve you. But I just want to be a part of your life. No matter how small. Please! Spend this one beautiful day with me. A friendly date is all I ask. I promise you will not regret it. I know you are going back tomorrow, Starz, and I might not be able to see you ever again! All I ask for is to spend one day with me to remember you by." He said all that in one breath, without breaking eye contact, and I could feel my heart hammering in my chest and my palms sweating.

"Just. One. Freaking. Day!" He asked again, leaning his face a few inches closer. His eyes were craving for me to say yes and I found myself getting trapped in their innocence and I nodded.

"Okay! Just one day!" I finally breathed out with a deep sigh.

"But right now, the only thing my eyes want to see is food!" A bad sense of humor was the only thing I had left to defend myself against the storm of emotions knocking at my heart's closed door.

The day had good vibes dwelling in it as we took our exit from the building and found ourselves roaming on the near-empty streets. It was a lazy Sunday afternoon, and I was pleased to feel the fresh breeze flowing through my hair. I felt like a honeybee in my yellow dress and black jacket. While Ethan was obviously looking like a fashion magazine model in faded denim and blue pullover when we strolled like lost tourists. Ethan looked back at me with the same playful smile that I was carrying throughout the stroll.

Lusciously strolling in the direction of the restaurant was Ethan's plan to explore the city, as well as to increase our appetite. There was something he asserted about neglecting the beauty around us and blah-blah-blah that didn't allow us to drive. Well, I was starving, so I just hoped he was not waiting for me to pass out before we reached there.

"Hola! Mademoiselle!" My head turned towards him, and my eyebrows waggled, noticing him waving at an old woman sitting outside the neighborhood grocery store. She gave him the brightest smile as if they were childhood friends, and Ethan bowed in fondness.

"I don't think you know, but you just spoke two languages. Hola is Spanish and your Mademoiselle with that exaggerated chivalry bow is French!" Ethan was still looking at her, smiling like a lovesick puppy. "I know, Starz! But who cares when she can't hear anything!" I couldn't help but stare at them with wonder. For a brief moment, her sight wandered over me and back to Ethan with questionable raised eyebrows.

"Oh, she is that nagging neighbor I've been telling you about the other day!" I gave a light punch on his forearm as I witnessed people around us were enjoying a good laugh. He unknowingly encircled his arms around me, and I shivered under his touch. I was having a hard time contemplating their friendship. It felt like it was his daily routine to come here and talk to her. She once again spoke her words through sign language, and I looked back at Ethan to understand what she was trying to say.

"No, no, we are not dating! I would never date a woman who snores like drowning pigs!" This time Ethan deserved to be elbowed by me on his side, and I was proud of it. He ducked, faking being injured, but all I could care about was a couple walking past us, enjoying the drama. "I got to go, gorgeous! This woman has no patience!" I almost rolled my eyes with a smile on my face. We waved goodbye to her and moved forward to our destination. This little encounter compelled me to wonder what other things he did all day.

After a whole fifteen minutes of still struggling to find the acclaimed well-known restaurant, I sighed in defeat. "You know we could've just ordered pizza?" I muttered when he squinted in every direction, clearly having a hard time figuring out the place.

"It was here! I visited it just the other day! Right here, where this dumb lingerie shop is!" I almost cackled when the salesgirl of that dumb lingerie shop came behind him and heard everything he just said. Her mouth dropped wide open when she was about to ask us to visit the store. Her gapping face was enough to express the insult she felt right at that moment.

"Maybe it only appears on a full moon night!" Ethan turned around with his brows snapped together in irritation when he got my joke. I was having a hard time controlling my laughter.

"I don't understand! Fine! Where do you want to go?" I could sense the disappointment in his words. He ran a hand through his hair, still contemplating the location of the restaurant. But his gesture made me admire his perfect jawline and the little twitch of muscle from being annoyed.

"Sometimes we should just stop planning everything and go with the flow, mate!" I tapped on his shoulder, making him look at me.

"You are so cute when you're annoyed! Now come with me! That place is looking equally delicious and I am famished!" Pushing his shoulders from behind, I almost dragged him to the café across the street. He gave a dirty glance at the old gray building.

Settling down on one of the seats, I noticed the place had hardly any customers, making it less noisy and perfect for enjoying a late lunch in serenity.

"Firstly, I'm not cute! I'm a dashing hot dude and secondly, if a tall old skinny man with bulging eyes walks through that door, I'll run on my heels." His cynical gaping at the place made me laugh. He leaned over the table and then whispered.

"This place screams haunted, look at the sign at the door!"

"That's a sign of a slice of pizza!" I whispered back, trying to sound as serious as him. "Oh, my bad! But..."

"Good afternoon!" Two things happened simultaneously. And I felt them in slow motion. Ethan's shriek and my snort came out at the same time when a tall, old, skinny man with bulging eyes came across our table and greeted us.

The server's hand shot up to his chest as Ethan gave him a minor heart attack! Wide-eyed, he looked down at Ethan as if trying to deduce whether he was having a seizure. I hid my face behind the menu when I couldn't help but crack further when Ethan was stealing eyes at him.

"Hello! I'll have a cup of coffee, hash brown, and a chicken club sandwich." I quickly ordered to break the unbearable silence, and he nodded at me, stealing a last glance at Ethan. "Same, but without the chicken!" He almost spat at the poor man's face and handed back the menus. My eyes glanced around the couple sitting across from us, giving weird looks. I guess we were lucky not to be thrown out from that lovely place.

Our food arrived in no time, and we dived in like two starving homeless kids. Taking a sip from my coffee, my eyes peeked at Ethan, who seemed to be lost in his own dreamy food world. With each bite, he closed his eyes, savoring every piece of it. *Perhaps this is what is called food porn.*

Watching him moaning over his sandwich did weird things to my body. A smile flashed across my face, noticing him finishing everything in a few minutes. Butterflies fluttered in my stomach when he licked his lower lip, savoring the taste of the sauce.

"You were right, Starz! This place has the best sandwich I've ever had!" I nodded unknowingly. Though his words fell into my ears, I was too busy drooling over him to comprehend them. *Get your shit together, girl!*

"Shit! I didn't mean to, Starz!" I gave him a puzzled look when he put down the half-eaten fry back on my plate. "I swear, I got so lost in the taste that I totally forgot about eating from your plate!"

"Relax, man! You are acting like I'm going to murder you for a piece of French fry." I shook my head, looking over his fearful expression.

"I see! For someone who almost strangled a man for extra chocolate chips just last night, you sound quite fine with sharing your food!" Now he had my full attention. I gaped at him, still holding the cup of coffee in my hand. He took the cup from my hand and carefully placed it on his side of the table, making every move very cautiously. Was he scared of getting hot coffee thrown at him?

"Oh, my God. I physically assaulted another human being? You weren't joking about being arrested? I can't believe I could be this monstrous." I was mortified! My hands cupped my mouth as I tried my best to hide the shame I was feeling.

"You really scared the shit out of me, Starz. Jumping off the counter and attacking that man! Where did you learn those ninja moves?" The impression of embarrassment was obvious on my face, but the way Ethan was narrating the story, I was having a hard time controlling my laughter. I couldn't believe I did all those things.

Tears of joy welled up in my eyes the moment he acted out the scene of me tucking at that man's pants while Ethan was struggling to drag me away from him. I lost my shit right there. And he wasn't done yet. I covered my face, bursting up into hysterical laughter. I winced when my stomach started to ache with a mad laugh. I didn't care if we were receiving weird looks from our surroundings. Because I didn't think I'd laughed so hard in years.

"Come with me!" Out of the blue, he threw some money on the table and grabbed my hand, making me drift off from the place the next second. "Where are we going?" I hardly managed to utter, still grinning at the moment.

"Go with the flow, mate!" I chuckled when he repeated my words. A strong breeze flew by my dress and I struggled, holding it down when Ethan dragged me with him. His fingers tightly wrapped around mine as we sprinted to cross the street. We walked down the busy sidewalk under the sun that warmed our hearts. My skin felt young and cheerful under the rays.

My eyes followed him, looking in every direction. "What are you looking for?" He was dragging me alongside in every way, not in the mood of letting go of my hand for a single second. "Ahh!" He exclaimed in utter joy and my forehead furrowed, seeking the cause of his grin. We were again on the run, but this time he knew the destination.

Our breaths collided with each other when we halted outside an on-rent bike stand and I scrunched up my face, knowing what was about to come. "Come on, Ethan!" I struggled to free myself from his grip, but all my efforts went in vain when he didn't let go of my hand. "Remember the flow, darling!" He looked down at me, giving me the best smile that could move mountains.

Within minutes, we were standing with our designated bikes in our hands. I whined like a baby who didn't know what to do with a bike handle. I attempted to look mad, but it seemed like my heart was too overwhelmed to let any negativity stir it.

"Let me help you!" Parking his bike, he came around, and before I could've attempted to fight back, he shoved a helmet on my head, messing up my perfect wavy curls. "Not my hair, dude!" My shoulders sagged in disappointment as my hands automatically went for my hair, but they were now buried under a stupid pink helmet.

"Safety first! Now, just swing your right leg over and start paddling one after the other!" I gave Ethan a once over, trying to figure out if he was genuinely giving me a bike lesson or being sarcastic. And I was right. He chuckled at my annoyed face. And that deserved a punch on the forearm. "I know how to ride a bike. Thank you very much, Sir!" He bowed down his head returning to his bike. With hesitation hovering over me, I twirled around to notice him saddling up.

"Are we seriously doing it?" I yelled back, mentally praying he would drop this stupid adventurous plan. He looked up and gave me his best serious, stern face, and I sighed.

"Yup, we are going to kill ourselves! It's a suicide mission and I don't even know why I am doing this!" I kept rambling to myself. I was scared shitless. Last time I rode a bike was in third grade and let's just say that it didn't end very well.

My head lifted to take a glance at the cars moving so viciously in front of us and I already imagined getting crushed by one of them. But right there, my lips took the shape of a mischievous smile when an idea popped into my head.

"I can't ride a bike in a dress, dude! You can imagine, one kick from the breeze and whoosh, everyone will know the color of my undies." I murdered my own self-respect for the sake of saving my life. He stifled a laugh, quickly taking off his pullover and fastening it around my waist.

"Here you go! Now no more excuses." Taking my hand in his, he gave it a tight squeeze and said, "I promise I won't let anything happen to you, Starz. Trust me." I was flustered by the sincerity in his voice.

He gave one determined nod, waiting for me to place my ass over the uncomfortable rubber seat. "Now you just have to paddle forward, keeping a sharp eye on the street! You got this, trooper." I nodded when it felt like Ethan was giving me a motivational speech as if I was going for a war! My trembling hands grabbed the handle as if my life depended on it and, in fact, it did. My left leg was still resting on the ground when I pushed the right paddle and started moving.

Looking at a distance, I forced my mind to forget about my distressed childhood memory of falling off the bike and breaking my wrist. The accident terrified me so badly that I never touched a bike after that day!

"There you go, girl!" His voice felt like a feather caressing my soft skin, fading subsequently into the background when I moved forward. I was holding my breath while giving my best shot at not falling on my face. I stumbled a little but quickly regained my balance.

"I am doing it, Ethan!" My voice was merely a mumble. Though the past incident took away my confidence to ride again, it never took away my love for biking. I always loved the feel of wind over my face. Getting my confidence back, I started to enjoy the ride. The warm draft was gushing through my hair and I felt like floating in the air. The excitement was written all over my face as I was smiling from ear to ear, while at the same time, my heart was pounding in my chest. The experience was making me feel alive! I was terrified, yet never wanted to stop.

"See! You're not that bad!" Soon, Ethan's voice touched my ears. I noticed him following after me on his bike from the corner of my eye. He was obviously looking hot as hell while cycling like a piece of cake. He grinned at me and I smiled back, stealing a glance at him for a second.

"Now, follow me. I know the best street in town to enjoy the ride in peace!" Following him, the first thing my eyes did was to land on his fine ass. And boy, the view was a treat for my eyes. I paddled faster when the distance between us started to increase.

Soon we were paddling parallel in confined alleys with small, aged buildings surrounded by willow trees. "I never knew I live in such a beautiful neighborhood!" I was amazed. My eyes gleamed, seizing the beauty around me.

"Didn't I tell you? It's going to be an amazing day!" He shouted to the sky, and I nodded in agreement.

"Now, brace yourself!" He winked at me with a smile that could steal a thousand hearts and faced forward with a captivating, amazed expression. Tracking his gaze, I found a steep slope coming ahead and terror stroked my soul.

"We are not getting on that lane, Ethan!" I shouted but still kept paddling.

"Just go with the flow, darling!" He squealed just before our bikes traced the first stone of the stone-paved lane.

"We are going to d… d… die!" I screamed in a stammering voice while my whole body bounced up and down. It was a suicide mission.

"Now. Push your legs wide open!"

"Excuse me?" I scowled at Ethan when I noticed him lifting his legs off the paddles and just stretching them out wide open.

"If we die, I'm going to bloody kill you, Stanton!" I screamed when his head looked up at the sky and he laughed.

"Just let go, Starz!" And I followed him. Followed my heart, for the first time in a very long time. Shutting out every rational thought coming from my scared mind, I just let go of everything. Every trouble.

Every worry.

Every fear.

Every uncertainty.

Despite being petrified and almost peeing my pants, I was feeling amazing. Though the picture of showing up toothless at the ER was pretty ugly. Enormous energy was buzzing through me right then as if I could do anything in the world.

My heart was pounding in my ears. I could feel the adrenaline rushing through every cell of my body. I was enthralled, like all the sunshine had been poured out on me, rejuvenating me.

The second we reached the clear ground, my fingers yanked the brakes and my head twirled around to search for Ethan. He was waiting for me, glowing from inside, looking at me with a beaming smile cracking through his luscious lips. And I ran. Leaving the bike on the ground, leaving all my fears behind, leaving everything behind that could stop me from enjoying this moment. I raced with all my might.

I jumped into his arms, wrapping my legs around his waist. I didn't care if I was strangling him on the street or if we had an audience. The happiness was flowing through me. His warmth and the sweet smell made me dizzy, overwhelming my senses.

He twirled me around and I giggled like a little girl. The sensation was a blend of conquering the world and feeling safe at the same time. *Sometimes little things make you so happy that you can't trade them for anything. It's a rare and invaluable experience.*

"Life is all about taking risks. Don't settle for ordinary when you can have something special if you're willing to take the risk." He whispered in my ear and I got my senses back. I acknowledged how my little self was wrapped around him, leaving no space in between. Unhinging myself from him, I took some steps back. Tucking my hair behind my ear, I lowered my head with my cheeks burning from embarrassment.

"It's okay, Starz. You can hug me anytime." He paused for a moment and then sniffed his shirt. "As long as I don't smell like a dying cat!" We paused for a moment. Our eyes interlaced each other like one candle blazing the other. And then suddenly we burst out laughing our ass off. I had no idea why we were panting. But our breaths synchronized with each other.

I knew he strived to make me comfortable around him. But at that moment, I saw something in his eyes, something so strong yet so fragile. His bright blue eyes peered at me in a way that made me see through that one emotion that was lurking behind his big smile.

The emotion of being in love with me. The emotion of holding himself back when he never wanted to let go. An emotion that cried out to me to hold his hand and never let go. But I had already lent out the things he was wishing from me to someone else.

꠷

Just as the sun was touching the horizon, the day turned into twilight. We returned our bikes and walked towards the benches that held the perfect view of the Tennessee River.

"I'll just get something to drink!" Ethan spoke as if reading my mind, and went to the nearby truck that was serving milkshakes and hotdogs. The riverfront was buzzing with life all around. I smiled, shaking my head at the silly faces he was making at me from afar, imitating the old lady who cut through the line in front of him.

I had messy hair and my thighs were twitching from that little adventure we had a little while ago, but I couldn't stop smiling. A soothing breeze was drifting through my hair, making them flow all over the place, but I couldn't care less.

My eyes followed the old lady taking her order to an elderly man waiting for her at the nearby bench. They exchanged a warm smile and my essence melted off, glimpsing at the delicate affection they held for each other. The man held out his hand for her as she settled down beside him.

The admiration was so fondling that I couldn't stop myself from shamelessly ogling them.

"They are amazing, aren't they?" I realized Ethan was back when he settled down beside me. I looked at him and felt happiness spread through every ounce of my body. The emotion was like ripples on the surface of the water, narrow on the inside and scattering wide with every coil. Letting you believe someone else had caused them, but in reality, it was only you. The happiness was coming from within, from a place somewhere deep inside of me that I thought didn't exist anymore.

"Back to earth, Starz!" I shook my head, coming out of a trance, and quickly snatched the milkshake from him and plunged into it, bowing my head down. We settled into a comfortable silence, observing the sky changing colors at sunset.

"One sec!" He suddenly darted towards a hawker selling some kitchenware. I smiled, watching him exchange some laughter with the lady. They suddenly looked at me, and I averted my eyes for a moment in embarrassment. I noticed him pointing his finger at me and I was forced to wave a greeting at them. And the next second I saw Ethan walking toward me with an empty glass jar. What? Are we going to catch fireflies now?

"What was all that about?" I asked as he advanced back, still not meeting his eyes.

"Nothing. She was asking me, 'Who's the lucky girl' that I'm buying this for?" And he handed over the jar, now filled with paper chits. And I had never been more confused in my life.

"Okay. Please don't take me like some creepy psycho guy." He sounded so nervous that I almost laughed.

"Well. This jar has forty-two notes. I had been writing them down since the day I found you back. And I would like for you to have them. You could keep them in the back of your cupboard. And take one out to read whenever you are feeling a little down or whenever something is not going according to the plan in your life."

"I actually wanted to make all forty-five and give them to you on your... you know... your big day! But if God permits, I will give the remaining three to you someday." My eyes shifted away when he began to stare at me with a gaze that had the power to break the walls that I had placed around my heart.

"You're so beautiful." I heard him whisper.

"Don't do this, Ethan!" I eyed him sternly at his failed attempt to flirt with me.

"Do what?" He asked innocently, tilting his head sideways.

"This! Trying to make me feel special like I'm the only great thing in your life. We don't belong together." I said, gesturing my hands between us.

"Hey, don't shut me out just yet. The day is not over and you promised to spend it with me, so bear with me here a little longer."

❧

"Where exactly are you taking me?" The sun had long drifted below the horizon and we were in a back alley without any street lights.

"You will see." I looked at his excited self and then at my surroundings. Dark, old walls in the vicinity. Frightening noises coming out from outdated air vents. Rusted staircases all around gave an impression of us wandering in some post-apocalyptic world.

Leaving the commotion and happy faces behind, I thought I was too credulous to believe anything he would say. It looked like I had stepped into some dark realm. Just a glance at this place made it obvious that this place was perfect for a serial killer.

"Please tell me we are not doing something illegal!" I was worried sick. Sweating profusely into my now greasy yellow dress, I took a quick glance at him and frowned, noticing he didn't break a sweat.

We paused in front of a rusted spiral staircase, and I cringed at the view. My head lifted, drifting away with each coil. It was worn out to the extent of collapsing any minute. I was sure it would not be able to hold our weight. My eyes were fixed on that flight of steps and I wondered where it was headed. But I kept my curiosity to myself for the sake of staying alive.

"It's the stairways to heaven!" I almost rolled my eyes at his use of words.

"That's exactly what I am afraid of. I'm confident we are going to fall over and break our necks." He rolled his eyes at me and before I could have sprinted away, I found myself climbing up. I looked down at our entangled fingers and then at his sparkling eyes, emitting such delight. I knew I should be scared, but I was pretty sure my heart was racing for all the wrong reasons. And soon we were facing a closed door. Now what?

I looked up in surprise when Ethan knocked at the door, and someone instantly opened it from inside. He clasped my hand tight as we finally walked inside.

"You don't buy bigger shoes, waiting for your feet to grow into them. You buy the perfect pair that slides in smoothly, making you feel this is exactly where you always belonged." He whispered in my ear, beaming with delight. My furrowed forehead cleared up when we finally arrived at our destination, and I took hold of my surroundings.

We were standing in the middle of a grand circular hall with embellished cream walls and huge velvet burgundy curtains. The roof was painted in a golden brown hue and a massive chandelier was hanging from the ceiling, making the place look like a 17th-century ballroom.

Reality surged my eyes to go wide in acknowledgment. And I finally gathered where we were standing. We had just entered through the emergency exit of my favorite theater in town, which showed classics.

But I still couldn't believe my eyes. Every show at the theater was sold out for the weekend. I checked it just yesterday. But here we were, standing in the central hall of a completely empty theater, lucky enough to be able to appreciate its beauty in serenity. My eyes stood frozen, taking in so much elegance. It was such an exquisite sight that I thought I might be dreaming. But this was way too colorfully detailed to be a dream.

I looked at Ethan, whose eyes were fixed on me and he squeezed my hand, making me believe this indeed was reality. "How?" I asked in astonishment. I couldn't recall discussing anything with him about my love for classics or this theater.

"I booked the whole place for tonight. But it was already sold out, so they had to put a canceled sign at the front and refund the tickets. So we had to take the back entrance." Saying I was astonished would be an understatement.

"But how did you know?" His smile stretched at my question.

"Let's just say I learned a lot about you last night." He winked at me and I turned crimson.

He tugged at my hand, and we entered the theater. There was a loveseat with blankets and popcorn placed specially for us to enjoy the movies in utter home comfort. We made ourselves comfortable as the lights dimmed down and Breakfast at Tiffany's started to play on the screen.

I remember peeking at him more often than not, admiring his smile while resting my head on his shoulder. My legs were folded under me and one hand was wrapped around his, with fingers entwined. We were wrapped under a blanket and I felt complete at that moment.

When Holly found the cat and Paul kissed her, Ethan looked at me with tear-filled eyes. I automatically leaned toward him and our lips met. The kiss was soft and tender and I could feel tears rolling down my closed eyes. It was a feeling of coming home after being lost for a long time. Like this was where I always belonged.

With a smooth move, he grabbed my hips and glided me onto his lap. Temptation hovered over us. We crossed over all our discomforts and disfigured past and got absorbed into each other. His hands skimmed down my back, sending waves of desire between my thighs. Every part of my body melted underneath him.

I was sweating from the heat seeping through him. The kiss was passionately engraved with need. It was demanding, a strong craving I had been stifling for far too long. My hands ran through his smooth hair, pulling him closer to the core. I shivered when I felt his hardness against my hips. It was sinful to feel delighted from making him this excited.

Suddenly, he pulled away, making me grimace at the loss of his touch. "Come back to me, please!" I attempted to pull him back when he resisted. "I swear on my life, I'm a better man now. I won't ever hurt you in a thousand years! I'll always keep you happy and safe." I was breathing heavily, and I bowed my head in disappointment. The moment had ended.

His warm hands curved around my face, tucking back a strand of hair. His eyes searched for the trail leading to my orbs. But I couldn't face him. He stroked the mark on my forehead, the mark he was responsible for.

"I could die a thousand deaths, but still can't amend the things I did to you. So all I can ask for is a fresh start. We could start all over again like you never knew me. And I will make you fall in love with me again. And this time I will not give you a single chance to regret it." This time, I lifted my head and met his weak eyes.

We were both crying by now. I didn't trust my voice at the moment, so I just nodded and hugged him tightly as if my life depended on it.

"I love you, Sarah!" Almost immediately, his body stiffened. He pulled me away to look in my eyes with an alarmed look at the words that had accidentally slipped off his mouth. His pleading eyes reflected back the fear of rejection. But I was far from being mad at him. I gave him a soft smile and slipped off from that couch.

"I need to use the restroom," I said, stifling my tears and moving away.

"Don't take too long. They are going to play Casablanca next." I nodded and quickly exited the place.

In a couple of minutes, I was back in the lobby and my eyes fell over the sign of the lavatory and I paced forward. My eyes fluttered, feeling the tiredness overpowering me. But there was scarcely any time to rest.

Walking towards the main exit, I witnessed a few questioning eyes on me. I pushed open the glass door, letting the cold night breeze stroke my face. I checked my cell phone, reading the messages from Ashely forwarding our flight details. It was a connecting flight, and I was glad she was assisting me. Catching a quick drive, I settled back in the backseat of a taxi when my phone hummed again.

'Where are you? They are going to start any second.'

I was about to shove my phone back into my purse when another message lightened my screen.

'You don't need a touch-up. Just smile and Tada! Now, hurry up, Starz!'

Hate! It was the only thing that could stop him. People say there is a thin line between love and hate. But what if I tell you the line was not that thin, and another emotion has been living on that very line? Numbness, when you are so torn apart, so hurt and disappointed that you don't suffer anymore.

It was okay if he was going to loathe me for the rest of his life. Nonetheless, I gave him a memory to recall every day and hate me even more.

I'd tried everything. Every single thing that could stop him. But couldn't break his resolve, his stubbornness was enduring. I didn't have anything left but to love him and then leave him. Being abandoned like this was a tremendous attack on his pride. All I wanted was to beat him down to the level from where he would come out with no other feelings for me except hate.

Hate would taint his soul. It would spread throughout his rationale, shutting down all other feelings for me. As the cab reached my building, I found myself staring up at his balcony, where he made me feel alive for the first time, after existing impassively for nine years, by shoving a guitar in my hand. I asked the driver to wait while I quickly brushed the memory away and climbed upstairs to take my bags and Finn.

I closed my eyes while walking past his door and rushed back down before I could change my mind. "To the airport, please!" I couldn't prevent my voice from breaking when the wheels rolled, leaving behind some of the best memories of my life.

With regret and sadness overpowering me, I brushed off the single drop of tear trickling down my left cheek and stared outside the window. I smiled manically, comprehending that betrayal was the only thing that has the power to fill him with bitterness. He would loathe me endlessly, and that's what I wanted. This was more for my own safety than his.

It was stupid to love someone expecting he would change one day for the better. Love doesn't come with conditions. But loving someone who is already best for you is the right thing to do. And Lucas was the answer to everything. He was my safety net.

A familiar tone patted my ears, making me aware of the ringing of my phone. I knew who would be calling me and I squeezed my eyes shut when I glimpsed at the name. My eyes welled up, turning my vision blurry. I tried to hide the pain inside as I whimpered in silence. After two missed calls, came a text message.

'It's such a dick move, Starz!'

This time I couldn't hold back a chuckle spilling out of my mouth, which quickly turned into loud sobs. I rubbed my tears away, smiling and crying at the same time if that was even possible.

Ethan Stanton got what he deserved! I gave him one day. One day, that was all he wanted from me. What I didn't know was that this one day would ruin me completely. It melted away every chain that I had welded around my heart.

I was no longer afraid of falling in love with him. Instead, I was afraid that I'd already fallen for the wrong guy once again. Because, after all, I was the same girl.

That foolish girl!

Twenty-nine

Ethan

NINE YEARS AGO

(The day of Sarah's accident)

From afar, anybody who looked at me, who knew me a little, would think that my life was perfect. But little did they know how it was being driven by someone else. How my life wasn't mine. How I was just a puppet being controlled by the flick of someone else's fingers.

Everyone had deduced me as the main character of a book. But what they didn't know was that my actions weren't mine. They were prophesied by my father, who was the founder of my life, the author of my book. My life was a bunch of opportunities carved out by him. Some scraped out or molded in his own way, as he preferred, where it could be profitable for him and his business.

I had no control over anything when it came to what I really wanted with my life. I loathed my father for controlling my every breath. Yet, all my actions somehow ultimately aimed to seek his approval. It had been so long that maybe I had grown used to being a puppet in his hands. A scared and dedicated pet to his master.

Nonetheless, nothing could justify my actions last night. Though I apologized a thousand times, I knew what I had done. How I behaved with Sarah could never be undone.

The deep, distant longing in Sarah's eyes that I had left behind kept flashing in front of my eyes as I climbed down her window earlier this morning. A sense of guilt hovered over my heart when I left her alone. Like a ton of weight pressing down my lungs, squeezing it so hard that it was getting hard for me to breathe. The guilt was the repercussion of accepting my father's absurd demands and once again putting Sarah after him.

I couldn't quite perceive if my car was going in the right direction. I was driving blind. My one hand remained fixed on the wheel while the other was busy pulling at my hair in utter annoyance. I could hardly concentrate on the road when my head was fuzzy with all the guilt and conflicting thoughts. I knew I was making a big mistake, yet I was unable to stop myself. It felt like I was being torn in half.

No person in his sane mind would ever ask his girl to do what I asked her to today. I was so ashamed that I wondered if she was ever going to trust me again. Or maybe she had already lost all her faith in me.

I should never have asked her to go alone, just because I was coward enough not to dare defer my father's plan. I was a chicken who had no guts to look into his own father's eyes and tell him once in a lifetime that I could not do what he had asked me to do. Not this time. Because it wasn't some stupid school day I was missing, it was much more than that. It was about a person. And that person was dearest to me than anything else in the world.

She needed my support more than ever today. I knew she was barely holding herself when I told her I couldn't accompany her. She looked so scared. So vulnerable that I wished to trade places with anyone just to be by her side.

I have been driving aimlessly for hours now. Trying to crush my anger and disappointment on myself with the break-neck speed of my car. But no more. I need to do something. Sarah needs me and I need to stand with her. I can't let her face the world alone.

By the time my vehicle entered the driveway of my house, I had made up my mind to defy my father. Screw him and his principles. That innocent girl was suffering all because of me and nothing mattered more than my presence by her side. I was the only person to blame who had brought tears in those beautiful, soulful, green eyes. It was all my fault that she was in such a mess.

I knew my father was not foolish and he must have sensed something fishy when I lied about my stomach ache last night. I had to do something just for the sake of canceling the business trip on which we were supposed to leave yesterday. But now I speculated if he would actually have forced me to leave, I wouldn't have backed out without a proper fight.

I loved that girl with all my heart. And I would always be with her, even if it meant going against my father's will. Her love had bestowed a strange kind of bravery in my heart that I believed was enough to fight for myself, for taking control of my life into my own hands.

After getting ready, I quickly stuffed my backpack with a small pillow, some snacks, and my mother's knitted scarf that I believed Sarah would find comforting. But then a frown etched my face.

I didn't have much money in my wallet. I had no idea how much it was going to cost. Nor could I ask my father for any help. So at last, I took out the stack that I had been saving for my college.

I knew my father planned to send me to the other side of the country to Stanford Business School, but I wanted to stay with Sarah in Baltimore, as she was heading to Johns Hopkins. Thus, I had been saving money to cover my own tuition for college as he would definitely disown me as soon as I would disagree with his plans for my future. Anyhow, I was going to be eighteen soon, and out of my father's grip. I hadn't shared this with Sarah yet. It was supposed to be a surprise for our graduation. But I guess this money needed to be put to better use now. We could figure out the college tuition later.

I checked the clock and hastily climbed down the stairs from my room. I was too late to pick her up from her house, but I could reach the hospital on time and make amends for my mistakes.

For once, I was grateful that it was still too early in the morning that there was nobody in the lobby to whom I had to justify my actions. Taking a water bottle from the kitchen, I sent a quick text to Sarah and slipped out of the backdoor. Pulling my backpack, I sprinted towards my car when my legs stopped dead on the gravel road. My mind screamed at me that it wasn't a coincidence that my father's black Lincoln was parked in the front like it was ready to depart.

"Good morning, son. I see you're feeling better now." My head jerked towards my father, witnessing him descending from the front porch stairs.

He had a winning smile on his face that I knew had nothing to do with my health.

"Good morning, father. I sure am much better now. But I don't believe I'm fit to…"

"Good, you are ready. We need to attend an important meeting. I will fill you up with the information on the way." My palms squeezed into tight fists when he ignored my words and didn't even let me finish my sentence. It wasn't the first time that he had totally neglected my wishes, but today it wasn't about me.

"I'm afraid to tell you, father, but there is something important that I have to attend to right now." A twitch of a muscle in my father's jaw would've stopped the coward Ethan right there, but nevertheless, I continued before he could have intervened.

"It is Sarah, father. I can't tell if you can recall her from yesterday, but she needs me right now. She is unwell. And I might be her only friend that can bring her to the doctor." A dry chuckle escaped my father's mouth, and I understood he didn't care about a word that I said.

"Don't be so foolish, son. Nothing should be more important in your life than your future right now. Now get in the vehicle. We are already late."

"But, father?" He sauntered towards his car, once again totally ignoring my pleas. "We will discuss it later!" His voice was so stern and commanding that my resolution to fight him back flew out of the window. I nodded and just followed my master like a faithful dog.

The air inside the vehicle remained thick as we proceeded further toward our destination. Nothing but a soft rumble of the engine echoed around us. No one made a sound. The unsettling silence around was making me even edgier. I tried to look outside, battling with my thoughts of how it was all going completely wrong. How I didn't belong there in that car.

My father's eyes remained glued to the newspaper in his hands. Skimming through every business article that could be beneficial for the company. A small, satisfying smile lingered on his face like he had won some game I had no idea we were playing. For a fraction of a second, I dared to steal a glance at him. Mentally begging him to listen to his son for once in a lifetime, when my phone started buzzing against my jeans.

I quickly pulled it out. Already mumbling a sorry to my father for disturbing his peaceful moment. Yet the moment my eyes noticed Sarah's name flashing on the screen, my hand shot to my forehead. I had to take that call. Yet I couldn't, as I could sense my father's scrutinizing gaze upon me. My legs started shuddering when it was too much for me to handle. Her name flashing on the screen was like her calling out to me from afar. The call disconnected and my heart sank as the screen went dark.

She might have reached the hospital. Maybe she was in need of something very important. There were so many possibilities that I almost growled with frustration. I had to be by her side at any cost. My hand racked through my hair when every single part of my body felt the bitterness I was dwelling into. I scorned at the situation I was forced to be in, as I never felt so lost in my life. So incompetent. The phone started ringing again and loathe surged in my chest against myself and my father. When the phone stopped buzzing, I got a notification of a voice mail.

"I remember when I was of your age, son." My back straightened up at my father's voice.

"I was so crammed with vigor and dreams which my father had built up in my head that I had nothing else to think about. He always made me remember that I was nothing without the word Stanton at the end of my name." I nodded at him. Trying my best to hide the distaste for his words. Because somehow I knew he had noticed the slight change in my body language.

"And so are you, Ethan. You are nothing. No one, without your family name. People don't respect who you are. But they do for where you had come from. It's all about power and money, son. The world is filled with dummies and boot-lickers. And so are most of your friends." My eyes bored into him when I finally saw what he was trying to convey. A chuckle left his lips when he neatly folded the newspaper and looked back at me.

"Women only love money, son. If you don't have that, you are nothing but a rejected and regular side character. Trust me on this, they won't care to give you a single glance if you don't have money." I felt a flicker of annoyance as I gripped the leather seat in my sweaty palms. The mere grin on his face made me sick to the pit of my stomach. "You have to focus on your career first. Soon you'll be off to Stanford and won't have time to take a second glance at these silly butterflies. If you want to prove yourself true to your family name, your legacy, then you should stop chasing these gold diggers."

"I'm sorry, father, but you are mistaken." He raised an eyebrow at me in challenge as I interjected. "Sarah is real. She is nothing like the person you think she could be." A humorless chuckle broke deep in his throat, but I paid no attention and continued.

"She is pure. She's true. She doesn't want my money. She just wants someone who could take care of her. Support her. And I am afraid to tell you, father, but she really needs me right now. And most of all, she is important to me. More than any of your business meetings could ever be." I tapped on the partition glass to instruct the chauffeur to stop the vehicle. My father remained quiet throughout as I grabbed my backpack and exited the car. But his stern gaze, sealed with bitterness and resentment, followed me till I was outside. Maybe he couldn't believe the revolting behavior of his dutiful son.

"Pardon me, but I don't mean to offend you, father. Sarah really…"

"You disappointed me, son." He just looked down at me with repugnance and dismay and turned to face forward. The wheels of his car rolled onto the freeway, as he didn't even let me complete my sentence.

I knew I had let down my father today. I was not the son I always promised my mother to be. But they weren't my priority today. I didn't give a damn if my reputation had been destroyed in front of my parents or if they were ever going to give their trust to me. Sarah was my first concern. I had to reach the hospital at any cost and be her strength. It was all that mattered at that moment.

My hand glided in my hair, and I groaned in frustration when I looked at my surroundings. I was in the middle of nowhere. Stranded on the freeway, where it was near impossible to get a ride back. I checked my phone and almost bit my lip when her frail voice echoed in my ears from the voicemail she had left me. She sounded so uncomfortable. So nervous.

So helpless. I damned myself for ever putting her in that position. I felt so ashamed. So awful and worthless.

By the time I reached the hospital, after bribing a cattle truck driver, I was sure I had missed the appointment. I couldn't even call Sarah because my phone's battery had already died. Talk about the worst luck. I glanced over the crowded front desk and, without waiting any further, I hurried down the hallway. My eyes scanned the information boards hanging from the ceiling, guiding me toward the designated floor. As I exited the lift on the fourth floor, my feet came to a sudden halt.

There was a loud commotion in front of the stairways. A crowd had gathered around the point where I witnessed a pool of blood staining the floor at the end of the flight of stairs. In that fraction of a moment, a strange fear clubbed my heart. I didn't know why that sight gave me terror. Why it made my breaths shallow and my heart throbbing against my chest manically. My eyes glanced over at the people standing there, and all I could gather was the expression of sorrow and disbelief.

"I'm sorry, but what happened here?" I asked one of the men who was comforting his weeping wife.

"Oh, a poor girl lost her balance on the stairs. Jesus! There was so much blood oozing out of her head. It was so horrible. I don't think she is going to make it." His words made his wife burst into a fresh spell of tears. But right at the moment, I could feel nothing but blind terror choking me from inside. No, it couldn't be what my mind was forcing me to think. It just didn't feel real. There were thousands of reasons that girl couldn't be my Sarah.

"I'm sorry to bother you, but do you happen to know her name? That girl who fell." The man shook his head and turned back to leave with his pained wife. I wanted to ask so many questions from him, but it felt like I couldn't bother them any further. They seemed deep in trauma, in shock. Thus, I fled the scene and rushed down to the OB/GYN OPD to find Sarah.

My hopeful eyes scanned the whole room, but she was nowhere to be seen. I even checked with the front desk lady, but she was too busy with the patients. I wanted to call her but I couldn't. I rushed towards the restrooms.

Asked every single lady for her, but no, she was nowhere to be found. For some strange reason, my sight diverted towards the stairs where the spilled blood was being cleaned, and I closed my eyes. I feared to imagine the worst. A stinging chill pierced my limbs. I was getting numb. Yet I decided to think positively and look at the brighter side.

Maybe she hadn't come to the hospital in the first place. Yes, there was a strong possibility that she had postponed the whole thing. Her voicemail didn't say anything about reaching here. I remembered her being reluctant to come here alone. To first attend the graduation and then tackle all this later. A tint of hope flooded my chest as I rushed to exit that building. I was actually dying from inside, desperate for the sheer sight of her. I wanted to see her face. See her smile. I needed to hug her and eradicate this uncertainty that was pressing me down.

But the fear didn't leave my side when I found the front door of her aunt's house locked. The apprehension broke my will, and I tried to rattle the doorknob as hard as I could, getting some stern stares from the neighbors.

I racked my brain for ideas. If she was not here or at the hospital, then she must be at school. Of course! Why didn't I think of that before? I ran as fast as I could to the school and searched every room, but she was not there either. I struggled to swallow down the frustration building in my stomach and decided to call her from a payphone, but her phone was switched off.

Where the hell are you, girl? I really want to see you. Just a glimpse of your face would be enough to put my racing heart to rest.

Days passed, but I was unable to trace Sarah. Her phone was off, her aunt's home was locked, and she never showed up for the graduation ceremony. There were a thousand types of rumors going around the town, and I didn't know what to trust and what not. My sanity hung with a thread. I wanted to scream at the top of my lungs. Apologize to her for my mistakes, for my sins that must have hurt her enough to abandon me like that.

It was like the whole universe was conspiring against me. Sarah never returned my calls. Never did I receive a reply to any of my thousands of texts and emails. Even her friend Ashley didn't want to see my face, let alone talk to me or acknowledge my endless pleas. The sheer sight of me disgusted her. Several times, I attempted to talk to her. Just to plead with her for any news about Sarah. But every time, she simply ignored me. I begged her to tell me where my girl had disappeared to. But she never talked straight to me.

I knew Ashley hated me. I was a low human being in her opinion, who was only there to hurt Sarah and break her heart, but she had no right to tell me that Sarah was better off without me. That I was just a bad chapter in Sarah's life that needed to be erased.

I wanted that miserable period to end. I was losing control over my senses. I craved that terrible feeling to vanish from my heart. As a result, I soon found myself drunk and high out of my mind for days to the end.

But that unsettling suffering only aggravated whenever I was sober enough to think straight. Every single day, I prayed I would find Sarah's home unlocked. I so desperately begged God for somebody to open the door and tell me she was in there. Or at least that she was doing okay. However, only disappointment welcomed me every time I crossed her street.

I waited at her door every single day. Till the light transformed into darkness and I was surrounded by the ghosts of misery and despair. And every time I returned home, more despair welcomed me in the impression of my father's utter disappointment for his son. And my mother's heartache for my terrible situation.

And then one day, out of nowhere, Ashley appeared on my doorsteps. I was caught off-guard and choked when my father asked if I knew her. I was stoned out of my mind at that moment and didn't know what I was saying until it was too late to take it back.

That night changed my whole life. It stole everything from me. My parents. Their love. Even my right to be called their son. They abandoned me for the sin I didn't even know I had committed before that night. My worst nightmare had come true. That poor girl falling down the stairs of the hospital that day was my Sarah. It was her blood that I had witnessed.

Soon I became the talk of the town. The disgraced monster who had played with an innocent girl's heart and then left her to die. My father urged me to reject all blames as being false accusations in front of everyone but I couldn't. And he hated me for that.

And everything went down from that moment. I went rogue. I refused to eat or work with anything that was related to my father. The madness to find her overtook me.

I searched every single hospital in Fairhope. But she was already moved to another city by the time I traced her. And this time, I had no patience to hear Ashley's bullshit. I didn't give a damn if she would insult me in front of the whole town. I just wanted her to spill out the name of the place where my Sarah had gone. However, once again, my doomed fate betrayed me when I found that Ashley had already left for college. Her parents refused to give me her contact details.

It was like I met dead ends everywhere I searched. The turmoil in my head swelled with every disappointment. Maybe I was getting nuts because somehow I always blamed my father for not being able to find Sarah. And maybe it was the sole reason my mother blackmailed me every time with her swollen eyes to leave the town and attend college. To start a new life free from the ghosts of my past.

I never wanted to let go of her memories. I knew I was going to find her in this very town where our story had begun in the first place. It was only here that I could amend my mistakes and discover my lost love again. But then I couldn't torture my mother any longer. She was as innocent as Sarah was. I could no longer neglect the pain on her face every time she begged me to go away. Far away from everything or everyone who was related to Fairhope.

And one day I decided to end her indefinite suffering. To pull my mother out of the misery that she didn't deserve to live in every single day. To free her from my father's perpetual rage and my sleepless nights and distress.

I disappeared from the town where my whole life existed. Yet I never stopped the very thing that was keeping me sane, keeping me alive.

I never stopped searching for her.

Thirty

Sarah

THE WEDDING DAY

"**I** know what I'm doing, Ash!"

"No! It's more like you think you know what you are doing, but actually, you have no fuckin' idea!" She grabbed my shoulders and made me look into her eyes.

"I'm sorry, but you are being a dickhead here! In order to save yourself from a 'plausible' heartache, you are ruining three lives!" She air coated the word 'plausible,' and an unexpected wave of fury crashed through me.

"If it's so bad to worry about my own safety, then I'm more than happy to wear that bitch crown, Ash." I shoved her hands away in frustration. I couldn't tell what had gotten into her. Earlier she was all about protecting me from repeating my past mistakes.

"You are being too stubborn! Look, he has accepted his mistakes. He is clearly sorry for whatever happened in the past. And moreover, he loves you and I can clearly see you feel the same way about him. Then what is compelling you to marry that… man? What's his bloody name?" Was she serious right now? I could sense a severe headache settling in my temples.

"Lucas!" I gave her a stern look.

"Whatever! It doesn't change the reality! Come on! Do you really want to spend the rest of your life with him? That dude is a statute of boredom!" Ash was never a fan of Luc, but this was her first time badmouthing him.

"You don't understand!" I replied with a sigh.

"Then, make me understand!" She almost yelled!

"I can't get hurt again! Okay? I wouldn't survive if he betrays me again!" I cried out, with a thousand emotions twisting inside me.

"Moreover, what makes you think he won't do it again? And as much as I can recall, you are the one who hated him throughout high school and asked me to stay clear of his tricks and lies. Since when did you join Team Ethan?" I asked, studying her intently for some answers.

"People fuckin' change, Sarah!" Her sharp voice was like an arrow to my chest. But she was not done yet.

"I have already told you how I think he might have been dealt a bad hand by fate. I was guilty of not giving him the benefit of doubt back then when he was begging me to know about your whereabouts. I was blinded by rage and revenge. All I saw was how hurt you were, both physically and mentally, because of him and I wanted him as far away from your life as possible. I even hijacked your phone and your e-mail id to make sure he was not able to contact you." My head yanked towards her when she averted her eyes with ripples of resentment consuming her.

My eyes stayed on her when she continued. "I saw you suffer from pain and depression. I died inside every day of guilt that I might be the one causing it, or at least I could end it by letting Ethan contact you. I never told you, but he used to call my house every year whenever I would be back home from college for summer breaks or Christmas holidays and ask me about you. But I really thought that you were better off without him. And I was happy seeing you forgetting everything and moving on in life." I was tongue-tied. She came close and made me sit across from her on the bed. Taking my hands in hers, she gave them a light squeeze.

"But the other day when you called me and told me what you are about to do, I realized that you never forgot anything. You never stopped loving him. And nor did he. That day when you told me about the differences between him and his father because of you, I called his friend Thomas and what he told me made me regret my every decision. He never abandoned you, Sarah. He never stopped looking for you. He has been searching for you continuously for the past nine years!" I could not take it anymore. I raised a hand in front of Ash to make her stop.

I stood up and swiveled to the large window of the bridal suite overlooking the ocean. Glancing at my reflection through the glass, I realized my face revealed two different stories. One aspect of it was tainted with great fear for the future, while the other was colored with hues of liveliness that dwelled inside me this past month.

Yet, my brain overpowered my heart at that moment and let me focus on the deep rooted fear of being abandoned again. Clouds of dismay filled my eyes, ready to rain havoc any second now.

Forty-five days... that's all he had.

Forty-five days to win my trust.

Forty-five days to earn my forgiveness.

Forty-five days to make me fall in love with him. Again!

I had no idea if it was enough time for him. But what I did know is that it was enough for me to see what had been buried deep in my heart. The part that never stopped loving him.

But it was too late now. What I did was supposed to be done. As far as I know Ethan from nine years ago, his ego was everything to him. And I believed nothing could stop him from chasing me but a firm blow on his self-esteem. Though he would hate me for the rest of his life, it was a win-win situation for both of us.

From the corner of my eyes, I looked at the jar filled with Ethan's notes sitting at the side table. He told me to read one anytime I felt low. Maybe I needed them the most right now. This might be the lowest moment of my life so far.

What if I trusted him and he betrayed me again? But, what if he was really a changed man now and I was making a huge mistake.

"Aloha! How's the bride doing?" My little trip to 'what ifs' was cut short when the door flung open and a gush of people poured in. My makeup artist quickly rushed toward me and pushed me on a chair in front of the mirror. In a few seconds, I was surrounded by my mother, my aunts, and my cousins. My eyes were suddenly witnessing a considerable amount of people in a rush. And it finally dawned on me that it was certainly my big day.

From the reflection in the mirror, I saw Ash shaking her head at me in disappointment before she disappeared behind the big door when my hairdresser yanked my face back to the previous position. I hated her for leaving me alone. I just sat there, quiet and lost, getting ready to marry someone I didn't even love. Perhaps he was doing the same. After all, Luc was marrying me because it was the right thing to do, not because he was head over heels in love with me.

After hours of makeup and hairstyling, I was assisted prudently to slip into the gown. My hands ran over the soft fabric, noticing the fragile work of strings of thread. It was similar to my fate. From afar, the fabric looked flawless. But coming closer, it was clearly visible that it was nothing but a bunch of patches sewn together, just like my heart.

My eyes were locked on the reflection of my room's door in the mirror, waiting for Ash to walk in any second and reassure me. To help me calm down my racing heart. We had a lifetime to debate about my bad decisions, but right now, I needed her support like a sister. Or maybe it was Ethan I was waiting for to show up and take me away.

A sharp noise made me jerk out of my thoughts when the fire alarm started buzzing. In that fraction of a second, a wave of panic rippled through the whole room. Everyone freaked out with a Déjà vu and started evacuating the room. I straightened up on my feet and tried to move fast in my heavy dress.

I was last to leave the room and as soon as I was in the corridor, a masked hand yanked at my mouth and I could sense two people pulling me into a janitor's closet. My eyes widened in fear as my nails dug into the hand covering my mouth. As the grip loosened, I dug my teeth in and a shriek echoed from my kidnaper's mouth.

"What the hell, girl? Are you going to bite off my fingers?" I was dumb folded hearing Ash's voice and turned around to witness her taking off the glove and blowing at her hand. Suddenly, a small light bulb flicked on and I found Thomas standing beside her with his hands in the air and fear in his eyes. Huh?

"Ashely? What the hell is happening?" My mind had gone blank. Saying I was confused would be severe minimization. I had never been so puzzled. I closed my eyes and shook my head to come out of the daze. But as I reopened them, my gaze fell on the third person standing behind them.

It was him.

"Look! Don't get mad, okay? I just tripped the fire alarm to hijack you for a minute and soon everyone would realize it was all a fluke and come back laughing. So you have maybe about ten minutes to talk. So… I am just going to leave you two alone." Ashley's voice echoed in my head as she walked out slowly, pulling Thomas along with her. The door closed back, and I was left alone with the last person I expected to see today.

Ethan stepped forward and tripped on his foot in the dark. His hands landed on my shoulders as my back hit the wall for support.

"Are you drunk?"

"What? No! God, no!" He quickly regained his balance and took two steps back. "I am just intoxicated by your beauty." I rolled my eyes at his attempt at flirting at this crucial time.

"I came to give you these." He handed me three neatly folded notes that he promised me the other day. He shoved his hands in his pockets and I just stared at him, dumbfounded.

I unfolded the one numbered forty-three and read it with a little difficulty in the dim light.

> You are the most kind-hearted person I know in this world. There isn't anything in my life, nor could there ever be anything as wonderful as the unconditional love you shared with me.

I glanced up at him, but his eyes were glued to the floor. So I opened the next one, number forty-four.

> Always remember there is someone in this world who is happy because you are happy, no matter where you are or whoever you are with.

I folded it back neatly and took out the last one with shaking hands. I read it with blurry eyes.

I love you, Sarah, always have and always will.

A tear slipped through my eyes and fell on the note, making the ink bloat into the paper. I looked up and saw Ethan staring at me with tear-filled eyes.

"No. This was not in the plan. You were never supposed to come here. It's all going off track. You were supposed to hate me." I shook my head.

"Wait, why would I hate you?" He paused, studying my face. "Oh!" and suddenly realization crossed his mind when he ran a hand through his hair, smiling bitterly. "You thought your plan of abandoning me that night was going to make you get rid of me? Is that what you think about me?" I lowered my head, not meeting his eyes.

"I'm not blind, Sarah. I saw your packed bags that morning. I knew it was your last night with me!" My head shot up and right there a flash of irritation crossed me once again.

"I'm leaving, Sarah!" He stepped forward and my heart almost froze at his words. Did I hear him right? Or was he playing with me? I searched his eyes for a hint of humor, but there was none. He was quiet, yet his words resonated inside my ears, inside my head, inside my whole existence. He had come to say goodbye. I should be happy with the news, but instead, I felt offended. *How dare he turn my life upside down and then give up on us like this?*

"I tried, Sarah. I really tried to make you believe, but I couldn't succeed." He said to the ground, as his head bowed like a fallen angel.

"Please, don't think I'm here to cause you or anybody any trouble. I just wanted to see you one last time. I won't take much time, but there are some things I need to apologize for." He slowly wrapped his fingers around mine.

"I'm sorry, Sarah! I was so wrong; so blinded by my selfishness that I couldn't see the fact that I was destroying your future. What was I even thinking? How thoughtless of me to force you for something that never did belong to me in the first place." His words poked my heart like an arrow, making me bleed in misery.

"I can only imagine how big a jerk I've been to you. It was hard for me to accept, but now that I can understand, I truly respect your decision." He never once glanced up at me, saying everything he was saying.

"Are you giving up on us?" His head shot up, taking into the words that unknowingly left my mouth.

"I tried, Sarah! I never wanted to give up, but I see now that what I've been doing is not right. I can't keep daydreaming about something that is never going to happen." When I felt like nothing could go any worse, his words hurt me like never before. I took in sharp traction of breath.

"You came into my life when I had made peace with my past. You grew like a hurricane and wrecked every safety wall, every closed door, and window I had placed around my heart. Raising havoc in my life, destroying everything that was binding me together all through these years." He kept staring at me, tears slipping through his eyes.

"And when I thought nothing could make me feel better, you overflowed my life with extreme joy, restoring liveliness in my soul." I took my hands from him and faced the wall in anger.

"Nine years, Ethan. Nine fuckin' years! I was not living; I was merely existing. Making futile efforts to overcome my past, to overcome you. And just when I was about to make peace with everything and move on, one day out of the blue, you happen to fall back into my life. Bringing back every single unpleasant memory with you. You shook me to the core once again." He didn't even care to utter a single word, and I felt offended.

"You brought back the Sarah that I had managed to bury all those years ago. But somehow I was breathing again. Living again. I felt a burden leaving my shoulders, making me afloat in joy." This time, tears welled up in my eyes and I scowled. I hate when my anger converts into sobs.

"Every single fuckin' time when I needed someone by my side in life. I wanted it to be you. When I was crying myself to sleep. I needed you!" I turned back around, facing him, and held his eyes.

"And now you are telling me you tried! You want to take everything away just like you did all those years ago?" He remained silent, and that fueled my anger.

"Answer me, Ethan!" I grabbed his collar and shook him, the pain in my chest swirling out into my words. I wanted answers.

"Sarah, I may have been a jerk to you, but I am a good enough person to let you go! To do what is good for you. I can happily live with the fact that you loved me once. Just remember one thing, my love was not fake, it was real and will always be." Taking a step closer, he held my hands once again.

"I don't know if you remember this, but you asked me once about my biggest fear. Do you want to know what I was most afraid of in my life? I feared I'm loving someone who won't ever see how madly I was in love with her. But I can see it in your eyes that you do see my love and I am not afraid anymore." I lowered my head, not able to face him anymore. But he placed a finger below my chin and made me gaze up.

"I want you to live your life with a person you would be able to look at without reliving the memories of your bitter past. You deserve better, Starz. Better than me." His stare bored into my soul. They were filled with guilt and remorse as tears ran down his eyes.

He leaned in and kissed my forehead with his quivering lips. I closed my eyes, letting his warmth seep into my heart, melting all the ice around it. But before I could've felt his warmth in my soul, he marched away; leaving nothing but a closed door and an empty Sarah behind.

A sinking sensation gripped my heart, leaving me scattered all over the place. Pitch-black darkness wrapped me in its fangs, carving me out like an empty shell. I was lost and there was no way for me to be found again without him.

My essence felt frozen; lifeless and withered, yet the pain inside me kept on growing. I felt alone and desolate. It felt like I was surrounded by these indestructible walls of despair and the whole world was screaming through them the fact that he was gone and so was my heart with him.

My heart dropped in my stomach, and my lungs felt constricted, making it hard to breathe. I never felt so helpless in my life. Clamping the armrest of the chair, I struggled to restrain my trembling essence, which was shattered into pieces.

My legs were quivering, and I feared I might lose my balance and collapse if I dared to stand up. Grabbing my head, I tried to reason out how I let this happen. Why on earth was this happening to me? Where did it all go wrong to find myself standing at the edge of this cliff once again?

I couldn't do much but accept my destiny. I was destined for this pain. It was getting unbearable. I wished for nothing more than to go back in time to when I first met him, only to turn around and never give him a chance to destroy me.

I tried everything to deter him. First bitterness, then understanding, and lastly the hate, but in between all these efforts, I never thought I would be the one falling for him.

I thought we were walking on two different paths that would never collide. Yet, he crossed my way, only to leave me tattered in the middle of a crossroads.

It was gut-wrenching remembering his tear-filled face, which kept on reflecting in front of my eyes, breaking me apart. I touched my forehead, remembering that throbbing kiss. He was damaged, but I couldn't do anything to help him. His soul was worn out, leaving all emotions bare on his face, begging with his eyes for me to come back into his life.

But then there was Lucas's pure heart, his selflessness. It was only his virtuous self that was holding me back. I couldn't destroy something like that. My betrayal would damage him. It was like repeating the atrocities of my past with someone, and this someone was too innocent like I was. He was too fragile to handle any of this. It was true I never loved him like I loved Ethan, but his fondness for me couldn't be deserted.

I sensed someone entering my room, and I hastily brushed away my tears. I couldn't afford to reveal to anyone how deep I was slumping into the dark pit. I bowed my head, concealing my withered face. My crying had died down to mere sniffles. And just when I thought I had composed myself, someone rested a hand over my shoulder, causing a shiver run down my spine.

"Are you okay?" It was Ashely. Witnessing her all dressed up in the maid of honor gown, I shattered into a thousand pieces.

"No!" I crashed into her arms, breaking down all over again.

I could barely let out any words. My body was so stressed out that I was losing control over it. It felt like I was screaming in an empty room submerged in darkness and there was nobody who could hear my voice.

"You know, choosing someone just because he is a safe option is not love." My head shot up just as my tear-filled eyes gazed at her.

"Ash, you don't understand." I stepped back, keeping a good distance from her now. Lowering my head in remorse, I tried to hide my trembling hands from her by facing my back to her. "It's too late now. This will break Lucas's heart! He is too fragile to endure such betrayal!" I shook my head. It broke my heart just by imagining his painful eyes. I couldn't do this. It was like butchering his soul.

"I don't know if you're understanding it, but marrying him like this would be the biggest betrayal you could ever cause him." I shook my head at her.

"I no longer know what I'm doing. It feels like, on one hand, I'm facing a bullet and on the other, I myself am the one pulling the trigger."

I stumbled down on the floor, losing myself. My back hit the wall, and I looked up, sensing my world falling apart. I never felt this terrible in my whole life. I noticed when Ash sat down next to me, giving me a comforting smile.

"Do you remember the day when we first met?"

"How can I forget? You called me a twat on the very first day we met." We chuckled, remembering the moment. It was unusual for me to sob and smile at the same time.

"Well, everyone almost believed in my magic tricks back in third grade, but you exposed me with your stupid facts." I stole a glance at her, looking at her, smiling softly.

"You know, love is just like magic; the more we believe in it, the more we find ourselves cut off from reality. The brain notices facts, but life is much more than just plain facts. That's why we have a heart, Sarah. To tell us what not to believe and take a leap of faith." She turned her head at me and I could see what she was trying to tell me at the moment. My face dulled, and I hugged her once again.

"Am I intruding on something?" Our heads shot up towards the door, noticing my dad's smiling face.

"Listen to your heart, babe!" Ash whispered, looking over at dad as we stood up.

"Sorry for making your daughter cry, Mr. Walter. We are just sad knowing she is going to shift to the other end of the country!"

"Oh, I see!" I managed to give him a quick smile, noticing Ash striding towards him.

"I believe a father-daughter talk is in order and I'm getting in the middle of that. I'll go fix my hair or something." She strolled towards the door, giving me a knowing look.

"Nice shoes, Ashely!" My dad remarked, and I chuckled softly, noticing she was still wearing her sneakers below that dress.

"Can't help it. I'm a sneaker girl, Mr. Walter."

She tapped his shoulder and then waddled away, closing the door at her back. I quickly brushed my tears away, taking in a deep breath. I bet my makeup was ruined, and I had puffy eyes and a red nose, but I tried my best to compose myself.

"You look beautiful, dear!" He opened his arms, and I fell into a welcoming embrace.

"I am proud of you, Ray. You are an intelligent, strong, and the most wonderful daughter any father could ever wish for. I'm so lucky to be blessed with you." He kissed my forehead. "You don't know how precious you are, Ray!"

Those last spoken words stirred my judgment. A memory reeled in my head. I'd heard those words before; same words but in a different voice. In that spur of the moment, Ethan's face flashed in front of my eyes. A smiling face with innocent dimples that had compelled me to play guitar that day. It was the very first time I felt raw bliss in my soul after a very long time and found a long-lost piece of my heart that had been missing from my life.

"You are going to share your whole life with him. Give him a chance by letting your guards down, Ray. When you open up to someone, you would be surprised to know how much love could flow in your life."

Everything seemed so confusing. Like my logical thinking was listening to him very carefully. But my critical thinking was compelling me to correlate his words with something entirely different.

Once again, my deliberations went back to a moment I had spent with Ethan. The day we shared a car ride to my parent's house. The journey brought a sensation of liberation with it. We gossiped like two long-lost best friends, no judgments, no bitterness, just plain white talks.

And everything went up from that day onwards. I opened up to him.

Day after day.

Bit by bit.

Not being aware that I was trailing off on a dangerous path.

"Your life is going to change, Ray! But it doesn't mean you have to change yourself with it. A man should love his lady the way she is. You don't have to pretend anything!" But I did pretend. Deluded by a belief that some dates, gifts, and kisses would make me fall for Lucas. I was misled by my past and unfortunately, I turned my eyes away from the truth.

"There is nothing like a perfect relationship. Sometimes you might not appreciate something about him, sometimes he might not appreciate your nagging. People fight, yell at each other, occasionally sleep in different beds, but that doesn't mean they don't love each other anymore. All it means is they care for each other enough to protect them from everything. If the person is worth fighting for, then it's meant to be." Suddenly, he took my hands in his, looking down at them for a while, and then glanced up, allowing me to see the vulnerability behind that soft smile.

"But remember, it is always worth taking some risks in life, Ray. The 'what ifs' have the power to destroy anyone's world." I stared at him, with tears flooding my eyes once again. My vision turned fuzzy, just like my thoughts.

I blinked, compelling myself to not miss a word he was saying, yet getting lost in the recollection that was flailing my subconscious.

Life is all about taking risks. Don't settle for ordinary when you can have something special if you're willing to take the risk.

At that very second, a jolt of emotions hit my core and my brain realized what my heart was trying to tell me all along.

Ethan. I wanted him. I needed him. I couldn't spend a day without him. Even when he was not around, he was always running through my thoughts.

Love has the power to heal anyone. Even a broken soul could be mended with unconditional love.

I had been in a dilemma, doubted his love, wasn't sure if it would ever be possible for me to love him again. But now I understand. I never stopped loving him. Now I realized it was that stupid jerk only that my heart desired to adore.

I no longer wanted to run away or hide my feelings from him. I wanted to give us a chance, a second chance. Because he deserved it. I deserved it. I craved to give a second chance to my first love. Because I knew I could wake up next to this man every morning and not get sick of him for the rest of my life.

"Dad, could you do me a favor and call Ashley in? I really need to fix this veil!" Now that I have realized how foolish and stubborn I had been, I didn't have much time to spare. He hugged me one last time and nodded with a smile.

Sorry dad, now I'm going to be selfish and think about my happiness first. I will finally follow what my heart desires.

Usually, I was a very patient person. I knew exactly when to stay put and not hurry to undermine the chances of getting the best apple. But today was different. It was absolutely conflicting, and I needed to act quickly or regret it my whole life.

"What happened?" I turned around, seeing Ashely barging in.

"Your dad said it's an emergency!"

"It is indeed. Now, take off your dress!" I was already pulling that stupid wedding dress off.

"Excuse me?" Her hands wrapped around her body like a caterpillar trying to hide from predators. Her befuddled eyes were staring at me like I had grown a second head.

"Ash, there is no time to explain. I'm going to be short and simple. I love him." My mouth was still open when she interrupted me.

"Who? I swear I'll punch you in the vagina if there is a third guy involved in this drama!" I frowned at her and gestured to her to zip her mouth shut.

"Ash, I was scared, terrified to get my heart broken again. Yet, I failed to notice that he is the only one who could join all my broken pieces together. I am alive only when I am with him. I went wrong on so many levels that I couldn't see the signs which were always in front of my eyes. I..."

"Finally, girl! You got your wits together!" With a mischievous smile, she pulled me into a hug.

 ⸺

"Tell me once again, why am I wearing your wedding gown?" Ash eyed me while I laced up her sneakers on my feet. I was wearing a janitor's overalls that we found in the janitor's closet where they took me after kidnapping just hours ago.

"Because I need to buy time to get away from all my relatives outside waiting for the bride. If they knew I was gone, they would form a search party and hunt me down in no time. And I am in no mood to face them at the moment." I straightened my back and held her by the shoulders.

"So you, being my best friend and the most amazing person in the whole wide world, have to hold the fortress for me for a little while." She rolled her eyes at me, but I knew she was sold by the compliments.

"But they will recognize me in an instant." She tried to argue half-heartedly.

"Are you kidding me? This veil is so coarse that I'm afraid you're going to bump your head into the wall and get a brain hemorrhage. Now, time for action, Ash." I gave her a tight hug before slipping out of the room in disguise. And I began my journey as a runaway bride.

I darted off towards the stairs, making my way through the closed doors in the corridor. My heart was pounding in my chest, with my lungs getting short of air. My skin tingled with the anticipation of seeing Ethan again as I climbed down the stairs.

"She is almost ready, getting some last-minute touch-ups with Ashley." Just when I overheard my father's voice at the end of the stairways, my head yanked toward the opposite direction. Catching sight of the unfolded doors of an elevator.

I couldn't afford to get caught. The needles of the clock were ticking and the probability of seeing him again was also slipping off my hand. So I slipped inside that elevator and took a sigh of relief taking support of the elevator wall when the door began to shut and... "Hey, hold up!" That sudden call and then a foot blocking the doorway forced me to let out a curse underneath my breath.

I quickly dropped my head, concealing my face with Ash's baseball hat that was quoting *'Hail to the queen'* when a bunch of guys entered the elevator. I shifted my small frame back when my vicinity soon grew a little crowded, and I found myself pressed to the corner.

"Dude, there is still some time left to change your mind and flee." One of the guys made a joke and everyone started laughing.

"No, mate. She is the real deal." My heart sank the moment I gathered that voice. I shifted on my spot, now being familiar with the fact that I had been surrounded by Lucas and his friends. I couldn't help but sneak a view. He was smiling, that same innocent laugh that deserved every happiness in this cruel world.

I knew what I was doing was absolutely wrong, and he didn't deserve this. But Ash was right. Marrying him while I loved someone else would be an even bigger betrayal than this. I unfastened the golden chain with the 'Forevermore' pendent from my neck and dropped it in Lucas's jacket pocket without anyone noticing.

I'm sorry, Lucas. Hope you could find in your heart to forgive me one day! I truly wish for you to find happiness in your life, just like I did.

With a ding of the elevator, the door opened on the ground floor and I waited for everyone to head out first before I darted towards the exit.

"Everything should be perfect! I want the photographer to catch every glimpse of the ceremony!" Out of the blue, my aunt's voice stroked my ears and my steps ceased watching her darting straight towards me. I dashed towards the nearest hideout behind a big fiber pot of fake palm tree. Mentally praying she wouldn't see me.

I bowed my head and tried my best to camouflage when she turned around towards the chapel. From the corner of my eyes, I saw the mound of people gathered there while Lucas took his place at the altar. I noticed my Mom fidgeting nervously, and I mentally apologized to her before scooting toward the exit.

A thick breeze pierced through my skin as I sprinted out of the driveway. I couldn't care less if I would be spotted now. I just wanted to escape those invisible glass walls that had been trapping me in for years now.

I was breathing heavily. Halting just outside the iron gates, I looked back and mumbled an apology to everybody who was going to get hurt today. And soon found myself walking on the pretty lively streets of that beautiful island. My small frame got lost in that crowd of wanderers.

To my left was the way towards the main market, and my right pointed straight to the airport. I patted my pockets but found that stupidly enough I had forgotten to bring my phone in all the haste. My head began to get fuzzy. My eyes longed to catch a glimpse of him, but they were getting lost in the crowd.

"Where are you, Ethan Robert Stanton? Don't you dare leave me alone this time!"

I fear that the day I will let go of you and your love, I will be lost. I'll just be sitting here, unwinding my thoughts on the sand, helping some kid build a sandcastle.

The words whispered around me, and a sensation of remembrance swaddled me. I sprinted towards the place I believed I would find him.

By the time I reached the shore, I was panting hard. The craving in my heart to see him, to feel him, to touch him was flourishing to madness. He was supposed to be here. He said I would find him at this very place. Yet I was alone, surrounded by strangers, and my heart plunged deep into my stomach.

The sensation that flowed within my heart was of a defeated warrior. My distressed body stumbled down on the sand. I was wounded and my willpower had been shredded in bits. My face was buried in my hands and I shook my head in disappointment. How stupid of me to assume he would wait for me. I felt so stupid for believing in some kind of happy ending. There was a voice inside my head that was laughing at my actions, mocking me at my idiocy. The worn-out feeling overpowered my wits, and I just wanted to lie down and get lost in a deep, never-ending slumber.

"Sarah!"

My head lifted towards the sky, desperate to put a face to that angelic voice. I frowned when the sun almost blinded my vision. I couldn't appreciate the face of the person hovering over me. But, as I stood up, the shadow shifted to the left, covering the blinding rays. My heart welled up with the feeling of coming home after being lost forever and I jumped over him.

"Whoa!" His body couldn't hold back my weight and we fell to the ground. My eyes squeezed shut in fear of getting hurt, but I never felt the hit. Sunrays caressed my back when my body glided over his as we were painted with golden sand. But I couldn't care less, as all I wanted was to hug the living daylight out of him. His strong arms wrapped around me like a warm blanket on a cold, rainy night. Relief flowed through our body and I felt alive once again.

"Sarah, is everything all right?" I looked into his luscious eyes and right there I was assured that I had made the right choice. I could stake my heart on the amount of enthrallment his eyes behold and then I hugged him even more tightly.

"I... I thought I would never see you again." My emotional stammering butchered my attempt to fight back the tears that were threatening to break free.

"What do you mean? I don't understand?" I let out a sigh when I knew it was my turn to confess the feelings I had been trying to bury all this time. I parted away to sit up straight, just to stare into those ocean deep eyes that were sparkling with a ray of hope.

"I'm in love with you, Ethan. Would you like to grow old with me? And…" He placed a finger on my lips, cutting me off immediately. I felt offended.

"Shhh… Not another word." He closed his eyes and let out a deep sigh. Tears flew down his cheeks as if they were waiting on the brink for his permission to overflow. But when he opened his eyes again, the world around us ceased to exist.

"I made some terrible mistakes in life, Starz. But I want to spend the rest of my life correcting them. You can shout at me; you can beat me. Hell, you can even humiliate me in front of the whole world, but please don't hate me. I need you, girl. Come back to me. Please!" He finally called me by that stupid nickname and strangely, it calmed down my nerves. He firmly held my both hands and yanked me towards him. My hands pausing at his chest allowed me to feel his racing heart, and I felt a passion shooting down my body. He brushed a strand of my hair behind my ear, making me shudder.

"Sometimes I say stupid things; even do stuff that I'm not supposed to do. But trust me when I confess my love for you, there is nothing but truth in it. I love you, Sarah Rose Walter." He clipped my face, looking into my wet eyes.

"It's not going to be easy, but I promise you that it's going to be worth a second chance, Starz," and then he grabbed my shoulders, straightening me up on my feet only for him to bend down at one knee, taking me by surprise. "You know I suck with timings. So, before you change your mind. Darling, can we start over?" I shook my head, covering my mouth as tears shimmered in my eyes. My actions made him lower his head, the sensation of disheartening painting his features.

"You are such a pain in the ass, Ethan. Your silly ploys test my sanity, and your flirtation makes my blood boil. Your pickup lines make me want to kill myself. Yet, I want you to keep on doing all those things. Always and forever. I want to take this chance, the risk of falling for the wrong guy once again. Because he is my Mr. Right." His head lifted to acknowledge the acceptance in my eyes as tears ran down my cheeks.

I pulled him up to his feet and hugged the love of my life and whispered in his ear…

"Because magic happens when we take risks!"

Epilogue

Ashley

STILL THE WEDDING DAY

Holy! Motherfuckin'! Shitballs!

This is so not happening. No way! This is bad, really-really bad. Why did I ever give her such an awful piece of advice? No, wait! Why did I even agree with her in the first place?

Oh my goodness, my heart is going to explode. Boom! Like a bloody water balloon over my head. Why is my heart hammering so hard against my ears? I am certain of having a heart attack right now. I completely messed up everything this time. Dug a grave for myself, only to be buried alive. When on earth am I going to stop having such terrible ideas?

What am I going to do now? Wait, what am I even doing here? I should have just run away with Sarah. Ethan would've given me a free ride to the airport. My thoughts were punching me from all directions, just as I was having a panic attack.

Pacing inside that small room, I slowly unlocked the door to have a peek outside. My heart was racing up while sweat built up on my forehead. I sneaked a view of the outside one more time and then instantly closed the door.

Why on earth do people invite so many guests to a marriage? As they say, marriage is just a union of two people who want to eat their favorite dishes until any funny business happens. Then why do they get fancy with the crowd?

"Dear, are you ready? It's almost time!" Sarah's Mom's voice gave me Goosebumps. I swear my jaw dropped to the floor. I was so very screwed.

"Argh! In a minute!" What now? Should I call in her parents and tell them the truth? Yeah, this would be a sane thing to do.

Carefully peeking through the door, my eyes fell over the mini Walter. He was my last hope. It was either him or jumping off the window, and I thought to give him a chance before breaking my bones.

"Hey! Pssst... Pssst." I struggled to catch his attention while he was too busy flirting with some chick in a backless. "Hey! Knucklehead!" A fleeting smile traveled through me when my voice caught his attention. He glanced first at his right, then left, and then ultimately at the ceiling. My eyes followed his gaze, and I cursed underneath my breath.

What on earth was he searching for on the roof? My voice from heaven? Wow, he was dumber than I thought. I wondered how this dumbass could be Sarah's brother. Was he really adopted, as she claimed?

And when I concluded it was not working, I looked around to throw something at him but found nothing but a bouquet of flowers. Squinting my eyes, I aimed for my target. Unleashing a deep breath, I flung a white rose at him and I cheered when it flawlessly hit his head.

"Yes! Little shit! Here!" Rubbing the side of his thick skull, his nose crinkled in shock just as he began to look everywhere but me. I was ready this time to throw my shoe at him when I eventually captured his attention. I smiled at him and hid the shoe behind me before he could have seen it.

I rolled my eyes when he gave me a puke-inducing smirk while leaning over his prey. He whispered something in her ear, on which she giggled, making me cringe so hard that I almost puked in my mouth.

I was fidgeting, dying with apprehension; anxiety was eating me alive, but he chose the most leisure walk while heading towards me. I wanted to beat the crap out of him just for his saunter. It was like he was taking a stroll in the park.

I waited and waited and waited and at last, when he was just within reach, I clutched his jacket, yanking him inside the room. He almost stumbled on his steps, but quickly regained the cockiness in his body language.

"Sweetheart, we can do this after the wedding. But, I can tell you a joke about my little friend, but it's too long, and you'll miss the ceremony!" I rolled my eyes so hard that I was certain I saw my bleeding brain at that instant.

"Holy shit! Why are you wearing my sister's wedding gown?" His jaw dropped when he understood my resting bitch face. "Where is my sister?" He dashed toward me in a matter of seconds and then swirled around my little self. A line appeared on my forehead seeing him searching for something and when he grabbed my gown, ready to look underneath, I grabbed his tie, yanking him at my eye level.

"Nice move, Asshat!"

"Did she run away? Tell me she ran away." The tension on my face was back, and I jumped out of my skin when he screamed. "I knew that! Aunt Rose owes me a hundred bucks!"

"Are you fuckin' kidding me right now? Can't you see we are in deep shit?" He scratched his head, giving me an innocent smile. News flash! I met a dumbass, and he made me kill myself with his dumbness.

"Oh, my God! I am not sure if I'm having a panic attack or I want to poop. And here you are, rather than coming with some plan and saving me and your family from the awaiting embarrassment, you're worried about your hundred dollars?" I started pacing in that stupid gown and in the end, tripped over the edge of the carpet, plunging straight towards the floor.

"We can tell my parents." My head lifted at him with hope sparkling in my eyes. "But just so you know, Dad is a heart patient. You go tell them and I'll go keep the ambulance ready." I couldn't believe what I was hearing from his mouth. My eyes squinted at him for a couple of seconds with an expression that suggested I could slaughter him any minute now.

"Are you really always this dumb or today is a special day?" He gave me a half shrug, and I groaned out in annoyance, standing up. Once again, I began to pace in the room, but this time holding the stupid dress up. I strived harder to plan something that could save both of us. But then our eyes shot towards the door when I heard a loud knock and then someone opened the door.

"I'll chop off your balls if you utter a single word!" I quickly threatened him, dropping off my veil.

"Ray, are you ready? It's time!" I internally slapped myself when Mr. Walter's voice hit my ears. My breath caught up in my lungs when he circled my hand around his forearm and squeezed my hand a little.

"Everything is going to be okay, Ray. Lucas is a nice man. He will keep you extremely happy." My nose crinkled at his remark. What the hell?

What era are we living in? I don't need a man to keep me happy.

It was possible he would never be happy after this day! Bullshit! I didn't think you would be happy after knowing I was not your daughter, Mr. Walter.

Just then, I saw Mr. Asshat coming to my rescue, standing in front of us. "Dad, grumpy has got a stomach bug. She has been leaking since morning. I think we should cancel the wedding before she embarrasses herself in front of the whole family." And right there I wanted to give him a standing ovation with the dumbest person alive award.

Mr. Walter threw his head back and enjoyed a good laugh at that little shit. While I had been staring at the window, mentally calculating the height of the room, in case I had to take an emergency exit.

"Angus! Don't tease your sister. She is already holding her breath."

As we exited the lift at the ground floor lobby the photographer attacked us with his camera. We walked quietly towards the chapel and I got cold feet when my eyes fell over the people sitting on either side of the aisle.

The room was pretty hot, and I was already sweating when I felt my hands getting clammy from holding that flower bouquet that kept on tingling my nose. I bloody loathed roses.

The music commenced to play and I swear I wanted to sit down and cry like a baby on that hideous red carpet. I still couldn't believe this was happening to me. How did I end up in this myriad of a mess? I couldn't marry him. Hell, I didn't even know his full name. Romanzo? Gonzo? Never mind! Mr. Walter caught hold of my hand tightly when I almost stumbled a little while walking down the aisle. I swear, I could feel a coin in my shoe.

You know a wedding is incomplete without a drunken uncle getting over-sentimental over Bride's entry. Well, in this case, it was my dad. My mother was making a great effort to console him, rubbing his back when he continued to cry on her chest. Dad, if you knew the bride was your own daughter, I bet you would be losing your consciousness instead of your tears.

On the other hand, the ivory veil was so long and heavy that I felt like someone was pulling my head back, making me bald with every step. I wondered what if someone stepped on it and my golden wig came off?

"I'm so proud of you, Ray. I'll always love you!" Mr. Walter whispered near me and I deduced I had been pushed down in an enormous dark hole till the point of no return. Or did I jump in on my own?

We finally reached the altar, but all of a sudden the soloist who was singing with a booming operatic voice started to cough loudly. And the song ended. He was trying hard to breathe as people came to rescue him while he uttered enough scratchy words to reveal that a fly went into his mouth. But before I could've enjoyed great manic laughter, my hand was passed over to the man I didn't even like in the very first place.

I kept staring at my shoes. "We are gathered here in the sight of God to unite this man and this woman in holy matrimony." Once again, my inner panic attack surfaced. I shifted in my place, but Gonzo squeezed my hands lightly, making me more uncomfortable.

"Into this holy estate, these two people present themselves to be joined. Today, they publicly declare their private devotion for each other." The priest continued as I strived to remain calm.

It's okay! Just breathe, Ash!

This will be over soon.

Soon? No! I was dying already. I tried to fool myself but failed miserably.

"If any of you have reasons why these two should not be married, speak now or forever hold your peace." My head turned towards the crowd.

Oh, come on! Where the heck are all my exes? I need you guys. Like right now!

But no one uttered a word, and the priest opened his mouth and I couldn't take it anymore.

"Well, sorry, I do have a problem. I'm sorry, but I can't do this." I lifted off my veil and in a fraction of a second, that dude's hand slipped off my arm like my skin burned his. Rude much?

Distant gasps and whispers flourished in the room, but I didn't leave my ground. "No offense, mate, but I can't marry you. Or anyone else present here! Just for the record!" I cleared my throat. "Okay, I'm sorry. Where was I? Right! From what I've heard about you from Sarah, you sound like a nice guy. Nice enough to forgive me and her for all this mess. Nothing personal, dude." I stepped down from the altar.

"Sorry for wasting the wine, I... I mean time... your time!" I looked around, witnessing people's eyes dangling outside their sockets.

"Ahem! I think I should go now. I'll just moonwalk away very slowly. Please to meet you all!" I started to head towards the exit door when I remembered something.

"Shoot! I almost forgot! Here is your ring. Lucas. Right?" And I saw him nodding with a scowl on his face before,

I broke into a run.

Acknowledgement

The only reason 'Darling, Can We Start Over? ' has come to life is because of my sister Komal who somehow took out whatever little time she got from her busy office hours and copyedited this whole book (Yes she edited this acknowledgement too).

As English is not my first language I struggled with laying down my thoughts out on paper, but she helped me to properly express myself and so in the development of the characters of this story.

Thank you so much sister from the bottom of my heart for every encouragement, every piece of advice to make the story more clear and realistic and also for giving me the courage to edit out some of my dearest yet unwanted scenes from the book. You've helped me convert my dream into reality.

Next, my best friend Garima, I am grateful to you for helping me out with the early plot outline of this novel. This wouldn't have been possible without you. Thank you.

Thank you dearest husband for believing in me and taking care of our toddler, thus allowing me some time to write this book.

And last but not the least I want to thank every blogger, bookstagrammer, and reader for believing in this book and a newbie author like me. Thank you for trusting and supporting me throughout this journey. You guys are the backbone of rocking my world with so much love and support. Thank you for everything.

If you liked 'Darling, can we start over?' please leave reviews on Goodreads, Amazon, Instagram and don't forget to tag #darlingcanwestartover.

About the Author

Monika Meena is a Doctor by profession who grew up in Rajasthan, India where she spent most of her life studying dentistry which ironically has nothing to do with writing romantic comedies.

While reading had always been a passion, Monika could never get away from her love for writing books full of hope, romance and happy-endings.

When she is not writing about hopeless romantic couples, you can find her chasing around her two kids, reading books, buying books, rearranging her bookshelves, or most of the time researching for her next work in progress while drinking too much coffee.

'Darling, Can We Start Over?' is the first book by Monika Meena. Visit her online at www.monikameena.com and follow on Instagram @authormonikameena.

.

Printed in Great Britain
by Amazon

84515149R00255